PRAISE FOR THE NOVELS OF MAUREEN MCKADE

"A story that will tear at your heart . . . terrific."
—*Rendezvous*

"Watch out when sparks start to fly!"
—*Affaire de Coeur*

"A Maureen McKade novel is going to provide plenty of excitement and enjoyment . . . Another triumph."
—*Midwest Book Review*

"Well-done, uplifting, and enjoyable."
—*Rocky Mountain News*

"With a clever storyline and sparkling dialogue she's created a town that will live in her readers' minds and keeper shelves forever . . . *Untamed Heart* is one of the must-read romances of the year!"
—*The Literary Times*

"One of the most original romances I've read in a long time. I look forward to reading more from this talented author."
—*All About Romance*

"Hard to put down . . . A great story."
—*The Best Reviews*

Berkley Sensation books by Maureen McKade

TO FIND YOU AGAIN
AROUSE SUSPICION
CONVICTIONS

CONVICTIONS

Maureen McKade

BERKLEY SENSATION BOOKS, NEW YORK

THE BERKLEY PUBLISHING GROUP
Published by the Penguin Group
Penguin Group (USA) Inc.
375 Hudson Street, New York, New York 10014, USA

Penguin Group (Canada), 90 Eglinton Avenue East, Suite 700, Toronto, Ontario M4P 2Y3, Canada
(a division of Pearson Penguin Canada Inc.)
Penguin Books Ltd., 80 Strand, London WC2R 0RL, England
Penguin Group Ireland, 25 St. Stephen's Green, Dublin 2, Ireland (a division of Penguin Books Ltd.)
Penguin Group (Australia), 250 Camberwell Road, Camberwell, Victoria 3124, Australia
(a division of Pearson Australia Group Pty. Ltd.)
Penguin Books India Pvt. Ltd., 11 Community Centre, Panchsheel Park, New Delhi—110 017, India
Penguin Group (NZ), Cnr. Airborne and Rosedale Roads, Albany, Auckland 1310, New Zealand
(a division of Pearson New Zealand Ltd.)
Penguin Books (South Africa) (Pty.) Ltd., 24 Sturdee Avenue, Rosebank, Johannesburg 2196,
South Africa

Penguin Books Ltd., Registered Offices: 80 Strand, London WC2R 0RL, England

This is a work of fiction. Names, characters, places, and incidents either are the product of the author's
imagination or are used fictitiously, and any resemblance to actual persons, living or dead, business
establishments, events, or locales is entirely coincidental. The publisher does not have any control
over and does not assume any responsibility for author or third-party websites or their content.

CONVICTIONS

A Berkley Sensation Book / published by arrangement with the author

PRINTING HISTORY
Berkley Sensation edition / October 2005

ISBN: 0-425-20850-8

BERKLEY® SENSATION
Berkley Sensation Books are published by The Berkley Publishing Group,
a division of Penguin Group (USA) Inc.,
375 Hudson Street, New York, New York 10014.
BERKLEY SENSATION and the "B" design are trademarks belonging to Penguin Group (USA) Inc.

PRINTED IN THE UNITED STATES OF AMERICA

10 9 8 7 6 5 4 3 2 1

CONVICTIONS

CHAPTER ONE

MURKY fog swirled around the streetlamp's glow as
Olivia Kincaid hurried down the nearly deserted sidewalk.
Her smoky shadow guided her, then shifted to her side, and
finally became a benevolent stalker.

Her sensible flats slapped the cracked sidewalk, the
only sound save the whispery rasp of her breath and the familiar hum of freeway traffic three blocks away. She shifted
her shoulder, trying to find a more comfortable position for
her leather briefcase strap.

She came to a cross street and, out of habit more than
necessity, paused to check for cars.

A shoe sole scraped concrete.

She whirled around, and her hair whipped across her
face. Shoving the strands out of her eyes, she searched the
enveloping darkness as her heart slammed against her
breast.

Damp silence seeped through her clothing and into her
pores. She trembled, tilted her head, listened, but only
heard the typical—and usually unnoticed—city backdrop.

With a gloved hand, Olivia clenched the strap on her
shoulder as she waited, poised, listening, for another footfall.

One that never came. Blowing out a lungful of air, she continued down the deserted sidewalk.

Blaming her taut nerves on the rape case she was prosecuting tomorrow, she inhaled and exhaled deeply as she lengthened her stride. Only two more blocks, and she'd be at her apartment building.

Then came the metallic ring of something—or someone—striking a garbage can in the dismal, smelly alley. Olivia's footsteps faltered, and her heart, which had eased into a more normal rhythm, kicked into high gear again. She moved faster, her shoes skimming the sidewalk now.

Not slowing her frantic pace, she glanced over her shoulder. Stygian shadows from the encroaching mist gathered and separated, like dancers shuffling to a funereal dirge. A soft cry escaped Olivia's lips and she jammed a knuckle into her mouth.

Was it him? The one who'd called her at least a dozen times a day over the past two weeks and left no messages? The one who'd sent her dead red roses? The one who'd left a message on her windshield while her car was in a locked garage?

She stumbled.

Fingers clutched at her arm.

Swung her around . . . toward a face with no face.

Olivia Kincaid jerked awake and opened her eyes to darkness. But it was, mercifully, a darkness devoid of pirouetting ghosts and empty faces. She bolted upright, biting back a moan when her healing leg protested the abrupt motion. Her satin nightgown, saturated with cold sweat, stuck to her clammy skin. Using her thumb and forefinger, she plucked the drenched material away from her breasts

Grimacing and wondering if she had any clean gowns remaining in her dresser, Olivia threw off the damp sheet and eased her feet onto the red, green, and blue braided rug covering the polished pine floor. After switching on the nightstand lamp, she pushed herself to her feet. She placed most of her weight on her right leg, which had become habit over the past two months. Her cane rested against the foot of her bed, but she ignored it as she tugged the wet gown over her head and tossed it toward her closet.

Goose bumps arose on her arms and legs, and her nipples puckered in the cool air. Ignoring her body's complaints, Olivia limped across the floor to her dresser and tugged open the third drawer. One nightshirt remained— actually it was an oversized T-shirt with a faded pink kitty on the front. It had been her favorite when she was a freshman in high school, over half a lifetime ago.

Olivia wrinkled her nose and donned the ancient relic. If her fellow assistant district attorneys could see her now, she'd never live "kitty" down.

But then, that was pretty unlikely with them being a thousand miles away and living in another world. A world she prayed she could return to someday.

Refusing to let depression gain a foothold, Olivia glanced at her digital clock radio: 1:28 a.m. *Lovely.* It was too early to rise, but there was no way she would be able to fall asleep again any time soon. Time for a hot chocolate fix.

She shrugged into a knobby blue terry cloth robe and debated using her cane. If she fell, or twisted her bad leg, it would set her recovery back another month. Easy decision. She hobbled back to her bed and grasped the smooth wooden curve at the top of the polished cane. It was easier to navigate with it, but Olivia still resented the need. But then, she resented everything about what had happened that night two months ago.

The familiar tap-slide, tap-slide of her footsteps accompanied her down the hallway to the spacious kitchen at the other end of the house. She passed her father's room and wasn't surprised to see a light shining beneath the closed door. He often read into the early morning hours. That hadn't changed in over twenty years.

She considered knocking on his door and letting him help chase away the remnants of her nightmare, but decided against it. It was past time to deal with them herself.

Olivia paused in the gourmet kitchen's entrance. Darkness gathered around her like the shadows in her nightmare—circling her and growing nearer. Dread twisted her belly. Her breathing became jerky and shallow as heaviness pressed down on her chest.

She threw out her hand and flattened it against the cool, smooth wall. Closing her eyes, Olivia concentrated on the solidness beneath her palm and not the coil of blackness that tightened its noose around her. She imagined the generations of Kincaids who'd lived protected within these very same walls. She reminded herself that her childhood had been spent in this house. There was nothing to be frightened of here.

Nothing.

"I am safe. I am secure. I am *not* afraid," she whispered.

The terror retreated and the anxiety eased, as did her labored breathing. Finally, she opened her eyes and lowered her hand. She felt like she'd just run a marathon. Brushing a hand across her sweat-dampened face, she limped into the kitchen and flicked on the light.

With steadier hands than she thought possible, she retrieved a saucepan and poured milk into it. No instant-mix-with-hot-water chocolate, but the honest-to-goodness stuff with cocoa, sugar, and a splash of vanilla. Anything less would've been blasphemous in the Kincaid household.

Olivia heard a faint shuffling and froze, then recognized her father's footsteps in the hallway. She was torn between wanting his reassuring presence and scorning her uncharacteristic dependence. She added another cup of milk to the saucepan, set it on the stove, and turned on the burner.

"There's enough for two," she said, looking at him over her shoulder.

Her father stuck his hands in his bathrobe pockets and studied her, as if seeing her for the first time.

Olivia grew concerned. "What's wrong, Dad?"

He blinked, and she almost believed he was blushing, but retired Judge Andrew Kincaid never blushed.

"For a second, you looked exactly like your mother," he said softly.

Olivia turned away to retrieve two cups from the cupboard and to hide the moisture sheen in her eyes at his unexpected comment. "Must be a trick of the light."

She heard the telltale slipper shuffle again as he came up behind her. "I'll take care of that. You sit down," her father said as he took the mugs from her hands.

Smiling despite her exasperation, she didn't bother to argue. Leaning on her cane, she limped to the breakfast nook. She pulled out a chair, its legs scraping quietly across the parquet floor, and sat down. She leaned her cane against the wall behind her and propped her elbows on the table.

"With or without cinnamon?" he asked.

"With," she replied, enjoying the rare moment of serenity.

"Is your leg bothering you?" he asked, keeping his back to her.

Olivia automatically massaged the scarred flesh above her knee. "A little."

"Ask your therapist about it."

"I might cancel tomorrow's session," she said, the tranquillity fading.

He looked at her over his shoulder. "Why?" He narrowed his eyes. "Does this have anything to do with the new batch of convicts coming in?"

Olivia considered lying, but ever since she was a little girl, she hadn't been able to slip a lie or a bluff past her father. It was a good thing she'd never had to face him in a courtroom.

"You know my feelings on the matter," she replied, her shoulders tensing under his steady gaze.

Steam rose from the milk on the stove, and her father poured it into the mugs and stirred. He brought them to the table and set one in front of Olivia.

"Thanks." She wrapped her hands around the mug's warmth and inhaled the familiar, soothing aroma of cinnamon and chocolate.

Her father sat across from her and mirrored her hold on his own mug. She glanced up at him and recognized the glint in his eyes. She almost wished she hadn't surrendered to the chocolate siren.

"I don't understand why you're against the work release program," he said.

Olivia clamped down on her frustration. "They're criminals, Dad. My job is to put men like them away for the longest sentence allowable by law. I don't work my butt off every day just so people like you can grant them early release."

He blew across his hot chocolate and then took a tentative sip. Olivia suspected it was to give him time to form a rebuttal.

"Prisons are overcrowded. There are incarcerated people who deserve another chance. Those are the ones I try to help," he said quietly but with an underlying steeliness.

Olivia gazed at her father, taking in the deeply etched lines in his tanned face topped by a full head of white hair. The steadiness of his gray eyes defied his seventy-one years. A lawyer for twenty years, a judge for nineteen, and a rancher all of his life, Andrew Kincaid should've been the poster child for the right-wingers. However, the fates had played a practical joke—he was the liberal and Olivia the conservative.

"And when they kill or beat or rob someone right after their early release, who explains to the victims and their families why this convicted felon was out on the streets weeks, even months, early?" She forced herself to hold his gaze and asked in a tremulous voice, "How did you feel when that victim was Mom?"

Her father didn't flinch. "She would've been the last person who'd want me to pull my support because of the actions of a few." He leaned forward and laid a large, callused hand over Olivia's clasped one. "Your mother's been gone for over twenty years, honey. It's time to let her go."

Olivia stared down at her father's hand on hers and

concentrated on keeping the lump in her throat from expanding. Ever since she'd returned to the ranch for an unexpected—and extended—visit, her emotions had wavered near the surface. For a woman who hadn't cried in years, she was blindsided by this continuing welling up of sadness. And yet, part of her felt almost detached from this maudlin side she hadn't known existed within her.

Her mother's murder, when Olivia was only eight, was the reason she became a prosecutor. She had never faltered from her goal, studying nights while her fellow high school students partied. During college and law school, she'd also ignored the social activities and worked at the courthouse when she wasn't hitting the books. She hadn't let anything get in the way of her goal, including emotions and relationships.

After a few moments, she cleared her throat and raised her mug to take a drink. Her father's hand fell away.

They sat quietly, sipping their hot chocolate. This would be the last night of peace for Olivia. Tomorrow the ranch would become a temporary home and workplace for five convicted felons—men who'd committed violent acts against innocent victims.

Men she would've eagerly prosecuted.

Men just like the one who'd murdered her mother.

As the prison van jolted down the country road, Hank Elliott soaked up the sights and sounds of freedom. Three months ago the concept of freedom had been an abstract one. With another year to go until he was eligible for parole, Hank had been taking one day at a time, keeping his nose out of trouble and his ass intact, just as he'd done the previous six years.

Six long, bitter years.

A rough nudge startled him back to reality, and he glared at the man across the aisle. "Keep your hands to yourself, Mantle."

The convict raised his cuffed hands and widened his eyes. "Ooooh, you're scaring me."

"Fuck you," Hank retorted. He deliberately cast his gaze back to the window and the undulating landscape of tans and browns.

Mantle was a coldhearted, sneaky bastard and was known among the other prisoners as someone to steer clear of, especially the younger men, barely out of boyhood. But he was also adept at showing those in charge what they wanted to see. He'd bullshitted his way into the work release program, and Hank vowed to keep an eye on him, to ensure he didn't do anything to endanger Hank's chance at an early release.

The road curved sharply, and ranch buildings came into view. Hank sat up straighter, anxious to see where he'd be spending the next three months of his life. Twelve weeks that would either free him or damn him back to prison. Hank had no intention of returning to the correctional facility.

"You think we'll each get a room to ourselves?" Barton, the youngest prisoner on the van, asked.

"You scared for your virtue, kid?" Mantle asked, lifting his eyebrows suggestively at the twenty-one-year-old.

"Leave him alone," Lopez, a swarthy Mexican convicted of assault, warned. A puckered scar down the Mexican's left cheek gave him a menacing appearance that had aided him in keeping alive in prison. However, Hank had found Lopez to be a decent man who'd done a stupid thing in a moment of passion, which had led to his imprisonment.

Mantle narrowed his ferrety eyes and leaned toward Lopez. "Or what?"

"Or you'll go back to the pen and rot for another ten years," the corrections officer interjected. Armstrong rested his hand on the heavy stick in his utility belt.

Mantle sat up straight and affected an air of remorse. "Yes, sir. Sorry."

Hank rolled his eyes as Armstrong accepted Mantle's apology at face value. Disgusted, he turned his attention to the window and watched the ranch take shape as they neared it. Although he wanted to whistle at the impressive corrals and horses that populated them, he kept his expression bland. A heavy-duty pickup was parked in the yard, and a two-ton truck was backed up to a large shed. A black Dodge Ram with a white trailer that had Ted Shandler, Farrier in bold black letters on the side was pulled up next to one of the two barns. A green tractor with four huge tires pulling a loaded hay wagon was moving away from the yard, probably off to feed cattle in one of the pastures.

Hank's family's ranch wasn't nearly this big or this neat. Of course, it wasn't the Elliott ranch anymore, either. Sold to pay off debts and lawyer fees, the ranch had been gobbled up by a sprawling corporation.

The familiar acidic bitterness burned his gut. He'd lost everything: his home; his dreams; and his sister, the only family he'd had left.

The van stopped, snapping him back to the present.

Armstrong stood and faced them. "All right, everyone out."

Hank donned his prison-issued black ball cap but remained in his seat, allowing his four fellow prisoners to exit the stuffy vehicle before him. He grabbed his bag, which held toiletries, underwear, another pair of blue jeans, and two more chambray shirts with Wilson Correctional Facility printed on the front pocket. Standing, he had to keep his neck bowed so he wouldn't hit the van's roof. He stepped out into the relative warmth of the late May sun.

Hank tipped his head back and gazed at a blue sky unbroken by clouds and iron bars. For a moment, he felt the sting of tears but quickly shoved the emotion deep inside. The weak were always the victims, and Hank had sworn his first day in lockup that he wouldn't be a victim ever again.

"C'mon, Elliott, get in line," Armstrong ordered impatiently, motioning with his stick toward the other convicts.

With his bag clutched in his cuffed hands, Hank swaggered to Mantle's side. He kept his body still, but his gaze roamed over everything. They stood facing an impressive house with a wide front porch and spectacular windows that currently had dark sheers drawn across them. Not even during its best days had Hank's home looked like this. Of course, he hadn't expected Judge Kincaid's house to be anything but imposing. Still, Hank couldn't hate the man; Kincaid had requested him personally for this work program.

The front door with its frosted oval window set in an oak frame opened, and a man wearing jeans and a wide-brimmed hat stepped outside. It took a moment for Hank to recognize him as the judge. He'd only seen the man in a suit before today. But seeing Kincaid in his own domain and wearing the clothes to match, Hank was even more impressed by the man's authoritative air.

"Welcome to the Kincaid Ranch, gentlemen," the judge said as he descended the porch stairs.

Hank and the other convicts nodded in acknowledgment of the greeting.

Kincaid moved to stand in front of them, his hands in his pants pockets. He eyed each man, his gaze coming to rest on Hank last. Although it was difficult, Hank held his probing look. When Kincaid blinked first, Hank felt a small measure of satisfaction.

"Remove their cuffs," the judge ordered Armstrong.

The CO opened his mouth as if to argue, but Kincaid didn't give him a chance. "Handcuffs make it damned hard for them to do any work," he said with the barest twinkle in his eyes.

Armstrong clamped his lips together and nodded shortly. After digging the key out of his pocket, he unlocked each of the prisoner's cuffs.

Once Hank's bracelets were gone, he rubbed his wrists. The CO who'd snapped the handcuffs on him at the prison had taken cruel pleasure in tightening them so they pinched the skin. But Hank hadn't complained. There were too many sadistic guards at the prison on the wrong side of the bars, and if a prisoner spoke up against them, the corrections officers would give the stoolie "special attention." It was simply another fact of prison life Hank had learned early on.

"I've spoken with each of you men personally," Judge Kincaid began once the convicts were no longer shackled. "You know what's expected of you. You also know that if you screw up, you will be returned to the correctional facility immediately, and the rest of your term will be served without possibility of early parole or being included in another work program."

Standing behind Kincaid, Armstrong crossed his beefy arms and smiled with brutal malice. Hank hadn't had a run-in with Armstrong, but he'd seen the CO beat the crap out of more than one prisoner without provocation. It wasn't like the prisoners were real human beings, after all.

Hank swallowed his resentment and stared straight ahead.

"As long as you do your job and obey the rules, you'll be treated like any other working man on my ranch," Kincaid said.

"Does that mean we get weekends off?" Reger asked curiously.

Kincaid smiled slightly. "It means you can rest and relax one day of the weekend if you've earned it, just like the hired men." His smile faded. "But you will not be allowed to go in to town until you've proven yourself, and that will only be to pick up supplies."

"So are we going to be locked in overnight, sir?" Mantle asked with exaggerated courteousness.

"That depends."

"On what?"

"On you." Kincaid stared at Mantle until the convict dropped his gaze.

Hank frowned, trying to decipher what the judge meant. Would they be locked in until they proved themselves? Or would they have the illusion of freedom, but there'd be a guard outside their door?

It didn't matter. Hank had no intention of fucking up his chance to get an early out from hell.

"You'll be fed well, better than the prison food you've been getting, but then you'll be working much harder than you did in there, too," Kincaid went on. "Breakfast is at six thirty, lunch at noon, and dinner at six thirty."

Hank's stomach growled, reminding him he'd eaten little for breakfast. He'd been too anxious to leave the harsh prison behind.

Kincaid glanced at Hank, and a smile lifted his thin lips. "Sounds like you haven't had lunch."

"No, sir," Hank said automatically, and then clamped his mouth shut.

With his head bowed to hide his expression from the judge, Mantle sniggered beside him. Hank fisted his hands, willing them to stay by his side.

"I'll have Connie fix something, and after you've all eaten, I'll take you around and get you started," Kincaid said. He turned and pointed to a long wooden building with a porch, set between two larger structures. "The middle building will be your home for the next three months. The bunkhouse for the hired men is next to it. On the other side of your new home is the kitchen and dining hall. You don't show up when the meal is served, you're out of luck until the next one." He held up his forefinger. "One word of warning. Don't tick off the cook."

Hank couldn't help but smile slightly. He remembered his father giving him the same advice when he was a kid, only it was his mother who'd been their cook. Abruptly, he crushed the trip down memory lane.

"Any questions?" Kincaid asked.

Nobody moved.

"This isn't prison, and you don't have to be afraid to speak out."

Not a twitch.

Kincaid took a deep breath and let it out slowly. "All right, if there aren't any questions, go ahead and pick out a bunk, then meet in the dining hall for some lunch."

For a moment, Hank was afraid to move, afraid that this was all some cruel joke, and Armstrong would cuff him and lead him back into the van. He mentally shook himself. It was going to take some time to get used to not being surrounded by bars.

He started toward their assigned building, following Mantle.

A horse squealed, and Hank spun around. Inside one of the smaller corrals, he spotted a stallion snubbed to a post and a burly man with a leather apron standing beside him. The frenzied horse tried to rear up, but the rope prevented him from doing so. However, as Hank watched, the rope snapped, and the stallion's front hooves dropped dangerously close to the blacksmith, who was trapped between the fence and the angry horse.

Hank dropped his bag and raced across the yard, vaulting over the corral fence.

Once inside the enclosure, he tried to gain the stallion's attention to give the blacksmith a chance to escape. He waved his arms at the horse and shouted, "Over here!"

The enraged animal spun around to face the new threat, and Hank slowly retreated. With any luck, he could roll under the fence before the horse could crush him beneath his hooves. Although he kept his attention on the pawing stallion, he saw out of his peripheral vision the farrier scramble over the fence with more dexterity than it seemed his bulk would allow.

The stallion suddenly charged, and Hank hit the ground rolling. He felt the brush of air as the horse galloped past him and around the inside of the pen.

"Are you okay, Elliott?" Kincaid asked as he offered him a hand.

Hank stared at the hand, for a moment wondering if there was a shiv in the other one. Realizing again that he wasn't in prison, he accepted the judge's help to get to his feet. But he released the man's hand as soon as he was standing.

"Fine," Hank replied tersely.

Behind Kincaid, Reger and Mantle exchanged money, and Hank wondered who'd bet on him getting smashed to a pulp.

Then he spotted the brawny farrier striding toward him and tensed, expecting . . . he didn't know what.

"Thanks, mister," the big man said, smiling widely and extending a meaty hand.

Hank fought back his learned aversion to a simple handshake and found his hand swallowed up by the farrier's ham-sized one. As soon as he could, he pulled his hand free. "It was nothing," he said awkwardly.

"It was more than that," Kincaid said. He introduced the farrier as Ted Shandler. "We owe you a debt, Elliott."

Hank merely glanced down and shook his head. He didn't want to be singled out. Survival depended on anonymity.

"You've worked around horses before," Shandler said, his arms crossed and his biceps bulging beneath his T-shirt sleeves.

Hank shrugged. "Some."

"If the judge agrees, I wouldn't mind having you give me a hand when I'm working with some of the surlier horses."

"Elliott's proven himself," Kincaid said, his eyes too knowing.

Hank looked from his new boss to Shandler's friendly face and felt something akin to a smile tug at his lips. "Sure."

Kincaid clapped his hands together. "Good. After you eat, give Ted a hand with that stallion and the other horses. All of the working stock have to be reshod."

With the excitement past, Hank headed toward his temporary home. He paused to pick up his bag and noticed a movement in one of the main house's windows. He narrowed his eyes and managed to pick out a woman's face framed by blond hair.

The curtain fell back into place, but not before Hank saw her mouth twist into an ugly scowl.

CHAPTER TWO

OLIVIA tried to concentrate on her book, an Oprah pick from a few years ago, but she'd reread the same page three times and still had no idea what was going on. She grimaced, dog-eared the page to mark her place, and tossed the book on the window seat beside her.

Pressing aside the gauzy sheers, she gazed out at the activity in the ranch yard. Men were milling about, getting their day's orders from Buck, the foreman. Despite her aversion to the convicts, she couldn't help but search for them among the legitimate hired men. They were fairly easy to spot with their black caps—most everyone else wore a wide-brimmed hat.

Buck directed the Hispanic and the youngest prisoner toward the farthest barn. By their expressions, they weren't pleased with their assignment. Olivia figured they'd been given the task of shoveling manure. She wrinkled her nose, not envying them but not sympathetic either. The shifty convict, who reminded Olivia of a fat-cheeked gopher, and the prisoner who looked like a wrestler were sent with a group of men into the back of a big truck. It appeared they'd drawn fence-mending duty.

Although Olivia knew her father handpicked the prisoners who came to work on the ranch, icy fingers of dread crawled down her back. Nobody could predict how those men would act once they were outside the prison walls. One of them could slip away from his work detail and find his way to the house . . .

Taking a deep breath, Olivia pictured the gun cabinet in her father's study. She knew exactly where he kept the key to it and which drawer the revolver was in. One day, not long after she'd returned home when her father was out talking to the foreman, she'd unlocked the cabinet and lifted out the gun. Her father had taught her how to shoot when she was a teenager and, with the weapon in her hands, she'd felt safe for the first time since the attack. Another day when he was outside, she'd timed how long it took her to get from the front room to the study to retrieve the gun. She'd wrapped that knowledge around her like a security blanket. No one would catch her unaware or unarmed again.

Feeling more in control, Olivia shifted her attention to the remaining convict, the one who'd spotted her peeking out the window two days ago, when they'd first arrived. He stood silently with his hands clasped behind his back as he listened to Buck give him his day's task. She had a clear view of the man's expression, which was bland almost to the point of insolence. Even from behind her glass wall, she could feel his cold resentment. She'd seen that kind of attitude before, from conscienceless murderers and heartless rapists.

The convict nodded to Buck, then pivoted slowly to face the window. His gaze locked with Olivia's as if he'd known she was there all along. She ordered her fingers to release the curtain, to let it shield her from his hypnotic glare, but they wouldn't obey her. Instead, she remained trapped by the prisoner's dark eyes, as helpless as she'd been when—

A cry escaped her throat and she stumbled back, dropping the curtain into place. She lurched away from the window seat but nearly crumpled to her knees at the weakness of her bad leg. Scrabbling for balance, she thrust out a hand and caught herself on the back of the sofa.

She registered the sound of the front door opening and heavy footsteps coming toward her. No time to get the gun. She'd failed to protect herself. Again.

Throwing an arm across her face, she cried, "No! Leave me alone."

"Olivia, it's just me, your father," came a calming voice. "It's all right, honey. There's nobody here but you and me. I promise."

Olivia's breath rasped raggedly. She focused on her father's soothing timbre, on the familiarity of the tone, and her terror faded. Lowering her arm, she opened her eyes and saw her father standing a wary distance away. She slumped against the sofa. "I-I'm sorry."

He closed the gap between them and carefully wrapped his arms around her. "It's all right, Livvie. You're safe here."

Her father's use of her childhood name should've reassured her, but instead, anger rose sharp and ugly. She pulled out of his embrace and reached for her cane, another reminder of the horrible night that had robbed her of something infinitely more valuable than money and physical health.

"I hate this," she hissed as she limp-paced behind the couch.

Her father dropped his gaze to the floor. "The doctor said it would take time to heal." He lifted his head, and apology shone in his eyes. "Both physically and psychologically."

"How long? It's been over two months." She stopped, closed her eyes, and tipped her head back, fighting tears. "Over two months I've been afraid of my own shadow. I just want to be like I was."

She heard her father's heavy sigh. "You were stalked and assaulted, Liv. A person doesn't recover from that overnight. Or even in a few weeks or months. The son of a bitch stole your feelings of security and safety."

Olivia had heard it all before—from her fellow assistant district attorneys and her shrink. Same old overplayed tune.

She opened her eyes and faced her father. "I know that and accept it, so why can't I move past it?"

"You can't run before you walk."

She managed a tight smile and raised her cane. "How appropriate, Dad."

Impatience twitched his lips. "Locking yourself away in this house isn't helping you heal."

"If you hadn't brought those convicts here, I'd still be taking my morning walks around the yard." She knew she was being irrational and petty, but she didn't care.

He shook his head, not falling for her offensive ploy. "They're an excuse. Any time you want to go outside, I'll walk with you." He paused and eyed her shrewdly. "Or don't you trust me?"

She should've known he'd use any weapon in his arsenal, including guilt, to get his way. "You know I trust you."

He arched his brow. "Then let's go see Misty's new foals."

"Foals?"

"She had twins—a filly and a colt—last night."

For a moment, Olivia forgot her fears. "Are they healthy?"

"Right as rain. And cuter'n two bugs in a rug." He canted his head, mutely asking her to accompany him.

Olivia's mouth lost all moisture. Walk outside? Leave her sanctuary?

"I d-don't . . ." She shook her head, hating herself for her cowardice.

"You say you want to be like your old self? You can't do that hiding in here," her father stated.

She hated it when he used her own words against her. But then, that's what a lawyer was trained to do. She should know.

She glanced down the foyer, at the solid oak door. All she had to do was swing the door open and step outside into the sunlight. Outside where the convicts were.

She turned to look down the hall, at the door to her father's study where the gun was kept. Maybe she could take it with her. Nobody would know if she tucked it into her jacket pocket.

I would know.

Wrestling with her fear, Olivia closed her eyes. She used to be called the "risk taker" in the Chicago district attorney's office. It was time to start living up to that name again.

Her heart hammered in her chest, but she nodded. "All right."

He smiled warmly. "Good."

Olivia braced herself and started to the door. Her father followed, and when she stopped, he gave her shoulder a gentle squeeze.

"Gotta walk before you can run," he repeated softly.

Olivia shook her head, amused in spite of her belly-cramping dread. With a shaking hand she reached out and turned the doorknob. Fresh air redolent of fresh-cut hay washed across her face as the door swung open.

Steeling herself, she hobbled out to stand in the center of the wide porch. The scent of juniper drifted past her, and Olivia took a deep breath of the pungency. Her father's familiar aftershave mixed with the juniper, and her pulse slowed its frantic beat.

"Whenever you're ready," he said.

Olivia gripped her cane tightly and kept her gaze averted from the activity around the corrals. Continuing down the steps, she used the porch post to help keep the weight off her bad leg. To get to Misty and her foals, Olivia would have to walk past the men saddling and loading horses into a trailer. Could she do it?

She had to—to prove she could.

Her father walked close beside her but didn't physically aid her. She was grateful for that. It was difficult enough to accept her emotional dependence on him.

He kept himself between her and the hired men, but many of them touched their hat brims and greeted her with sincere respect and pleasure. Some had worked on the ranch for years, since before she moved away, and Olivia relaxed amid the familiar faces.

She glanced over at the corral and met the remaining prisoner's cold eyes. Her footsteps faltered.

"Is something wrong?" her father asked.

"Which one is he?" she demanded.

He followed her line of sight. "Hank Elliott. I'll introduce you." Before she could argue, he called out, "Elliott. Come here."

The rangy man swaggered over to them and stopped a few feet away, one hip cocked. "Yes, sir?"

"This is my daughter, Olivia. Olivia, this is Hank Elliott."

"Ma'am," Elliott drawled.

Olivia couldn't have spoken if her life depended on it. All she could do was nod.

"We were just going to peek in on Misty's foals. Care to join us?" her father asked him.

Olivia shot him a disbelieving look, but he didn't seem to notice.

Elliott didn't reply, but he fell into step on the other side of Olivia. Her heart hammered in her breast as the man's intensity battered her already-strained defenses. She could easily visualize him in the defendant's chair in a court-room, his expression contemptuous as he dared the jury to convict him. And if Olivia had been the prosecutor, she would've fought to have him put away for a very long time.

His long legs moved with smooth, stealthy motions as his thighs surged against denim. He swung his arms easily, and Olivia couldn't help but notice the flexing of his fore-arms beneath the rolled-up sleeves of his chambray shirt. Pure masculinity radiated from him like blinding rays of sunlight, and both were equally scorching.

Attracted to him despite everything, Olivia reminded herself that Ted Bundy had been good-looking, too. So was the man who'd stalked and attacked her.

To deflect her downward-spiraling thoughts, she

glanced away and found her attention captured by the worn brown boots encasing Elliott's feet. Something told her he was no stranger to ranch work. That insight made him seem somehow more human, and her fear diminished slightly.

At the entrance to the barn, Olivia went in first with her father behind her. Elliott brought up the rear, but Olivia was hyperaware of his presence. Her father's hand on her back guided her past a half-dozen stalls before they arrived at Misty's.

Olivia leaned against the gate and peered through the slats to see the newborn foals. Their spindly legs appeared too thin to hold them upright, but the young horses were surprisingly steady. The colt was suckling one of his mother's teats while the filly butted her brother.

Momentarily forgetting about the convict, Olivia laughed softly at the foals' antics. "They're beautiful."

"Without Hank, they wouldn't have survived," her father said.

Olivia straightened in surprise to glance at him.

Her father answered her unspoken question. "The first one had to be turned before either of them could come out. The vet wasn't going to get here in time, but Hank was able to do it and save them both."

Olivia turned her attention to the flat hazel eyes that gazed at her. Her mouth grew dry, but she forced herself to ask, "How did you know what to do?"

Elliott shrugged, insolence written in the careless gesture. "I grew up on a ranch."

"He wants to be a veterinarian," her father added.

A flash of annoyance streaked across Elliott's face, but he only shrugged again. "*Wanted* to be a veterinarian."

"So what happened that kept you from going to vet school?" Olivia asked, her natural curiosity asserting itself.

His hard lips curled upward, but there was no warmth in the expression. "Prison happened."

She lifted her chin. "The consequences of breaking the law."

His jaw muscle knotted. "Yes, ma'am."

Although the words were correct, his disdainful tone caused her to flinch.

"You should get going. The men probably have the horses loaded up," her father said to Elliott.

"Yes, sir." He spun around and stalked out of the barn.

Olivia scowled at the convict's back. "How can you trust him?"

"Don't judge him until you get all the facts, Liv," her father said with a glimmer of his stern judge persona. "As a lawyer, you should know that."

"Obviously he's already been judged and found guilty, or he wouldn't have been in prison. What did he do?"

"Accessory to felonious assault. He pleaded not guilty."

Olivia snorted. "They all plead their innocence. It doesn't mean a damn thing."

"Right. Every person in prison deserves to be there." His tone was rife with sarcasm.

"You said it. I didn't."

Her father shook her head. "The system isn't perfect, Liv. You know that. Sometimes the innocent are convicted."

"And too often the guilty aren't."

"You have your mother's stubbornness."

"And that's a bad thing?"

"Only when you let it blind you."

Olivia gripped her cane tightly. "Stubbornness didn't blind me to the bastard who did this." She glanced down at her leg. "He'd already stalked and assaulted at least two other women. I tried to put him in prison where he belonged."

"You did your best."

"And look where it got me. I'm thirty years old and living with my father because I'm too scared to live on my own." She choked on the last word, hating herself for what she'd become.

Her father put his arm around her shoulders, but she threw it off and moved away from the stall. Knowing he was only trying to help made her feel guilty, but she was too full of self-disgust and anger.

Outside the barn, she stood for a moment, taking long breaths to loosen the constricting band around her chest. A clang caught her attention, and she looked over to see Elliott closing the back end of the horse trailer.

As if knowing she was there, he turned and swept his hungry gaze up and down her body. Elliott wore his virility like a suit of armor and wielded his sultry gaze like a sword. Even suspecting this knight possessed no chivalry, Olivia couldn't deny the arrow of heat streaking through her.

Although Olivia's attacker hadn't raped her, lying in her hospital bed afterward, she'd believed she would never experience a woman's desire for a man again. But this convicted felon stirred something deep and primal within her.

Something she thought was as dead as her self-confidence.

"Do you want to continue walking?" her father asked from close beside her.

Olivia jerked, startled. Before she could answer, Elliott spun away and joined three other men in the quad cab of the pickup. She watched the truck and horse trailer bump down the driveway.

Breathing a sigh of relief that Elliott was gone and the yard was now deserted, she replied, "Yes. It's nice to be outside."

Although he didn't say anything, Olivia knew her father was pleased that she didn't scurry back into her hidey-hole. She linked her arm with his, and he patted her hand as they continued walking.

"Where are they going?" she asked, motioning toward the departing pickup and trailer.

"Antler Creek. Some cattle are getting out in that area. They're going to gather up the strays, then find the break in the fence."

"I'm surprised you let Elliott go with them. Aren't you afraid he'll keep riding?"

"No. He won't chance ruining the possibility of getting

out a few months early. Besides, he's already proven himself. Right after he got here."

"When he saved the farrier?"

"You saw that?"

"I was looking out the window," she admitted.

"Then you know he put himself in danger to help a stranger. In my book, that's not the act of your typical convict."

"Maybe he only did it to gain your trust." Olivia wasn't about to let Hank Elliott off the hook that easily.

Her father shrugged. "It's possible, but it seemed more instinctive than calculated."

Olivia pressed her lips together, not accepting the prisoner's supposedly selfless motives as quickly as her father. She had yet to meet a convict who didn't have an agenda, an angle. She'd discover Elliott's, one way or another.

"BREAK'S over. Back to work."

Hank stifled a groan and pushed away from his comfortable lean against a cottonwood. After being in the saddle for four hours, it had felt damned good to be standing on his own two feet.

Keeping his discomfort and thoughts hidden, he tightened his saddle cinch and mounted. His thigh muscles protested, but he ignored them.

"Ready to return to your comfy cell, Elliott?"

Hank schooled his face into a blank mask and turned to his persecutor. Rollie. No surprise there. Rollie had been riding his ass ever since Hank started working at the ranch. The man was a bully with a gut that hung over his belt and mean snake eyes.

"Why don't you crawl back into the hole you came from?" Hank asked conversationally.

Rollie's eyes narrowed as he smiled coldly. "You think you got it made with the boss, but I wouldn't bet on it. Once a con, always a con. Something happens, and you're gonna be the first person everyone turns on."

"You threatening me?"

"That ain't a threat. Just a friendly warning."

"Knock it off, ladies. We've got work to do," Buck said, riding up behind them.

Hank nodded at the foreman, glad for the interruption. He nudged his horse away from Rollie. Hank had allowed his prison-learned defenses to slip. Being away from the palpable violence and hopelessness behind the walls, Hank could almost imagine he was back in the world he'd grown up in. But Rollie had reminded him it was only an illusion.

Kincaid's daughter was also a reminder of his less-than-human status. He hadn't seen a woman like her in over six years, and his body wasn't shy about reminding him how long it'd been since he'd been laid. Those snug blue jeans hugging her pert ass and the blouse that did little to hide her firm, high breasts had him as hard as an iron bar in record time.

But the disgust in her eyes told Hank she didn't share her father's sense of fairness, and that it'd be a cold day in hell before she shared her bed with someone like him. Not that he blamed her. Like Rollie said, once a con, always a con.

Still, Hank couldn't dismiss Olivia Kincaid that easily from his thoughts. In addition to disgust, he'd recognized fear in her eyes. Fear and pain. Someone had hurt her. Badly. A swell of protectiveness cracked through his bitter wall.

A cow burst out of some brush, and Hank was grateful for the distraction.

He didn't want to feel anything for Olivia Kincaid . . . or anyone else.

Chapter Three

Olivia limped into the kitchen minus her cane and was greeted with the radio announcer's, "Welcome to *Swap Shop*. Our first caller on the line this morning has canning jars and lids for sale." She smiled at the small-town radio show she'd often listened to as a child.

The coffeepot was nearly empty, a testament to her father's caffeine habit. Although it wasn't good for his health, she knew she'd have more success convincing a suspect to confess to murder than convincing her father to cut back. She poured the remainder into a cup and put on another pot, then joined her father in the breakfast nook.

"Are you looking for anything in particular?" she asked.

Her father glanced up from the newspaper, his brow furrowed in puzzlement. "What?"

"You're listening to *Swap Shop*."

It took another moment before his expression registered that he understood her reference. His lips curled in amusement. "Oh, no. I listened to the local news and forgot to turn it off."

He reached over, and the caller trying to find a rear

bumper for his 1971 Ford truck was cut off in midsentence. "How did you sleep?" he asked.

Olivia smiled. "Actually, better than I have in weeks. I only woke up twice and didn't have any trouble falling back to sleep."

He nodded, obviously pleased by her progress. "Getting outside every day helps." He folded the newspaper and set it aside. "I know it's been difficult for you since the prisoners got here, and I'm proud of your progress."

Olivia's cheeks heated, but she held his gaze. "I still don't like having them here. They're dangerous men, Dad."

He leaned forward, his forearm resting on the table. "I've always been careful, taking only prisoners I believe are nonviolent and who deserve the chance to prove themselves. The rewards substantially outweigh the minor risks."

Olivia shuddered. "That's *your* opinion."

Her father sighed and dragged a hand across his face, but his gaze was determined and his voice resolute when he spoke. "I helped establish this program, and I'm not about to abandon it."

She took a deep breath, struggling to contain her impatience with his stubbornness. Although she respected and admired her father, she hated this blind spot he possessed. "Fine. We agree to disagree."

His disappointment made Olivia cringe inwardly, but she wouldn't—couldn't—agree.

She carried their empty cups to the sink, rinsed them, and set them by the coffeepot. Leaning against the counter, she watched out the window at the men gathered in the yard, waiting for their day's assignments.

She'd learned the convicts' names from her father and sought out each one now, to ensure they were all accounted for. Lopez, the Hispanic, and the youngest con, Barton, were standing beside one of the corrals smoking cigarettes. Reger, a husky, nondescript man with brown hair and washed-out features, was hunkered on his haunches a few feet away drawing in the dirt with a twig. Mantle, the furtive, gopher-cheeked man, was talking it up with Rollie, one of the hired men.

Her gaze automatically sought Hank Elliott's lean figure. With his arms crossed, he leaned his shoulder against a corral post. His cap was tugged low over his eyes, but Olivia suspected he was observing and taking mental notes of every person around him. His face had lost its prison pallor and gained a deep golden tan, enhancing his good looks. His hands and forearms, too, had been darkened by the sun. If anything, her unexplainable reaction to him had grown stronger, which only increased her wariness.

The appearance of an unfamiliar car wending its way up the long driveway stole her attention from Hank.

"Are you expecting someone, Dad?"

"No. Why?"

"There's a white car coming in."

He joined her by the sink and swore under his breath.

"Who is it?" Olivia asked, puzzled by his reaction.

"Melinda Curry Holcomb." He growled out the name.

Olivia flashed back to a bouncy brunette in a cheerleader outfit demanding Olivia fork over her homework so she could copy it. The memory wasn't a pleasant one. "I went to high school with her."

"She reminded me of that when I ran into her about a month ago," her father said dryly.

"What does she want?"

"She writes a gossip column for the county paper. When I saw her, she said she wanted to come out and interview you. I told her you weren't feeling well."

Olivia's mouth grew cottony. It was bad enough that her father and coworkers knew of her near breakdown. "I don't want to talk to her."

Her father patted her shoulder. "You stay here. I'll get rid of her." He strode out of the kitchen.

Olivia curled her fingers around the edge of the counter as she watched her father step off the porch. Her attention shifted to Melinda, who was getting out of the sedan. Al-

though it had been twelve years since high school gradua-
tion, Olivia had no trouble recognizing her former classmate. Melinda's former shoulder-length dark hair was now
cut in a short, sassy style, and she wore a fire engine red
halter top, skintight white capris, and heeled sandals that
matched her blouse.

The conversation between her father and Melinda was
punctuated by hand waving and stiff body language. It
didn't look like she would take no for an answer.

Irritated with both Melinda and herself for allowing her
father to fight her battles, Olivia squared her shoulders and
limped outside onto the porch.

Melinda spotted her immediately and dodged around
Olivia's father. The woman's staccato heels echoed on the
wooden porch.

"It's been a long time, Olivia," Melinda said, her voice
as brassy as her clothing.

Not long enough.

"Yes, it has been." Olivia crossed her arms, hoping she
looked more composed than she felt. "What do you want?"

"An interview. I've already talked to the Chicago police
and the district attorney's office about your attack. I could
write my story with what I have, but I thought it might be
good to hear it from you."

"Olivia?" her father asked, clearly wondering how she
was handling Melinda's prying.

Olivia didn't like it, but if she didn't talk to her, Melinda
would put her own spin on the story.

"It's okay, Dad. I'll answer her questions."

He seemed relieved. "I'll leave you two alone then."

Olivia was oddly relieved he wouldn't remain and be
party to her half-truths. He gave Olivia a nod of encour-
agement, then strode toward the barn.

"Why don't we sit down?" Olivia asked, pointing to one
of the wicker chairs on the porch.

Melinda sank into one. "So how did you hurt your leg?"

She'd obviously noticed Olivia's limp when she'd
come out of the house.

"You should know," Olivia replied. "You talked to the police."

Melinda had the grace to glance down, but her penitence didn't last long. She met Olivia's gaze with her own haughty one. "I only received the official version. I'd like yours." She tugged a small notebook and pen out of her purse.

Olivia gritted her teeth and looked beyond the porch to the men milling about. Many of them were watching her and Melinda with unabashed curiosity. She quickly glanced down, fighting the urge to flee into the house, and cleared her throat. "My kneecap was smashed, but the doctors did an excellent reconstruction job."

"So why are you still here? Surely you've recovered enough to go back to work."

Olivia wasn't about to explain her personal demons to this woman and have them splashed across the front page of the county paper. "I'm still on medical leave. As soon as I've healed completely, I'll return to my job."

"I was under the assumption you were seeing a psychologist."

Olivia's face heated with both anger and humiliation. The only people who knew she had gone to a counselor were her fellow prosecutors in the DA's office. Who disliked her so much that he or she would divulge the confidentiality?

"I visited one twice while still in Chicago," she answered curtly.

"But not here?"

Olivia shook her head, afraid to trust her voice.

"Why did Peter Larsen attack you?" Melinda asked, not pulling any punches.

Although the jagged memories came fast and furious, Olivia managed to keep her face and voice cool. "I had tried to indict him for stalking and assaulting two women, but there wasn't enough evidence. I didn't succeed. He made me his next victim. End of story."

"Surely there's more to it than that."

Olivia clasped her hands and rested them in her lap to hide the trembling. "Those are the facts."

"But how did you feel during the attack? Were you frightened?"

Fragments of that night strobed through Olivia's mind: Larsen swinging the bat at her knee, his leer as he slapped her, his hand on her breast. She choked back the bile rising in her throat and struggled for a calm that wasn't there. "Only a fool wouldn't have been frightened, Melinda, and I'm no fool. I'm only trying to put it behind me now."

Melinda leaned forward, looking like a shark going in for the kill. "So you *are* having trouble dealing with it."

Irritation cut through the lingering fear. "It isn't something a person recovers from overnight, but I'm handling it."

"Are you? No one has seen you since you returned."

"I visit my physical therapist twice a week in Walden." Olivia stood. "If there's nothing else . . . ?"

Melinda reluctantly returned her notebook and pen to her purse, then rose. "I think you've answered my questions."

Olivia didn't like her tone. It implied Melinda had read more into her censored answers.

The highly strung stallion neighed from its corral, drawing Olivia's attention. Her father had bought him a few months ago for breeding. Only the more experienced ranch hands could get near him. It was no surprise the farrier was still having trouble with him.

"What a beautiful animal. I'd like to take a closer look," Melinda said, her gaze on the corral.

The woman didn't strike Olivia as the type to be interested in a horse. Did she suspect Olivia was frightened of leaving the house and wanted to have her theory proven correct? Though she had gone outside every day since she'd seen Misty and her foals, and had even started helping Connie prepare lunch and dinner for the men, she only went out after the yard was empty. Now, there were a handful of hired men still standing around, including the convicts. Her father was by the barn, talking to Buck.

Olivia steeled her shaky resolve. She wouldn't let Melinda see her fear, or it would be broadcast around the entire county in the next edition of the *Jackson County Sentinel*.

"Let's go," Olivia said with forced brightness. She descended the steps carefully, her mouth dry and her heart thumping. Her legs wobbled, and she wished she'd brought her cane. However, she lifted her chin and looked out across the yard, only to have her gaze snared by Hank Elliott's. Even across the distance separating them, she felt the heat of his eyes, thawing her icy dread and turning it into something hot and volatile but no less frightening.

Conscious of the gazes following them, Olivia forced herself to ignore them. Besides, it was likely their gazes were locked on Melinda and her well-endowed curves plainly visible beneath her snug clothing rather than Olivia in her baggy sweatshirt and jeans. *Thank goodness.*

Olivia gritted her teeth as she limped across the uneven yard. Melinda's heels weren't made for traversing ranch yards, and Olivia felt a smug sense of satisfaction at the woman's gracelessness.

At the corral, Olivia leaned against a post, taking some weight off her bad leg. Melinda stood beside her and raised one foot, then the other, checking to see if her impractical heels were still intact. Despite her uneasiness, Olivia had to bite back a smile.

Melinda glanced up, but instead of looking at the stallion, she peered into another corral where the farrier and Hank were putting new shoes on one of the mares.

"Who is that?" Melinda asked, pointing at Hank.

Obviously Melinda was more enthralled with the human stallion.

"He's one of the convicts here on the work release program," Olivia answered blandly.

"Oooh, a bad boy."

Olivia didn't know whether to laugh or gag. "A *very* bad boy. I thought you were married."

"Not anymore."

"I'm sorry," Olivia said, fumbling for something to say. "I'm not."

Before Olivia could comment, the stallion trotted up to them and blew noisily, showering Melinda with droplets of horse snot.

"Ewww," Melinda said, her nose wrinkled with disgust as she brushed ineffectually at her hair and ruined blouse. Then she glared at the stallion and smacked his nose with her fist.

The excitable animal whinnied shrilly, and his eyes rolled upward. He raced away from them, and before Olivia could shout a warning, the stallion tried to leap over the fence. His right foreleg caught on the top pole, and the horse toppled to the ground inside the corral with a hair-curling scream.

Olivia nearly screamed herself, but slapped her hand over her mouth.

The stallion surged to its feet, and Olivia breathed a sigh of relief. Then she noticed the horse favoring his right leg.

"Damn," she whispered hoarsely.

The farrier, Shandler, and Hank Elliott were the first to reach the stallion. Lopez, Reger, and Barton were next, followed by the hired men who remained in the yard. They approached the animal warily. Shandler managed to grab the stallion's halter, and Lopez clipped a lead rope to it. The convict tied the horse to a post with calm, unhurried motions. Surprisingly, the stallion behaved, as if knowing they only wanted to help.

Olivia's father hurried toward her and Melinda, his expression stormy. "What happened?" he demanded.

"It was an accident, Judge Kincaid," Melinda said in a whiney voice. She plucked at her damp shirt. "He ruined my blouse, and I lost my temper."

"She hit him," Olivia said flatly. "It scared him."

Melinda flashed Olivia a reproachful glance. "It was an accident," she repeated to the judge.

"I think you should leave now, Ms. Holcomb," he said firmly.

Melinda lifted her chin. "Fine. At least I have my story."

She pivoted, nearly lost her balance on her heels, then wobbled back to her car. This time Olivia couldn't even dredge up a smidgen of amusement at her awkwardness.

"I'm sorry, Dad. I had no idea she'd do anything like that," Olivia said, guilt and misery pressing down on her.

Her father's arm settled around her shoulders. "It's not your fault, Liv."

She and her father watched Hank and Shandler examine the horse's leg. Finally, they stood back and released the stallion. He trotted away, favoring the leg only slightly.

Her father sighed in relief. "It doesn't look like he was seriously hurt."

Olivia nodded, also relieved. "Thank heavens."

"I have to talk to Buck about a couple more things. Do you want me to walk you back to the house first?" he asked.

Now that the excitement was past, fear encroached Olivia's thoughts again. She pressed it back. She'd come this far with Melinda; she could walk back by herself.

"Go ahead. I'll be fine."

He gazed at her for a moment before giving her shoulder a gentle squeeze, then walked away.

She glanced around and spotted the ferrety convict Mantle staring at her. His thin lips were curved upward in a lecherous smile. Olivia quickly turned away to begin the long trek back to the house. Her shoulders tight with tension, she could feel Mantle's lewd gaze on her. Why was he watching her? What did he want?

Her breath came in harsh gasps, and the distance to the house seemed an impossible chasm to cross. Her injured knee burned with agonizing pain, but she couldn't slow down. She had to get to safety . . . to the gun that would protect her.

A hand settled on her arm, and she spun around, seeing a black cap and a chambray shirt with Wilson Correctional Facility printed on the pocket. A scream crawled up her throat, but her bad leg buckled, stealing her breath.

Hank kept a firm hold so she didn't collapse to the ground. "Careful, Ms. Kincaid." His smooth-as-melted-butter voice slid through her.

An odd mix of relief, panic, and desire flooded Olivia when she realized it wasn't Mantle. Still, she struggled to free herself from his firm but gentle grasp. "I-I can do it myself."

He released her and stepped back. Olivia barely managed to remain upright with the loss of his support. She panted like she'd run up Longs Peak, and the unwelcome sensation of light-headedness swam through her.

"Where's your cane?" Hank asked.

Olivia pulled in a few more deep breaths, and the wooziness faded. "In the house."

He frowned, and the expression pulled at the corners of his sensuous lips. "Helluva lot of good it's doing you there."

Olivia's earlier fear faded even as her knee's pain intensified, and she snapped, "Tell me something I don't know, Mr. Elliott."

His eyes darkened. "If you won't let me help you, let me get your cane."

"So you can get the layout of the house?"

He appeared confused, but it was quickly replaced by cynicism. "Look, if you don't want my help, fine. Stumble up those stairs yourself."

He spun away and headed back to the corral.

Trembling, Olivia took a step toward the house. Pain flashed like lightning up and down her leg. Tears filled her eyes, and she damned her weakness. She looked around, but her father was nowhere in sight. But Mantle was still there, watching her like some damned snake ready to snatch a mouse. She may have lost much of her confidence, but Olivia was no mouse.

"Mr. Elliott?" she shouted.

He stopped and looked back at her over his shoulder, his expression cut from granite.

"I think I will accept your assistance," she said past the dryness of her mouth.

After a moment's hesitation, he ambled back to her side.

"Do you want to lean on me, or would you like your cane?" he asked, his low timbre wreaking havoc on her already weak defenses.

The scent of male sweat tickled Olivia's nose, and she could almost taste its brackish flavor. Harsh memories of another man's caustic sweat in her nostrils surfaced, and she cringed. Although she didn't want Hank in her sanctuary, she was more fearful of a flashback. "My cane. In my bedroom. Down the hall."

She barely saw his nod through her hazy vision, but she felt his physical withdrawal with a keenness that shocked her. Hank Elliott was a convict, someone to be distrusted, yet Olivia *wanted* to trust him.

A headache throbbed in her temples, keeping rhythm with the beat of her heart. If the knee pain didn't upset her stomach, the headache would.

"Here's your cane, Ms. Kincaid," Hank said, holding it out to her.

Her estimation of him rose a notch. He kept his distance, as if knowing his proximity bothered her. She extended her hand, and her fingers closed around the polished wood of the curved handle. She quickly put it to use, immediately easing the pressure on her bad knee. The relief was so profound, she nearly wept.

"Thank you." Her voice was faint, sounding nothing like the strong ADA's from Chicago.

Hank nodded. "I'll walk you to the porch."

Olivia nodded, again sensing she could rely on him. She made it to the bottom of the steps without embarrassing herself. In fact, her pain had abated, and the nausea had disappeared.

She turned around and lowered herself to the second step, then stretched out he bad leg in front of her. Kneading the flesh above the knee, she noted that Hank remained a good six feet away. Close enough to assist her, but far enough away to give her a sense of safety. His actions could be a ploy, but even if they were, she owed him her gratitude.

"I appreciate your help, Mr. Elliott." She found it was tougher to say the words than she expected.

"Contrary to what most people think, just because I'm a con doesn't mean I like to see people hurting." Resentment twined through his words.

Olivia was obviously in the "most people" category. Three months ago she wouldn't have cared, but now the comment drew a trickle of guilt.

She tilted her head back to look up at him, noting the defensive clench of his jaw and the challenge in his eyes. Remembering that he'd wanted to be a veterinarian, she said quietly, "I take it that goes for animals, too."

He blinked and shrugged, though Olivia guessed he wasn't expecting her comment. "They're living creatures, too."

But Olivia caught a glimpse of something behind his harsh mask. "Is that the reason you want to be a vet?"

"Wanted," he corrected sharply. His penetrating gaze skipped over her face, then settled on a butte in the distance. "Too late now."

She felt unexpected sympathy for the convict. Just like any other person, he'd had dreams, too, before he was incarcerated.

"That's too bad. From the way you examined the stallion, you'd be a good one," she said quietly.

He brought his gaze back to her, and she thought she spotted a flush in his cheeks, though his expression didn't change. "Who was that woman?" Hank asked.

It took Olivia a moment to switch mental gears. "A former high school classmate."

"Not a friend."

It wasn't a question.

"Hardly. She was one of the popular girls. You know how it was in high school. It was a long time ago." Olivia shrugged, although for the first time it bothered her that she hadn't taken time to have fun in high school or college. "Where are you from?"

"Small town south of here. My graduating class was thirty-one students."

Olivia smiled. "Mine had forty-four. I think most of them still live around here."

"Same here." He sent a quick look at the farrier. "I should get back to work."

Olivia pushed herself to her feet, surprised but grateful that Hank didn't extend a hand to help her. She hobbled up the steps, aware of his scrutiny but knowing he wouldn't get any closer.

She paused before opening the door. "I appreciate your help, Mr. Elliott." She glanced down, thinking she owed him some kind of explanation yet not understanding why. She met his curtained eyes. "I was assaulted in Chicago. He smashed my knee so I couldn't run away." Those two sentences cost her most of her remaining strength, and she entered the house.

WITH *her nose in the air, she acts like she owns the whole goddamned country. Well, she's not going to be so high and mighty when she has to pay for what she did. It's my responsibility to rid the world of people like her. My duty . . .*

CHAPTER FOUR

AFTER spending the remainder of the day inside resting her bad leg and trying to figure out Hank Elliott, Olivia checked her e-mail after dinner. She found a note from Susan, a fellow ADA and as close to a friend as she had in Chicago.

> *Liv, guess what? The old man gave me the Brubane case! This is big, Liv! If I can get a guilty verdict, the old man promised to give me more cases like this. I just hope I can do half as well as you did with your first big one. Cross your fingers for me.*
>
> *So how are you doing out there in the boonies? How's your leg? Does it look like you'll be coming back soon? We miss you.*
>
> *Everyone here says hello and get better soon. TTYL, Suse.*

Olivia smiled and clicked the Reply button. After setting her fingers on the keyboard, she froze. What should she tell her friend? That the thought of stepping into a courtroom made her sick to her stomach? That the biggest risk she could take was stepping out of the house alone and walking to the cookhouse? That going back to Chicago anytime soon was as likely as flying to the moon?

She curved her hand around the mouse and canceled the reply, logged out of her e-mail account and off the Internet. The familiar depression crawled through her, and she sought solace in oblivion. She brought up the Spider Solitaire game on the screen and clicked on the four-suit option.

Five of hearts to six of spades. Queen of diamonds to king of diamonds. Eight of clubs to nine of clubs.

The rhythm of clicking and moving the mouse to carry cards from here to there soothed her just like it had the first time she'd played not long after moving back home.

She hit the end of her run with no more cards to turn over. Another loss. She started a second game, lost that one, and then a third and fourth and on and on. Never winning, but always certain the next game would give her the satisfaction of a victory.

A knock sounded, and her concentration shattered. Time resumed its normal pace.

Her father stuck his head in the office doorway. "Are you busy?"

She cleared her throat. "No. C'mon in."

He joined her. "More solitaire?"

"Spider solitaire," she corrected. "More challenging."

His sigh was soft, but Olivia heard it. "How many hours have you been at this tonight?"

Irritation cut through her as she glanced at the anniversary clock on the bookshelf: 10:45. She'd come in to check her e-mail at 7:30. She covered her shock quickly. "Two, maybe three hours."

"Try closer to three and a half."

"Why did you ask if you already knew?" Olivia asked peevishly.

"This won't help you step back into the world, Liv."

Knowing he was right but not wanting to admit it, she started the computer shut down sequence.

"I came in to remind you I'll be leaving for Denver

early in the morning," he said. "I have a nine o'clock meeting. Was there anything you wanted me to pick up for you? Maybe some more books?"

Olivia shook her head. "I just ordered three online last week. I wish you didn't have to go." As soon as the words left her mouth, she wanted to snatch them back.

His smile disappeared. "I'll cancel if you want me to."

Self-contempt rolled through her at how relieved she was by his offer. "No. I'll be fine," she said firmly, more to convince herself than her father. "I'll give Connie a hand."

"She told me yesterday that she appreciates your help. She's never complained, but she's not getting any younger, either."

The Hispanic cook had been working at the ranch for so long that Olivia couldn't remember a time when she hadn't been there. Instead of being gratified by Connie's thanks, Olivia felt guilty for not helping her more.

"I don't do that much, but I do peel a mean potato," Olivia said, forcing a teasing grin.

"You do more than that, according to Connie." He glanced at the clock. "It's late. You should go to bed, Liv. I'll be home in time for dinner tomorrow night." He kissed her forehead. "If you have any trouble, go to Connie."

He didn't specify what kind of trouble, but they both knew. If she felt an anxiety attack coming on, she would seek out Connie. "I'll be okay."

He nodded, but she could tell he wasn't completely assured. "Good night, Liv."

She watched him go, feeling the leaden weight of fear drag her down again. Savagely, she reminded herself this wasn't the first time since she'd run back home with her tail tucked between her legs that he'd left the ranch for a day.

But it is the first time since the convicts arrived.

Olivia reassured herself with the knowledge that she could get to the gun in her father's room from any place in the house in fifty-seven seconds or less.

•　　•　　•

HANK threaded the leather strap through his fingers, examining it closely for wears and flaws. The bridle was an old one, but it had been well cared for. Not finding any part that needed mending, he pulled the strap between an oil-soaked cloth. When he returned the bridle to its nail, it gleamed.

He didn't mind working alone in the tack room. No one bothered him here, and he could relax his guard. The scent of leather reminded him of his father teaching him how to care for the saddlery. Sometimes the images of his father were so clear, Hank almost forgot he wasn't here by choice. Then Rollie or Mantle or one of the other men would come by and remind him of the stark reality.

As he replaced a latigo strap on a saddle, he heard muffled voices arguing outside the tack room. He listened closely but couldn't make out the words. He warily moved to the door that led into the main part of the barn.

Although it was dim, Hank could make out Mantle and Barton not more than twenty feet away. Barton was holding his hands up, as if warding off Mantle.

"No."

Barton's single word told Hank all he needed to know. There was no doubt as to what Mantle wanted from the good-looking kid. The son of a bitch had been eyeing Barton like a vulture readying to feast on fresh carrion ever since they arrived at the ranch. Barton could probably handle himself in a fair fight, but Mantle knew too many dirty tricks.

Hank strode over to the two men. "Something going on here?" he asked with deceptive blandness.

"Butt out, Elliott. This is between me and the kid," Mantle said.

Hank looked at Barton, although he kept tabs on Mantle out of the corner of his eye. "Is that right, Barton? Do you want some time alone with Mantle here?"

Barton's hands clenched into fists at his sides, and his eyes were wide, filled with panic and humiliation. "No. I just came in here to get a halter, and Mantle followed me."

"Bullshit. You wanted me to follow you," Mantle accused the younger man.

Barton's face paled. "No, I never . . ."

For a moment, Barton's features blurred, becoming another young man, one Hank had tried to help. He reburied that jagged memory. "Aren't you supposed to be mucking out the stalls in the other barn, Mantle?"

"Fuck you, Elliott," Mantle said.

"I thought that was *your* specialty." Hank smiled coldly. "Keep your filthy hands to yourself."

Mantle matched Hank's hard smile. "Don't get in my way again, Elliott, or you'll be sorry." He swaggered out of the barn.

"Thanks," Barton said, his voice sounding even younger than his years.

"Mantle's a mean bastard. Sleep with one eye open, kid," Hank said gruffly. "Don't forget what you came in here for."

Barton followed him into the tack room, and Hank plucked a halter off a peg. "Here."

Barton nodded his thanks and left.

Shaking his head, Hank sat back down to continue working. Why did he even bother? Barton wasn't his responsibility, just like Lenny hadn't been. But then, Lenny wasn't anyone's responsibility anymore.

Dead men didn't need protection.

Hank looked up to see the foreman enter.

"Need you to run into town, Elliott," Buck said without preamble.

"Why?" he asked warily. He hadn't expected the opportunity to drive off the ranch by himself.

"Christ, I'm not setting you up, if you're worried about that," Buck replied impatiently.

Hank scowled, remembering the setup that had landed him in prison. "Can't be too damned careful."

"Leroy was supposed to make the run this morning, but the damned fool got drunk last night and sprained his ankle getting off his barstool. Everyone else is out working. I'd go, but we have a buyer coming in for some stock, and since the boss isn't here, I've gotta take him out to look at the beeves."

Hank met the foreman's gaze. "You trust me?"

"Not especially, but the boss does. Don't make a liar out of him."

Hank respected the foreman's honesty. He owed the judge, but more importantly, he wasn't going to screw up his chance at freedom—legal freedom. "Where do I need to go?"

"Grocery store. Back up to the delivery door. They'll have everything ready. You just gotta load it up and sign for it."

"Which truck?"

Buck tossed him a set of keys. "Dark green Ford pickup. And don't let Sheriff Jordan catch you speeding."

Hank jangled the keys in his palm, savoring the thrill of them in his hand. He froze, remembering one tiny detail. "I don't have a driver's license."

"You don't know how to drive?"

Hank scowled. "My license expired while I was in prison."

Buck waved a hand. "Don't worry about it. As long as you drive the speed limit and don't do anything stupid, the sheriff doesn't care. He knows the judge has cons working for him."

Hank was surprised but didn't show it. "Yes, sir."

"Get outta here, Elliott. I'll expect you to be back and have the supplies unloaded before lunch."

Sorely tempted to run to the truck, Hank forced himself to walk casually, as if he were entrusted to drive every day.

The ten-year-old pickup wasn't locked, and Hank jumped in like a kid taking his first driving lesson. He stuck the key in the ignition but didn't turn it. Instead he caressed the steering wheel, the knobs on the dashboard, and the stick shift on the floor. The acrid scents of gas and oil were as sweet as perfume.

Funny how he used to take driving for granted before he

went to prison. He pressed the clutch with his left foot and turned the key. The Ford roared to life, and Hank shifted into gear. An unexpected jolt jerked his head back, but as he crawled through the ranch yard to the driveway, his driving skills returned.

Just like making love.

And damned near as good.

By the time Olivia finished eating breakfast and shower-ing, it was nine thirty. Connie probably had the men's lunch under way, but there would still be tasks Olivia could do.

As she stepped outside, she noticed the green truck tooling down the driveway at a speed only a gray-haired grandmother could appreciate. She wondered who was be-hind the wheel since most of the hired men tended to drive like NASCAR wannabes.

The yard was quiet, and Olivia enjoyed the birdsongs and light rustle of the wind. The sky was pure blue with none of the afternoon clouds creeping in over the mountain peaks yet. If not for her limp and the residual touch of ap-prehension, she could almost believe she was merely home for a vacation.

A horse snorted from one of the corrals, and she noticed the farrier was working alone today. Hank must have been assigned a task out on the ranch someplace, which meant she wouldn't be seeing him. She should be relieved, but in-stead felt . . . abandoned.

The dining hall door was open to let in the cooler air. Tantalizing smells of baking bread and bubbling tomato sauce filled Olivia's nose. When she entered the cafeteria-type room, she spotted Connie sitting by one of the four long tables.

"*Hoa*," Connie said with a gap-toothed smile on her broad face.

"Good morning. Sorry I'm late," Olivia said.

Connie waved her hand that was holding a paring knife.

"You're just in time to help me peel these apples. I thought I'd give the men a treat tonight—apple crisp."

Olivia's mouth watered. She'd have to snitch some for her and her father when it came out of the oven.

She plucked a knife from a drawer and joined Connie beside two pails of green apples. They spoke little, only commenting on the weather and the judge's trip to Denver.

Olivia picked out the last apple from the pail, but before she could begin paring it, she heard a vehicle backing up to the door.

"Looks like the men will eat tonight after all," Connie said, winking at Olivia.

"Like you would ever let them go hungry," Olivia teased.

She followed Connie outside. The driver had his back to them as he opened the truck's tailgate. Olivia recognized the shoulders, slim hips, and fine-looking butt at the same moment she recognized the shirt and jeans. Looking around, she couldn't see one of the regular hired men with Elliott, which meant he'd gone alone. She wanted to ask him how he'd finagled a solo trip into town, but her mouth was too dry and her senses too busy cataloguing his presence.

"Did you get everything?" Connie asked him.

"I think so, ma'am," Hank replied.

"Bring it in."

"Yes, ma'am." Hank turned, and his eyes widened, clearly not expecting to see Olivia. "Shouldn't you be off that leg?"

She found her voice. "It's fine." She reached for a box in the truck bed.

"You shouldn't be doing that."

"I don't need a babysitter."

Hank's lips pressed into a firm line. "You obviously know what's best, Ms. Kincaid." He strode past her into the cookhouse.

Connie raised her eyebrows, but Olivia ignored the unspoken question.

After four trips carrying groceries inside, Olivia recognized her knee's limit. Although she wanted to feel useful, she didn't dare risk injuring her knee permanently.

She settled into a chair and stretched out her bad leg, then absently massaged the scarred flesh. From her position, she had a clear view of Hank carrying in the supplies.

A few minutes after she sat down, Hank strode in without his shirt. His biceps flexed as he piled two boxes on a table, and his rippled abdomen gleamed with a layer of sweat. This show was almost as good as the Chippendales performance she and Suse had gone to in Chicago two years ago.

Then Olivia reminded herself how Hank had attained that hard body—not by honest labor, but by working out in a prison gym.

"That's everything, ma'am," Hank said to Connie. "Would you like some help putting it away?"

"Opening the boxes would be good," Connie said. "Then Olivia and I can put things in their place. Do you mind helping, *chica*?"

Olivia stood but kept her distance from Hank's smooth-as-glass chest. "Not at all."

Just as they got started, muted music sounded, and Connie reached into her apron pocket to draw out her cell phone. As she answered it, she moved outside to boost the signal.

"Everyone must have one nowadays," Hank said, shaking his head, but whether it was in disgust or amazement, Olivia couldn't tell.

Olivia tried to keep her gaze on his face, not the well-developed pectorals or the sparse arrow of hair above his waistband. "Cell phones? Yes, I suppose so."

"There were a few around before, but they were a lot bigger."

"How about computers?"

"They've changed a lot, too. There was a computer lab in Wilson. I spent a lot of time there."

"Doing what?"

He shrugged. "Took some classes. Read the local newspapers. Stuff like that."

"What kind of classes?"

Hank handed her two extra-large bags of frozen vegetables, and she placed them in one of the freezers.

"Biology grad courses," he answered.

"You have a degree?"

His eyes narrowed, and his nostrils flared slightly. "Does that shock you?"

"Not many convicted criminals do."

Hank clenched his teeth and continued unpacking. Obviously, she'd touched a nerve with her assumption that most criminals were high school dropouts.

"I didn't mean anything," Olivia said. "I just assumed—"

"That's right. Most of your kind do."

" 'My kind'?"

He glared at her. "Prosecutors. You all *assume* we're guilty."

"You usually are," she shot back.

Hank laughed, but it wasn't a nice sound. "Or we wouldn't have been arrested in the first place, right?"

Before Olivia could react, Connie returned, tears streaming down her face.

"What is it?" Olivia asked anxiously, stepping toward the woman.

"My mother. She collapsed this morning. She's in the hospital in Santa Fe."

"I'm so sorry," Olivia said, wrapping her arms around the stout woman.

"I have to go, *chica*," Connie said, drawing out of Olivia's hug.

"Yes, of course. Do you need anything?"

The cook pulled a white handkerchief from her apron and wiped her cheeks, then blew her nose. "No, my sister, she'll drive. She's going to pick me up in an hour." The cook surveyed the kitchen and tables. "You'll have to give the men their lunch, *chica*. There is lasagna in the oven and salad in the refrigerator. Slice the fresh bread for them, too."

Olivia's pulse doubled. "I-I don't . . ."

Connie grasped her hands. "You must. Perhaps one of the men will help you."

"I can."

Olivia had almost forgotten about Hank.

"I'm sorry, Olivia, but I have to leave," Connie said, moving to the door. "Please tell your father why I had to go so quickly."

"He'll understand. Call to let us know how your mother is doing."

"I will." Connie paused in the doorway. "There are thawed chickens in the refrigerator for dinner. You can make chicken and dumplings." Then she was gone.

Rooted in place after Connie's abrupt departure, Olivia felt the full impact of what had just occurred. Even if a temporary cook could be found, it would take more than a day or two, which meant the cooking responsibilities would be hers.

Olivia could no longer hide from the world.

CHAPTER FIVE

HANK watched Olivia as she brushed a strand of blond hair from her heat-flushed cheek. She inhaled deeply, drawing his appreciative gaze to the silhouette of her breasts. Lust slammed through him, subtle as a stripper in a monastery. His body's lightning-fast reaction shouldn't have surprised him. Six years of celibacy added up to a hell of a lot of frustration. Damned good thing he'd learned a thing or two about control, although her proximity was making it hard—in more ways than one—to ignore his libido's return.

She turned toward him, oblivious to the effect she had on him. "Well, at least we won't starve." She peered past Hank, dismay and something akin to panic flooding her features. "Connie was going to make apple crisp."

He glanced at the two buckets of peeled apples and felt compelled to reassure her. "Don't worry. No one's going to miss it."

"No. I can't let these apples go to waste," she said firmly, her lips thinning.

Hank frowned, wondering why she thought it was such a big deal. It wasn't like the end of the world if some apples had to be thrown out. He shrugged. "Let the men eat them that way, or cook them down to sauce. They won't care."

Olivia nibbled on her lower lip, and Hank imagined he was the one doing the nibbling. Turning away from Olivia before she saw the evidence of his arousal, he spotted one of the ranch vehicles barreling up the driveway. "Forget about the apples for now. The men are coming in for lunch."

She glanced over her shoulder, then back at Hank. Dread seized her pale features.

He frowned at her odd reaction. "Connie said the meal was ready. It just needs to be set out."

Olivia blinked and nodded rapidly. "That's right." She seemed to shrink into herself as the truck braked in front of the bunkhouse and the men climbed out. "The tables have to be set."

As Hank placed plates and silverware on the tables, Olivia pulled out the pans of lasagna from the two large ovens and cut them into generous pieces. Hank then carried the pans to the tables, and Olivia sliced the still-warm bread with an electric knife.

"The salad is in the refrigerator," Olivia called to him.

He nodded and set them down, too, then divvied up the plates of sliced bread. Just as the tubs of butter had been placed on the tables, the men flooded the dining hall. A few of them appeared surprised by Olivia's presence. Although she often helped Connie, she was never around when the men arrived to eat.

"Do you need any more help?" Hank asked Olivia.

She shook her head, but her face appeared pinched, and she took a step back. "Go ahead and eat. I'll just stay in the kitchen in case anyone needs anything."

Puzzled by her skittishness, he suddenly remembered that she'd been assaulted. The image of someone hurting Olivia sent scalding anger flowing through his veins. He clenched his jaw, fighting the irrational wave of protectiveness.

Hank nodded curtly to Olivia and joined the other men to eat lunch. The only place left was beside Mantle, and he sat down reluctantly.

The furtive man leaned across the table, his leer on Olivia as he spoke to Hank. "You gonna share or keep that sweet ass all to yourself?"

Mantle's crudeness made Hank want to shove the man's teeth down his throat. He managed to rein in the murderous impulse and said sotto voce, "The judge might take exception to your description of his daughter."

Mantle laughed, a thick braying sound. "When did you get to be a fucking choirboy?"

Hank forced his muscles to relax. "Look, I'm only trying to keep my nose clean and get out of prison."

"Then that's something we got in common." Mantle leaned even closer. "But that's the only thing we got in common. You keep out of my business, and I'll keep out of yours, then we both get what we want."

There was no doubt Mantle was threatening him again, but Hank knew better than to get into a pissing contest. Mantle might be a son of a bitch, but he was a smart son of a bitch. He'd turn things around so Hank would be the one returning to prison if anything erupted between them.

Hank glared at Mantle, who was helping himself to the lasagna. If he or anyone else tried to screw up Hank's bid for an early out, he'd do what he had to.

There was no way he was going back to prison.

TOO anxious to eat lunch, Olivia cleaned up the kitchen, then finished putting the groceries away. Her head whirled with the tasks ahead, turning her belly into a churning vat of acid.

As a lawyer, she'd juggled cases ranging from shoplifting to theft to assault and murder. Yet she'd never felt as overwhelmed and inadequate as she did now. Preparing a brief seemed like child's play compared to preparing a meal for twenty men.

She comforted herself with the knowledge it would only be for two, maybe three days. Until her father found someone else to take the job. Someone infinitely more qualified than one burned-out ADA.

The murmur of men's voices rose, and chairs were pushed back. Footsteps faded as they left the dining hall, and Olivia breathed a sigh of relief.

Buck appeared in the kitchen's doorway, his hat in his hand. "Where's Connie?"

"Her mother is in the hospital," Olivia replied. "She had to leave right away."

"If you want, I can get one of the men to do the cookin' until the boss can hire someone."

Olivia considered it but knew her father was already shorthanded for this time of the year. Besides, a part of her had enough of hiding out. "No, that's all right. I can do it."

He appeared relieved. "If you need any help, let me know, and I'll get one of the men to give you a hand."

"Hank Elliott was in here unloading supplies, so he helped me set the tables."

"If you want, I'll have him stay and help you clear off the tables then."

Grateful, Olivia nodded. "Thanks. I appreciate it."

With one last respectful nod, Buck walked away. She saw him stop by Hank and speak to him. Hank's gaze shifted to her, and she turned away to fill the sink with warm, soapy water. Just as she turned off the faucet, Hank brought in a stack of dirty dishes.

"Where to you want these?" he asked.

"Set them on the counter."

From her peripheral vision, she saw his sun-darkened hands set the pile on the counter. His short, blunt fingernails were amazingly clean, devoid of the typical ground-in dirt. However, tiny scars on his knuckles told Olivia he'd participated in a fistfight or two, and she shivered at the evidence of his violent side. But then, maybe he'd been defending himself, and she couldn't fault him for that.

While she rinsed the dishes, then placed them in the

industrial-size dishwasher, Hank made several trips with dirty pans and plates.

"Do you need anything else, Ms. Kincaid?" he asked with a molasses drawl that sent a shiver of desire up her spine.

Olivia cleared her throat. "No."

Hank's boot heels echoed dully on the wood floor, leaving silence in his wake. And an odd hollowness in Olivia's chest.

The remainder of the afternoon flew by as Olivia attempted to fill Connie's shoes. Pasty mixtures of flour and water dotted the countertops, but chicken and dumplings simmered happily on the stove. She'd taken Hank's suggestion and made applesauce, which added a zest of cinnamon to the air amid the stomach-growling scent of chicken.

Once the dishwasher was done, Olivia set the table with the now-clean plates and silverware in preparation for dinner. She made fresh coffee in the large restaurant-style coffeepot. Her stomach growled at the mouthwatering smells.

At six o'clock, a knock on the door startled her. She opened the door a crack, and when she saw it was Hank, she swung it wide open.

"Do you need some help?" he asked.

"Yes, thank you," Olivia said, pleased that he'd returned.

Hank simply nodded and came inside. Olivia's nose twitched from the smell of soap that wafted in his wake. He'd obviously washed up before coming over to offer his help, but the soap couldn't cover the scent of leather and masculinity that was distinctly him.

"Are you doing all right?" Hank asked when he came back for another hot kettle of chicken and dumplings.

She brushed back a strand of damp hair from her forehead and offered him a tired smile. "I don't know how Connie does it day after day."

He shrugged. "She's used to it. You've been recovering."

Olivia stiffened at the reminder. "For too damned long."

Hank regarded her silently. "The men will be coming in pretty soon. Are you ready?"

Her shoulders tensed, but she nodded.

She dined in the kitchen as the men ate. The low hum of voices was surprisingly soothing, as long as she kept her distance.

After they'd eaten, the men left the dining hall. Olivia knew most of them would end up in front of the television in the main bunkhouse. Hank and his fellow prisoners would probably join them. The hired men were, overall, pretty accepting of the prisoners. Those who didn't approve of them rarely stayed on the payroll for long. Olivia's father wanted them to work as equals on the ranch and culled out the troublemakers.

Olivia didn't miss the irony; she was probably the worst naysayer, but he could hardly fire his own daughter.

Hank appeared with an armload of dirty plates. "I'll clear the tables," he said simply.

Startled out of her thoughts, Olivia got to work. Once everything was rinsed and put in the dishwasher, she let the water out of the sink.

"Would you like some help in the morning, Ms. Kincaid?" Hank asked.

He was wearing his aloof mask, but she couldn't deny the heat that shimmered between them, like a wavy mirage above a hot highway. There, yet not. "If Buck doesn't mind."

"He won't." Without another word, he left.

Startled by his abrupt departure, Olivia hobbled over to the window and saw Hank pause outside the barracks where the convicts slept. She studied him in the dim light. He shoved his hands in his pockets and turned to look out toward the dim outline of the mountain peaks in the distance.

Olivia wondered what he was thinking. Was the ranch any different than prison for him? Hank and the other four convicts weren't allowed off Kincaid land without permission. They continued to wear their Wilson Correctional Facility chambray shirts and ball caps. It was their mark, their badge of dishonor.

Her gaze traveled across Hank's shoulders and back, and down his long, muscular legs. She gave in to her feminine curiosity, and her attention lingered. She'd worked around men in suits for so long, she'd forgotten the allure of denim over a tight backside. Her fingers remembered, though, and she curled them into her palms.

After the attack, she'd lost control of her emotions, and now her body betrayed her. Her life was screwed up enough; she didn't want or need the complication of Hank Elliott. Yet she couldn't escape him if she continued to cook the meals because, in spite of everything, he'd be the one she'd turn to for help.

She glanced toward the mountains, which were lit with an eerie orangish glow as the sun dropped behind the peaks. Olivia grabbed her cane and left the cookhouse, intent on getting to the house before the sun disappeared completely. The skin between her shoulder blades tingled, and she suspected it was Hank's gaze that followed her.

However, Olivia wasn't certain if the tingle was one of trepidation or excitement. Or which was more dangerous.

BITING back a frustrated sigh, Hank watched Olivia disappear into the big house. She hadn't even glanced at him when she'd passed. What had he expected, that she would smile seductively and ask him to follow her into that fancy house, down the hall to her fancy room, and make love in her fancy bed?

He closed his eyes, envisioning her bedroom. He'd only been in it long enough to retrieve her cane, but he clearly remembered the feminine scents: a hint of violets and powder, and Olivia's unique musk that had taxed his control only minutes ago in the cookhouse. Surprisingly, her room contained frilly curtains and a pale pink, blue, and green bedspread, revealing a soft underside to

Olivia's rigid exterior. He'd noticed a stack of books beside her bed and had no trouble imagining her lying in bed, alone except for a book held between her long, slender fingers.

Instead of holding some book at night, a passionate woman like her should be caressing a flesh-and-blood man—a man like him who could appreciate her touch, and who would be more than willing to reciprocate.

Arousal tightened Hank's muscles, and he opened his eyes to escape the scorching visions that fired his blood. The damned woman was going to be his downfall if he didn't gain control of his rampant lust.

Instead of dwelling on Ms. Kincaid, he ought to be figuring out a way to find his sister. In the three weeks since he'd been on the ranch, he'd been unable to find out anything about her.

His mood surly, Hank steeled himself and entered the sleeping quarters. His four roommates glanced up, but only Barton gave him a slight smile and nod of greeting. Mantle had his nose buried in a skin magazine that he must have gotten from one of the hired men. Hank shook his head in disgust and turned away.

"Elliott, you seen the article on the boss's daughter?" Reger asked from where he reclined in his bunk.

Hank stopped to send Reger a glare. "What article?"

"Hey, don't shoot the messenger." Reger held out a newspaper, and Hank stepped closer to look at the headline. "Olivia Kincaid Returns Home to Heal."

"Says she was attacked by some bastard in Chicago where she was a district attorney," Reger said. "No man ought to treat a woman like that."

Hank snatched the newspaper from him.

"Help yourself," Reger said sarcastically, crossing his arms.

Hank dropped onto the edge of his own bed and skimmed the story. The details of the attack on Olivia were painfully eloquent, with descriptive words like "brutal," "ruthless," "vicious," and "atrocious." The reporter hinted at more than simple assault but never went so far as to say Olivia had been raped.

The article explained a hell of a lot about Ms. Kincaid's attitude. It was no wonder the woman kept her distance.

Sickness climbed up his throat as rage boiled. He thrust the paper back at Reger and shot to his feet. Frustrated rage tied his gut into a knot. Wanting to hit something—or somebody—Hank didn't trust himself to be around his fellow prisoners. He strode outside and grasped the porch rail, bracing himself against it as adrenaline coursed through him. His fingernails dug into the wood.

Long minutes passed until sanity seeped back into Hank, and he eased his iron grip on the rail. He flexed his cramped fingers as he tried to make sense of his reaction. Why did the thought of some man abusing a woman he hardly knew bring out these murderous impulses? Why did he care that she had been injured in some city a thousand miles away?

Why the hell did he care that Olivia Kincaid might never be able to trust again?

OLIVIA jerked awake, her heart pounding in her breast. Her frantic gaze searched the brightly lit room until her memory kicked in. She lay on the living room sofa, and the dazzling artificial smile of a local newscaster glowed on the television screen.

What woke her?

"Olivia?" her father called.

She sighed in relief and swept back her tangled hair as she sat up. "In here, Dad."

Her father entered the room with his suit coat over his arm and his loosened tie askew. "I thought you'd be in bed."

"I was trying to stay awake until you got home." She smiled wryly. "Didn't quite make it."

His expression turned somber, and he lowered himself to the couch beside her. "Did something happen?"

Olivia laughed, but there was no humor in it. Ever since she was a child, he had ESP when it came to his daughter. "You could say that. Connie's mother is in the hospital in New Mexico. I asked Connie to call us when she knew anything." She slumped into the cushions. "She left right before lunch."

Her father shook his head. "That's a shame. I got the impression Connie and her mother are pretty close."

Connie had worked for the Kincaids since Olivia was ten. At one time Olivia had suspected her father and Connie of being more than friends, but if they were, they'd hidden it well. Now all Olivia could see between them was a comfortable relationship born of long years of acquaintance.

"So how did the men get fed?"

His question startled Olivia out of her musings. "Connie had lunch made already, and Hank, uh, Mr. Elliott helped me. I muddled through dinner, and so far none of the men have collapsed from food poisoning."

He smiled, relaxing visibly. "So *Mr. Elliott* gave you a hand?"

The way her father enunciated Hank's name told her he hadn't missed her gaffe. "Yes."

"Did Connie have any idea when she might return?"

"No."

He sighed. "That leaves us in somewhat of a pickle."

Whatever cobwebs remained in Olivia's head disappeared. "You know most of the people around the area. Can you think of someone who can cook and could use the extra money?" she asked, trying not to sound desperate.

"A lot of folks could use extra money, but there aren't many who can cook for a crew like we have here." He turned his head to meet her gaze squarely. "It sounds like you could do the job."

Olivia's heart skipped a beat, and she shook her head vehemently. "No. No way, Dad. I can't."

"You've already proved you can."

Her insides knotted into a hard fist. She pushed herself

to her feet and flinched at the stiffness in her bad leg, but her anxiety made the discomfort negligible.

"I only did it because I didn't have a choice. No one else could do it," she said, her words coming out too fast.

Her father shrugged nonchalantly, but Olivia spied the shrewdness in his eyes. "You could've asked Buck to find someone to take care of the meals. I'm sure one of the men could've thrown something together for dinner, even if it was just soup and sandwiches."

"Buck offered to find someone," she admitted. "But I know how shorthanded you are already."

"I see."

Although there was no sarcasm in his voice, she recognized that tone. It was the same tone he used when chastising an overeager lawyer in his courtroom. She wasn't certain she liked the analogy.

He laid his coat on the arm of the sofa and clasped her arms. "You didn't have to cook, yet you did. Personally, I think that's a good sign. It means you're ready to take another step forward."

Her insides quaked, and her skin felt clammy. "I don't think—"

"I do," her father interrupted smoothly. "You can do it, if you put your mind to it." He released her and added gently, "But I'm going to leave the decision up to you, Liv."

Despite Olivia's misgivings, she *had* succeeded in feeding the men. A quiet thrill of satisfaction washed through her. It was a feeling she hadn't experienced since . . . since before the attack.

Could she accept the responsibility until Connie returned? Or would she crumble like she'd done over and over the past few months?

Cooking three meals a day didn't come close to facing a judge and jury in a courtroom, but it would be a step in the right direction. If she could conquer her fear of dealing with the ranch hands and, more importantly, the convicts, she would move closer to regaining her former life. The only life she'd ever wanted.

"All right." She cleared her throat. "I'll do it. But I'd like an assistant, another woman. And when Connie returns, she can stay on and help her until the fall when there won't be so many men to cook for."

He frowned. "And where do you expect this assistant to stay, in the bunkhouse with the men?"

"Of course not," Olivia replied impatiently, her mind racing for a solution. "How about the spare bedroom?"

"You wouldn't mind a stranger living in the house?"

"Not if it's a woman."

He appeared deep in thought for a long moment. "You make a good argument. It might work."

Olivia tilted her head and crossed her arms. "Well, Your Honor, will you grant the defendant her request?"

"You drive a hard bargain, ADA Kincaid." His face relaxed, and he smiled. "I'll run into town tomorrow and see who I can come up with."

Although she'd won, Olivia found it a Pyrrhic victory. She wouldn't have to work so closely with Hank Elliott, but she wouldn't have any walls protecting her from the convicts, either. She'd see them, but more dangerously, they'd see her. What if one of them was as ruthless as the man who'd attacked her after watching her for weeks?

She shuddered inwardly and took a shaky breath. No, no longer could she let what-ifs control her life. Besides, this was her father's ranch, her home. If she couldn't regain a sense of safety here, where could she?

Her father reached for his jacket and pulled a folded newspaper from the pocket. He handed it to Olivia. "Melinda Holcomb's story is in this week's paper."

Olivia stared at the newspaper. With a shaking hand, she reached for it but didn't attempt to unroll it. "How bad is it?" she asked hoarsely, her gaze aimed at the paper.

"Read it." Picking up his suit coat, he said, "It's been a long day. I'm going to lock up, then go to bed." He kissed her brow. "Good night, Liv."

"Night," she replied. Faintly aware of her father's leaving, Olivia lowered herself to the sofa. Light-headed with trepidation, she unfolded the newspaper, and the headline on the front page leapt out at her.

Olivia sank back into the cushion. Her mouth was bone dry, but morbid curiosity kept her from going into the kitchen to get a glass of water. The article taunted her with the same gory fascination as a traffic accident.

As Olivia perused the cold, hard facts, she separated herself from the woman described in Melinda's story. The litany of her injuries could've been a grocery list, and the charges against the assailant only brought to mind the customary sentences for each crime. Olivia had read countless reports about victims like this one as an assistant district attorney.

Only this victim was herself.

Olivia crushed the paper between her hands and threw her head back against the couch. Closing her eyes, she tried to erase the words from her mind, but the final sentence refused to be obliterated.

"Ms. Kincaid is currently in seclusion at her father's ranch, and hoping to someday overcome the horrors of that tragic night to return to a normal life."

Melinda basically stated that Olivia was a nutcase. But then, hadn't Olivia called herself that a thousand times since the "tragic night"? However, she hadn't announced it to the world. She'd hidden from it instead. She'd gone into "seclusion."

Melinda had laid out the black-and-white facts, but the way she'd spun them together left too many shades of gray. People would add their own hues and tints to the unanswered questions and come up with their own Technicolor version. Perhaps if Olivia had been more forthright with Melinda concerning the details, there'd be less for folks to speculate about. Or not.

People tended to believe what they wanted to believe, and anything more Olivia might have added would've only further fueled their imaginations. Besides, Melinda would've put a spin on those other details, too.

Damn the woman for turning her into Jackson County's most pitiful victim.

I silently come up behind her, looping the leather around her neck and twisting. I can smell her terror and cheap perfume and foul muskiness. Leaning closer, I close my eyes, breathing in the purity of leather. I hold on for another minute, ensuring she is gone. The innocent are now safe from her evil.

CHAPTER SIX

THE following morning, Olivia, with her father's and Hank's assistance, served the men a hearty breakfast of scrambled eggs, sausage, and toast. Hank was stiffly polite, and she was grateful her father was there to act as a buffer between them.

After the men went to work, the sound of a vehicle coming up the driveway drew Olivia out of the dining hall. She shaded her eyes against the morning sun and recognized the county sheriff's SUV. Limping to the house, she arrived there at the same time as the sheriff. Her father came out of the house to join Olivia.

Sheriff Caleb Jordan stepped out of the four-by-four and strode over to greet them. He had stopped by the house a month ago to visit, and Olivia wasn't surprised the county sheriff she remembered from several years ago had long since retired. Sheriff Jordan didn't have a potbelly hanging over his belt like old Sheriff Mitchell had, and he appeared to be only in his early to midthirties.

"Judge Kincaid," he said, extending his hand. He removed his wide-brimmed hat, revealing a head full of dark hair that curled over his ears and down to his collar.

His blue-green eyes met Olivia's. "Good morning, Ms. Kincaid."

"Hello, Sheriff," she said with a smile. Despite his formal manner, the lawman made her feel comfortable and safe.

"Come on inside and have some coffee," her father said. "Join us, Olivia?"

She nodded, glad to be included, and led the men into the kitchen. After they all had cups of coffee, her father asked the sheriff, "So what brings you all the way out here?"

"Do you know Melinda Curry Holcomb?" Sheriff Jordan asked without preamble.

Olivia glanced at her father, who seemed as puzzled as her.

"Yes, we both do," he replied.

"Melinda and I went to school together," Olivia added. "She was here about two weeks ago." She shifted uncomfortably. "Interviewing me for a story for the county paper."

Jordan nodded but didn't display any reaction. "Did she mention anything about going out of town?"

"Not to me."

The judge lifted his hands and shook his head.

Jordan took a deep breath and sighed. "She's missing. Her mother went over to see why she hadn't returned her calls from the day before, and it looked like Ms. Holcomb hadn't been home for a few days. No one has seen her, and her car is missing."

"Maybe she took off for a week or two. She's done it before," the judge said wryly.

The sheriff shrugged. "That was my guess, too. Some folks I talked to said she was planning a trip to Las Vegas, but her mother insists she would've told her if she was going out of town."

Her father grimaced. "I think Melinda doesn't tell her mother everything she does."

Olivia didn't know Melinda very well but suspected she was still the type who'd do *what* she wanted *when* she wanted. However, Olivia's experience as an ADA wouldn't allow her to totally dismiss her former classmate's disappearance as a lark. There was always the possibility, no matter how remote, that Melinda hadn't left of her own free will.

Sheriff Jordan traced his cup handle with his forefinger and thumb. "I've talked to nearly everybody in this county, and no one's seen her. I'll put an APB out on her car and check her credit cards to see if she's charged anything lately."

"I'm sure she'll turn up eventually," her father said. He frowned. "What else is bothering you, Caleb?"

She had noticed the weary lines in the sheriff's face, too, and wondered if Melinda's case had put them there.

The lawman rubbed his eyes. "Two days ago the remains of a woman were found just over the state line in Wyoming. The state crime unit said she was murdered seven or eight years ago. They'll have a better idea of time after the autopsy."

"That's not your jurisdiction," Olivia said.

Sheriff Jordan glanced at her. "No, but since the body was found so close to the Jackson County line, our office has been enlisted to help with the investigation."

"Have they identified the body yet?" the judge asked.

"Not yet, but they're hoping to by the end of the week."

Olivia shivered. Who was the victim? Was she somebody from the rural area, somebody whose picture was on a missing person's poster? Or was it someone nobody had missed?

Sheriff Jordan finished his coffee and stood. Olivia rose so she wouldn't get a crick in her neck from looking up at him. She followed the two men out the front door.

"How's that boy of yours, Caleb?" her father asked, his grim expression giving way to a genial grin.

The sheriff's smile transformed his stoic features into breathtakingly handsome. And Olivia couldn't help but wonder why she was attracted to a convict like Hank Elliott, rather than this lawman.

"He turned five last week," the sheriff replied, his eyes glowing with pride. "It's hard to imagine it's been that long since—" He broke off and glanced away.

The judge clapped his shoulder. "He's a fine boy, Caleb. You have a right to be proud of him."

When Jordan turned back to the judge, he'd regained his composure, but there was a hint of melancholy in his eyes. "I am, Judge. He's the one thing Jeannie gave me that I'm grateful for."

The two men shook hands, then Sheriff Jordan nodded to Olivia. "Good-bye, Ms. Kincaid."

"How did the sheriff end up back here?" Olivia asked her father as Jordan drove away. "I thought he joined the army after high school."

"He did. He married a gal he met while he was in the service. Six months after he got out and moved back here, she took off with another man. Last Caleb heard, she was living in Omaha with her third husband. Not once has she come back to see her son." Her father shook his head in disgust. He glanced at his watch. "I need to drive into Walden and look for a cook's assistant."

"Good luck, Dad," she said fervently.

LUNCH passed uneventfully, with Hank coming to the dining room fifteen minutes early to help her get the food on the tables. She was startled by how much pleasure she felt when he arrived.

This time she remained close to the kitchen doorway, watching the men eat. Although she was somewhat nervous being the only woman in the roomful of men, the irrational fear was absent. Buoyed by her progress, she ate the hamburger casserole she'd made as she studied the men.

Nobody paid her undue interest, and her gaze settled on the end of one of the tables, where the prisoners sat together. The youngest one, Barton, was talking with Lopez, a Hispanic with a scar on his left cheek. On first glance, Lopez appeared to be a dangerous man, but his quiet laughter dispelled that impression. The brown-haired prisoner with washed-out features was shaking his head at Hank, but there was a hint of a smile on his face. Olivia wondered if maybe she'd judged the convicts too harshly, that her father could be right about them. They were only men who'd made a bad choice but who were basically decent human beings.

But then Mantle caught her eye, and the wink he gave her made her skin crawl. She gave her attention to her food, although her appetite deserted her. There was something about Mantle that reminded her of a rat leaving a sinking ship.

Restless, she pushed her plate back and rose. Ignoring the men and her cane, she went out the back door and leaned against the wall.

A warm breeze mixed with the scents of sage, horse, and grass flowed gently against her face. She closed her eyes and breathed in the familiar fragrance. Muted voices and the occasional laugh drifted to her, and that, too, was familiar—achingly so.

Childhood memories, innocent and carefree, contrasted sharply with the adult Olivia's dark thoughts. For a minute, she wallowed in those childhood reminiscences. Even chores she'd disliked as a child—shoveling manure and hauling hay bales as big as her into the barn—brought a dull pain of longing for the past. Things were simpler then. What did a young girl know about perverts and stalkers who liked to hurt women?

"Hello, Ms. Kincaid."

Olivia jerked and turned to see one of the convicts standing about ten feet away. Instinctively, she tried to take a step back, but she was literally against the wall. However, the prisoner, Reger, wasn't lunging toward her, and his hands were in his pockets.

Her heart racing and her palms sweating, she managed a stiff nod of greeting.

"Lunch was real good, ma'am. My mom used to make something like it when I was a kid," he said.

"I-I'm glad you liked it." Olivia slid her gaze to the cookhouse door and estimated how long it would take to get inside and lock the door behind her.

Reger studied her, and Olivia used every ounce of willpower to stay in place. She didn't see any sign of arrogance or cruelty in his expression, and she breathed deeply to allay the hysteria she courted so closely.

"I saw the article. I'm sorry for what happened to you," he said.

Olivia's mind blanked for a moment before she determined what he was referring to. "You saw it?"

"Yes, ma'am. We all did."

So they all knew she was a victim. Her throat, as well as her stomach, convulsed, and she was glad she hadn't eaten much. She raised her chin and spoke with a dry mouth. "As you can see, I'm perfectly fine except for my leg. And that'll heal in time."

"I'm glad to hear that, Ms. Kincaid." He touched the brim of his ball cap and dipped his head, then walked away.

Hysterical laughter bubbled up, but she forced it back down. The moment she'd talked to Melinda, she'd known her life would be in the spotlight. So why did the knowledge that Reger and the other convicts knew of her attack disturb her? Once a victim, always a victim? Would she forever carry this fear inside her?

And what about Hank? Was his recent reticence related to the newspaper story? Did he pity her?

Nausea washed through her. She wasn't some helpless creature to be pitied, yet that's how Melinda had painted her. And isn't that how Olivia had been acting, like some damned victim afraid of her own shadow?

She slipped back into the kitchen, and for the next few hours, she focused on her tasks so she didn't have to think about fear or pity or being a helpless victim. If she did, she was afraid she'd fly into a million pieces.

It was midafternoon when she heard the return of her father's truck. She limped onto the porch and used her hand to shade her eyes against the bright sun to watch her father park in front of the cookhouse.

"Mission accomplished," he said as he stepped out of the truck.

Olivia shifted her gaze to his passenger, who got out and looked around curiously. The young woman appeared to be only nineteen or twenty, with long brown hair caught in a ponytail that hung halfway down her back.

Olivia leaned toward her father and said in a low voice, "She's awfully young."

He shrugged. "She was the only one I found who was interested." He turned to the new employee. "Dawn, come over and meet my daughter."

Olivia smiled slightly as the girl slid her hands in her pockets and gave her a measuring look.

"Olivia, this is your new assistant, Dawn Williams," her father introduced.

Olivia stuck out her hand, and Dawn stared at it a moment before slowly withdrawing her right hand from her jeans pocket and shaking Olivia's. "Nice to meet you, Ms. Kincaid."

"Call me Olivia." She turned to her father, who was looking more than a little pleased with himself.

"I happened to run into Dawn at the post office, and we started talking. She said she needed a job, and I said I needed a cook's assistant." He smiled at the girl. "Worked out for both of us."

Dawn shrugged. "I just finished my first year of college and was looking for a summer job. Like Mr. Kincaid said, it was sheer luck that put him in my path."

"Lucky on our part," Olivia amended. "Would you like to see where you'll be staying?"

She shrugged. "Sure. I'll get my bags."

Dawn had only two bags. She carried one, and Olivia's father carried the larger suitcase into the house. Olivia led them past her own bedroom to a smaller room at the end of the hallway. It had a double bed, dresser, desk, and bookshelf.

Dawn walked around the room, touching the furniture

and running a hand across the quilt on the bed. There was little expression on the girl's face, and she remained silent during her examination.

Olivia frowned and glanced at her father, who appeared as puzzled as her by the girl's behavior.

"I know it isn't much, but—" Olivia began.

"No, it's fine," Dawn reassured. She glanced down, but not before Olivia thought she spotted moisture in her eyes. "It's just that I've lived in foster homes around Denver since I was thirteen, so I'm not used to having a room of my own. I've always had to share with other girls."

Sympathy filled Olivia. "I'm sorry."

Dawn shrugged, and there was no sign of tears in her eyes when she raised her head. Instead, her chin tilted pugnaciously. "Don't be. I'm used to it." She set her bag on the bed. "Your father said I'd probably be starting work right away. I'm ready."

Dawn marched out the door and down the hallway.

Olivia leaned close to her father. "She doesn't seem to be a slacker."

He shook his head. "No, I don't think that'll be a problem."

"But something else might be?"

"She told me about the foster homes but didn't mention any family. I have a feeling she might have a chip on her shoulder."

"But you hired her anyway?"

"She was desperate, and my instincts were telling me to trust her."

Olivia hoped her father's instincts were right.

"You'd better get out there before she takes over your kitchen," her father teased.

"She does know how to cook, right?"

He furrowed his brow. "Well, I didn't exactly ask her flat out if she could."

Olivia laughed. "If she doesn't, she will soon." She noticed as her father rubbed his left shoulder and grimaced slightly. "Something wrong, Dad?"

"Nothing some Ben-Gay won't cure. I keep forgetting I'm not as young as I used to be."

Olivia patted his arm. "None of us are."

She followed in the wake of her new helper and found Dawn looking around the cookhouse.

"So what do I do?" she asked when Olivia entered.

"There's a pail of potatoes in the pantry. You can peel them while I get the meat ready for the oven," Olivia said.

Dawn wrinkled her nose but didn't comment.

Olivia smiled to herself as she unwrapped the huge package of pork chops and began to line the first of four flat oven pans with them.

"How did you like your first year of college?" Olivia asked.

Dawn kept paring a potato. "It was okay."

"What kind of degree are you going for?"

She finished one and picked up another. "I'm not sure yet. Biology's kind of interesting."

"Maybe something in medicine?"

"Maybe."

Awkward silence grew between them.

"You said you spent time in foster homes?" Olivia asked gingerly.

Dawn nodded.

"What happened to your family?"

The girl glanced away. "My parents died in a car accident."

Olivia suddenly wished she'd kept her curiosity in check and her mouth shut.

"What happened to your leg?" Dawn suddenly asked.

Tit for tat. Not that Olivia blamed her. "A man hit it with a baseball bat."

Dawn's eyes widened, and she paused in her task. "On purpose?"

Olivia turned away and set the first pan filled with pork chops on the counter. "Yes."

"That sucks."

Olivia chuckled, relieved by her response. "Yeah, it

sucks all right. But I'm pretty lucky the limp isn't permanent."

"Yeah, lucky." Dawn didn't sound convinced.

All in all, Olivia was pleased with her father's choice of an assistant. It was only Dawn's age and prettiness that made her uneasy. She could be a temptation the hired hands, especially the convicts, might not resist. She would just have to ensure Dawn wasn't put in direct contact with them.

By the time the men were returning from their day's work, Dawn had the tables set. While the ranch hands were cleaning the day's grime off, the girl put out the food.

Hank Elliott entered the dining hall first. His gaze caught sight of the new employee, and he froze, his eyes wide. "Dawn?"

Olivia hardly recognized the hoarse voice as Hank's.

The girl froze and pivoted slowly. Her eyes flashed, and her lips pressed into a thin line. "Hello, big brother."

CHAPTER SEVEN

HANK'S vision tunneled in on his little sister, and all he could hear was the virulence in her voice lingering in the air. Although he hadn't seen her in two years, he recognized her immediately. Those same hazel eyes met his each morning in the mirror. Her chin, raised pugnaciously, was a smaller version of his, though the cleft was less noticeable. Her dark brown hair, too, matched his, but her thick hair was wavy while his was too short to be anything but straight.

He took one step closer but no more. "What're you doing here?"

"I work here," she replied flatly. She motioned to his shirt. "I see nothing's changed—you're still a jailbird."

Hank glanced down at the words Wilson Correctional Facility stenciled above the left breast pocket. He'd become so accustomed to it, he rarely thought about the label that branded him a prisoner. He suddenly wanted nothing more than to rip the damned shirt off, but instead crushed the ball cap he held between his hands. "Only for another few months."

"Congratulations." Dawn's voice oozed with sarcasm.

"Don't bother inviting me to your getting-out party." She turned away.

Before Hank could stop himself, he grabbed Dawn's wrist.

"Mr. Elliott," Olivia cried out.

He glanced at her, noting her pale complexion and wide, frightened eyes. "Stay out of this, Ms. Kincaid," he said with a layer of steel. Then, remembering the article about her attack, he felt the need to reassure her and added softly, "This is between my sister and me."

Olivia glanced at Dawn, whose stony expression gave nothing away. "Dawn?" she asked deliberately.

The girl relinquished her glare long enough to say, "It's all right, Olivia."

Hank knew Olivia wasn't completely convinced, but she eased off to stand by the kitchen—close enough to observe but far enough away that she wouldn't overhear a low conversation. He gave her a tight nod of gratitude, but she only folded her arms beneath her breasts and narrowed her eyes. Even with the bombshell of seeing his sister here, Hank felt a jolt of awareness for Olivia settle in his gut.

Peeling his gaze away from her, he focused on his little sister, who had matured into a beautiful young woman. "What happened to you? After you turned eighteen, you disappeared." Concern and anger made his words come out like an accusation.

Dawn pulled away from him. "Why do you suddenly care about me now? You didn't give a damn six years ago when you got yourself thrown in prison."

He jerked back, as if her words had slapped him. "I was innocent, Dawn. I never robbed that store." He reached for her, and she retreated a step. Anguish churned in his gut at her rejection. "You have to believe me, Pumpkin, I didn't deserve to go to prison."

She blinked at his use of the nickname he and his parents had called her since she was a baby. For a moment, Hank thought he was getting through to her, but her next words dashed his hope.

"The jury thought you did, which left me a ward of the state," Dawn said. "Do you know what that was like? Do you have any idea how many places I've lived since you left? Everything I loved was taken away from me. Everything!" A tear rolled down Dawn's cheek, and she dashed it away with an angry swipe of her hand. "You were the only family I had, and you left me."

Hank's heart ached for what she'd endured. "If I could change the past, I'd never have given Carl a ride to the store." He held out his hands, imploring her to believe him. "I swear to you, I didn't know he was going to rob it and use me as his wheelman."

Dawn sniffed, but there was only disdain and antagonism in her face. "Same old tune, Hank. And I'm sick and tired of hearing it. That's why I disappeared when I turned eighteen. I couldn't stand to see you anymore after the hell you put me through. I have my own life now, and I don't need you." She paused and fixed him with a cold glare. "I don't *ever* need you again."

Dawn spun around and ran out of the building.

Ice settled in Hank's heart. He dropped into the nearest chair and buried his face in his hands. Just as he'd lost the family ranch and his self-respect, the sweet little sister he'd known was gone, too. Another casualty of his imprisonment.

His lungs felt tight, and it was impossible to drag air into them. Moisture burned his eyes, but he savagely fought the tears into submission.

A touch on his arm startled him.

"I'm sorry," Olivia said, standing above him.

"Yeah, so am I," Hank said gruffly. He stood, ignoring the dull ache in his chest. "I bet I'm living down to your expectations of me."

Olivia's brow furrowed in confusion. "I don't understand."

He laughed, but it was a jagged, scathing sound. "You can add abandoning a thirteen-year-old sister to my list of crimes."

"From what I heard, you didn't abandon her." Her cheeks reddened, as if she'd just realized she'd admitted to eavesdropping on their conversation.

"She believes I did." Hank turned away from Olivia to step out onto the porch and gaze at the mountains, where the sun sank toward the peaks. She followed him. "Hell, maybe she's right. I'd known Carl since we were in kindergarten. He always was a troublemaker, even back then. But it was a small school, and there wasn't a whole lot of choice in friends." He shrugged, remembering some of the wilder things he himself had done in high school.

"In our senior year, he got a girl pregnant and married her. I didn't see him much after that. Until I came home from college after Mom and Dad were killed in a car accident. Dawn was only twelve, and I was twenty-three." Rancor welled in his throat. "I went from being a carefree college student to becoming a surrogate parent and running a ranch overnight.

"It was almost a year later when I ran into Carl. The ranch was getting farther and farther in debt, and I didn't know a damned thing about raising a teenaged girl. When he suggested we buy some beer and get drunk, I couldn't get him over to the store fast enough." He chuckled without humor. "And the rest, as they say, is history."

Olivia didn't speak, and only the rustling of leaves outside broke the silence. Hank tipped his head back and closed his eyes, wishing like hell the earth would open up and swallow him. But with his luck, it'd spit him right back out.

"Were you really innocent?" Olivia's quiet voice drifted to him.

He sneered. "Innocent isn't a word people would use to describe me."

"You know what I mean." A shred of impatience cut through her tone.

Taking a deep breath, he opened his eyes and turned to face her. Her complexion wasn't as wan, and her clear blue eyes didn't hold the shadows he'd seen so often before.

"I was guilty of ignorance and bad judgment," he confessed. "And if that was worth six years in prison, then I guess I got what I had coming." Even he cringed at the bitterness in his voice.

Before Olivia could say anything more, the men headed their way for dinner. Hank barreled through the incoming group to escape to the barracks he shared with the other convicts.

"Mr. Elliott," Olivia called after him.

He stopped and looked over his shoulder at her, noting how the sun's slanted rays wrapped her in an odd, ethereal glow, like she wasn't real. But Hank knew how real she truly was.

"You didn't get any dinner," she said.

"I'm not hungry, ma'am."

She pressed her lips into a thin line, and he turned away. All he wanted was to be alone to think about his sister and her harsh words—words he deserved more than he cared to admit.

After over a year of worrying about Dawn and wondering if she was safe, he'd stumbled across her purely by accident. He still didn't know what she was doing with her life or why she was working at the ranch, but he was determined to find out. As long as she worked there, he could keep an eye on her and try to talk with her.

And maybe someday she'd forgive him.

"ARE you all right, Miss Olivia?" Buck asked as he joined her on the porch.

She drew her gaze from Hank's retreating form and nodded at the foreman.

"What's Elliott's problem?"

"The girl Dad hired to help me is his sister. They hadn't seen each other in some time," she answered him.

Buck swore under his breath. "Sounds kind of fishy to me. Her taking a job at the one ranch where her brother is working."

Although troubled by the coincidence, Olivia said, "I doubt if she's here to help him escape."

"You don't know that. Does the judge know about them being family?"

"Not yet. I'll tell him."

Buck scowled. "Don't wait too long. Who knows what they might be up to. Could be like that time—" He coughed and scratched his cheek. "I'd best go eat. Night, Miss Olivia."

Watching his retreat into the dining room, she pondered his obvious slip. What did he mean? Had something happened that she didn't know about?

She'd ask her father tonight if he'd ever had trouble with a convict in the program. If he had, why hadn't he told her? Or maybe he had, and she'd forgotten.

Guilt assailed her. She'd always looked forward to getting a letter or e-mail from her father while she was in Chicago, but more often than not, she'd read the note quickly, then put the contents out of her mind. There was always so much work at the DA's office, and she'd never been able to catch up. Looking back, it was hard to believe how much her life had revolved around her job. Her personal life was almost nonexistent. The first dates she'd had rarely evolved into a second or third. Not that she blamed them—she'd told each man flat out that her career would always take priority.

Olivia wondered if maybe it was because those men had never made her feel much of anything. Unlike Hank, who made her feel too much.

Someone walked across the yard toward her, and she recognized Dawn's petite form.

"I'm sorry," Dawn said as she joined Olivia on the porch.

"For what?"

"For making you witness that little family reunion." Her lips curled into a grimace.

"You didn't seem very happy to see him." *Understatement of the year.*

"Would you be happy to see someone who abandoned you?"

"It wasn't like he had a choice."

The flash in Dawn's hazel eyes reminded Olivia too much of her brother.

"He had a choice, and he made the wrong one," Dawn said.

"It seems odd that you just happened to get a job at the same place where your brother is working," Olivia said, not bothering to hide her suspicion.

"I happened to be in Walden to visit a friend from college, but she was on vacation with her family. I decided to check out the ads on the post office bulletin board to see if I could find a job when I ran into your father."

Olivia narrowed her eyes, noting how Dawn kept her gaze aimed over Olivia's shoulder. The girl was lying, but why? Should she tell her father? Or merely keep an eye on her? Then another thought struck Olivia. "Why is your last name different than Hank's?"

Dawn slid her hands into her back jeans pockets and scuffed a tennis shoe against the wood floor. "Williams was my mom's maiden name. I didn't want Hank to find me."

"But it seems you found him."

The girl wrinkled her nose. "Bad luck, pure and simple. Are the men done eating yet?"

There was nothing subtle about her changing the topic.

"Not yet," Olivia replied.

"It won't hurt to go in there and start gathering the plates."

Olivia latched onto Dawn's arm. "No. I don't want you getting close to the men."

"They aren't going to do anything." Exasperation crept into the girl's voice.

Olivia knew she was overreacting and that Dawn was probably right, but it still didn't ease the irrational fear that clenched her insides. If only her father had brought back someone more Connie's age, she wouldn't have to worry so much. She forced her voice to remain calm. "I know your brother is one of the convicts, but you don't know the other four. It's been a long time since they've been around a woman, especially one as young and pretty as you. We don't know what they might try."

Dawn rolled her eyes but nodded. "Fine, but I can handle myself, you know." She moved to the other side of the porch, away from Olivia.

"That's what I used to say, too," Olivia whispered to the evening.

An hour later, Olivia and Dawn dried the last of the hand-washed pans and put them away. The dishwashers were both running, taking care of the dishes, cups, and silverware.

"We'll empty the dishwashers tomorrow morning," Olivia said to Dawn.

The girl yawned. "I can't believe how tired I am."

Olivia smiled. "I'm pretty exhausted myself."

"But you have an excuse. You're old." Dawn's eyes twinkled impishly.

Olivia laughed and was surprised at how good it felt. "I'm only eleven years older than you."

The girl sobered. "That makes you a year younger than my brother."

The lighthearted moment disappeared, and Olivia and Dawn left the cookhouse together.

"Does it hurt much?" Dawn asked quietly, glancing down at Olivia's leg.

"More than it did this morning," Olivia admitted.

"Are you sure you should be on it as much as you were today?"

Surprised and touched by the girl's concern, Olivia answered, "After a good night's sleep, it'll be fine."

Once they entered the house, Dawn said, "I'm going to unpack, then go to bed."

"You're more than welcome to watch TV and help yourself to anything in the kitchen," Olivia said.

"Thanks, but I'll pass tonight."

"There are towels in the linen closet at the end of the hall."

Dawn nodded. "Good night."

"Good night," Olivia echoed.

She heard a muffled clatter from the kitchen and hobbled over to the doorway. Her father was stirring something in a pan on the stove.

"Hey, Dad," Olivia said in greeting.

Startled, he turned toward her and put a hand over his heart. "Give your old man a heart attack, why don't you?" he teased.

She grinned, crossed the floor, and kissed his cheek. "You're as healthy as a horse."

His smile grew. "I've seen some pretty sick horses in my time."

She slapped his arm playfully, then leaned over the pan. "Tomato soup? I should've saved you some dinner from the cookhouse."

"Nah, this is fine. Sometimes I get a hankering for tomato soup and a grilled cheese sandwich." He shrugged as if embarrassed. "It reminds me of your mother."

Olivia studied her father for a moment, noticing for the first time the deeply etched lines in his brow and at the corners of his eyes. There was also something else, a sadness in the curve of his lips.

"You still miss her," she said, surprised.

He handed her the wooden spoon. "Here, make yourself useful."

Olivia stirred the soup as her father made a cheese sandwich and slapped it in a frying pan.

"I miss her every single day," he finally said. "It seems lately I've been missing her even more. It's been twenty-two years. You'd think it'd become less painful rather than more."

Tears pricked Olivia's eyes, and she blinked them back. Laying a hand on her father's arm, she said, "Maybe it's because you have more time to think about her than before you retired."

"Maybe." He flipped the sandwich over to grill the other side. "Or maybe I'm just getting maudlin in my old age."

Olivia managed a halfhearted smile. Ever since she'd come home after being assaulted, her father had been her rock. He was always there to listen and lend his shoulder to her tears, but now there seemed a subtle shift in their relationship. Perhaps she was finally opening her eyes and looking outward rather than focusing solely on herself.

"Do you want one, too?" her father asked, pointing at his sandwich.

"No thanks."

As he deposited the grilled cheese sandwich on a plate, Olivia put the heated soup in a bowl. She carried it to the table and set it down in front of him.

As her father ate his dinner, Olivia poured herself a glass of milk and joined him. She remembered the confrontation between Hank and Dawn, and Buck's warning.

"Something interesting happened at the cookhouse," she began.

Her father glanced up, an eyebrow arched in question.

"It seems Dawn Williams is Hank Elliott's sister," Olivia said.

"What?"

"Hank recognized her. Dawn didn't deny it, but there's no love lost between them. At least, not on Dawn's side. She said she was using her mother's maiden name so he couldn't find her."

Her father set his spoon down and placed his elbows on the table. His eyes narrowed. "Yet she ends up here?"

"According to her, it was all one big coincidence." She shook her head. "But I don't believe her."

"Do you think she'll be trouble?"

Olivia considered his question, using her instincts to guide her impression of the girl. "No, but I think she has some reason for finding him." She sighed. "She really laid into him about abandoning her. He seemed pretty shook up by her accusation."

Her father scowled. "Elliott doesn't deserve that."

"But he did get himself arrested and thrown in prison."

"For something I don't believe he did."

Olivia made rings on the table with the bottom of her damp milk glass. "You said before that you thought he was wrongly incarcerated."

"So you *were* listening."

"I listened, but I didn't believe you."

"And now?"

She recalled Hank's resentment, and the pain and vulnerability she'd glimpsed in his face when he'd told his story. "Now I'm not certain. He told Dawn he didn't know his friend was going to rob the store, but I've heard that excuse before."

"I have, too, more times than I can count." He paused. "But this time I believe it."

Olivia trusted her father's judgment, but it was still difficult for her to let go of her suspicions, despite her attraction toward Hank. Working with Dawn, she could get a better picture of Hank Elliott, although she had doubts about his sister, too. But, then, Olivia was trained to ferret out the truth.

"Buck wasn't happy to learn Hank and Dawn were related. He said something about hoping it wasn't like another time." Olivia kept her gaze on her father. "Do you have any idea what he meant?"

Her father stood and carried his empty soup bowl and plate to the sink. He threw out the quarter sandwich that remained and rinsed his bowl.

She stood and joined him, her anxiety level rising at his continued silence. "What did Buck mean, Dad?" she reiterated more firmly.

He turned around, leaned against the counter, and crossed his arms. "Two years ago one of the convicts in the program tried to escape. His girlfriend stopped by, pretending to be some kind of salesperson. She tried to get him a message, but Buck was watching her. He came to get me, and we confronted her. She pulled a gun out of her purse."

Olivia gasped. "What happened?"

He shrugged. "Nothing. She didn't know much about guns. She didn't realize it couldn't be fired with the safety on. I took the gun from her and called the sheriff. Caleb came and arrested her, and took the prisoner back to the correctional facility."

Olivia's mind raced, imagining a far different scenario, one where the woman was more knowledgeable about guns. Fear made her muscles turn to jelly. "Why didn't you tell me?"

He shrugged, his face suddenly appearing haggard. "You had enough on your mind. You had just started working in the DA's office. I didn't want to worry you."

Anger surged through her, obliterating the fear. "Worry me? Damn it, Dad, you're the only family I have left."

His eyes narrowed, and his lips thinned. "And what would you have done? Call to lecture me on the folly of the work release program? You've been against the program since the beginning. You would've used the incident as more ammunition against it and, to be honest Olivia, I was sick and tired of listening to your criticism."

Stunned, Olivia knew her mouth was gaping and her eyes were wide. Her father had never before spoken to her this way.

He took a deep breath and let it out slowly. When he met her gaze, there was regret in his eyes. "I'm sorry, honey. I guess I'm more tired than I thought." Holding up his hands, he said, "That was the only incident like that in all the years I've been doing this, and to my way of thinking, that's a damned good record."

She hadn't known how much her protests had bothered him. She'd only been trying to help him, and she'd ended up upsetting him. Opening her mouth to apologize, Olivia was interrupted before she could speak.

"I'm going to bed, Liv. I'll check the locks. Could you make sure all the lights are out?"

She only had time to nod before he walked out of the kitchen, his shoulders hunched and his footsteps heavy.

He's gotten old.

The realization brought a sharp pang to her heart. While she'd been following her dream, her father had grown old alone. His only passion seemed to be the program, and she had repeatedly maligned it. No wonder there was little mention of the convicts who worked at the ranch in her father's letters. It was a vital part of his life, yet he'd kept it from her. And it was her own fault.

She owed her father so much. The least she could do was bury her aversion for the program—and the convicts—and give her father her tolerance if not her approval.

CHAPTER EIGHT

OLIVIA was pleased at how quickly Dawn picked up on the tasks and routine of her job. Although the teenager seemed preoccupied at times, they worked together well. On Dawn's fourth day on the job, there was another awkward moment when she wanted to clear the breakfast dishes before the men left the dining area. Olivia tugged her into the kitchen.

"They aren't going to try anything," Dawn said, rolling her eyes at Olivia's concern. "Most of them have wives and girlfriends."

"It doesn't matter," Olivia insisted. "When I was in Chicago, I saw a lot of women who had your attitude, up until they were beaten or raped. Many times both." She trembled inwardly, even as she kept her voice steady. There was no way she'd let anything happen to Hank's sister, not while she was under Olivia's supervision.

The girl sighed in exasperation. "That was Chicago. We're in the middle of nowhere. Nothing like that ever happens out here."

A shiver slid down Olivia's spine. Was it the memory of her attack, or was something else making her skin grow clammy? Something like the Jane Doe that Sheriff Jordan had told them about? Of course, that woman had been killed a long time ago. Her murderer was probably long gone.

Probably.

And what about Melinda, who was still missing? Had she run off to vacation in Las Vegas like most people believed, or was she lying somewhere out there in the hills like the recently discovered Jane Doe?

"Please, just humor me," Olivia said to Dawn.

The younger girl rolled her eyes. "Whatever."

Olivia heard the men departing. "Now you can clear the tables."

"Fine."

Olivia wondered if she'd been as stubborn at that age. She limped out of the kitchen and almost ran into Hank. He caught her arms and instead of aversion, she fought the urge to lean closer. Before she could pull away, he released her.

"I'm sorry you had to witness our little family reunion, Ms. Kincaid," he said, his voice a mix of chagrin and sullenness.

Olivia blinked, startled by the lame apology. Annoyed, she lifted her chin. But then she saw evidence of sleepless nights and felt a wave of compassion.

"That's all right. I imagine it was quite a shock to see your sister here," she said stiffly after ensuring Dawn was far enough away that she wouldn't overhear them.

Hank smiled wryly, easing the defensiveness in his posture. "That it was."

Suspecting he wanted to know about what his sister had been doing, she said, "Dawn just finished her first year of college in Fort Collins."

First surprise then pride softened Hank's features. "Thanks for letting me know."

She tilted her head to the side in acknowledgment.

His sister came over to pick up the dirty plates from a nearby table.

"Morning, Dawn," Hank said.

She nodded curtly and returned to the kitchen bearing a pile of dishes, not seeing his flinch of pain.

"Thanks for the breakfast, Ms. Kincaid," Hank said formally, then left.

Olivia wanted to slap some sense into his sister. "He's trying," she said to the girl as she finished clearing the last table.

Dawn wrinkled her nose. "Too little too late."

"He says he was innocent."

"I believe him."

Olivia stared at the girl. "But you said—"

"I said he left me." Dawn spun away.

Shaking her head, Olivia returned to the kitchen to rinse the plates and wash the pans before placing them in the dishwasher. As she worked, she couldn't help but think about Hank and Dawn Elliott. Dawn believed her brother was innocent, yet she couldn't forgive him for abandoning her. Of course, Dawn had barely been a teenager at the time. All she understood was she no longer had a home, and it was her brother's fault. But Dawn was no longer a girl. Couldn't she forgive him and move on?

If Olivia had been fortunate enough to have siblings, she couldn't imagine disowning them. Surely in a few years Dawn would regret her attitude, but the time in between would be lost forever. And once Hank was out, he'd need as much support as he could get. In fact, Olivia suspected both brother and sister would benefit from having the other to lean on.

Maybe she could help them. She wasn't certain how, but she used to be able to figure out a solution after examining a problem from all different angles. Perhaps if she studied both Dawn and Hank, she'd find a way to help them reconcile.

By doing so, Olivia could repay Hank for his assistance over the past month. It would also assuage her conscience for readily believing the worst of the man because he'd been in prison.

• • •

THE next day a front came through, bringing a steady rain that clearly had no intention of ending soon. Everybody on the ranch, from the hired hands to the horses to the barn cats were miserable and on edge.

On the second day of the deluge, Olivia listened to the rain on the roof as she and Dawn finished cleaning the lunch dishes and started preparing dinner. Although it was Saturday, June was a busy time, so the only day off was Sunday. This evening many of the men would go home to their families who lived in Fort Collins, Longmont, and even Denver. They'd spend the rest of the weekend with their loved ones, then return to the ranch early Monday morning for another six-day week. Those who remained, including the convicts, would have to scrounge for their own meals on Sunday so Olivia and Dawn could have a day off, too.

Olivia was definitely looking forward to the free time. She'd only checked her e-mail twice since she took over the cook's job, and she hadn't had any time to play spider solitaire. She smiled to herself, deciding that was probably a good thing—she'd become obsessed with the damned game.

She glanced up from her task and noticed Dawn standing motionless as she stared out a window. Frowning, Olivia laid down the carrot she was cleaning and silently came up behind the girl. She looked over her shoulder to the wet world outside and immediately saw who had captured Dawn's attention: the youngest prisoner, Barton.

"He's one of the convicts," Olivia said quietly.

Startled, Dawn jumped, but her attention returned to the poncho-covered young man. "He walked me to the house yesterday." Her voice held an innocent girl's wistfulness.

Scowling, Olivia wondered how that had escaped her attention. "That doesn't mean he's harmless," she warned. "He's in prison for shooting a man."

Dawn turned, her eyes wide. "Why'd he shoot him?"

Olivia returned to the sink to continue cleaning carrots for the dinner stew.

"He must've had a good reason," Dawn said, following her.

She obviously had a crush on Barton.

Olivia repeated what her father had told her, "The man he shot had sold some drugs to his brother, who died from an overdose."

"So he's really not a criminal," Dawn said almost triumphantly.

"He took the law into his own hands."

"But it was for a good cause."

Olivia managed to restrain a sigh of impatience. "Vigilantes are just as bad as the criminals they go after, since they're breaking the law, too. Barton should've gone to the police with his information rather than shooting the drug dealer."

A petulant frown took residence on Dawn's face. "If you'd had the opportunity, would you have shot the man who attacked you?"

Olivia's breath whooshed from her lungs like she'd been kicked in the belly. She grasped the edge of the sink as light-headedness swam through her. That night flashed through her mind in disturbing detail.

Pale light splashing across his gaunt face.

His shadow moving over her.

The odor of garlic, old sweat, and unwashed clothing.

Excruciating pain in her knee.

Hot tears on her cheeks.

She breathed deeply to dispel the sensory images, and the terror leached away. She hadn't had an anxiety attack in weeks and had even gone for two or three hours without thinking about what had happened. Why did Dawn's words bring it all back in shocking detail?

"Would you?" Dawn prompted.

Olivia remembered her helplessness, and rage swept through her. "Yes," she replied in a firm voice. "If I had a chance, I'd shoot him." She'd never been so certain of anything in her life.

Dawn crossed her arms and lifted her chin. "Doesn't that make you no better than Johnny Barton?"

Weariness washed away Olivia's anger. She took a shaky breath. "But *I* didn't shoot anyone."

"Only because—"

"The stew won't make itself, so unless we want a mutiny on our hands, we'd better get back to work," Olivia interrupted, wanting nothing more than to change the subject.

She turned on the radio to fill the uncomfortable silence and caught a warning for flash flooding around the area. With all the rain, it didn't surprise her.

As Olivia helped Dawn set the long tables, her leg bothered her more than usual. It was probably the damp weather that made it ache. She gripped the back of a chair and took some weight off it.

"Sit down, Olivia. I can finish," Dawn said.

Olivia opened her mouth to argue, but the stubbornness in Dawn's face reminded her so much of her brother's that the words died in her throat. She nodded and hobbled to the kitchen to sink into a chair.

She sat there, breathing deeply to dispel the remnants of the sharp pain. Some time later, she realized that Dawn should've finished the task. She rose and limped in to the dining area. When she spotted Dawn, irritation washed through her. The girl smiled flirtatiously as she leaned toward Barton, who spotted Olivia and stepped back.

Dawn turned, and her eyes widened. "Olivia," she said, sounding both surprised and guilty.

"I got worried when you didn't come back to the kitchen," Olivia said tersely. Yes, she was worried one of the men might take advantage of her, but it looked like Dawn was a willing accomplice, if not the initiator.

Dawn's lips flattened in exasperation. "I told you I can take care of myself."

"And you know what I said about staying away from the con—" she broke off, then finished, "the men."

"Um, maybe I should leave and come back when dinner's ready," Barton said, his anxious gaze shifting between Dawn and Olivia.

"No," Dawn said. "You weren't doing anything wrong. Neither of us were."

Olivia gritted her teeth, her aggravation—and concern—for Dawn overcoming her wariness around the convict. "Come back to the kitchen. The rest of the men will be coming any minute now."

For a moment, Dawn looked like she was going to rebel, complete with stamping her foot and pouting. But Barton said something to her in a low voice, and Dawn's expression softened. She nodded grudgingly.

Without a word, she swept past Olivia, leaving Olivia alone with Barton.

"I hope she's not in trouble," Barton said. He seemed amazingly young and naive for having spent the last five years in prison. "I know I was early, but . . ."

"It's all right, this time," Olivia said, surprisingly unafraid of the tall, husky blond.

"I haven't seen a girl close to my age since I was put away," Barton said.

"Do you know she's Hank Elliott's sister?"

Barton's eyes widened. "Neither of them said anything."

Before Olivia could decide how much to tell him, the clatter of tromping boots sent her pulse skyrocketing. The men filed through the door, talking and laughing.

"Stay away from her," Olivia advised Barton, then fled to the safety of the kitchen.

Olivia joined Dawn at the small table to eat dinner.

Dawn pushed the stew around on her plate. "You can't forbid me to see Johnny."

It took a moment for Olivia to realize she was talking about Barton. "Maybe I can't, but my father can. He's responsible for those men, who are technically still prisoners. And he's responsible for you because you're an employee."

Dawn gave up the pretense of eating. "But what I do on my off time isn't anyone's business but mine."

"But what Johnny Barton does is my father's business." Olivia laid her fork down and leaned toward the girl. "You could hurt Barton's chance at parole. Is that what you want?"

"No," Dawn replied without hesitation. "But—"

"The bottom line is if you want this job, you have to follow the rules."

Dawn stared down at the tabletop, and Olivia wished she knew what was going through her mind.

Finally the girl lifted her gaze to Olivia's. "I don't want to lose this job, so I'll toe the line." A crooked smile tipped her lips upward. "I'm sorry, Olivia."

The capitulation was almost too easy, but maybe Dawn really didn't want to mess up Barton's chance at getting out of prison. Or maybe the girl was only appeasing her and planned to meet clandestinely with Barton. Olivia wouldn't put it past her.

"You're forgiven," Olivia said, taking Dawn at her word. For now. She reached across the table and laid a hand on her arm. "And I'm glad you want to stay here."

Dawn's cheeks reddened. "Thanks." She stood and carried her plate to the sink, where she scraped the remains of her stew into a bowl that would be carried out to the barn cats.

Later, after Dawn had cleared the tables, she asked Olivia if she could go to the house. Olivia, still working on scrubbing the pots, nodded. "As long as you're not meeting Barton."

Dawn rolled her eyes. "I'll go straight to the house, Mom."

Olivia barely managed to restrain an eye roll herself. "I'll be in soon."

Dawn grabbed her raincoat and left Olivia alone. Ten minutes later, Olivia donned her poncho. She spotted the bowl of table scraps. She should've had Dawn carry it out to the barn for the cats, but she'd forgotten. She picked up the bowl, and after turning out the lights, she left the cook-house. The air was cool, but despite the rain and clouds, it wasn't completely dark yet.

Olivia figured nobody would be outside in this weather, so she felt safe going to the barn alone. Once there, the blessed dryness and relative warmth felt heavenly. She turned on a light as five cats gathered around her, rubbing against her ankles and meowing loudly. She leaned over and set the bowl on the straw-covered floor. The cats immediately deserted her for the food.

Enjoying the peace and quiet, she leaned against a post and watched the cats eat, laughing quietly at their antics. The rhythm of the rain on the roof further lulled her and gave her a sense of security she hadn't felt in her own company for some time. Maybe her return to her former life in Chicago wasn't that far in the future. Olivia's spirits rose.

The barn door on the far side creaked open. Her sense of well-being fled, and she froze. Beyond the pool of light it was dark and gloomy, so she couldn't see who'd entered the barn. Her heart pounding, she eased around the post, even though she knew it provided inadequate cover. She gripped the post, her fingers cramping as her gaze frantically searched for a safe place.

Who would be out on a night like this? Should she call out? Maybe it was her father or Buck.

Or it could be Mantle.

She shivered and clamped her teeth together to keep them from chattering. No matter how hard she concentrated, she couldn't hear anything over the rain on the roof and her own frantic heartbeat.

What if she was being stalked again? She wouldn't know until it was too late. Until she was attacked . . . again.

Suddenly the door behind her opened, and she spun around, forgetting about her bad leg. She gasped and grabbed a nearby post to keep her balance.

"Olivia?"

Hank's familiar voice brought a wave of relief so profound she nearly collapsed.

He took a step closer. "What's wrong?"

"I-I thought I heard someone c-come in the other door." She eased her iron grip from the post. "I couldn't see who it was."

His lips flattened, and his gaze flicked past her to the other side of the barn. "I'll check it out."

Olivia caught his arm. "I'm going with you."

She readied herself for an argument, but after only a moment, he nodded tersely and took her hand in his. It struck her that she should be frightened, but the thought disappeared as quickly as it came. She followed him closely, her fingers wrapped securely around his.

She strained to see through the murkiness and could make out shadows but little else. Finally they arrived at the other door and stopped. Hank released her and hunkered down to lay his palm on the barn floor.

"Damp. Someone was in here," he stated.

Olivia trembled. "Who?"

Hank rose and shook his head. "Why didn't you just call out to whoever came in?"

She crossed her arms. Her face warmed with embarrassment. "I was scared. I know that sounds stupid."

Hank looked down at her, and she wished she could see his eyes, but they were hidden by his cap brim's shadow. "It doesn't sound stupid, not after what you've gone through. But it's a lot different here."

Olivia smiled without humor. "Funny. Your sister said the same thing."

After a moment's startled hesitation, he shrugged. "She's right."

She didn't feel like arguing and instead asked, "What're you doing out here?"

He removed his wet ball cap and shook droplets from it. "I come here once in a while to get away from everyone," he admitted.

"I suppose it's not a bed of roses sharing living space with four other people."

"Especially when I don't trust them," Hank added with a shrug. "But then, they don't trust me either. So we're all even."

"Except they committed crimes and, according to you, you're innocent."

His low laughter stole through Olivia and settled in her belly. A seductive smile claimed his lips, and Olivia forgot to breathe. Although he had a five o'clock shadow and his hair was plastered to his scalp from the rain—or maybe because of those things—masculinity radiated from him in undeniable waves. She swayed toward him, but her head caught up to her body, and she stilled.

Hank's smile deepened, as if he knew the battle that clashed within her. He stepped closer. Olivia resisted the urge to retreat, but not because of the fear that had been with her since the attack. Instead, it was the feelings he evoked that frightened her.

"You never have to be afraid of me, Olivia," he whispered close to her cheek. "Never."

Her eyelids fluttered as his warm breath stirred embers of desire and lust. Maybe he'd never physically harm her, but there were other kinds of hurt. Like the hurt of wanting but being too afraid to reach for it, or the hurt of losing something you didn't even know you possessed until it was gone.

"I'm not afraid of you," Olivia said honestly. *Not the way you think I am.* Although her voice was husky, she kept her gaze locked with his.

He brushed her cheek with his thumb. "Good." Then he abruptly stepped away, as if he couldn't stand to be close to her. "I'll walk you back to the house."

Frustrated and unaccountably hurt, she opened the barn door and stepped back into the pouring rain. She heard Hank behind her, closing the door, and then the light touch of his hand on her back.

He accompanied her to the porch.

"Thanks," she said.

"No problem."

By the tone of his voice, she could've been nothing but a lost calf returned to its mama.

As he turned to leave, she remembered something. "Was everyone in your barracks when you came to the barn?"

"Mantle and Reger weren't," he replied. Then Hank stepped off the porch and disappeared into the wet darkness.

Cold fear slithered through Olivia.

What if the silent visitor to the barn had been one of the two convicts?

CHAPTER NINE

LATER that evening Dawn joined Olivia in the living room. Some half-hour comedy Olivia had never heard of played on the television. But it was obvious by Dawn's comments and laughter that she was familiar with the program.

After another incomprehensible joke, Olivia realized she was a total cultural pygmy when it came to the current TV shows.

"I'm going to make some popcorn. Want some?" Olivia asked Dawn, restless and wanting something to do.

"Sure."

Olivia smiled and pushed herself to her feet. Her knee had grown stiff, so it would do her good to move around.

As she shuffled toward the kitchen, the front door swung open, and her father, wearing a dripping raincoat and a grim expression, entered the foyer.

"Dad," Olivia said, startled. "What's wrong?"

He removed his hat and shook the water off onto the rug. "We've got to get the cattle moved out of Winnie Canyon," he announced gravely. "The stream's already overflowed its banks."

"Oh no." Then she remembered the mass exodus of men after dinner. "But most of the hired men are gone."

He nodded somberly. "Buck's gathering everyone he can to go up there and move the cattle out."

Olivia glanced down at her knee.

"Not you, honey. Your leg," he said, reading her mind.

She rubbed her thigh with her fist. "After my last appointment, my physical therapist said I could start riding again."

"You haven't even sat a horse since you came home. Riding at night trying to move cattle is out of the question."

"I can help," Dawn said from behind Olivia. "I used to help my brother herd our cattle. It was a long time ago, but I still remember how."

"It's going to be wet and treacherous in the dark," he warned the girl.

"I'll change into my boots." Dawn hurried off toward her room.

"I want to help, Dad," Olivia said. "I may not be up to riding yet, but I want to go with you. If nothing else, I can stay with the vehicles and watch the extra horses, or even block with one of the trucks."

Worry showed in his eyes, and he rubbed his jaw. "You'll be sitting out there by yourself."

She knew what he was asking. "I won't lie and tell you it won't bother me, but I can do this. I *want* to do this."

"All right, Liv. Go put on some warm clothes. It's going to be cold and ugly out there tonight."

Olivia smiled, grateful for his understanding. "Thanks, Dad."

Fifteen minutes later, she stepped outside wearing a rain slicker, her wide-brimmed hat, and the riding boots she hadn't worn in years—boots that felt like old friends. To keep her shoulder-length hair dry and out of the way, she put it up under her hat.

She squinted to see through the gloominess, noting the controlled chaos surrounding the corrals. The handful of remaining men were busy roping and saddling horses, then leading the animals into one of the two trailers already hitched to the pickups. As she limped across the muddy yard, she spotted Dawn's slight figure leaning against a corral post. She was more than likely watching Barton. Or was it her brother who stole her attention?

Ignoring the temptation to search for Hank, Olivia joined her father and Buck.

"Just the person we were talking about," her father said to her.

"How's it going?" Olivia asked.

"We've got eleven men, counting Buck and myself. And with Dawn, that gives us an even dozen riders. We'll have to make two trips to Winnie Canyon to get everyone and the horses over there," he explained.

Olivia glanced at the two trailers—one held four and the other only two horses. "Which group are you going with?"

"The second. Buck's taking the first crew to the canyon, then he'll stay with them to start moving the cattle. I'll send Dawn with that group." He adjusted the brim of his hat and scowled. "With all those flash flood warnings, I should've had those cattle moved out of there yesterday."

In the dim light, her father's creased face appeared waxy and haggard. Olivia had the urge to guide him back to the house and insist he go to bed rather than head out to a flooded canyon at night to save some cattle. But she knew him well enough to know he'd never shirk his responsibilities, even if it impacted his health. It was one of his qualities she both admired and loathed.

"I should've thought of it, too, but we haven't had this much rain at one time for a few years," Buck said with a disgusted look. "It's a good thing we got them five prisoners."

"Do they all know how to ride?" Olivia asked.

The judge nodded. "Elliott's the best horseman, but Barton and Lopez grew up on ranches, too. In fact, those

three were working with the wild horses at the prison before I brought them here. Reger and Mantle can ride, but
they haven't done it much. Reger will be in your group,
Buck. Keep an eye on him. I'll keep Mantle with me and
do the same."

"Will do, boss," Buck said.

"We're loaded," Lance, a reed-thin hired hand called out.

Buck shouted orders, telling which hands to get into the
two trucks. Olivia didn't miss the fact that Dawn entered
the one with Barton. Her heart skipped a beat as she wondered how safe the girl would be with all those men
crammed in the cab.

Stop it!

She was overreacting again. Dawn would be safe, especially with Barton. Oddly enough, after talking to the
young convict in the bunkhouse, Olivia was inclined to
trust him. She just hoped their hormones wouldn't make
them do something stupid, which might lead to Barton losing his chance for an early release.

Like you *should talk.*

Olivia frowned at the irritating little voice inside her.

"Olivia, I want you and Hank to go with them and drive
the trucks and trailers back," her father said.

She opened her mouth to ask her father why Hank was
being used as a driver when he was so good with the
horses, but then she caught the shrewd look in his eyes. He
knew she was fairly comfortable around Hank so volunteered him to be the second driver. "Thank you," she said
softly to her father.

He smiled and winked at her.

She glanced at the trucks, and her heart missed a beat.
Now she would have to get into a truck filled with men,
too. She reminded herself these were the same men she
saw every day, and they'd already had numerous chances
to try something. She squared her shoulders and started toward one of the trucks, but her father's hand on her arm
stopped her.

"Are you sure you're up to this, Olivia?" he asked for her ears only.

A frisson of unease scampered up her spine, but she ignored it. "I'm sure."

Hank Elliott paused beside her. "Which truck do you want to ride in?"

Although she could barely see his shadowed face, she could hear the consideration in his voice. "It doesn't matter."

"You both have to ride in this one," Buck hollered. "The other one's full."

Olivia smiled slightly and was rewarded with a crooked grin from Hank. The man in the front passenger seat relinquished it to Olivia. Disappointed she wouldn't be able to sit beside Hank in the back, she allowed him to help her into the truck. She more than liked his firm but gentle grip on her hand and arm and felt bereft when he stepped back and closed the door.

What was wrong with her? She was behaving like a teenager who couldn't sit next to her boyfriend on the school bus.

Once Hank settled in the backseat, Buck pulled out, following the other truck across the muddy, bumpy road. Olivia and Buck were the only two in the front, and Hank was directly behind her.

A metallic jangle told her they were driving over the cattle grate across the road. The nearly full moon momentarily broke free of the clouds and provided some needed light.

Since she had to drive the truck and trailer back to the ranch, she concentrated on the route to the canyon. It had been a long time since she'd been to that part of the ranch, and although she'd once known the land like the back of her hand, time and weather had brought changes to the rugged terrain. Night also gave the landscape an alien appearance.

The moon disappeared behind another moving cloud, and the silver glow vanished. Only the headlights outside and the dashboard lights inside breached the darkness.

"How're you doing?" Hank asked quietly, leaning close to her.

She turned slightly in her seat. "I'm okay."

He reached around between her seat and the door and gave her arm a gentle squeeze. She was tempted to place her hand on his, but he retreated before she found the courage to do so.

The last mile was the most difficult, with water-filled potholes and slippery mud. Buck put the truck into four low and crawled along the narrow road. Finally they arrived, and everybody exited the cab.

Olivia hunched her shoulders against the damp coolness and stood out of the way as the men led the horses from the trailers. Hank joined her after helping lower one of the trailer gates. He crossed his arms beneath his slick poncho.

"She won't let me help her," Hank said, his gaze following Dawn, who was checking her saddle cinch.

"She's independent."

Hank snorted. "A little too independent."

Olivia knew she was treading on dangerous ground. "It sounds like she had to be. She lost her parents, then a year later, she lost her brother."

"I didn't die."

"No, but to her it probably felt that way."

The moon peeked out again, giving Olivia enough light to see Hank's stark face. For a moment, he reminded her of a marble statue, but she knew he wouldn't be cold beneath her touch. No, she suspected passionate fire seethed beneath his calm surface, banked for six years while he was cut off from everyone he cared for.

"I wish she wouldn't do this," Hank finally said, his voice lower and tired-sounding. "I don't think she's done much riding since we had the ranch."

"She said she used to help you move cattle."

"She actually acknowledged me?"

Olivia scowled at his sarcasm. "She doesn't hate you."

"Could've fooled me."

Olivia turned to face him, not bothering to hide her impatience with his attitude. "You admitted you were going drinking with this so-called friend of yours the night you were arrested because of problems with the ranch and your sister. Don't you think she knew that?"

Hank stared straight ahead, but Olivia knew he wasn't seeing the dark night. She opened her mouth to press her point, but abruptly closed it. He could figure the rest out on his own.

She turned her attention to what she could see of the long, narrow canyon. Normally, the stream meandered through the rich, grassy area this time of year. But now it looked like a fast-flowing river. She could make out shadowy blobs on the slope and knew those were the cattle they'd be moving tonight.

"Okay, take them back," Buck called to her and Hank.

Hank waved at the foreman, who mounted his horse and led the riders into the narrow valley. Olivia picked out Dawn among the bunch and wasn't surprised to see her riding next to Barton.

"I'll double-check the trailer gates, then take the lead truck," Hank said.

Olivia nodded and limped back to the truck she'd ridden in, except this time she climbed into the driver's seat. When Hank pulled out a few minutes later, Olivia followed. She hadn't driven a truck and trailer for some time, and it took her a few minutes of white-knuckling the steering wheel before she grew more comfortable with the rig.

The trucks and trailers crawled through the mud. Olivia sighed in relief when they hit a better stretch of road, and she put the truck back in four high. She kept her eyes on the trailer lights ahead of her, turning and slowing when Hank did.

Brake lights suddenly flared ahead of her, and she drew to a halt with a sinking feeling in her stomach. She felt a momentary twinge of fear being out in the middle of nowhere with a man she hardly knew.

His door opened, and he put his head down against the

rain that had started up again. Hank's shadowy figure moved toward the front of his truck and disappeared from view.

Olivia debated whether to go out and see what the problem was or stay in the truck and wait for him to come to her. She didn't have to wait long as Hank coalesced out of the gloom. She quickly rolled down her window a couple of inches but left her door locked. Not that she thought Hank might try something, but since the attack, it had become habit.

"What's wrong?" she asked Hank as he stopped by her door.

"Flat tire," he said in disgust. "I'd have you go on to the ranch ahead of me, but I don't think you can get around me. The road's too narrow."

"If it was dry, that wouldn't be a problem."

"If it was dry, we wouldn't be out here tonight."

Olivia acknowledged his wry words with a nod, then dug into her pocket for her cell phone. "I'll call Dad and let him know what happened."

Hank hooked a thumb over his shoulder. "I'm going to start working on the flat."

Olivia nodded as she switched on her phone.

No service.

Great. Either this area normally had no service, or the weather was playing hell with reception.

For a full minute, she sat in the truck with her hands on the wheel staring at the trailer canted at a slight angle ahead of her. She couldn't see Hank, so she figured the flat tire was on the truck's passenger side. She'd stay warm and dry if she waited in here, but it didn't feel right with Hank out there probably drenched and shivering in the night. If nothing else, she could hold the flashlight and hand him tools.

She climbed out of her vehicle and slogged through the mud, biting back a grimace at the stiffness in her bad leg. When she came around the corner of the trailer, she spotted Hank kneeling in the mud with a flashlight lying on the

ground. She could hear him mumbling but wasn't certain
what he was saying, although she had a good idea. Her
own vocabulary would consist of four-letter words if she
were in his position.

"Can I help?" she asked.

He turned his head sharply toward her, obviously startled by her presence. A scowl captured his lips. "You
should've stayed in the truck."

She shrugged. "I thought you could use a hand." Leaning over, she plucked the flashlight from the mud and
aimed it at the jack Hank held. "How's it going?"

He sighed, as if knowing he couldn't convince her to
get out of the rain. "The mud is making it hard to get the
jack to stay in place."

Olivia kept the flashlight on Hank's dirty hands as he
scooped away the top wet layer of mud. When he found
harder ground, he placed the bottom of the jack on the
relatively dry spot and began levering it upward. It held,
and when the flat tire was elevated above the mud, he
stopped.

She shifted her weight as he removed the loosened lug
nuts. The flat came off next. She straightened when Hank
stood and followed him with the flashlight to the back of
the pickup.

He placed the flat tire in the bed and held out his hand
for the flashlight. "I have to go under the back end to get
the spare."

"I'll get the tire iron for you."

After retrieving the tool, Olivia stepped back. Between
the sound of the falling rain and the iced tea she'd drunk
earlier, she needed to take a nature break.

"I have to use the bushes," she said to Hank.

"Okay."

"Um, I'll only be a minute or two."

"No rush." Hank disappeared back under the truck to
free the spare tire.

Glancing around at the nearly black surroundings,
Olivia shivered but more from the cold then fear. She was

safe out here in this beautiful, sparsely populated land. The fear that had been her constant companion for weeks was absent. It was a heady feeling, like the rush she got after winning a big case.

Her bladder reminded her she needed to find a semiprivate area to take care of business. She considered going behind the horse trailer, but Hank might come around there for some reason.

So, carefully placing her feet, Olivia kept the glow of the flashlight in view as she moved away to find a suitable spot. The ground sloped downward more sharply than Olivia expected, and her bad leg gave way beneath her. She put out her hands to brace herself as she fell forward and sank into mud almost up to her elbows. Disgusted, Olivia rolled onto her back, sat up, and wiped her hands across her jeans. She wasn't certain if her hands or jeans had more mud on them. At least no one had seen her less-than-graceful tumble.

Fortunately, her leg didn't seem to have suffered any major trauma. But standing up was going to be a bitch. She shifted again to get her hands beneath her and her left hand landed on something other than mud. Moving her hand, she leaned forward to see what it was.

A scream crawled up her throat and tore through the darkness. Olivia scrambled backward on all fours, away from the human arm she'd touched, barely noticing the pain in her knee. She came up against something solid behind her, and another scream passed her lips.

"Olivia, what's wrong?"

The voice was familiar, comforting even, and she pushed herself more firmly against Hank. She pointed in the direction of the arm and panted, her heart pounding with desperation.

Strong hands gripped her shoulders. "What is it? What's down there?"

"A-an arm," she managed to stammer out. "I-I touched it."

"Somebody's down there?"

Olivia nodded vehemently, the back of her head hitting Hank's chest. "A body."

He rubbed her upper arms and leaned close. "Take it easy, Olivia."

Olivia managed to gain some control over her terror, and her shakes turned to minute tremors. Her heart slowed its rapid beat, and her breathing became more regular.

She'd seen countless dead bodies before, many of the deaths the result of atrocious trauma, but those had been crime scene photographs or remains laid out on a stainless steel table in a sterile morgue. They hadn't been out on her father's ranch where it was supposed to be safe and crime-free.

"How are you doing?" Hank asked, his head close to hers.

"B-better," she replied. "I just didn't expect to find a body out here."

He gave her a gentle squeeze. "I'm going to take the flashlight and check it out. You stay here."

She clutched his hand. "No. I'll go with you."

"You don't need to see it again."

She took a deep, steadying breath, and her panic receded. "I've seen dead bodies before. I'm just not used to finding them myself. This time I'll be ready."

Hank looked like he wanted to argue, but Olivia said softly, "I'll be all right."

He clenched his teeth but nodded. After standing, he pulled her to her feet. With his arm around her waist, Hank helped Olivia descend the slope. The flashlight's arc caught the body's hand first, and Olivia flinched only slightly.

"It's a woman," she said softly, as if her voice would disturb the dead.

"Looks like it."

They stopped, and Hank moved the flashlight downward to the woman's feet. She wore red high-heeled sandals that looked oddly familiar, but she couldn't place them. Slowly, Hank brought the light up the woman's body, which lay in a few inches of water. She wore snug black jeans and a red shirt. When the beam illuminated the woman's mud-encrusted face, Olivia couldn't help but gasp.

"It's Melinda," she whispered hoarsely.

CHAPTER TEN

HANK wrapped his arm around Olivia, feeling the violent shudders that rocked her. In his mind, he could still hear the echoes of her horrified scream, cutting through the night. Although he had only a faint memory of dashing headlong into the darkness to locate her, he recalled his dizzying relief when he'd found her. And when he'd embraced her . . .

Banishing the memory of her soft curves nestled against him, Hank reluctantly turned his attention to Melinda. Nausea crawled up his throat at the sight of the bloated body, and he swallowed convulsively.

He tore his gaze away. "Are you sure it's her?"

Olivia nodded, her damp hair brushing his jaw.

He remembered the flamboyant woman and how she'd frightened the stallion into trying to jump the fence. At the time, Hank had been tempted to horsewhip Melinda.

"Let's go back to the trucks," Hank said.

"What about . . ." She motioned toward the body.

"We can't do anything for her now except call the sheriff."

Although Olivia seemed reluctant to move, she allowed

CONVICTIONS 113

him to guide her across the uneven ground. At the truck, she retrieved her cell phone and attempted once more to make a call.

"No service." She tossed the phone back into the cab. "A lot of good having one when the damned thing doesn't work when a person needs it."

Although Hank agreed, he kept his opinion to himself. "I'll finish changing the tire. Why don't you wait in your truck?"

"I'll help you."

"No. You need to get warm." He paused and asked awkwardly, "Do you still have to answer the call of nature?"

She shook her head and smiled wryly. "I couldn't go now if I tried."

Hank nodded in understanding and waited until she was sitting in the vehicle. "It'll only be another five or ten minutes."

Her nod was barely visible in the gray darkness.

As he hurried back to the lead truck, he heard Olivia start her truck's engine. Good. At least she'd be warm.

He endured the drizzle that seeped through his clothing and into his pores as he worked. After what seemed an eternity, Hank finished changing the tire.

Olivia rolled down her window as he approached.

"I'm done." He wiped at his face but realized he was probably just smearing the mud. "We could probably find this spot again, but to be certain we'll leave your trailer. Can you back it off the road?"

She glanced behind into the darkness and nodded. "I think so."

Hank stepped back and Olivia put her truck in reverse. She backed up, easing the trailer far enough off the road that vehicles could get by, but keeping her truck from sinking into the shoulder's mud.

"That's good," Hank hollered.

He released the two-horse trailer with quick efficiency and rejoined her. "Follow me, but not too closely. If I stop fast, I don't want you running into my trailer."

She scowled. "I know how to drive."

"Sorry." Hank gritted his teeth, knowing they were both on edge with a corpse lying less than a hundred feet away.

Because of the muddy roads it took twenty minutes to return to the house. Judge Kincaid rushed over to Olivia's truck, and Hank joined them after he'd parked.

"What happened? Why are you so late?" Concern and impatience warred in Kincaid's voice.

"My truck had a flat," Hank replied.

The judge turned toward him. "Where's the other trailer?"

Hank opened his mouth to answer, but Olivia, still seated in the truck, beat him to it.

"We found Melinda." Her voice was amazingly steady. "Her body is in a gully just off the road, about five miles from here. We left the trailer there to mark the location."

Kincaid's eyes widened, and he grasped Olivia's arms. "Are you all right?"

"I'm fine. It's just not every day I literally trip over a body."

"Damn. And here everyone thought she'd run off for a week in Vegas." Kincaid shook his head, obviously feeling guilty. "I'll call Caleb and tell him. He'll have to call the state lab in Fort Collins to get the forensics team out here." He helped Olivia out of the truck as he glanced at Hank. "You'll take them to the body."

Caleb must be the sheriff. Hank nodded. "Yes, sir."

"I'll go, too," Olivia said.

"No. The only place you're going is into the house to take a hot shower and put on some dry clothes." Her father steered her toward the house.

Olivia balked and nearly slipped in the muck. Hank reached out to steady her, but Kincaid beat him to it. She pulled away from her father. "I'm the one who found the body. I'm the one who has to go with them. You and Hank need to go to the canyon to help with the cattle."

"For Pete's sake, Liv, I can feel you shivering all the way through your coat. If you go back out in this, you'll catch pneumonia."

Hank shook his head at her stubbornness. "The judge is right, Ms. Kincaid. I can show them where the body is."

She glared at him. "You're just as wet and dirty as I am, and probably colder, since you were changing the tire while I was sitting in a warm truck."

"But you're—"

"Don't even start with the I'm-a-man-you're-a-woman shit, all right?" she interrupted.

He resisted the urge to shake his head. "I was only going to say that you had quite a shock finding the body," he said curtly. "There's no reason for you to see it again."

"I've seen a lot worse in Chicago. I can handle it."

Hank stuffed his hands in his wet jeans pockets. He'd forgotten about her background, which gave her an edge over him in viewing dead bodies.

"It's going to take Caleb about half an hour to get here. You both have time to shower and change before he arrives. I'll tell Slim and Mantle to fill the horse trailer and drive over to the canyon to give the men a hand. I'll go with you two and the sheriff." He spun around and headed to the barn.

Olivia remained rooted in place.

"You heard the boss. Shower," Hank said, keeping his gaze averted from her. The image of Olivia showering was one he didn't dare dwell on.

"I'll see you in half an hour," she said.

Hank merely grunted and strode toward the quarters he shared with the other convicts. At least he would have some privacy while he showered and changed.

When he stepped under the hot spray, he sucked in his breath as the heat struck his icy cold skin. With his head lowered, he merely stood under the water, letting it wash over his body and chase away the chill.

Some minutes later he shut off the water and grabbed his towel. He dried himself and dressed in the last clean set of clothes he had. As he struggled to tug on his wet boots, he wondered if Olivia would actually come with them to show the sheriff where the body was. If the boss had his way, she wouldn't, but Hank suspected father and daughter were cut from the same cloth. Both stubborn and strong-willed.

Hank shrugged back into his poncho and stepped onto the porch to see the sheriff's SUV and another county car park by the house. Hank loped across the yard and came up behind the lawman just as Judge Kincaid opened the door.

"Caleb, come in," the judge said, waving a hand expansively. "And you, too, Hank. I'm sure the sheriff has some questions for both you and Olivia."

Hank stood behind the sheriff as both his slicker and the lawman's jacket dripped water onto the floor.

After a somber round of greetings and an introduction of Hank to the lawman, Sheriff Jordan cut to the chase. "Are you sure it was Melinda's body?"

Olivia wrapped her arms around her waist. "Yes. She was wearing the same sandals she'd worn when she interviewed me."

"I'm going to need statements from both of you," Jordan said, looking from Olivia to Hank. "But right now, I want to go to the scene."

Hank rode with Olivia and her father as they led the sheriff in his SUV and the two deputies in an official sedan down the muddy road. The rain had stopped completely, and the clouds were thinning, revealing stars and a glimpse of the moon.

Bundled in a heavy coat, Olivia sat in the front seat, her arms crossed. A part of her wished she'd done as her father said and stayed at the house. But the prosecutor in her wanted to get a closer look at the scene.

She spotted the abandoned trailer on the side of the road. "There it is."

Once there, Sheriff Jordan and two of his deputies were shown Melinda's corpse. The youngest deputy, who wasn't more than twenty-one years old, stumbled away. Olivia grimaced at the faint sound of retching. This was probably the first dead body the kid had ever seen. He'd better get used to it, since it probably wouldn't be his last.

Sheriff Jordan pressed his lips together in a grim line as he hunkered down a few feet from the body. He shone his flashlight on the corpse, and Olivia glanced away. A hand on her shoulder made her look up, expecting to see her father. Instead, it was Hank who lent his quiet support, and she thanked him with a smile.

"It's her all right," Jordan said, ducking his head to examine the body more thoroughly without moving closer. He obviously knew not to contaminate a crime scene any more than Olivia had. "It looks like she was strangled."

Olivia, who'd kept her gaze averted from the body, now turned to look at it. She hadn't noticed the strap around her neck. "That rules out an accident," she said, keeping her tone professional.

Jordan glanced at her. "The forensics folks are on the way from Fort Collins, so it may be another hour before they get here." He shook his head. "They won't find much. The damned rain probably washed away whatever evidence there might have been."

"If she put up a fight, there might be trace evidence under her fingernails."

Jordan nodded, then straightened. "What were you two doing out here at this time of night?" His suspicious gaze encompassed Olivia and Hank.

"They were bringing back two trucks and trailers from Winnie Canyon," her father answered for them. "With all the rain, we have to get the cattle out of there."

"How did you see the body in the dark, Ms. Kincaid?" the sheriff continued his questioning.

Suddenly nervous, Olivia pressed her fists deep into her jacket pockets and told him.

"That's a hell of a coincidence, getting a flat tire so close to the body," Jordan said, his mild tone not fooling Olivia.

"Are you insinuating something, Sheriff?" her father demanded before Olivia could.

"No, sir. I'm only trying to get answers." Jordan turned his attention to Hank, who'd been silent since they'd arrived. "You're one of the convicts in the work release program, aren't you?"

Olivia turned to see Hank's reaction. But his expression was flat, with no hint of his thoughts or feelings.

"Yes, sir," Hank said, his voice one note away from surly.

"What were you in for?"

"Accessory to a felony."

"Did you know Melinda Curry Holcomb?"

A flicker of something touched Hank's face, but it was gone before Olivia could identify it.

"I saw her when she was at the ranch a couple of weeks ago," Hank answered in a monotone.

"You can't believe he had anything to do with her death," Olivia exclaimed.

"I don't believe anything, Ms. Kincaid. I'm just asking questions," the sheriff said dryly.

"Easy, Olivia," her dad said. "He's only doing his job. You know how it works."

Hank shifted his weight from one booted foot to the other as he half listened to the verbal volleys between the sheriff and the Kincaids. He glanced at Melinda's body, then quickly looked away. Contrary to popular opinion, not all convicted felons were unperturbed by dead bodies. He had only seen one other dead body before tonight, and that had been his cell mate.

Although this corpse wasn't covered with blood, her bluish marblelike skin and the frozen, unseeing gaze nearly brought Hank's dinner up. Hell, Olivia was handling it better than he was.

"Mr. Elliott, would you answer the question?" the sheriff asked in a way that told Hank he'd been trying to get his attention for more than a few moments.

"I'm sorry. What?" Hank asked, drawing his attention back to Jordan.

"Did you know Ms. Holcomb before she came to Judge Kincaid's ranch?"

Hank shook his head. "I'd never seen her before that day."

The interrogation was bringing back bad memories—memories of being questioned about a crime he had known nothing about until after the fact. Surely he didn't have to worry about being accused of killing this woman—she was basically a stranger. Hank had no motive. But Sheriff Jordan was looking anything but appeased by his answers.

The arrival of three more vehicles put an end to the questions. For now. Hank had an idea he'd be seeing more of the sheriff.

"Why don't you wait in your vehicle while I talk to the forensics team?" the sheriff suggested.

"I'd like to go up to Winnie Canyon to see how my men are doing," Kincaid said.

"I'd like to go, too," Hank said, jumping at the chance to get away. Besides, he wanted to make sure his sister was all right. He hadn't liked the way she'd cozied up to Barton.

Sheriff Jordan shook his head. "You and Ms. Kincaid have to stay here." He turned to the judge. "You can leave, though, sir. Your daughter and Mr. Elliott can wait in my vehicle."

"But—" Kincaid began.

"I'm sorry," Jordan interrupted. "They were the ones who found the body. Forensics might have some questions for them."

"We'll be fine, Dad," Olivia said. "I know you're anxious to see if they've gotten the cattle moved."

Indecision crossed the older man's lined face, but finally he nodded. "I'll be back." He gave his daughter a quick hug and turned to Hank. "Keep an eye on her and make sure she doesn't find any more bodies."

"Dad." Olivia scowled.

Despite the worry gnawing at his gut, Hank smiled at the man who'd given him a chance and his trust. "I will, sir. Could you check on my sister? Make sure she's okay?"

Kincaid slapped Hank's shoulder. "I will."

"My vehicle's unlocked. Wait in the backseat." Sheriff Jordan motioned to his SUV.

Hank assisted Olivia into the back of the sheriff's SUV, then got in on the other side. With less than two feet separating them in the confined space, Hank was acutely aware of Olivia's presence, of the flowery shower soap she'd used and the slight herbal fragrance of her clean hair. When was the last time he'd savored the scent of a woman? Too long, if his body's reaction was any indication.

He shifted in his seat, hoping Olivia wouldn't notice his restless movement.

"Why couldn't I have waited until we got back to the ranch?" Olivia suddenly asked.

"What?"

She turned her whole body toward him. "If I had waited to use the bathroom at the house, I wouldn't have found the body, and we wouldn't be here right now. We could be out helping move the cattle."

"And Melinda would still be missing," Hank said quietly.

He sensed more than saw her embarrassment.

"You're right. It's selfish of me to be thinking about that when Melinda is dead."

Hank shrugged. "Life goes on. You're worried about your father."

"He's worried about the men and the cattle, and now there might be a murderer on the ranch."

Hank hadn't thought of it that way, but he supposed everyone would be suspect, including Olivia and himself. Could someone from the ranch have killed Melinda?

As if reading his mind, Olivia said, "It's hard to imagine someone around here being a murderer." She seemed to shrink into herself.

"Just because the body was found on your father's land doesn't mean someone who works here killed her. Maybe someone figured this would be a good place to dispose of the body, hoping it wouldn't be found."

Olivia remained silent, but he could almost hear the cogs in her head turning. Finally she said, "That makes sense. If the killer buried the body, he probably thought no one would ever find it. That's usually a dry creek bed, but with the rains, the water could have swept away the dirt covering her." She shook her head. "I thought it was safe out here. But now there's Melinda's murder, and then there's the skeleton that was found just over the Wyoming state line a few days ago."

"What skeleton?"

"A woman. She died over six years ago, at least that's what the sheriff said. When he told us about it, they hadn't learned anything yet." She paused. "I'm just being paranoid. But that's par for the course lately." She laughed, but Hank could hear the effort behind it.

"You have a right to be," he said.

"No, I don't. This isn't Chicago, and the man who stalked and attacked me is behind bars. He's serving ten to fifteen years." She touched his arm, startling him. "This isn't who I am."

Hank tried to see her expression in the dim light. "Then who are you?"

He could feel her gaze on him, and then she abruptly turned away to stare out the window. "I wish I knew."

The pain filling the soft statement made Hank want to offer her comfort, like he had after she'd found the body. But he suspected she'd resist this time. He'd seen young men, almost boys, in prison after they'd been brutalized. They, too, had lost themselves. Some never found their way back.

In the silence that followed, Hank tried to divert his thoughts from his companion. Six years of abstinence made the temptation that much more compelling. However, despite the hell he'd been living in, the morals his parents had drilled into him remained. Besides, Olivia wasn't someone a man picked up in a bar for an easy lay.

The lust he felt was threaded with concern and protectiveness. A dangerous combination for a man like him.

The minutes crawled by in uneasy silence until Sheriff
Jordan returned and climbed into the front seat. He
switched on the overhead light.

Hank blinked in the sudden brightness.

The sheriff turned so he could look at them. "It looks
like she was murdered five or six days ago. The ME will
know more after the autopsy." He removed his wide-
brimmed hat and rubbed his brow, leaving behind a
smudge of dirt. "Do you know of anyone who might have
had a grudge against her?"

"We went to school together, but I hadn't seen her in
over ten years until the day she came out to the ranch to interview me," Olivia said. "I don't know anything about her
personal life."

"What did you think of the story she did on you?" Jordan asked a little too casually.

"As little as possible."

Hank frowned at her sharp reply.

"Come again?"

"I wasn't happy about it."

"You didn't have to agree to the interview."

"If I hadn't, she would've printed her own version of what
happened to me in Chicago," Olivia snapped. "I felt like I
had to do it, but I wasn't happy with the final product."

"Were you angry enough to kill her?"

Olivia narrowed her eyes and clenched her jaw. "No,
Sheriff, I was not angry enough to kill her."

"She's Judge Kincaid's daughter," Hank spoke up,
more than a little irritated with the sheriff's heavy-handed
interrogation.

"I'll be talking to the judge, too. Standard procedure,"
Sheriff Jordan said flatly.

"It's okay, Hank," Olivia said, making a visible effort to
calm herself. "He's right."

Jordan shifted his attention to Hank. "Ms. Holcomb was

a beautiful woman, and you've been in a prison a long time. Maybe she turned you down and things got out of control."

Hank sneered. "And maybe Ms. Holcomb didn't tempt me even after six years in prison."

"You don't like women?"

"Not self-centered ones like Ms. Holcomb."

"You have standards, Mr. Elliott?"

"You're badgering him, Sheriff," Olivia cut in, clearly irritated.

"He's not on the witness stand, Ms. Kincaid. I'm just trying to get some answers."

"By insulting him? Keep to the subject of Ms. Holcomb's death."

Jordan rolled his eyes. "As an ADA, I thought you'd be on my side."

Olivia smiled with saccharine sweetness. "I'm on the side of justice and equality."

Hank grinned. Before this moment, he'd had trouble imagining Olivia in a courtroom. Now, he had no problem seeing her in front of a judge and jury.

"As unbelievable as it sounds, I do still have *some* standards," Hank replied to the sheriff's question, his tone sarcastic.

The sheriff glared at him, then Olivia. "It's after one in the morning. We're all tired. Tomorrow, I want you two to come to the office and give your statements."

Hank and Olivia nodded.

"I'll give you a ride back to the ranch," Sheriff Jordan said as he maneuvered around to sit behind the steering wheel.

Olivia pointed to a bobbing set of headlights coming down the road toward them. "I think that's my father."

She got out of the SUV, and Hank followed her. The sheriff stepped out, too.

Kincaid braked to a halt and his door flew open.

"Olivia, Hank, get in."

The urgency in his voice caused Hank to clasp Olivia's arm and help her move more quickly toward her father's vehicle.

"What's going on, Judge?" Sheriff Jordan asked.

Kincaid's distressed gaze settled on Hank. "It's your sister. Her horse came back without her."

CHAPTER ELEVEN

THE moment Judge Kincaid stopped his four-by-four at the mouth of Winnie Canyon, Hank jumped out and surged toward the horse trailer. Someone grabbed his arm, and Hank whirled around, fists raised to counter the interference. Kincaid's commanding voice stopped him.

"Hold on, Hank. You can't just go off half cocked. You won't do yourself or your sister any good."

"Damn it, she's probably hurt out there somewhere." Hank made an encompassing wave toward the darkness.

"And it won't help her to get yourself lost or hurt."

"Dad's right, Hank," Olivia said, coming around to stand beside him. "You need to coordinate your search with the other men."

Hank fought the impotent anger and fear coursing through his veins. If something happened to Dawn just when he'd found her again . . .

But the judge and Olivia were right. He took a deep breath and found himself trembling, but not from the cold.

"We'll find her," Kincaid said, releasing him. "Half of the men are getting the cattle moved over to Barker Flats, while the other half are working in pairs to find your sister.

You and I will ride together." He turned to Olivia. "You stay here in case Dawn shows up."

She opened her mouth to argue but abruptly closed it. What else could she do? She nodded once, feeling useless.

"Stay in my car and lock the doors." Judge Kincaid held up a finger to punctuate his order. "The person who killed Melinda is still out there somewhere."

Although Hank didn't like the sudden apprehension on Olivia's face, he understood why the judge had warned her. She needed to be on her guard.

What if the killer was nearby and had already claimed a second victim—Dawn?

He fought back the clawing panic. He had to keep a clear head if he was going to be of any use in finding his sister.

Olivia slanted Hank a glance, then asked her father, "Is the gun under the driver's seat?"

The older man nodded somberly.

"I'll be okay," she assured him. She looked at Hank, then back at her father. "Be careful."

"We will." Her father kissed her brow and nudged her toward his SUV.

Hank caught her worried expression as she took one last look at them. He tried to give her a smile but knew it fell flat.

Hank paused by the horse tied to the side of the trailer, its head hanging down. This was the mare Dawn had been riding. He swiftly and efficiently ran his hands over the horse's rain-soaked hide and down each muddy leg. Heat emanated from the right front knee, and Hank could feel the swelling.

"She's lame," he pronounced. "Probably stepped in a hole."

"Which means your sister was more than likely thrown," Kincaid said. "And maybe hurt."

"Better than being murdered," Hank said grimly.

Kincaid nodded, equally grave. He handed Hank a flashlight, which he tucked into his waistband. Then the two men quickly backed out the two horses that remained in the trailer. After tightening the cinches, they mounted up.

Suddenly torn, Hank peered through the night at the dim outline of Olivia in the vehicle. By searching for Dawn, Hank was leaving Olivia vulnerable to the at-large killer. His stomach knotted.

Then Olivia raised her hand and nodded to him as if reading his thoughts and wanting to reassure him.

"Olivia will be all right," Kincaid said, gazing at his daughter. "She's a fighter." The last was spoken with more than a note of pride.

Hank couldn't argue with that. Olivia Kincaid was turning out to be more than he had bargained for. But whether that was good or bad, he had yet to decide.

He allowed the judge to lead the way through the inky darkness broken only by their flashlight beams. As they rode deeper into the canyon, the darkness thickened. They could hear the muted rushing of the swollen creek less than a hundred yards away.

For over an hour they rode through the canyon, calling out Dawn's name. The sound of the fast-moving stream faded, and the quiet grew oppressive within the confines of the steep walls surrounding the mountain valley.

With each passing minute Hank's frustration grew. The night hampered them, and they could've ridden within a yard of an injured Dawn and not even seen her. When they reached the far end of the canyon, they made a wide arc and swung around. Their flashlights cut through the darkness but illuminated nothing but rocks, bushes, grass, and the occasional mouse.

As they started back toward the canyon entrance, Hank yelled, "Dawn!"

There was no answering shout.

He swore under his breath. "Why'd you let Dawn ride with the men?" Hank, exasperated and cold, asked the judge.

"She wanted to help."

"So did your daughter, but you didn't let her."

"Her leg is still healing." Kincaid nudged his horse alongside Hank's. "I know you're worried, but Dawn is an adult. She can make her own decisions."

"Just like you let Olivia make her own decisions?" Hank knew he was pushing, but acid churned in his stomach, fueling the fear for his sister's safety.

The older man stiffened. "Don't presume to know what's going on with my daughter."

"I don't have to presume. I read the paper, too." Hank turned away and hollered, "Dawn! Where are you?"

They continued on, with Hank calling out Dawn's name every minute or two.

"You don't know everything," Kincaid said, startling Hank. "Her mother was killed by an armed robber in a convenience store when she was a child. Olivia saw it happen."

Hank cringed inwardly, imagining the young girl watching her mother die. She must've been terrified.

"After that, Olivia put all her energy into becoming a prosecutor," the judge continued. "She never did the things normal kids did that gave their parents gray hairs. She was the perfect daughter: responsible, studious, the top of her class."

Hank had no trouble seeing Olivia as a serious child, and for some reason it bothered him.

"I didn't see her much after she left home to attend college, then law school. But I was proud of her. What man wouldn't be proud of a child who followed in his footsteps?" The older man's voice resonated with pride, but there was also a trace of unexplained bitterness. "Three months ago I got a call from the Chicago district attorney telling me my daughter had been attacked. I flew there immediately and found a shell of the girl I knew. That bastard hurt more than her body. He stole her confidence as well as what made her who she was. I wanted to kill the son of a bitch."

Hank's hands tightened on the reins, understanding the

rage that Judge Kincaid must've experienced. What if it had been Dawn who was attacked?

"Yes, I make decisions for my adult daughter, but only because she gave me that right." Pain was evident in Kincaid's steely voice. "God knows I don't want it. I want the Olivia who fought tooth and nail to get into the district attorney's office, then put her heart and soul into putting criminals behind bars."

Stunned by the judge's passionate speech, Hank stared straight ahead, unable to think of anything to say. His mind swirled with memories of the prosecutor who'd put him behind bars and how angry he'd been by the man's ability to turn Hank's innocence into guilt.

Try as he might, he couldn't imagine Olivia twisting the truth like his prosecutor had. But he also remembered what she had said while they'd been waiting for the sheriff.

"This isn't who I am."

Did that mean the feelings Hank had for her were for someone who didn't exist?

Hank heard the dull report of a shot and jerked back on the reins. "Did you hear that?"

Kincaid drew up alongside him. "Hear what?"

Another shot sounded.

"Gunshot." Hank's heart lodged in his throat even as he tapped his heels against his horse's sides. Judge Kincaid was right beside him as they rode hard for the canyon's exit.

IT seemed to Olivia she'd spent all night sitting in vehicles. She crossed her arms and glared out the windshield. Her leg ached, and she had to keep shifting to relieve the stiffness.

Turning on the dome light, she checked her watch. Almost three a.m. Dawn had been missing for over two hours. She switched off the light and stretched her bad leg so her heel rested on the passenger side floor. The doors were locked, but she'd lowered the two front windows an inch or so to keep the glass from fogging up.

At first, she'd jumped at every little noise, but now she was only tired and bored. And stiff and cold. Peering outside, she searched for returning men, but there was nothing to see.

It wouldn't hurt to get out and walk around to shake off the exhaustion that tugged at her. But what if the man who killed Melinda was out there?

Olivia's gut instinct argued against her rationality. She was out here with no other living person in sight. A two-minute stretch outside the vehicle should be safe enough. Besides, she had protection.

She picked up the revolver from where it lay on the passenger seat and checked the chamber. There was a cartridge in it. If someone attacked her, all she had to do was squeeze the trigger.

Feeling more confident with the weapon, Olivia eased open her door and stepped out onto the damp soil. She stumbled slightly but quickly caught herself. The air was cold but refreshing after the staleness of the vehicle's interior.

With the revolver in her right hand, she stretched her arms upward. The kinks and knots in her back, shoulders, and neck began to unravel. She walked around the vehicle, then over to Dawn's mare and spoke soothingly to the animal. As she stroked the horse's neck, she gazed out at the shadowy darkness surrounding her. Nothing moved. For a moment, it seemed like she and the mare were the only two living creatures left on earth.

Scuffling caught Olivia's attention, and she froze in mid-pet.

Olivia wrapped both hands around the revolver and strained to hear the sound again. When she did, she turned in the direction the odd noise emanated from.

"It could be just a coyote or skunk," she said under her breath. But her thundering heart didn't buy it. She stifled the urge to call out in case the murderer was searching for a second victim.

Her palms grew damp from sweat. Moving with infinite care, Olivia stepped back toward her father's vehicle.

Something scraped against rock.

Olivia peered into the murkiness and struggled to see what lay hidden by the shadows. Fear pulsed through her veins, and momentary dizziness plagued her.

"Keep it together," she murmured to herself between uneven pants. "It could just be one of the men."

Like Mantle.

If anybody on the ranch killed Melinda, Olivia would bet it was Mantle. The man made her skin crawl.

She took another step backward, and her foot landed on a rock. Her ankle turned slightly, enough to make her flail out an arm to find her balance. She risked a glance behind her, and her stomach dropped when she realized her objective was still fifty feet away.

Grasping the revolver between her hands, she slowly turned in a circle. A shadowy movement caught her eye, and she brought the gun to bear on it.

"Olivia," came a woman's voice. "Is that you?"

Trembling, Olivia lowered the weapon. "Dawn?"

"Oh, God, it is." The girl lurched out of the shadows toward her.

Olivia caught Dawn's arm. "Are you hurt?"

Dawn shook her head and managed a shaky smile. "Only my pride."

Olivia nearly staggered in relief. "Everyone is out looking for you."

"I'm sorry. I didn't mean to cause so much trouble. My horse stumbled. I wasn't expecting it." She shook her head wryly. "A good rider always expects it."

"Mistakes happen. I'm just glad that you're all right." Olivia guided her toward her father's vehicle. "Get in. I'll start the engine so you can warm up."

After Dawn was ensconced in the SUV, Olivia went back outside. She wanted to let the men know Dawn was found, and the only way she could think of was to fire a couple of rounds in the air. She did so, flinching at the loud reports that broke the silence.

Back in the SUV, she placed the weapon under the

driver's seat. Warm air blew full force from the vents. Dawn needed what Olivia had needed earlier: a hot shower and dry clothes. Hopefully, it wouldn't be long before her father and the others returned.

"I feel so stupid," Dawn said, pushing back the wet strands of hair from her dirt-streaked face. "I wanted to help and only made it harder on your father and everyone else."

"Weren't you riding with Barton?" Olivia asked curiously.

The girl's face reddened. "I haven't ridden a horse in about five years, and Johnny rode like he'd been born in the saddle. When we saw a group of cattle, we went in opposite directions to gather them. Once we had them together, I told him to take them by himself and I'd check for stragglers."

"And that's when you were thrown?"

Dawn wrapped her arms around herself. "Yes. Stupid of me."

Olivia rubbed the girl's arm. "Quit beating yourself up. Even the best riders make mistakes."

A tear slid down Dawn's grimy cheek. "Do you think your dad will fire me?"

"No, of course not. He'll understand." Olivia gave her a teasing smile. "But he probably won't let you play cowboy again."

"Cowgirl." Dawn's moisture-filled eyes held a hint of feistiness.

Olivia laughed, and the knot of worry in her chest unraveled.

Abruptly Olivia's door was jerked open, and a man's face peered at them. Olivia screamed, and her mind flashed back to that horrifying night. Seeing her attacker's sneer; hearing his spewed filth; feeling his fists and feet against her stomach, her face, her whole body. Then the excruciating pain of a bat striking her knee.

She curled into herself, shielding her head with her arms and drawing her knees to her chest.

"Move over. Let me talk to her." Arms enfolded her. "It's all right, Liv. You're safe."

The soothing voice crooned close to her ear, and she fought to escape the suffocating memories. The scent of horses, leather, and familiar aftershave completed her journey to reality . . . and sanity.

"Dad?" she whispered.

"Are you all right, Liv?" her father asked. He loosened his arms around her.

It took her a few moments to remember where she was.

"It happened again." Disgust roughened her voice. "The flashback."

Why did she keep remembering? Why couldn't she put the attack behind her?

"It's okay, honey."

Irrational anger surged through her, and she pushed away from her father but couldn't go far in the driver's bucket seat. "No, it's not all right. One minute I'm fine, and the next, I'm a basket case."

"I'm sorry I scared you," came a low voice from the passenger side.

She shifted so she could make out Hank standing outside the open window. She glanced from his somber expression to her father's severe one. "What happened?"

"I surprised you," Hank said. "And it must've reminded you of . . ."

He let the sentence hang, but Olivia could fill in the blanks. She'd thought Hank was her attacker and had freaked out. God, he must think she was certifiable.

"Dawn found her way back here," Olivia said, needing to change the topic.

Hank's gaze swung to his sister, who was leaning away from the passenger door, as if trying to keep as far from her brother as she could. "I see that," he said impassively.

Despite her own emotional shakiness, Olivia saw the hurt in his eyes. She clasped Dawn's hand and spoke to the girl. "He was frantic with worry for you."

Dawn stared at the dashboard.

"What were you thinking?" Hank suddenly demanded of his sister. "You could've been killed out there."

Dawn's eyes snapped with anger equal to her brother's as she leveled her gaze on him. "I was thinking I could help. I didn't plan on falling off the damned horse."

"But you did, and you were damned lucky you weren't hurt. Or murdered."

Dawn laughed without humor. "There's no one out here but us."

Hank's jaw muscle clenched and unclenched. "We found a woman's body tonight, only a few miles from here."

Dawn's mouth dropped open, and she turned to Olivia for confirmation.

"It's true," Olivia said quietly. "She was murdered."

In the silence that followed, she heard the low murmur of men's voices. Olivia peered past Hank to see the gathering of hired hands and their horses. How long had the men been there? Long enough to witness her breakdown?

"Let's get back to the house and get some sleep. I think we can all use it," Olivia's father said. He turned to someone behind him. "Buck, did the cattle get moved out of the canyon?"

"All but maybe a straggler or two," Buck replied. "Do you want me to send a few men back in?"

"No. Have everyone head home."

"Yes, sir."

As Buck carried out the orders, Olivia got out of the SUV to let her father drive. "I'll ride in the backseat."

"Are you sure you're all right?" her father asked.

She managed a weak smile. "I'll be fine after twelve hours of sleep."

She climbed into the backseat and moments later, her father turned around and drove back to the ranch. Olivia turned to look out the back window, and in the shadowy night, she could make out Hank's lone figure watching them.

CHAPTER TWELVE

ALTHOUGH she'd gotten to bed sometime after four a.m., Olivia was awake at eight thirty. Listening to the silence of the house, she figured her dad and Dawn were still asleep. She moved and stifled a groan at the aching stiffness of her bad leg. Unable to find a comfortable position, she knew it would be a waste of time to lie in bed any longer.

Cobwebs filled her head after a restless night of half-remembered nightmares. As she showered, her mind cleared and focused on the mystery of Melinda's death. She'd told Hank it could've been someone on the ranch. What she hadn't said was he and his fellow convicts were probably prime suspects. But what would've been the motive? Rape? Olivia didn't like to dwell on that possibility, but it was too apparent to reject. She wondered if Sheriff Jordan would allow her to see the medical examiner's report.

Her mind racing with different scenarios, she quickly dressed and hobbled down the hallway. Once in the kitchen, she realized she wasn't hungry. She made a pot of coffee, moving quietly so she wouldn't wake her father or

Dawn. She would have breakfast later with them once they woke.

As she waited for the coffee to finish, she glanced out the kitchen window. Nothing stirred except for one person who stepped out of the convicts' barracks carrying his boots. Her heart kicked up a notch when she recognized Hank's familiar tall, lean body.

Knowing Hank would appreciate some coffee, she filled two thermal travel mugs and headed outside. She lifted her face to the sun that shone from a sky so blue it almost hurt her eyes. After three straight days of rain, the warmth and sunshine felt heavenly.

Her courage wavered for a moment, then she limped across the yard to the porch where Hank sat in one of the warped wooden chairs. Ignoring the quiver in her knees, she carefully climbed the steps.

Hank's eyes were closed, and a slight smile framed his lips. Fascinated by how much the expression softened his features, she allowed her gaze to roam, and it settled on his lap. Olivia had rolled her eyes at her friends when they'd talked about men's "packages," but she wasn't rolling her eyes now. Despite her embarrassment, she couldn't help but wonder if he was naturally well-endowed, or if he was having some very pleasant daydreams.

Shaking herself free of the erotic images, Olivia took a deep breath. "Hank?"

His eyes flew open, and she detected a tinge of red touching his tanned cheeks. "What're you doing up so early?"

Hank's voice was husky, and she hoped he wasn't catching a cold after spending so much time in the rain last night.

She tilted her head to the side. "I could ask you the same thing."

He remained seated, which surprised her. Until she glanced briefly at his crotch. Maybe he had a reason for not standing.

Hank shrugged. "I couldn't sleep any longer."

"Same here. Dad and your sister are still sleeping, so I decided to come out and join you. I hope you don't mind."

Disappointment flared within her when it looked like he was going to refuse her company. Then he smiled. "Is one of those for me?" He motioned to the thermal mugs.

"I'm not usually a two-fisted drinker." She grinned and handed him one.

Hank waved to the chair beside him. "Have a seat."

She glanced at the closed door behind them. "We won't wake them, will we?"

He shook his head. "I doubt anything short of an earth-quake will bother them."

As they sipped their coffee in comfortable silence, Hank kept his gaze aimed at the mountain peaks. It was safer than focusing on Olivia. He was pretty certain she'd noticed his hard-on but hoped like hell she didn't know she'd starred in his erotic daydreams.

But as pleasant as his thoughts had been, he appreciated her company even more. It'd been a long time since a woman had brought him coffee and spent time with him.

This scene was a world away from prison. It was peace-ful and quiet here without the violence that simmered just beneath the surface in the pen. Yet violence was found here, too. A woman's body in the heart of the ranch, and a killer who might be less than a hundred feet away.

Dread gripped him. Had the murder been one of pas-sion? Or something else?

His hand tightened on the mug as he thought of his sis-ter. Was she in danger? What about Olivia?

He opened his mouth to verbalize his fears, but clamped it shut. It was too nice a morning to spoil with talk of mur-der. There'd be more than enough speculation later.

"Do you like the coffee?" Olivia asked.

"It's good."

"Starbucks—one of my vices. I got used to drinking it in Chicago."

He leaned forward and planted his elbows on his knees. "So how long have you been home?"

"Three months now. It seems like forever since I was in the city."

"Sounds like you miss it."

"I suppose I do. They're holding my job for me."

"As an assistant district attorney?" Some of his contempt for prosecutors slipped out.

She met his gaze head-on. "What's wrong with being an ADA?"

He shrugged. "Nothing, if you enjoy bullying people."

"So you think I enjoy bullying people?" There was a razor edge to her voice he'd never heard before.

He shifted uncomfortably. "I didn't say that."

"You implied it."

Hank rose and leaned his shoulder against a porch post, staring into the distance.

"I take it your prosecutor bullied you," Olivia said with way too much perception.

"You take it right." It was easier to talk when he wasn't looking at her. "Son of a bitch told the jury I knew all along what Carl was planning. He *implied* I'd even helped plan the robbery."

"He was only doing his job."

"His job sucks."

"His job is to put away criminals so they aren't a threat to innocent people."

"But what about when they put innocent people away?"

There was an uncomfortable lull before Olivia said, "It happens."

Hank bit down on his lower lip so he wouldn't say something he'd regret later. Although he'd confided in Olivia more than he had anyone in over six years, she was still the boss's daughter. She had the power to send him back to hell if she chose to do so. All it would take was a few well-chosen words to Daddy.

"Dad told me you were involved in the wild horse program at the prison," Olivia said.

Surprised she'd changed the subject, he turned to face

her. When he spotted only curiosity in her face, he relaxed. "That's right."

"I've only read a little about it. How does it work?"

"The government sponsors wild horse roundups each year. We get some of them at the prison, and our job is to tame them so they'll be adopted instead of euthanatized."

"It sounds like a mutually favorable program."

Hank shrugged. "I suppose." He gazed down into his coffee. "Some of the mustangs can't adapt to being captured and imprisoned. Those have to be put down."

He had seen the same type of thing happen among the convicts, only they hanged themselves with sheets or slashed their wrists with a shiv.

"They sound a lot like people," Olivia said, echoing his thoughts.

He shrugged. "Strip away our freedom, and people are nothing more than animals."

Her face became thoughtful. "Yes, I suppose." Then she smiled crookedly and tried to lighten the mood. "When it boils down to it, all living things came from the same primordial ooze."

Hank chuckled. "And in prison, a lot of them ooze right back into it."

"You were in six years. Why didn't you?"

His amusement fled. "Dawn. She was all I had." He paused and added in a low, bitter tone, "And then she left."

"But you didn't . . ." Olivia seemed at a loss for words.

"No, I didn't," he said flatly. He calmed himself. "Then I had the horses."

Olivia stood and joined him, so close he could smell the herbal scent of her hair. Out of self-preservation, he shifted farther away from her beguiling scent.

"I'm going to walk around and try to work out the stiffness in my leg. If you're not doing anything, I wouldn't mind the company," she said.

"Sure."

Her smile of gratitude sent a shock of awareness straight to his groin. If her smile was that potent, he wondered what he'd do if he actually kissed her. It was humiliating to even think about. Yet he couldn't brush away the thought.

They left their empty coffee mugs on the rail. He guided her down the steps, his slightly trembling hand grazing her lower back.

You're going to have to learn how to treat a lady all over again, Elliott.

He matched his pace to Olivia's uneven one.

"My limp is always worse in the morning," she admitted.

"After last night, it's probably worse than usual."

She nodded. "We'll have to drive in to Walden to give our statements to Sheriff Jordan today."

"Yeah, I know." Hank wished they could've ignored the inevitable for a little longer. "I'm sure I'll be grilled about where I was when she was murdered."

Olivia sighed. "I know, and I'm sorry. Fair or not, you and your fellow prisoners are going to be at the top of their suspect list."

"Nothing new there."

Olivia stopped and placed her hand on his bare forearm, sending shocks of awareness arcing through him. "If you're innocent, you have nothing to worry about."

He laughed, the sound sharp and cutting. "They told me that the last time I gave a statement, too. Hell of a lot of good it did."

Her lips pressed together tightly, and her brow creased. "What's with the attitude?"

"Look, I've been through our so-called justice system once, and I sure as hell don't want to experience it again."

Olivia raised her hands, palms out. "You're getting way ahead of yourself, Hank. Even if you had the opportunity, you have no motive. He has no reason to book you."

Irrational bitterness spilled through him. "Doubt if that'll stop him. Once a criminal . . ." He paused by the corral.

The stallion stood in the center of the enclosure, pawing at the ground and tossing his head.

Olivia stood beside Hank and grasped the top corral pole. She remained silent, but she was chewing her lower lip, and he could tell her mind was racing.

"Was Dawn all right last night?" Hank asked before she could defend her precious legal system.

Olivia seemed startled by the question. "Cold and tired, but not hurt. Didn't you talk to her?"

He tamped down his frustration and shrugged. "Tried to. Just said she was fine."

"Give her time. She'll come around. You're still her big brother."

Hank grunted at her platitudes. "She could've been killed last night, like that reporter woman." He leveled his gaze at her. "Unless you think I'm the murderer."

Her cheeks flushed. "I never said that."

He took a step toward her and felt a measure of satisfaction when she had to tilt her head back to look at him. Some perverse part of him wanted to push her, to make her admit that she believed him. "You've talked all about motive and opportunity, but not innocence." Her gaze skittered away, and Hank hid his hurt behind a mask of resentment. "Maybe you'd better run back to the house so Daddy can protect you."

Her head snapped up, and anger sparked from her blue eyes. "I'm not afraid of you."

"Maybe you should be."

Doubt flitted across her features, but she didn't back down. "Don't pull any of that hard-ass crap on me, Hank. You're pissed off at the world because you've spent the last six years in prison for a crime you didn't commit." She jabbed his chest with her forefinger. "But I'm not going to be your whipping boy." She clamped her mouth shut and visibly calmed herself. "If the sheriff tries to pin this on you, I'll be in your corner. Believe it or not, I'm on your side."

Hank stared down into her impassioned face, admiring the fire in her eyes. He'd gotten what he'd wanted from her. Or at least, part of what he wanted. His gaze slid down her face and over the baggy sweatshirt that hid the fullness of her breasts. He could almost feel their soft plumpness in his palms and taste the sweetness of her skin. Would she be as passionate in bed as she was at defending him?

He cleared his throat and his mind, then met her steady gaze. "Thank you."

Olivia smiled. "You're welcome." Her analytical lawyer look returned. "It's possible the murderer might have been someone passing through. More than likely, he stole Melinda's car and is miles away by now."

"Is that speculation or hope?"

"Both." Her expression turned fierce. "Then again, if it was one of the prisoners, it's going to hurt Dad. He's put his heart and soul into the work release program."

"Liv."

Olivia heard her father's call and spotted him striding toward them, dressed in his work clothes.

"Morning, Dad. What's up?" she asked.

"Caleb called. He wants you and Hank in his office by eleven thirty."

Olivia glanced at her wristwatch. "That only gives us an hour."

"Then you'd better get going. Have you eaten breakfast?"

She shook her head. "We'll get something in town. What about you?"

He shrugged. "I'll scrounge something from the cookhouse with the men. Then I'm going to see how much damage the rain caused and hope we didn't lose any cattle."

Although she didn't like her father driving around the ranch by himself, especially with a murderer loose, she nodded. But it didn't stop the worry from knotting her stomach.

"I have to change. I'll meet you in about ten minutes," Olivia said to Hank.

She went back to he house and exchanged her sweatshirt for a white blouse with a light blue scoop-necked knit shirt underneath it. Brushing on some blush and mascara for the first time in weeks, she scowled at her reflection.

"Okay, so I'm putting on some makeup. What's the big deal? It's not a crime," she muttered.

Fortunately, the woman in the mirror didn't comment.

She returned to her bedroom and heard padded footsteps. Glancing up, she saw Dawn dressed in an oversized T-shirt and white socks shuffle past the bedroom door.

"Morning, Dawn," she called to the girl.

Dawn backed up two steps and peered at Olivia. The younger woman's hair was frizzed, and her eyes looked half-closed.

"Where are you going?" Dawn asked.

"Walden." Suddenly Olivia realized she might be able to use the trip to bring the siblings together. "Would you like to come?"

"Now?"

"If you can be ready in ten minutes, you can ride with us."

Dawn suddenly looked more awake. "Us? Who else is going?"

"Just your brother."

She shook her head vehemently. "No way."

Olivia mentally kicked herself but tried to keep a casual front. "C'mon, he really wants to make things up to you."

"It's too late for that." Dawn disappeared down the hall and a few moments later, Olivia heard the bathroom door close.

She sighed.

I tried.

After one last critical look in the mirror, she grabbed her purse and limped outside. Her father was standing beside his SUV. He tossed her the keys.

"Take my car. It'll be more comfortable," he said.

She grinned crookedly as she flipped the keys in her palm. "Thanks." She glanced around. "I figured Hank would be waiting impatiently."

"He'll be ready in a few minutes. I loaned him a shirt."

"He won't be waring his prison-issued one? Isn't that against the regulations?"

Her father shrugged, but his eyes twinkled. "Sue me."

She laughed. "You like him, don't you?"

"Out of all the inmates I've had go through here, he shows the most promise. But he has to let go of his anger and bitterness if he's going to make something of his life."

Olivia recalled Hank's defensiveness and understood too well. "I like him, too, Dad."

Her father canted an eyebrow. "Even if he is a convict?"

"Sue me," she tossed back at him.

He chuckled, then grew serious. "Don't let the sheriff bully him. Caleb's a good man, but he's never had to deal with a murder in his jurisdiction, and Hank makes too good a suspect."

"So do the other convicts."

He grimaced. "I know. Some of the people around here have made it clear they don't like my involvement with the work release program. They might try to use this to get the program shut down."

"Even if one of the prisoners is booked for the murder, you won't quit, will you?"

"No. I won't let one bad apple destroy all the good that's been done over the years and that can still be done in the future."

Although reluctant to do so, Olivia realized he had a point. However, the possibility that they might be housing a murderer bothered her more than she wanted her dad to see.

"Do you think Dawn is in any danger?" Olivia asked.

"No more than you are."

"If you're going to be away from the house all day, you might ask Buck to keep an eye on her."

"That's not a bad idea, but she'll probably stay in the house."

Olivia shook her head. "Not if she sees Johnny Barton outside. She's got a crush on him."

"Great." Her father scowled. "That's all we need."

"I warned her to stay away from him, and she agreed to, but she gave in too easily."

"I'll take care of it, Liv." He glanced behind her. "Here comes Hank."

Olivia turned around, and her breath caught in her throat. The chambray prison shirt had been replaced by a cream-colored dress shirt and blue tie, which contrasted handsomely with his suntanned face. Her father's navy, tan, and brown herringbone suit coat covered his shoulders and made them appear even broader. Although he still wore his blue jeans and boots, the outfit gave him a casual dressy look that would've turned even the most sophisticated woman's head in Chicago.

"Sorry. Damned tie took me a few minutes to figure out," Hank said. "It's been awhile."

Olivia's father slapped his shoulder. "Don't worry about it. Looks good. You still have some time to spare. Right, Liv?"

Olivia snapped her mouth shut and nodded. "Uh, right. Do you want to drive, Hank?"

Despite his obvious eagerness, he said, "If you don't mind."

"Go for it."

His fingers brushed hers when he took the keys, sending a shiver through her.

Her father hugged her, and after a round of good-byes, Hank drove down the driveway.

"You look good," Olivia commented.

"Your dad loaned me the shirt and jacket."

"He told me." She noticed his white-knuckled grip on the steering wheel. "Is something bothering you?"

He shot her a glance. "Nothing we haven't already discussed."

"Don't worry."

"Easy for you to say." Hank took a deep breath and let it out slowly. "I'll be okay."

Olivia studied his hawklike profile and resisted the urge to brush back a dark curl from his forehead. He hadn't been to a barber since coming to the ranch, and his short hair was growing out, revealing a tendency to curl like his sister's.

They remained silent as Hank turned onto the paved state highway and accelerated down the deserted two-lane road. He set the cruise control at three miles above the speed limit.

Olivia flipped on the radio and found the one AM station that came in with a minimum of static. They were talking about hog futures and the price of corn.

"We can either listen to this or one of Dad's George Strait CDs. Any preference?" Olivia asked Hank.

He grimaced. "Do I have another option?"

"We could talk."

"George Strait."

Disappointed but not surprised, Olivia put the disc in and settled back in her seat for the long ride.

CHAPTER THIRTEEN

THE CD ended, and Hank listened to the muffled thunk-thunk of the tires on the road. It was hypnotic, and he had to be careful not to nod off with the steady rhythm. With only an occasional car and a glimpse of a solitary golden eagle to break the monotony of the landscape, he could've easily fallen asleep.

He glanced at Olivia, pleased to see she hadn't wakened when the music ended. She'd fallen asleep five minutes into George Strait. Her mouth drooped open, and Hank figured she'd probably be mortified if she knew. But he didn't mind seeing her like this. In fact, it pleased him in an odd, chest-tightening way that she trusted him enough to let down her guard.

He would've enjoyed the drive, and Olivia, more if he weren't so anxious about what lay ahead in Walden. He and Olivia were only supposed to give their statements, but Hank knew the sheriff wouldn't miss the chance to interrogate him. Unless the murderer was already captured, which was unlikely.

A sign announced Walden was only four miles ahead.

Olivia would probably appreciate some time to shake off the effects of her nap.

"Olivia, we're almost there," he said quietly, not wanting to startle her.

Her body jerked, and she stared wild-eyed out the windshield. She reminded Hank of the mustangs when they were first brought into the prison program. "It's okay. We're almost to Walden," he said, using the same soothing voice he used on the untamed horses.

She turned to him, and awareness replaced the frantic look in her eyes. Visibly relaxing, she brushed her hair back with a slightly shaking hand. "Sorry."

"For what?"

"For being such rotten company."

He chuckled. "Believe me, you're the best company I've had in years." He winked at her. "Even sleeping with your mouth open and drool gathering on your chin."

She swiped at her chin, her face red. "I wasn't drooling. Was I?"

"No. I just wanted to see your reaction."

Olivia punched his upper arm lightly. "It's not nice to tease the groggy woman."

"Maybe not, but it is fun."

She merely rolled her eyes heavenward. Flipping down the sun visor, she checked her hair and face in the small mirror and wrinkled her nose at what she saw.

"There's nothing wrong with the way you look," Hank said.

Olivia huffed a laugh. " 'Damn with faint praise,' " she quoted.

"I meant that as a compliment." He shook his head, chagrined. "I must really be out of practice."

She leaned toward him and laid a hand on his arm. "Or maybe the lady is out of practice receiving compliments."

Hank glanced at her, noting the pink flush in her cheeks that made her natural beauty even more striking. "Any man who didn't notice you would have to have both feet in the grave."

Her blush deepened, but she smiled. "Thank you."

He caught a whiff of her subtle perfume and tightened his grip on the steering wheel. The ache to kiss her, touch her smooth skin, hear his name from her passion-swollen lips almost overwhelmed him. He'd known riding into Walden alone with Olivia would be a test of restraint for his long-ignored libido, but he was unprepared for the intensity of the attraction.

He concentrated on the collection of houses and businesses that lined both sides of the road. The Walden sign proclaimed the town at an elevation of 8,099 feet, with a population of 734, give or take. At eleven o'clock on a Sunday morning it appeared that the citizens of Walden were attending church services.

"Where's the sheriff's office?" Hank asked Olivia, obeying the twenty-five mile per hour speed limit through town.

"Keep going north. It's in the courthouse." A few minutes later she said, "Turn left here."

Hank did so and immediately spotted the stately looking county courthouse with its four pillars. Since it was Sunday, he had his pick of parking places and chose a close one so Olivia wouldn't have to walk far.

With his pulse racing, he followed her to the door. The last time he'd been in a courthouse, his life—and Dawn's—had been forever altered. Taking a deep breath and wiping away the film of sweat on his brow, Hank entered. Only the swish of their clothing and the dull thud of their soles on the shiny floor broke the tomblike silence.

Moments later, they entered the sheriff's office.

A young deputy glanced up from his desk. "Can I help you?"

"We're here to see Sheriff Jordan," Olivia said. "He's expecting us."

The freckled deputy's eyes widened. "You're the ones who found Melinda Holcomb's body."

And you're the one who lost his dinner, Hank thought peevishly.

"Could you let the sheriff know we're here?" Olivia asked the deputy.

The young lawman picked up the phone and hit one of the buttons. "Sheriff, those two are here to give their statements." He listened for a moment, then nodded. "All right." He looked up at Olivia but ignored Hank. "He wants one of you to wait here while the other gives his or her statement."

"I'll go first, since I found the body," Olivia said.

Hank noticed a tremble in her chin, but her voice was steady. "All right."

"Go down the hall and take the first left, Ms. Kincaid," the deputy said respectfully. "It's a conference room. The sheriff will be with you in a minute."

Hank watched Olivia until she disappeared into the room. He glanced around and spotted two straight-backed chairs against the wall, which he assumed was the waiting area. He lowered himself into one and rubbed his face.

God, he hated it here. Everything reminded him of his arrest and subsequent trial. He closed his eyes to block out the uniformed deputy, the wanted flyers on the wall, the fax machine, and tried to imagine he was somewhere else. However, the smells of ammonia, an overworked Xerox machine, burned coffee, and the kid's cheap cologne wouldn't let him be distracted.

He opened his eyes and stared at the deputy until the younger man looked up, then Hank glanced away. He continued to play the stupid game until Olivia returned with Sheriff Jordan. The lawman's eyes were bloodshot, and dark smudges lay beneath them. If Hank didn't dislike police officers on general principles, he would've felt sorry for the guy.

"I appreciate you coming in, Ms. Kincaid," the sheriff said in a solicitous tone.

"Standard procedure," she said with a tremulous smile.

Jordan smiled back, making Hank glare at the lawman as jealousy made his already short-fused temper rise. He crushed the emotion. What right did he have thinking of

Olivia Kincaid that way? Sheriff Jordan was a much better match for someone like her than some ex-con.

"Mr. Elliott, your turn." The sheriff's tone wasn't nearly as friendly as it'd been with Olivia.

His muscles stiff, Hank rose.

Olivia touched his arm, and her eyes were warm and reassuring. "Don't worry. It's a piece of cake."

His tension eased, and he gave her hand a grateful squeeze, then followed Jordan down the hallway. The lawman motioned for him to sit down at a scratched and pitted table in a room that looked suspiciously like an interrogation room. Hank slouched into the seat, ignoring the apprehension that made his palms sweat.

"I just need you to tell me what happened last night. How you found the body," Jordan said without preamble. He moved over to a video camera mounted on a tripod and made some adjustments. "I'll be taping your statement, then someone will type it up, and you'll be asked to sign it."

Hank nodded. It wasn't the first time he'd done this, but he hoped like hell it would be the last.

"Describe in your own words what happened the night you and Ms. Kincaid found the body," the sheriff said.

Hank took an unsteady breath. He related how he and Olivia were driving back to the ranch when his truck had a flat tire; how he heard Olivia's scream and ran to her, only to see the body. The statement was almost verbatim what he'd told the sheriff the night before.

When he was done, Jordan asked, "Is there anything you'd like to add, Mr. Elliott?"

He started to shake his head, the spoke aloud. "No. That's all."

Jordan turned off the video camera and perched on the corner of the table, only a foot from Hank. "Where were you Monday night?"

Hank clenched his jaw. Just as he thought, he was going to get the third degree. "Sleeping in my bed at the Kincaid ranch."

"Do you have any witnesses?"

"No, not unless one of the other convicts woke up and saw me."

"Do you think that happened?"

"How the hell should I know? I was asleep." He didn't bother hiding his frustration. "I didn't kill her, Sheriff. I had no reason to."

"Did you have reason to kill Sandra Hubbard?"

The name blindsided Hank, and his memory spiraled back in time. "We grew up in the same town. She disappeared about eight years ago."

Sheriff Jordan nodded, as if he already knew this. And he probably did, damn him.

"Her remains were found last week just over the state line in Wyoming."

Hank's stomach churned with shock. "She's dead?"

"That's right. Where were you eight years ago?"

Déjà vu washed through Hank, bringing a sense of being on a runaway train. "Going to college in Fort Collins."

Sheriff Jordan stood and invaded Hank's personal space. "Mrs. Hubbard said her daughter was going to Fort Collins to visit an old boyfriend before she disappeared."

Hank glared at him. "You don't think I killed her."

Jordan held out his arms. "I don't think anything. I'm just asking you some questions."

Hank's hands clenched and unclenched in his lap. He'd expected to be asked about his whereabouts during Melinda's murder, but Sandra's death came out of left field.

"I'll tell you the same thing I told the police eight years ago. The last time I saw her was the summer before she disappeared. I was home, and we went out a few times. Had some laughs. That was it."

"She was strangled, just like Melinda Holcomb."

The sheriff threw out his statement like a bone tossed to a dog. Hank crossed his arms and refused to play fetch.

Jordan leaned down, so close that his nose almost

touched Hank's. "They say confession is good for the soul. You're already in prison. What's the big deal?"

Red fury surged through Hank, and he rocketed to his feet, forcing the sheriff to back off. "Goddammit, I didn't kill anyone."

Jordan placed a heavy hand on Hank's shoulder. "Sit down, Elliott," he ordered coldly.

Adrenaline dodged through Hank's veins, inciting him to fight or flee. He fought the instinct and drew a shaky breath. Forcing his knees to bend, he lowered himself to the wooden chair.

Sheriff Jordan crossed his arms and stared down at him. "Five weeks ago you began working at Judge Kincaid's ranch. Two days ago a strangled woman is found on Kincaid property. A woman goes to visit you in Fort Collins and she disappears, only to be found eight years later, strangled. Both women were buried in shallow graves." He paused and narrowed his eyes. "I don't believe in coincidences, Elliott."

Hank struggled to remain calm. "I never saw Sandra after I went back to college, and I didn't even know the other woman. I didn't kill them."

Jordan remained still and silent, like a hawk eyeing a field mouse. Hank refused to cower and kept his gaze locked on the lawman's.

Sheriff Jordan broke the staring contest. "We don't have enough to arrest you, but the lab is going over everything with a fine-tooth comb. If they find *anything* that leads me to you, I'll have your ass back in prison so fast you won't know what hit you. In fact, I'm going to recommend to Judge Kincaid that you be placed back in the penitentiary until this mess is sorted out."

Panic reddened Hank's vision, and it took every ounce of self-control to resist taking a swing at the sheriff. If he went back to prison with these murders hanging over his head, he might as well eat a bullet. He clamped his lips together, afraid to say anything.

"We're done." Jordan paused deliberately. "For now."

Hank remained frozen in place and had to consciously unlock his jaw. "Can I leave?"

The lawman nodded.

Hank pushed himself upright, his knees weak and wobbly. He reached for the doorknob.

"One other thing, Elliott," Jordan said.

Hank stopped but didn't turn around.

"Anything happens to Ms. Kincaid, and you will regret the day you were born. Understand?"

He turned his head slowly toward Jordan, whose uncompromising expression made his threat a promise. "I understand." Hank's voice trembled with pent-up rage.

Hank jerked the door open and strode back to the front office where Olivia waited for him. She glanced up at him, and the smile forming on her lips vanished. Concern creased her brow.

"Hank?" she asked tentatively.

Hating to see her worry, he forced a smile. "I'm done."

Sheriff Jordan entered the front office. "Remember what I said, Elliott."

Hank's lower lip curled. "I'm not likely to forget, Sheriff." He spoke the last word with derision.

Olivia looked from Hank to the sheriff and back. "What happened?"

Jordan's coldness was replaced by a reassuring smile. "Thanks again for coming in, Ms. Kincaid. Say hello to your father for me. Could you let him know I'll be stoping by tomorrow?"

She nodded, her uncertain gaze darting between the two men. "Good-bye, Sheriff."

Hank opened the office door for Olivia and followed her out. Feeling like a teakettle about to blow off steam, he concentrated on getting his emotions back under control. He was aware of Olivia darting troubled looks his way, but he was afraid to speak. Afraid he'd take out his bitter frustration on her.

By the time they arrived at the car, Hank's anger had receded to be replaced by desperation. Lightning wasn't supposed to strike twice in the same place, but Hank was proof that it did. First to be imprisoned for a crime he was innocent of, and now to be accused of two murders he didn't commit.

"Would you like to eat lunch before heading back?" Olivia asked once they were seated in the SUV.

Hank's stomach protested at the thought of food, but he suspected Olivia might be hungry. They hadn't had any breakfast, and it would be close to an hour before they got back to the ranch.

"Sure," he said.

She seemed relieved that he'd finally spoken. "There's the River Rock Inn on Main. The food's pretty good."

Hank remembered seeing the restaurant when they'd entered the town and drove there without Olivia prompting directions. There were cars parked up and down the main thoroughfare, and he turned off on a side street to park.

He got out and removed the judge's sport coat and tie and laid them over the seat. He didn't want to risk spilling something on them in the restaurant. By the time he got around to Olivia's side, she was already standing on the sidewalk.

At the restaurant, the uncomfortable silence continued as they were led to a booth. Curious stares followed them, but Hank ignored them. He slid onto the vinyl cushion on one side, and Olivia sat on the other.

Once the waitress left, Olivia peered into Hank's face. "So what happened?"

Hank shook his head. "Nothing for you to worry about."

She leaned forward and spoke in a low but intense voice. "Don't patronize me, Hank. Did Sheriff Jordan give you the third degree?"

"Nothing I couldn't handle." Hank was accustomed to keeping his problems to himself. Besides, there was nothing Olivia could do if he told her what had happened.

The waitress returned with two glasses of water with ice and a lemon wedge in each. "Do you know what you want?"

The menus lay untouched on the table.

"Could you give us a few more minutes?" Olivia asked.

"Sure. No problem." She bounced away.

Hank picked up the well-used menu and scanned it, barely comprehending the selections. When the waitress returned, he ordered a house burger and fries—it seemed the easiest thing to decide upon. Olivia had a salad and half a club sandwich combo.

Olivia took a sip of water. "So, what is it that you can handle so well that you look like you're ready to go one-on-one with Sheriff Jordan?"

Despite his frustration, Hank's lips curled upward at the corners as he imagined himself and Jordan in a grudge match.

She continued to look at him, waiting patiently.

Hank drummed his fingers on the table. What would she say if he told her everything? And who would listen—Olivia the friend or Olivia the assistant district attorney? Of course, she'd find out sooner or later. It might be better if she heard it from him first.

He took a sip of the water to dispel his mouth's dryness. Glancing around at the other customers, he kept his voice low. "Sheriff Jordan asked me where I was Monday night when your friend was killed. I told him I was sleeping, but of course I can't prove it."

Olivia nodded, her expression somber. "But that will hold true for the other convicts as well. None of you can alibi the other unless someone was awake; then the in-evitable question would be why that person was awake in the middle of the night." Her lips quirked upward. "Be-yond the obvious, of course."

Hank's smile was less forced, but he sobered quickly. "Remember the woman's remains that were found last week?"

She nodded, puzzled.

"They identified the woman. I knew her. Sandra Hub-bard. We grew up in the same town and dated one summer when I was home from college. She disappeared eight years ago, supposedly on her way to see me at Fort Collins."

Olivia's face paled, and her eyes widened. "No."

Hank smiled without amusement. "Yes. There's more. Both women were strangled."

"Same MO, and you knew both women, plus you had opportunity." Olivia closed her eyes. "Shit."

"My thoughts exactly."

She opened her eyes, and misery shone from them. "This is so not good."

"Sheriff Jordan said he's going to suggest to your father that I be returned to prison." Steely determination strengthened Hank's resolve. "I won't go back, Olivia. I was innocent the first time, and I'm innocent now."

"Dad won't do it," she said without hesitation. "You haven't been arrested, so there's no reason for you to be placed behind bars. He'll back you."

Some of the coiled tension eased in Hank's chest.

"Did the sheriff say what kind of evidence they had?" Olivia asked.

He shook his head. "It didn't sound like they'd determined anything except cause of death. What could they find? Anything on Melinda's body would've been washed away, and Sandra—" He swallowed hard, picturing her how he remembered her, not as a pile of bones in an unmarked grave. "Sandra has been dead for eight years."

"If Melinda fought her attacker, there might be traces of his skin or blood under her fingernails, maybe even something clenched in her hand if she grabbed the killer's clothing." She rattled off in a clinical tone. Obviously, this woman was Olivia the assistant district attorney.

"But how could they tell Sandra was strangled, too?"

Olivia frowned. "There's no way forensics could have determined that with only skeletal remains. They must have something they're keeping under wraps."

"Like what?"

She thought for a moment. "Maybe the murder weapon?"

Hank's mind backtracked. "Sandra was strangled with a leather strap, too."

"Good assumption." Her gaze became unfocused. "I need to find out what they have."

"Why would they tell you?"

"They might not tell *me*, but I bet they would tell a retired judge." Her eyes glittered with excitement.

"I'm glad someone's enjoying this," he muttered.

She blinked and focused on him. "I didn't mean it that way. It's just—it's just that it's been a long time since I've wanted to get involved." She wrapped her smaller hand around his fist, which lay on the table. "And I want to help you, Hank. I want to prove you didn't do it."

"And how do we do that?"

"By finding the real killer."

CHAPTER FOURTEEN

THE waitress arrived bearing their lunch, and Olivia hastily removed her hand from Hank's. The young woman placed their plates in front of them.

"Can I get you anything else?" the girl asked.

"We're fine," Hank said curtly.

Olivia munched on her salad, barely tasting it. Although Hank was eating, it seemed more out of necessity than enjoyment.

She studied him, trying not to notice how his forearms flexed below the rolled-up shirtsleeves or how the dark hairs peeked out of the vee where the top two shirt buttons were undone. The last thing he needed was her thinking with something other than her brain. She needed to concentrate on how to help him legally, not how to get him into bed.

Disconcerted by her erotic meanderings, she focused on the problem at hand.

"How well do you know your fellow prisoners?" she asked.

He paused, a French fry halfway to his mouth. "Not very." He popped the fry into his mouth.

Olivia pushed aside her empty salad plate and the remainder of her sandwich. "Tell me what you know."

"Why?"

"Because there's still a murderer out their, and it could very well be one of those men."

He bristled. "You're the same as Sheriff Jordan. You got some cons in the vicinity, so pin at least one of the murders on them. Bonus points if you get both pinned on one."

"Who do *you* think killed Melinda?"

"How the hell should I know?" Heads turned in their direction, and Hank lowered his voice. "Did she have any enemies? Was she seeing someone? Had she pissed off anyone lately?"

Okay, so Olivia had been a little overzealous. Even though it was a small county, there were still more than enough suspects, not counting the convicts or the hired hands on the ranch. However . . .

"It might not have been someone at the ranch, but my gut is telling me otherwise. The place where she was buried was on a road that isn't used much. Nobody would know about it unless they were familiar with the area," she said.

"What if it was someone who used to work for your father?" He paused and added with a sour note, "Maybe a former convict who went through the program?"

Olivia considered his theories, and although they were possibilities, she didn't think them very probable. "Maybe, but I think we should concentrate on those who are working on the ranch now."

"And what? Solve the crime?" he demanded with incredulous sarcasm.

Her impatience flared. "I don't know. Maybe. It's better than not doing anything at all."

"Excuse me."

Olivia glanced over at a woman wearing dark slacks and a black-and-white blouse who approached their booth. She looked familiar, but Olivia couldn't place her. "Yes?"

"Olivia Kincaid?" the woman asked.

She nodded warily. "That's right."

"I thought that was you. I'm Brenda Whitelaw."

The name didn't ring any bells, and Olivia shook her head.

Brenda laughed nervously. "You probably remember me as Brenda Rogerson. I was two years behind you in school."

The faint memory of a pigtailed girl came to mind, and Olivia smiled. "That's right. How are you doing, Brenda?"

"Just fine." She motioned to a table where a slightly overweight man was trying to get two hyperactive boys to mind him. "That's my husband and two children. I do some part-time bookkeeping here in town." Her expression brightened. "But look at you, a big-time lawyer in Chicago. At least, you were."

Embarrassed, Olivia glanced at Hank, who gave her an encouraging nod. Bolstered by his support, she said, "I'll be going back once my leg is healed."

"Yes, I read about that. How dreadful for you." The woman leaned closer. "The word around town is that Melinda Holcomb was murdered on your father's ranch."

Olivia suddenly remembered something else about Brenda—she always stuck her nose in where it didn't belong.

"Her body was found there, but it hasn't been proven she was killed there," Olivia clarified, knowing the facts would be out soon enough.

"People were talking about it after church service this morning. Nothing like this has ever happened around here."

"And it probably won't again," Olivia assured her, although she wasn't certain of that herself. She wondered how much had leaked out about the skeletal remains found last week, and if anyone knew the two deaths could be related. In Chicago, the connection would've been kept from the press, but out here, word of mouth was far more efficient than any big-city newspaper.

"We don't know that." Brenda glanced around and lowered her voice. "Women are scared. I respect your father and all, Olivia, but it's just not right the way he lets prisoners roam around his ranch like they were as respectable as the rest of us. If you ask me, one of them killed Melinda."

Olivia intentionally kept herself from glancing at Hank, but she could sense his rising anger. Her own temper wasn't far behind. "My father carefully screens every prisoner who comes into the program."

"Mistakes can be made."

And you just made one. Olivia bristled at the slight against her father. She deliberately looked past Brenda to her children, who were racing between the tables and drawing disapproving looks from the other customers. "Aren't those your boys, Brenda?" she asked in a sugary sweet tone.

Olivia felt more than a twinge of satisfaction at the woman's red face. Without a word, Brenda scurried off to grab her sons and talk to them in a low voice. The boys didn't appear fazed by the scolding.

"Are you done eating?" Hank asked curtly.

She nodded.

Hank reached for the check, but Olivia nabbed it.

"My treat," she said, knowing he had very little money. "You can get it next time."

"Next time."

Olivia shivered under his smoldering gaze, and her body reminded her how long it'd been since a man had looked at her as a woman. And how long since she'd looked at a man with something other than fear or indifference.

She scooped up her purse and carried the bill to the register by the door. Hank shifted his weight from one foot to the other as she paid. Leaving the tip with the cashier, Olivia joined him, and they left the restaurant.

"She didn't mean anything," Olivia said, guessing at Hank's preoccupation.

"It wasn't just her." Hank made an irate motion toward

the restaurant and said with a heavy dose of sarcasm, "She isn't the only one who disapproves of having us cons around decent folks."

"Did you hear other people talking?"

"I didn't have to. I saw the way they were looking at us."

Olivia waved aside his concern. "They were just staring at me because of that article in the paper."

"It was more than that, Olivia. In prison, I learned how to recognize anger and fear, and most of those people were filled with both."

They arrived at the SUV, and Hank opened Olivia's door for her, then went around and slid in the driver's side.

"Even if you're right, they're not going to do anything. People in small towns love to gossip. That'll be the extent of their actions," Olivia said, putting on her seat belt.

"I'm not so sure of that. When people get scared, they do stupid things." He stuck the key in the ignition but didn't turn it.

"You think they'll come out to the ranch in hooded robes and demand that Dad turn you and the other convicts over to them?" She was being facetious, but Hank's worry seemed over the top.

He turned, laying his right arm across her seat back. "All I'm saying is that the pressure will be on your father until the murderer is caught."

"All the more reason for us to investigate on our own." She crossed her arms stubbornly.

Hank took a deep breath, and his features softened. "Are you sure you're up to this, Olivia? You still have a hard time being around people."

Trepidation made her heart skip a beat, but there was a new certainty budding within her. Although only a splinter of her past self-assurance, her confidence was growing slowly. She'd proven that by simply eating in a restaurant.

"I appreciate your concern, Hank. I really do. But I'm starting to feel something else besides fear." Her clenched hands pressed into her thighs. "I need to do this, for Dad and for you, but even more for myself. Can you understand that?"

"Yeah," he said with reluctant acceptance. "But I don't want you taking chances. You were badly hurt once. I don't want you hurt again."

The concern in his voice made Olivia blink against unexpected tears. She'd never leaned on a man before, had prided herself on her independence, but she found herself wanting to lean on Hank's strength. He was the first man, other than her father, whom she trusted enough to support her. Ironic that he was a felon, the type of man whom she spent most of her life loathing and taking pleasure in prosecuting.

"I'll be careful," she promised.

"Good."

The word was a bare whisper that sent a tendril of heat curling through Olivia.

She expected Hank to start the car and head back to the ranch. Instead, he continued to gaze intently at her. His attention sparked a fire in her belly that expanded, threatening to melt her muscles.

Deliberately, she lifted her hand and laid it against his cheek. The rasp of his whiskers against her palm shocked her with its eroticism, and her breath grew shallow. She was gratified to hear Hank's labored breathing, as if he'd been running for miles.

"It's been a long time, Olivia."

She heard the evidence of his passion in his husky voice.

"Can I kiss you?" he whispered.

Olivia's breath stumbled in her lungs. Her vision narrowed to Hank's rugged, tanned face and the smoldering hunger in his hazel eyes. "I hope so," she managed to say above the thundering of her heart.

A tiny smile twitched Hank's sexy lips, and Olivia couldn't wait a second longer. She leaned close and tilted her face upward. Unerringly, her mouth found his, and his lips slid with a sensuous glide over hers. After seeing the burning desire in his eyes, she was surprised by his exquisite gentleness. He made her feel treasured, protected, cherished—all the things an independent woman should disdain. So why didn't she?

She groaned and increased the pressure, her tongue tentatively brushing his lips. He opened to her without hesitation and swept in to taste her. She sighed into the kiss as he wrapped his hands within her hair, holding her, guiding her. Hank became more insistent, kissing her with more intensity and gentling it a moment later. He nibbled at her lower lip before deepening the kiss once more.

A car horn sounded, and Hank pulled away.

Olivia gasped at his abrupt retreat as her lips tingled and burned.

For a long moment, there was only the sound of their harsh breathing, each raspy breath a counterpoint to the other.

Without a word, Hank started the engine and pulled out onto the street. Stunned by her reaction to the kiss, Olivia sat rigidly as he turned around and got onto the highway headed southeast, back to the ranch.

Her body throbbed and hummed in a way she hadn't experienced in years, if ever. And even if Hank was wrongly imprisoned, he was still a convict and she was an ADA. There were a hundred reasons why the kiss had been a mistake, but at the moment she couldn't give a rat's ass about any of them.

Cool it, girl.

As long as the suspicion of murder hung over Hank, there was no way she could let herself get too close to him. Though never would she have imagined she could feel this way about a convict, Hank Elliott was a decent man—a man who had six years of his life stolen away because he'd been in the wrong place at the wrong time.

And she'd be damned if she let circumstantial evidence steal the rest of his life.

NOT long after returning to the ranch, Hank carried a bulging cloth sack into the laundry room of the bunkhouse.

He'd hoped it would be empty, but as usual, his luck had skipped town. Rollie, the ranch hand who went out of his way to make Hank's life miserable, sat in one of the old chairs looking at a magazine with a scantily clad woman on the cover.

Rollie glanced up at Hank and smiled without warmth. "If it ain't the boss's favorite con."

Hank ignored the jibe as he started up one of the three washers and added some detergent. After the tense scenes at the sheriff's office and in the restaurant, Hank didn't need Rollie's shit.

"I seen you leave with little Miss Priss. I don't know what you're selling, but you sure got both Kincaids buying it," the stocky man said.

Hank closed the washer lid and leaned against the machine, facing the hired hand. "What's your problem, Rollie?"

The man set his girlie magazine aside and stood, using his bulk to try to intimidate Hank. "My problem is you, Elliott. The way you got the judge wrapped around your finger, you *could* get away with murder." He tilted his head and squinted at Hank. "And maybe you did."

Anger seethed in Hank, but he said flatly, "Seems to me the person pointing the finger is more likely the one trying to hide something."

Rollie narrowed his eyes. "You calling me a killer?"

Hank shrugged deliberately. "It wasn't me."

The hired man curled his hands into fists. "You son of a—"

"Something going on here?" Buck stood in the doorway, and his jaundiced gaze moved between the two men.

Rollie kept his glare aimed at Hank. "Nope."

Hank crossed his arms over his chest and lazily slid his gaze to the foreman. "Nothing at all, Buck."

A dryer's timer buzzed, breaking the tension.

Rollie grabbed his laundry bag and stuffed his dry clothes in it. He slung the pack over his shoulder and swaggered to the door. Buck remained blocking the doorway for a moment longer, then stepped aside. Rollie's foot-falls grew fainter as he strode away.

Buck strolled into the laundry room and leaned against a dryer. "Rollie ain't a bad sort. He's just had a run of bad luck."

"And that makes it okay for him to be an asshole?" Hank asked, rolling his shoulders to dispel the tightness.

Buck glanced down. "No, but maybe if you'd stop pushing him, he wouldn't be itching for a fight."

Hank laughed without humor. "He's the one who's pushing, Buck. All I want to do is keep my nose clean and do my job."

"Seems to me trouble finds you. Two women dead and you in the middle of it."

Hank frowned, wondering how Buck had learned he was the main suspect in the two murders.

But before he could ask, the foreman explained. "The sheriff called not long ago and talked to the judge. Told him his suspicions about you." Buck took a deep breath and let it out in a sigh. "From what I've seen, you're not a bad guy, Elliott. But I swear you've got the worst case of hard luck I've ever seen."

Hank couldn't help but chuckle. "Sure seems that way, doesn't it?" He sobered. "If I get arrested and convicted for something I didn't do, this time I won't be coming out except in a pine box."

Buck slapped Hank's arm. "Don't worry, son. You got the judge behind you and from what I seen, Ms. Olivia, too." The foreman started to leave, but paused. "Oh, I seen your sister with Barton earlier today."

Hank stiffened. "How'd you find out she was my sister?"

"Ms. Olivia told me." Buck paused. "Far as I know, no one but me, the judge, and Ms. Olivia know you two are related. Might be best if it stays that way."

As Hank watched Buck leave with his usual rolling gait, he digested the information. He'd noticed Dawn's interest in the youngest prisoner but had hoped it was merely an infatuation. She deserved better than a convicted felon.

Especially if it was Barton who'd strangled the Holcomb woman. It was doubtful he'd killed Sandra Hubbard, though. Barton would've been only thirteen or fourteen at the time. As much as he wanted to find the real killer, Hank knew it probably wasn't him. He wasn't the type to kill a woman in cold blood. Hell, Hank even kind of liked the kid. If it'd been Dawn who'd overdosed on drugs, Hank might have done the same as Barton.

He sank onto one of the folding chairs and propped his elbows on his thighs. His life was galloping out of control like a runaway horse . . . again. It was about time he reined in that horse. Olivia was right. In order to clear himself, he had to find the real killer.

But he wouldn't allow Olivia to risk her life to help him. If something happened to her, the price of his freedom would be too damned high.

THAT evening Olivia finished cleaning up the kitchen after a light dinner with her father. Feeling stifled in the house that had been her sanctuary for weeks, she stepped out onto the porch. The ringing of horseshoes against a metal stake caught her attention, and she turned to watch four of the men playing a lively game.

Two of the convicts—Lopez and Reger—were pitted against Buck and another hired hand. She crossed her arms and studied Lopez and Reger. Could one of them have killed Melinda?

Lopez had beaten his wife and her boyfriend after he'd found them in bed together—a crime of passion, which made it statistically unlikely that he'd killed Melinda. Reger had been convicted of bilking elderly widows out of their savings. Although Olivia thought he was a despicable human being, it was rare that a con man committed murder, so he went to the bottom of her suspect list, too.

The door opened behind her, and she knew without looking it was her father. He joined her, placing a hand on her shoulder. "I see Ted is back."

Olivia followed his gaze and noticed the farrier's familiar truck and trailer. "I thought he was done."

"John Nestler had a couple of horses come up lame, so Ted said he'd finish trimming and reshoeing our stock after he took care of John's."

The sound of whooping drew Olivia's attention back to the horseshoe match. It appeared the game was over as the four men ambled away. Once they were gone, Hank and Ted took their places.

"What do you say we challenge them?" her father asked her with a wink.

Although Olivia knew they didn't have a snowball's chance in hell against the two men, the temptation to be near Hank was compelling. Besides, her natural competitiveness was returning, which she took as a positive sign in her recovery.

She smiled. "Let's show 'em how it's done."

Olivia limped slightly, but her leg felt better than it had since the assault. She wasn't certain how well she could toss the shoes, but she was game to give it a shot.

"Glad to see you're back," her father said, shaking Ted's hand. "Any trouble at the Nestlers?"

Shandler's ham-sized hand swallowed up her father's, and he grinned. "Turned out to be not as bad as John made it out."

"Glad to hear it." Her father motioned toward the horseshoes. "Care to take on the Kincaids?"

Aware of Hank's gaze on her, Olivia smiled. "I have to warn you, it's been a few years since I've played."

"When she did play, she was a formidable opponent. Take it from someone she's trounced more than once." Her father winked at her.

Olivia's cheeks heated, but she didn't look away. "Careful, Dad, you might scare them off."

She was rewarded with a smile from Hank, which set her pulse skittering through her veins.

Hank glanced at Ted, who nodded. Ted flipped a coin to

see who started, but Hank caught the quarter in the air. "Ladies first."

"Famous last words," Olivia said with a cheeky grin.

Her father smiled, his pleasure at her burgeoning confidence obvious from the twinkle in his eyes. He took the four horseshoes from Hank, and he and Olivia went to their stake.

"Ladies first?" her father teased, holding out two horseshoes.

Olivia grasped the metal shoes, their weight both familiar and foreign in her hand. She moved one to her left hand and hefted the other in her right. Turning the horseshoe until the grip felt comfortable, she took a deep breath, drew back her arm, and let it fly. The ring of metal told her she'd hit the stake, but it rolled away. No score.

She glanced at Hank down by the stake, and he gave her an approving nod.

"Good one, Ms. Olivia," Ted called.

The vestiges of nervousness faded, and she threw the next horseshoe with more confidence. This one caught the stake.

"Ringer," her father shouted.

Hank and Ted clapped.

The flush of success touched her cheeks with warmth, and she bowed at the waist with a flourish.

The game continued, interspersed by the clanging ring of the shoes against the stakes and good-natured ribbing. Olivia enjoyed the closeness with her father and the farrier's affable nature. However, it was Hank's presence that provided her the most pleasure.

The sun dipped behind the mountain peaks, and Olivia shivered in the rapidly cooling air. She and her father threw for the last time to win by two points. They exchanged a high five.

Olivia's bad leg grumbled about its overuse, but she tried to keep her discomfort from showing. She'd had too much fun to spoil it.

Shaking his head but smiling, Hank picked up the horseshoes to carry them back to the barn.

"Looks like we'll have to practice before a rematch," Ted said as he slapped Hank on the back.

"It just proves beauty and brains always win over brawn," her father said, his eyes twinkling with amusement.

Everyone laughed.

Her father yawned. "I don't know about you youngsters, but after the late night, this old man is ready for bed."

Olivia realized she, too, was exhausted after too little sleep and the trip into Walden. But then her gaze caught Hank's, and the smolder in their hazel depths nearly made her gasp. She wondered if he remembered their kiss as vividly as she did.

"Good night, Judge," Ted said respectfully.

"Good night, Ted, Hank," her father said with a wave. "Olivia?"

"If you don't mind, I think I'll take a walk," she said.

Her father opened his mouth but closed it abruptly when his gaze darted between Hank and Olivia. "That's fine. I'll see you inside later."

Once her father walked away, the farrier smiled knowingly. "I'm kind of tired myself. Good night."

Olivia and Hank echoed his good night, then stared at one another in the growing dusk. Attraction flickered like a live wire between them. Olivia took a step toward him.

"I don't think this is a good idea," Hank said, holding up a hand.

"What's not a good idea?" Olivia asked softly.

Hank retreated a step. "You. Me. Us."

"It was a good idea this afternoon."

"Was it?"

Olivia frowned. "You liked it."

"Hell, yes, I liked it. I haven't kissed a woman in over six years." Hank shifted the four horseshoes from one hand to the other. "Next time I might not be able to stop with just a kiss, Olivia."

She wasn't certain whether she should be frightened or flattered. Right now, she was only confused and hurt. "I see."

"No, you don't." Hank glanced away and took a deep breath, then returned his attention to her. "I care for you, and I won't take the chance that I might hurt you. Besides, I have a killer to catch."

"*We* have a killer to catch."

"I don't want you involved, Olivia."

Her mouth dropped open. "If you recall it was *my* idea in the first place."

Hank nodded reluctantly. "Yes, but I won't take a chance with your life. You stay out of it, Olivia. Do you hear me?"

Although Olivia appreciated his protectiveness, she wasn't the frightened woman he'd first met. "I hear you, but I don't agree. Sheriff Jordan will tell my father and me things he won't tell you. I've worked with law enforcement and I know what to ask, what to look for. You need me, Hank."

She could tell by his clenched jaw that he didn't want to need anyone. Her heart softened. "Please, let me help you."

His inner battle reflected in his face, but he was smart enough to recognize the truth of her words. If he wanted his freedom, he'd have to accept her assistance.

Finally, his lips pressed together, he nodded. "All right. But I'll talk to the men. You talk to the sheriff."

Olivia nodded at his assent. No matter if he'd agreed with her or not, she planned to investigate. She was trained in ferreting out the truth, and it was about time she put her training back into action.

CHAPTER FIFTEEN

WHEN Hank entered the dining area the following morning, he immediately homed in on Olivia standing at the front of the room. Usually she hid in the kitchen, but he'd watched her transformation over the weekend. He didn't know what exactly caused it but suspected the murders gave her something to think about other than her attack.

Her gaze met his, and Hank's groin tightened at her slight smile and nod. Despite his anxiety of being under suspicion for two killings, he hadn't been able to forget the passionate kiss they'd shared. Erotic dreams of her writhing beneath him in a satin-sheeted bed had tormented him overnight. When he awoke, he'd been hard and aching but had ignored his body's betrayal.

He had nothing to offer Olivia, not even a good name.

"Get moving, Elliott," Rollie said and shoved him with his shoulder.

Hank stumbled forward and spun around, his fists raised.

Rollie smiled coldly. "Go ahead, Elliott. Take a swing. See how fast they throw your ass back in the pen."

Hank's chest heaved as he fought to gain control of his anger. If he had allowed someone to bully him in prison, Hank would've ended up dead or worse. But this wasn't prison, and there were new rules.

Buck pushed through the circle of gawking men and inserted himself between Hank and Rollie. He shook his head in disgust. "You two are worse than two bulls in the springtime. Get something to eat, then get your asses outside."

Rollie showed his teeth in a caricature of a smile, then joined a handful of other men at one of the tables.

Hank found himself alone, except for Barton, who merely said, "Buck's right. Let's eat."

Hank nodded, and he and the younger man sat at the end of a table, somewhat separated from the others. Hank glanced up, his gaze instinctively returning to Olivia. Her lips were pressed into a tight line, and her face had lost some color, but it didn't look like she planned to run and hide. Instead, she appeared disappointed. In him?

Irritation made him scowl. She had no clue what kind of life he'd had to live in prison. Survival of the fittest didn't pertain only to animals in the wild.

"Rollie's not worth losing your freedom," Barton said quietly so no one would overhear.

Hank's grip tightened on his fork. "I know."

Barton glanced around, then leaned forward. "Then don't let him get to you. Next time turn around and walk away."

Hank stared at the younger man, for the first time realizing maybe he wasn't as naive as Hank had believed. He consciously released the tension in his shoulder muscles. "I'll try."

They ate in silence, until Dawn came by, refilling coffee cups. He was relieved to see she was treated respectfully by the men, even Mantle . . . although the slimeball let his gaze linger on her longer than necessary.

When she stopped by Barton, she ignored Hank and gave the younger man her complete attention. Barton shot a nervous glance at Hank as Dawn filled his cup. If Hank were a gambling man, he'd bet Barton knew he and Dawn were brother and sister.

"Oops, ran out of coffee," Dawn said to Hank, sounding more mocking than contrite.

Her tone was worse than a slap, and he glanced away, hiding the hurt. Once she disappeared into the kitchen, he stared at Barton, who shifted uncomfortably.

"She's my kid sister," Hank said, his voice pitched low.

Barton flushed, but he didn't look away. "I know. Ms. Kincaid told me."

Although he was surprised Olivia had spoken to Barton, Hank didn't let it show. "I don't want Dawn getting involved with an ex-con."

Barton's jaw clenched, and he shoved back his chair from the table. Without a word, he strode outside.

Hank swallowed the last of his lukewarm coffee with a grimace, then followed in Barton's resentful wake.

While Hank waited for the other men to finish eating, he wandered over to the farrier, who was already busy. A sorrel mare was snubbed to the corral while Ted trimmed her hooves.

Hank leaned against the top rail. "Need any help?"

Ted glanced up from his hunched position, and a smile creased his broad face. "Got it under control, but thanks anyway."

Hank watched him work. "How long have you been doing this?"

"For a good while now."

"Not that much work for farriers anymore, is there?"

Ted let down the mare's leg and moved toward his work area where his forge, anvil, and tools were all set out in precise order. "You'd be surprised. At last count there were over ten million horses in the country, and as long as you don't mind traveling to your work instead of having work come to you, it's the perfect job." He grinned. "Of course, you have to like horses, too."

Hank chuckled. "No problem there."

Ted grew serious. "You interested in being a farrier?"

"I hadn't really thought about it."

"Maybe you should. I'd be willing to apprentice you."

With his dream to be a veterinarian lost, maybe becoming a farrier wouldn't be a bad choice. "I'll think about it."

"You do that. You're the only person I've ever made that offer to." He paused. "I get the feeling you care for horses like I do."

Hank smiled, knowing that was a high compliment. "Thanks, Ted."

Hank wandered off to get his day's assignment from Buck as he considered Ted's offer. He just hoped he got the chance to make his own decision about his future.

HANK used his bandanna to wipe the sweat from his face and neck. He'd wanted a solo task, and he'd gotten his wish. However, stacking forty-five-pound hay bales onto a flatbed wagon to take out to the cattle wasn't exactly his idea of a good time.

He swigged down the rest of his bottled water and drew the back of his hand across his lips. Though tempted to remove his long-sleeved shirt, Hank knew the hay would irritate his skin if he did. With a sigh, he pulled his work gloves back on and returned to his task.

The flatbed was backed into the storage shed, up to the first row of bales, which were stacked fifteen feet high. Hank climbed the bales like stairs to get to the highest tier. After tossing another couple of dozen bales down, he descended to pile them on the wagon.

As Hank did the tedious task, his mind wandered to his sister and Olivia. With the possibility of a murderer on the ranch, he was glad they spent most of the time together. The killer might be long gone, but the possibility remained that he was even now searching for another victim. Why was there so much time between Sandra's murder and the Holcomb woman's? Maybe the killer was a transient.

Hank's sixth sense snapped him back to the present, and

his gaze shot to top of the stacked hay. His eyes widened as the uppermost bales toppled toward him. He jumped off the wagon as a heavy one grazed him, throwing him off-balance. His head connected with the edge of the trailer, bringing pain and encroaching darkness. A bale fell directly on his side, and he groaned. Driven by instinct, he rolled under the flatbed.

After what seemed forever, the avalanche ended. The abrupt silence seemed eerie and somehow expectant. He opened his eyes and for a moment, he thought he'd been blinded. But it was chaff and dust that surrounded him within the confines beneath the trailer. He quickly covered his mouth and nose with his hand but was too late to prevent a sneezing fit.

Hank frantically heaved aside the hay bales piled around the trailer. He crept out from beneath it and crawled over the jumbled mound of bales as his eyes watered and his sneezes changed to hoarse coughing.

Wiping at his tearing eyes with one hand, he waved the other to disperse the dwindling dust cloud. His coughing lessened and, once he could see clearly, he looked up at the empty place where the fallen bales had been. If they'd been piled haphazardly, Hank could understand the accident. But the bales had been solidly stacked.

Had someone pushed them? But if that had happened, wouldn't Hank have seen the person come into the shed? Not if he came in the back door and climbed the stack from the other side. Hank had been too busy protecting himself to look upward.

Hank moved his arm and flinched at the soreness of his right side. His pain faded with the escalation of his anger. Who the hell would try to kill him? And why?

He strode out of the storage shed and toward the corral, where Ted was shaping a hot shoe on the anvil.

"Have you seen anyone around the yard?" Hank asked the farrier without preamble.

"What happened to you?" Ted demanded.

Hank blinked. "What?"

"You're covered with dust and got a knot growing on your forehead."

Hank fingered his brow and flinched when he found the bump. "Shit. I almost got buried by some hay bales. Did you see anyone around the shed in the last ten minutes?"

Ted shook his head. "There've been a couple fellas cleaning out the barns, but nobody over there. Are you thinking someone did it on purpose?"

Hank sighed, his adrenaline draining away. "I don't know. Maybe. Or it just might've been that when I pulled a bale out, it made the whole stack unstable."

Ted's face darkened. "Report it to the sheriff."

Hank turned and noticed that Jordan's official SUV was parked by the house. That's right—Olivia had said he'd be coming today to question everyone about the woman's death.

"Tell him what happened," Ted said. "If someone is trying to kill you, maybe the sheriff can find out who it is."

Although correct in theory, Hank doubted Jordan would give him the time of day, much less look into an attempt on his life. However, maybe informing him of the incident would make Hank look less like a suspect.

"Is he in the house?" Hank asked.

"Chow shack. There's been a steady stream of men going in to talk to him, one at a time. I hear he's asking everyone about Ms. Holcomb's death."

At least the lawman hadn't decided to merely pin her murder on Hank. "Thanks."

"No problem." Ted returned to the mare.

Wrapping his left arm around his waist, Hank shuffled across the yard to the dining hall. The door was ajar, and he knocked then entered without waiting for a reply.

Sheriff Jordan glanced up, and irritation creased his brow. "What do you want, Elliott?"

"I'm here to report an assault."

Jordan's eyes widened slightly, as did Slim's, whom he was questioning. Out of his side vision, Hank noticed Olivia step out of the kitchen, her expression both frightened and grim. She'd obviously heard his announcement.

Jordan turned back to Slim. "That's all for now. Thanks for your cooperation."

Slim stood. "Sure. No problem, Sheriff."

Clearly not wanting to get involved, the lanky man ducked out.

Jordan got to his feet and approached Hank, his expression suspicious. "What're you up to, Elliott?"

Hank's temper, already shortened by his body's aches and the adrenaline rush, neared its end. "Somebody just tried to bury me under a ton of hay bales."

Jordan eyed the bump on Hank's temple and his general dishevelment. "Looks more like you ran into somebody tougher than you."

Olivia stepped forward. "Sheriff, this man is reporting a crime."

Jordan cast a skeptical glance at her. "I thought you'd be more cynical, you being a big-city ADA."

Olivia tilted her head to the side and crossed her arms. "And I thought you'd be more understanding, you being a small-town sheriff."

Jordan clenched his jaw. He clearly didn't like her throwing his words back at him.

"Tell us what happened, Hank," Olivia said, her tone professional but concerned.

He described how the wall of bales had tumbled down and how he'd managed to save himself from serious injury. Hank had to give Jordan credit—despite his skepticism, he jotted down notes on his pad.

"Who would want to hurt you?" Jordan asked.

"Could be half a dozen different men," Hank replied.

"Do you go out of your way to piss off people?"

Fuck you. Hank barely managed to suppress the words. "No, but other people seem to go out of their way to piss *me* off." He glared at the sheriff deliberately.

Jordan's jaw muscle jumped. "Show me where it happened."

Hank led the way and was aware of Olivia following them across the yard. Once in the shed, he pointed to the mess of bales on the ground. "I was in the middle of that."

"This looks more like attempted murder than assault," Olivia said.

"Yes, ma'am," Hank said.

Jordan wandered among the bales, then stopped and looked up from where they came from. Without a word, he climbed up the stored bales to look around.

"Were you hurt?" Olivia asked softly.

He turned to find her standing close, and words deserted him for a moment. The concern in her expression almost made up for Jordan's indifference. "Bruised, but nothing serious."

She touched the knot on his forehead, her fingers cool. "Did you black out?"

"No," he said, his voice made husky by her proximity. "Just grayed out some."

"You should go to the hospital. You could have a mild concussion."

"Wouldn't be the first time." He captured her hand and lowered it before her touch drove him crazy. "I'm fine."

Sheriff Jordan rejoined them, his expression somber. "The bales are packed pretty solid up there. It's doubtful they came down on their own."

"So you believe me?"

"I believe those bales were probably pushed down intentionally." Jordan narrowed his eyes. "I also think that someone trying to throw suspicion off himself might try a stunt like this."

Hank started toward him. "You son of a—"

Olivia grabbed Hank's arm. "Stop it." Her glare shifted to Jordan. "If Mr. Elliott did do this to draw attention away from the murder investigation, how did he get hurt?"

Jordan eyed the knot on Hank's forehead. "I don't know," he said grudgingly. "I'll ask around. Maybe someone saw a person hanging around the shed, but that's about all I can do."

"Fine," Hank said through gritted teeth.

Sheriff Jordan nodded to Olivia, and his long legs carried him out of the shed.

It took a moment for Hank to realize he and Olivia were alone. "You should get back."

"Come with me and I'll get you some ice for that bump," she said.

"It's all—"

"No, it's not." She took a deep breath and let it out in a shaky gust. "Damn it, Hank, you could've been killed."

He shrugged. It felt odd having someone worry about him. He wasn't sure if he liked it or not. "But I wasn't."

Olivia's chin lifted, revealing her stubborn streak. "Do you think this was related to Melinda's murder?"

Buying time to come up with an answer, he scratched his back where the chaff and dust had settled. "No. The killer wouldn't gain anything by getting rid of me. As long as I'm the main suspect, the investigation is centered on me."

"Did you talk to anyone about the murders?"

"I'm not an idiot, Olivia," he snapped.

She drew back. "I didn't say you were," she said softly. "But if you're starting to nose around, maybe someone is getting nervous."

Hank thought a moment. "Yesterday Rollie and I had a few words. He practically accused me of killing the Holcomb woman."

"Could he have killed Melinda?"

Hank had already considered that angle, but although the bully couldn't seem to speak two words without provoking him, he wasn't certain. "He might have. Buck mentioned something about Rollie having a run of bad luck." He snorted. "He doesn't know what bad luck is."

"I'll ask Dad about Rollie, find out what he knows about him."

He arched an eyebrow.

She held up her hands. "Just Dad. I promise." A cunning

look entered her eyes. "I'll bet Sheriff Jordan will be talking to Rollie this afternoon, since he hasn't yet."

"Olivia," he warned.

"I agreed I wouldn't talk to the hired men or the other inmates, and I won't." She grinned. "But it's amazing how voices travel in the dining area."

Olivia's obvious enjoyment at playing spy made it hard for Hank to be annoyed. "Be careful."

"Don't worry." She looked at the fallen bales, and her confidence disappeared, replaced by grimness. "Nobody tried to bury me under fifty hay bales."

Buck and the judge entered the shed, their expressions somber. If they were surprised to see Olivia with Hank, they didn't show it.

"Sheriff Jordan just told us what happened," Judge Kincaid said.

"Did he tell you it was deliberate?" Olivia asked.

"He said it could've been accidental, but he didn't think it was." Kincaid's breathing seemed to be labored. "Why would anyone do this?"

"It's not exactly a secret that some of the men aren't fond of him," Buck said, motioning to Hank.

Kincaid shook his head. "I don't pay the men to like each other. I pay them to do their jobs."

Hank had never heard the older man so upset. "It's okay, sir," he reassured. "Whoever did this probably won't try anything else."

"That doesn't matter. I don't want someone like that working on my ranch."

"I'll do some asking around, Judge," Buck volunteered. "If it was one of the men, I'll find him."

Hank opened his mouth to argue, to tell Buck he'd take care of his own problems. But then his gaze strayed to Olivia, who stood there, her face thoughtful but her eyes filled with worry. For him.

And for the first time since Hank was placed in prison, he had friends in his corner.

•   •   •

THE son of a bitch will be punished. It's my duty and my right to rid the world of scum like him so the others will be safe. I caress the leather and allow the pure scent to calm me. Until tonight . . .

CHAPTER SIXTEEN

WITH a dish towel over her shoulder, Olivia wandered out of the kitchen into the dining hall. Connie had called last night, letting them know she'd be back in a few days. On one hand, Olivia was glad she was returning to take over the cooking, but on the other, she'd come to enjoy the job. But then, she had her real job waiting for her in Chicago.

Sheriff Jordan sat at a corner table, obviously not wanting any eavesdroppers while he interviewed the hired men. She wiped the tabletops, using the task as a means to get closer to the sheriff, who was questioning Mantle.

"Had you seen Ms. Holcomb prior to her visit to the ranch?" Jordan asked the rat-faced prisoner.

"No, sir," Mantle replied respectfully, his hands folded in his lap.

"Did you ever speak to her?"

"I only saw her from a distance when she was here, Sheriff."

"Where were you the night she was murdered?"

"Sleeping." He leered. "Alone."

Sheriff Jordan grunted, and Olivia got the impression he'd gotten that same answer countless times today.

"One last question, Mr. Mantle. Where were you living eight years ago?" Jordan asked without inflection.

Mantle's eyebrows drew together. "Eight years ago?"

Olivia had the impression he was stalling for time. Jordan caught her gaze and frowned slightly.

Oops. Busted.

She moved to the next table and kept her back to the two men but remained near enough that she could still hear them.

"Um, I was in Omaha, working in an insurance office," Mantle finally replied. "I can give you the name of the company if you'd like, Sheriff."

"What was it?"

Mantle rattled off a name, which was probably legitimate. Although as smarmy as a crooked politician, he was also too smart to give a fake company name. In this day and age, information like that was too easy to confirm or disprove.

"Is that all, Sheriff?" Mantle asked.

Jordan leaned back in his chair and eyed him. "Did you know a Sandra Hubbard?"

"No, sir. Should I?" The prisoner's pious attitude made Olivia roll her eyes in disgust.

"That'll be all, Mr. Mantle. Thank you for your cooperation."

"So I can go?"

"You can go back to work," Jordan said with a note of finality.

Keeping her head down, Olivia could see the prisoner leave out of her side vision. She started back to the kitchen.

"Ms. Kincaid," Sheriff Jordan called out.

So he wasn't going to let her off the hook. She pasted on a smile and turned to face him. "Yes, Sheriff?"

"Your act didn't fool me for a minute." Although his tone was serious, a slight smile twitched his lips. "So, what did you think?"

Seeing this as an opportunity to pry for information, Olivia approached the lawman. "I think Mantle would sell his mother if the price was right."

Jordan shrugged. "He said he didn't know either woman. And although he may have had the opportunity, so did almost everyone else on the ranch, including your friend Elliott."

The way he said "friend" made it sound like she and Hank were involved in a hot and heavy affair. "Hank didn't kill anyone."

"He had means and opportunity for both victims. All we're missing is his motive, but once we find that, we've got him."

"Even if—and it's a big if—you come up with a motive, you still couldn't convince me he's a murderer."

Jordan shook his head in exasperation, then stood and stretched. Olivia heard the muffled popping of joints and bones.

"When are you going to interview Rollie?" she asked.

Jordan frowned and glanced down at the list of employees her father had printed off from his computer records that morning. "Roland Pepper?"

The name caught her unaware. "Probably. I just know him as Rollie."

"Why are you interested in him?"

"He's been giving Hank grief since the prisoners got here." She paused, wondering how much Hank had told the lawman. "He might've been the one who pushed those bales."

The sheriff narrowed his eyes. "So why didn't Elliott mention him?"

"Because he figured you wouldn't do anything about it." She arched an eyebrow, challenging him to deny it.

Jordan's cheeks flushed as he stiffened. Olivia didn't need a body language dictionary to tell her that she'd struck a nerve. But she wasn't about to pussyfoot around the issue, not when a man's life was in danger. And that life was Hank's.

"I sure can't do anything about it if he doesn't tell me," Jordan grumbled.

"When you talk to Rollie, ask him where he was this morning."

The sheriff stared at her a moment longer, then jotted something in his notebook. "So what sparked the bad feelings between Elliott and this Rollie?"

Olivia shrugged. "You'll have to ask Rollie."

Jordan rubbed his eyes, which looked bloodshot and tired. "Would you happen to have some fresh coffee back there?"

"There's some left from lunch. I can—"

"That's all right. I'll get it." He started to the front where the big restaurant-style coffeemaker sat, but paused and turned back to Olivia. "I'm bringing this Rollie in next. I'm not too proud to admit that you've probably had more experience with witnesses than I have. If you want to listen in, go ahead, but I expect you to be discreet about what you hear. Understand?"

Olivia smiled with satisfaction. She was being offered more than she'd expected. "Yes, sir."

Ten minutes later, Rollie swaggered into the dining hall. His gaze roamed across Olivia who stood by the kitchen door, but didn't linger.

"Thank you for coming, Mr. Pepper." Sheriff Jordan motioned to the chair where the other men had sat. "Have a seat."

Rollie shrugged and settled on the chair.

With Rollie's back to her, Olivia moved closer, so that she could listen in on the interview without being obtrusive.

"I knew Ms. Holcomb—used to see her at the Watering Hole in town on Friday and Saturday nights," Rollie said without prompting.

"How well did you know her?" Jordan asked.

"Not as well as I'd a liked, but then she didn't go for the hired help. She went straight to the ranchers, or anyone who might have more than a hired man's wages in his pocket. She didn't care if he was married, either."

"You're saying she was promiscuous?"

Rollie frowned. "What does that mean?"

"It means she slept around," Jordan explained.

"Guess so."

"When was the last time you saw her there?"

"Been over a year. I haven't been there since I got this job."

"So you don't go out anymore?"

"Not since I quit drinking."

Olivia frowned. Was he an alcoholic?

"Are you an alcoholic?" Jordan asked, reading her thoughts.

"Not anymore."

Apparently no one had told Rollie that once an alcoholic, always an alcoholic.

Jordan merely grunted. "Where were you the night Ms. Holcomb was killed?"

"Sleeping," Rollie replied.

That seemed to be the standard reply.

"Did you ever hear anyone talking about Ms. Holcomb? Maybe someone who got turned down by her?"

"I've heard some talk, but nothing like that. Mostly it was just stuff guys talk about."

Olivia swallowed back her disgust, knowing all too well how that kind of "stuff" sometimes led to assault, rape, or murder.

"Did any of it seem more than just guy talk?" Jordan asked, calm and professional.

Rollie thought a moment then shook his head. "Nah."

Jordan jotted down some notes. "Where were you eight years ago, Mr. Pepper?"

"Why?"

"Just answer the question, please."

"I don't see why—"

"Answer the question," Jordan said, staring hard at Rollie.

"Prison," he answered, anger ringing in his tone. "Satisfied?"

Surprised, Olivia leaned forward.

"What were you in for?" the sheriff asked.

"I beat up some asshole in a bar in Montana. Got three years in the state pen."

"Where were you this morning between ten and ten thirty?"

"Working."

"Where?"

"In the south barn, cleaning out stalls."

"Was there someone with you?"

"Slim."

Jordan glanced up and caught Olivia's gaze. He lifted an eyebrow that asked if she was satisfied. Although something niggled at her, she couldn't pin it down, so she nodded.

The sheriff rose. "Thank you for your cooperation, Mr. Pepper."

Rollie stood and crossed to the door, where he paused. Fierce anger and something else blazed from his eyes. "If you ask me, it was Elliott that killed Melinda."

"Why do you think he did it?" Jordan asked.

The husky man shrugged. "He was pissed off at Mel— Ms. Holcomb for hitting the stallion."

Olivia restrained an impatient sigh. Hank wasn't the only one angered by Melinda's fool stunt.

"Thank you," the sheriff said in dismissal.

Once Rollie was gone, Olivia said, "If he's going to base his accusation on that, you'd have to add my father, Buck, myself, and half the hired men."

"What exactly happened?" Jordan asked.

She described the incident that led to the stallion trying to jump the corral.

Jordan raked his hand through his hair. "Ms. Holcomb wasn't exactly a paragon of virtue."

Olivia couldn't help but chuckle at his dry tone. "Don't ask me. I'm prejudiced."

Jordan eyed her thoughtfully. "You mentioned before that you weren't real happy with Ms. Holcomb's article in the paper. Do you think Elliott could have killed her because he knew she upset you?"

Disbelief bubbled up in Olivia. "No way, Sheriff. Hank and I are friends, sort of." How could she describe their relationship? *Lover wannabes?* "He's helped me out, and we've gotten to know each other a little. But we're not lovers."

"Maybe he's obsessed with you."

This was going from ludicrous to ridiculous. "And maybe you're reaching for straws, Sheriff Jordan," she said coolly. She stepped up to him. "If he killed Melinda for me, how do you explain Sandra Hubbard's murder?"

"Maybe he was obsessed with her, too, and when she came to break it off with him . . ." He let it drop, his insinuation as clear as her grandmother's crystal.

Olivia's first reaction was to simply deny his words, but she couldn't use emotion. If she wanted to convince him, she had to use reason. "Except you're talking two very different motives. If Hank is obsessed with me and killed Melinda in a twisted display of affection, then you can't use the same logic to say he killed Sandra. He either kills *for* his obsession or he *kills* his obsession, not both."

"Why not? For all we know, if you don't return his affection, he'll kill you next." Sheriff Jordan paused. "Are you willing to bet your life he isn't the killer?"

Olivia opened her mouth to reply affirmatively, but the ADA in her stilled her voice. People wore many faces, and nobody could predict who might or might not commit a crime, especially one of passion. Oftentimes, friends and family members of criminals didn't even have a clue until after the fact.

Although she hated to admit it, she answered, "No. But that doesn't mean I think he did it."

"Then give me another suspect," Jordan said, his patience obviously wearing thin.

"Are you absolutely certain both Melinda and Sandra Hubbard were murdered by the same person?"

"According to the forensic evidence, pretty damn certain."

Olivia's confidence wavered. "Was Melinda raped?"

Jordan glanced down. "No."

"What about fingerprints on her body or the murder weapon?"

"Since she was underwater, the lab folks aren't very optimistic about finding any good prints. But they'll let me know." Jordan glanced at his watch. "If you'll excuse me, I have three more men to interview."

"Just one more thing, Sheriff. Are you going to check Rollie's alibi for this morning?"

He sighed. "I'll get to it, Ms. Kincaid."

Although unsatisfied by his answer, Olivia returned to the kitchen.

"Is it time to start dinner?" Dawn asked.

Startled, Olivia glanced at the girl who sat by the small table, leafing through a magazine. "I suppose."

Dawn frowned. "What's wrong?"

Unaccountably irritated, Olivia stared down at her. "Aren't you the least bit worried about your brother?"

Dawn blinked and lowered her gaze, but not before Olivia spotted a spark of something: concern, maybe?

"A little, I guess." She looked back up at Olivia. "But you told me he wasn't hurt."

Olivia dropped into the chair beside her. "Not this time. But what if something like this happens again, and Hank isn't as lucky?"

Dawn squirmed in her seat. "He can take care of himself."

Olivia laid her hand on the girl's shoulder. "What about the murders? Do you think he killed those women?"

Dawn tensed. "Women? I thought there was only one."

"Do you remember a Sandra Hubbard?"

Dawn's brow wrinkled. "I—yeah, I do. She was one of Hank's girlfriends. I think she disappeared or ran away a long time ago."

Olivia supposed eight years was a long time ago for a nineteen-year-old. "She was murdered."

Dawn's mouth gaped.

"And since Hank knew her, and he kind of knew Melinda, they think he may have killed both of them," Olivia finished. She didn't reveal that they'd each been strangled with a leather strap.

"He didn't do it." Righteous anger sparked the girl's eyes and voice.

Surprised by Dawn's vehemence, Olivia leaned back in her chair and studied her a moment. "You do love him, don't you?" she asked softly.

Dawn's eyes glistened as she stood and wrapped her arms around her waist, as if protecting herself. "He's my brother."

"So why do you act like you don't care?"

"Because he hurt me, and I want to hurt him back." A tear ran down the girl's cheek, and she dashed it away with the back of her hand.

Olivia stood and hugged her. "He didn't mean to hurt you."

"I know," came the muffled reply. "But I get so mad sometimes."

"Don't you think he gets mad, too? He was put in prison for a crime he didn't commit. He's the one who's had to live behind bars for six years."

Dawn's shoulders shook, and Olivia rubbed her back soothingly, allowing the girl to cry. After a few minutes, Dawn eased away and drew her sleeve across her cheeks. She lifted her head and looked at Olivia. "What will happen to him if they arrest him for the murders?"

"He'll go back to prison to await his new trial. If he's found guilty, he could get the death penalty if they establish premeditation." Olivia didn't sugarcoat the possibility. She wanted Dawn to understand exactly what her brother faced.

"But they haven't arrested him yet, right?"

Olivia nodded. "That doesn't mean they won't. The sheriff has to take his report to the district attorney, and if they find there's enough circumstantial evidence against your brother, they'll issue an arrest warrant."

Grief filled Dawn's face. "You're a lawyer, right?"

"Yes."

"Then you can defend him."

Olivia shook her head. "I'm a prosecutor in Chicago."

"Does that mean you can't practice law in Colorado?"

"No. I'm licensed here, too."

"Then why couldn't you?"

How could she tell Dawn that because of her assault and the emotional fallout, she might not be able to enter a courtroom again? And even if she got past her personal demons, that she'd become too emotionally involved to be effective as Hank's defense lawyer? She laid a hand on Dawn's shoulder, giving her the only promise she could. "If it comes down to him being arrested, I'll make sure he has good counsel."

Dawn's expression fell, but she didn't push the issue. "All right."

Troubled by the girl's obvious disappointment, Olivia forced a smile. "We'd better make dinner, or we'll have a room full of unhappy and hungry men."

Dawn nodded and they went to work in leaden silence.

FEELING more at ease now in the company of the hired men, Olivia waited in the dining hall as they drifted away until only Hank remained. He stood and gathered the dirty dishes around him.

"You don't have to help us." Olivia reached out to take the stack from him.

He sidestepped her. "I don't mind," he said over his shoulder.

Going through the doorway into the kitchen, he almost collided with Dawn, who was coming out.

"Uh, sorry," Dawn murmured, her cheeks flushed.

Surprised she'd apologized rather than reamed him a new one, Hank stopped. "It was my fault. Sorry."

Her gaze darted across him but came back to rest on the bump on his forehead. "Olivia told me what happened this morning."

Hank's thoughts ground to a halt. His sister was speaking to him without anger for the first time. "She did?"

Dawn nodded and slid her hands into her jeans pockets. "She said you were all right."

"I am." Hank knew he sounded like an idiot, but he was shocked by Dawn's civility.

"I'm glad." Then she hurried into the dining area to help Olivia.

Warmed by his sister's concern, Hank placed the dirty dishes in a deep sink filled with hot soapy water. Why the change of heart? Or was it only a reprieve?

Olivia brought in an armful of plates and cups and set them in the sink, too.

"You told her what happened this morning," Hank said.

Olivia leaned her hips against the sink and nodded. "She was in the house when you came in here to tell the sheriff. I thought she'd want to know."

"Did you talk to her about anything else?"

Olivia tilted her head. "Like what?"

Hank narrowed his eyes, recognizing her attempt at misdirection. "Like anything?"

"Define anything."

She was acting like a damned lawyer. "Her attitude is different," he said with a hint of annoyance. "Like she might even care what happens to me."

"She does care about you, Hank. Don't doubt that."

Hank knew Olivia wasn't telling him everything, but had no clue as to what she might be hiding . . . or why. However, he also suspected she wasn't about to tell him either.

"Head hurting?" she asked, motioning toward his forehead.

He shrugged. "I'm fine."

Olivia leaned forward and straightened his collar. "Sure you are."

The oddly intimate touch and the gentle smile that accompanied her words made his chest tighten and his blood race. He tucked a glossy strand of hair behind her delicate ear. The sensual pleasure of touching a woman made him linger, his fingertips caressing her velvety softness.

Olivia's eyelids fluttered shut, and her mouth opened slightly. She brushed her tongue across her lower lip, leaving it pink and gleaming. And so damned tempting. One taste of her sweetness hadn't been enough.

His fingers curled, gripping her silken hair, and he tilted her head upward as he leaned down to kiss her. Olivia's mouth was warm and firm and tasted oh so sweet. Blood roared in his ears, and his body pressed against hers. She rotated her hips slowly, like a dancer performing exclusively for his pleasure. He hardened and knew she felt him when she groaned and pressed more firmly against him.

Suddenly she pushed him away, her hands flattened against his chest. Although Hank would've rather faced a charging bull than release her, he drew back. His heart thundered, and his breath came in shallow pants.

"Dawn's out there," Olivia said in a hoarse whisper. "I don't want her . . ."

So he was good enough to tease, but she couldn't let anyone see her kissing a con . . . and enjoying it.

"Sure. Whatever," he muttered.

He spun around to leave, but Olivia grabbed his arm with a surprisingly strong grip.

"What does that mean?" she demanded.

"What do you think it means?"

"I wouldn't be asking if I knew."

He glared down at her hand on his arm, and she released him.

"Tell me," she said through clenched teeth.

"I'm good enough to practice on, but can't let anyone find out Ms. Olivia Kincaid, big-city ADA, gets off on kissing a con," he said, keeping his voice low but intense.

First shock, then anger flushed her face. "I'm going to pretend you didn't say that. Because if you think I could actually use someone like that, you don't know me at all." Her voice shook.

"Then why do you care if Dawn catches us kissing? We're all adults."

Olivia stepped right up to him, her toes touching his. "Because I warned her to stay away from Barton." Her cheeks reddened. "And if she sees us together, she'll think I'm a hypocrite."

Barton had mentioned Olivia didn't want him and Dawn to see each other, so that part was the truth. But Hank didn't know if Olivia was sincere or if it was only a convenient excuse.

"So why don't you just take your own advice and stay away from me?" Hank asked, keeping this expression blank.

Olivia's gaze slid away. "Because I *am* a hypocrite. I don't want to stay away from you."

The angry pressure in Hank's chest eased away. He hooked his forefinger beneath Olivia's chin and raised it. She didn't fight him, but she kept her eyes downcast.

"It's okay, Olivia," he said, feeling awkward. "I'm sorry."

Finally, she looked at him, and a spark of defiance lit her eyes. "You should be. I don't become a hypocrite for just anyone."

Hank laughed, and the rest of his tension drained away. He put some distance between them so he wouldn't be tempted again. "Buck told me that Dawn spent time with Barton yesterday while we were in Walden."

A shadow filled the doorway. "So everyone thinks they have to babysit me?" Dawn's furious tone left no doubt she'd overheard him.

Olivia stepped toward her. "You told me you'd stay away from him."

Dawn had the chagrin to look away, and she stomped over to a counter to plop her handful of dishes down. "I'm old enough to decide who I see and who I don't." She glared at Hank. "You're a few years too late to start acting like a big brother."

"You never gave me a chance," Hank argued.

"Fuck you," she swore, startling him. To Olivia, she said, "I feel sick. I'm going to the house."

Like a tornado, she was gone, leaving an awkward void in her wake.

Hank rubbed his brow and said sarcastically, "That went well."

"She really does care for you," Olivia said.

Ten minutes ago he had believed Olivia. This time he wasn't so certain.

CHAPTER SEVENTEEN

ALTHOUGH angry with Dawn for leaving her to take care of the dinner cleanup, Olivia didn't have the heart to go after her. It helped that Hank volunteered his services. Although he was more reticent than usual—most likely due to Dawn's hurtful words—Olivia was glad for his company. So she kept quiet, allowing him peace and space.

It was after eight when they finished. Olivia picked up the bowl filled with scraps for the barn cats and ushered Hank out of the dining hall.

"Do you mind if I walk you down there?" Hank offered.

She flashed him a grateful smile. "I'd like that."

Olivia limped across the yard, though she hardly noticed the dull ache in her knee. Either she'd grown accustomed to it, or her leg had gotten better. Or Hank's presence acted like an analgesic.

Hank Elliott—better than Tylenol.

She shook her head at the silly thought, wondering if she was more tired than she realized.

Since it was one of the longest days of the year, the sun was just beginning to slip behind the western peaks. Long shadows moved ahead of them as they approached the barn. Hank opened the door, allowing her to enter ahead of him, then he flicked on the light switch and closed the door behind them.

The scents of hay, horses, and leather mingled in the air, and a wave of nostalgia swept through Olivia. For a moment, she was seven years old again, currying her pony under her father's watchful eye.

A mother cat and her four kittens tumbled out of an empty stall and gathered around Olivia's ankles, bursting the bubble of memories. She set the bowl on the ground and grinned at the animals' antics.

Hank squatted down beside the cats, and his big hands were amazingly gentle as he petted them.

"Hey, don't be such a pig," he said with a smile as he lifted the fattest kitten up and away from the bowl. The animal meowed loudly in protest. Hank chuckled and set the squirming critter behind his siblings.

Olivia crossed her arms and leaned a shoulder against a support post. She smiled, enjoying Hank's rapport with the cats. Even if she hadn't know, it was obvious he had a soft spot for animals.

"You'd be a wonderful veterinarian," she said.

He snapped his head up, and his expression lost all the enjoyment and warmth she'd just witnessed. "Don't."

Instead of frightening her, his harsh tone saddened her. She squared her shoulders and met his glare. "Why not? Just because you got sidetracked for six years doesn't mean you can't go back to school when you get out."

His laughter's harsh ring should've bothered her, but she knew it was prompted by pain rather than anger.

"And how the hell would I pay for it? I have maybe a hundred dollars to my name. Every form I fill out, I'll have to put X in the box that asks if I've ever been convicted of a crime. Then I'll have to answer their questions. And by the time I'm done, nobody's going to let a convict onto their campus, much less loan me money."

"My father would help you."

He shook his head, and his spine stiffened. "I've never leaned on anyone in my life."

"Then maybe it's time you did."

Her soft words seemed to unbalance him, and some of his bitter anger faded. "You wouldn't understand, Olivia. You've always had your father to rely on. I don't have anyone." His tone was matter-of-fact rather than self-pitying.

"I've been on my own since I started college," she argued.

"But you always knew he was here." He paused and took her hands in his. He caressed her knuckles with his thumbs. "When you were assaulted, what did you do?"

She'd come home . . . to her father. "That's different."

His smile was a mixture of regret and sadness. "No, it's not." He took a deep breath. "You're going to get better, Olivia, and you're going back to Chicago to follow your dream. Don't waste your time worrying about me. I'll be fine."

Tears burned Olivia's eyes. "But—"

"I'll be fine," he repeated firmly.

Stubborn pride showed in the clench of his jaw and the firm line of his lips. Olivia didn't know if she wanted to smack the damned fool or kiss him. Her body made the decision before her mind, and she placed her palms on either side of his face and pulled his head downward. She pressed her lips to his, hungry for the taste and feel of him after the appetizer in the kitchen.

Hank reacted after only a moment of hesitation. Wrapping his arms around her, he tugged her close. His mouth opened to hers, and Olivia swept her tongue into his warm moistness. The lingering taste of coffee and his own unique flavor made her dizzy with desire.

His hardness pressed into her belly, stealing the breath from her lungs. She drew back, gasping with the powerful waves of need cresting through her, making her ache with hollow longing.

Panting, Hank rested his forehead against hers. He caressed her with firm strokes, his hands moving up and down her back, but not going below her waist. "So help me, if we don't stop now, I'm going to take you right here. Right now."

Olivia shuddered from his rough, husky tone. After what had happened to her she should've been afraid. He was taller, bigger, stronger than her. He could take what he wanted without asking . . . but she knew he wouldn't. Just as she knew he was no murderer. Despite his prison record and the corded muscles that flexed beneath her hands, he was a gentle, sensitive man.

Heat and passion flowed through her veins. Lowering her shaking hands to his shirt, she undid one button, then another and another.

Hank clasped her wrists. "Are you sure, Olivia?"

She raised her gaze to his smoldering hazel eyes and saw the fire he tried to tamp down. But she didn't want him to temper the fire. She wanted to be consumed by the flames that burned within him. "Yes. I'm sure."

Her acceptance snapped the last strand of his control. He growled and cupped her ass, then lifted her. Olivia wrapped her legs around him as Hank claimed her lips with near-savage intensity. She welcomed his powerful passion, eager for his hard heat that pulsed between them.

Hank carried Olivia to an empty stall lined with fresh straw and knelt down, never breaking their kiss. He laid her down gently, his knees straddling her thighs, and slid his hands beneath her rumpled sweatshirt. His fingertips skated over her bare skin.

She retreated from the kiss and gulped in needed air. Frantically grabbing the hem of her shirt, she jerked it upward, tossing it aside. Taking Hank's hands, she placed them on her breasts.

"Liv, oh, God," Hank murmured. He feared he might come in his shorts, something he hadn't done since he was fifteen and accidentally saw his best friend's older sister naked. Biting his lower lip to stall the inevitable rush, he molded his palms over the lace-covered flesh and rolled each nipple between his thumb and forefinger.

Olivia arched upward as she panted beneath him. Hank leaned down, kissing her sculpted collarbone and following an imaginary line down to the tip of her breast. He sucked tenderly, felt the nipple pucker into a hard pebble beneath the moist lace. She thrashed beneath him, her hips pumping upward, rubbing his erection.

So close . . . He forced himself to kneel above her, high enough that her bucking pelvis couldn't touch him. Hell, even without the stimulation, he was damned close to the edge.

He unbuttoned the top button of her jeans and unzipped them, then waited. Olivia opened her eyes, which were filled with confusion and frustration.

"Why'd you stop?" she asked.

Hank stared down into the face that haunted his nights and made him wake hard and aching. "Last chance, Olivia."

He could see her comprehension in the widening of her eyes and the flaring of her nostrils. Instead of replying in words, she answered by pulling his shirt out of his waistband and lowering his zipper. She laid her hand against his erection, and only the worn cotton of his briefs lay between them.

Knowing even a slight motion of her hand would shatter what pitifully little control he had, he shifted away and removed Olivia's remaining clothing. God, he'd suspected her baggy clothes hid a trim body, but he had no idea how sexy the entire package would be. He nuzzled her pale thigh and her soft curls tickled his nose, as did her musky, feminine scent. He'd almost forgotten the perfume of a woman, the music of her soft moans and the silk of her skin. Throbbing with near-bursting desire, Hank removed his own clothing.

"Condom?" Olivia whispered.

The request should have broken the mood, but her husky voice only increased his arousal . . . if that were possible. He nodded. "My pocket."

He dug a condom out his jeans pocket, now glad that he hadn't turned them down from the prison health nurse. Trembling so much, Hank couldn't open the packet, so Olivia took it from him. He watched as the foil gave way and when her fingers touched him, he nearly climaxed. He turned away, unable to watch her slender fingers roll the latex over him.

"Now, Hank," she said, and he was glad to note her voice wasn't all that steady. "Please."

Hank wanted to go slow, but his body had been denied the pleasure of a woman for too long. He thrust into her, and her snug, slick heat surrounded him. His hips bucked once, and his control vanished in an abrupt, mind-numbing orgasm. He lay in a mindless heap as aftershocks rippled through him.

"Hank," Olivia said, close to his ear.

Humiliation washed through him. *Goddammit.* He'd come faster than a teenager who just discovered *Playboy.* "I'm sorry, Olivia," he murmured.

She stroked his hair with gentle hands. "Don't be. It was a compliment."

He could sense her smile and gathered his courage to look at her. There was no hint of ridicule or anger in her flushed face. "I feel like a stupid kid."

She laughed, and her breasts jiggled against his chest. A bolt of desire licked through his veins, and he was shocked to find he was ready for another round. But this time he vowed he wouldn't leave Olivia behind.

"I don't think you feel like a kid at all," she finally said, dragging a fingertip down the middle of his chest.

Hank was grateful for her understanding, and it only made him that much more determined to ensure she was satisfied this time. He captured her roaming hand and kissed each fingertip. She squirmed beneath him, and he gasped at the unexpected pleasure of her surrounding pressure and heat.

He eased out of her and replaced the condom with a new one. Glancing up, he saw Olivia watching him closely, her eyes dilated and surrounded by only a sliver of blue. A steamy smile teased her lips.

"Ready for another ride, cowboy?"

Her sultry voice and twinkling eyes made him throb. Even as an adolescent, he didn't remember being this horny. But then, Olivia's charms and the long years of enforced abstinence were a lethal combination.

For a long moment, he merely gazed down at her smooth, pale skin, small breasts, and the evidence between her thighs that she was a true blonde. "God, you're beautiful, Liv," he said.

Her cheeks reddened, but she replied saucily. "You're not bad yourself."

"Men can't be beautiful."

She arched a light-colored eyebrow. "I didn't peg you for the sexist type."

A knee on either side of her hips, he leaned down and kissed one corner of her mouth, then the other. "I can be very sexist," he whispered.

Her laughter stirred warm air across his face. "Sexy."

He kissed the pulse point at the base of her neck. "Thank you."

Then he nipped, kissed, sucked, or licked nearly every delicious inch of her. And fulfilled his vow of bringing her over the edge moments before his second release claimed him.

Hank lay on his back with his arms around Olivia, who'd curled up close to his side, her head resting on his shoulder. Her right arm rested across his waist while her left hand splayed through his chest hair. The bitter anger that usually burned in his gut was absent, and a surreal sense of peace surrounded him.

Olivia shifted, and her muscles tensed.

"Olivia?" Hank asked, fearful she was regretting what happened between them.

"Sorry. My bad knee cramped." A hitch in her breath told him it was still hurting.

"Maybe I can help." He eased out of her arms and moved downward to examine the scarred knee.

"It's ugly," she said softly.

Brushing his fingers across the incision, he shook his head. "It's part of you, so it can't be ugly."

She chuckled. "I thought you were supposed to sweet-talk the woman *before* taking her to bed."

"Did I forget to do that?" he teased. "I'll have to remember next time." His caresses on her knee turned into a gentle massage.

"Will there be a next time?" Olivia asked.

The doubt and trepidation in her voice made him pause as he considered her question. "That's up to you, Liv."

She remained silent, and he resumed kneading her leg. Her skin was warm and smooth despite the scarring.

"I don't usually do this," she said.

Hank couldn't help but smile. "Lie in a barn naked while a man rubs your leg?"

Her snort sounded suspiciously like a chuckle. "That, too, but what I meant is I've only had two other lovers, and I dated them for weeks before . . ." She covered her eyes with her forearm.

Hank moved back up to lie beside her. He skimmed his hand along her bare flank. "What you're trying to say is you're not usually this impulsive?"

She lowered her arm and met his gaze. Pink tinged her cheeks. "Yes." She curved her palm around his jaw. "I think we both needed this, but I know nothing more can come of it."

Indignation boiled up, and Hank forced it down. She was right on both counts. And wasn't she only saying what he believed, too? "Friends?" he asked.

A relieved smile caught her lips. "Friends."

A friendly fuck wasn't exactly how he'd describe what he and Olivia had done, but he didn't have the words to express it. However, making love came damned close.

He took a deep breath and managed a weak smile. "Friends."

Irrationally feeling as if Olivia had cheapened what they'd shared, Hank stood and extended a hand to her. He pulled her to her feet, and they dressed in silence. A piece of straw stuck out from Olivia's hair, and he plucked it out.

"Thanks," she said, looking everywhere but at him.

He suspected she was regretting her recklessness. "No problem."

Hank ushered her out of the barn, and a man stepped out of the shadows. Olivia stumbled back and barely stifled a scream.

"Enjoy your evening?" Mantle asked in a slimy voice that left no doubt he knew what had transpired between them.

"What're you doing here?" Hank demanded.

"I saw you and the lady here go into the barn, and when you didn't come out, I thought something might have happened." The leer in his expression exposed his real reason for spying. "Then I realized what you were doing, so I thought I'd see if I could get in on the action. Share and share alike." Mantle's gaze slid down Olivia, leaving her feeling like a lap dancer in a third-rate strip joint. "But I was too late."

Hank moved in front of Olivia as if to protect her, but she'd had enough of Mantle's innuendos. She sidestepped him to confront the weasely prisoner.

"What I do and where I go and who I am with is none of your business," Olivia said. She narrowed her eyes. "Besides, Hank is more than man enough for me. Why would I need—or want—anyone like you?" She curled her lips into a haughty smirk.

Mantle widened his eyes as if surprised. "Funny, Lenny didn't think he was man enough."

Olivia gasped, and her shocked gaze darted to Hank.

He growled and took a menacing step toward Mantle. His hands clenched into fists, and Olivia had the impression he wouldn't hesitate to beat the crap out of the smaller prisoner.

Despite her bewilderment, she inserted herself between the two men, facing Hank, and was shocked by his feral expression. Bracing her palms against the rock-hard chest she'd only minutes before been lying on, she said, "Don't."

"Get out of the way, Olivia," he said in a near snarl.

Olivia's gut clenched in fear, but she held her ground, believing in Hank's innate gentleness. She kept her voice low so Mantle wouldn't overhear. "No. You start something, and you'll be tossed back in prison to serve the remainder of your term. Is that what you want?"

Seconds seemed to stretch into hours as she waited, not giving an inch.

"Didn't he tell you about his little Lenny?" Mantle suddenly asked.

Although Olivia's back was to him, she could sense his cocky sneer. "Shut up, Mantle."

"Sure, no problem. But next time you should know more about a man before letting him screw you."

Mantle's words ate at Olivia like acid, and sickness churned through her. "Get out of here."

She listened to his dull footsteps fade away, and Hank's muscles lost some of their tension.

"I'm okay," Hank said.

She stared at him, willing him to meet her eyes, but he looked past her. Releasing him, she took a step back, and the shakes hit her. She crossed her arms to hide her telltale trembling. "You want to tell me what that was all about?"

He glanced at her but didn't hold her gaze. Instead, he moved away to the corral and leaned against the top pole, his back to her.

Uncertain if she wanted to know who Lenny was, Olivia couldn't ignore the air of misery around Hank. She joined him and studied his silhouetted profile in the evening's darkness. "You owe me an explanation."

His jaw muscle jumped into his cheek, and he clenched the post so tightly his knuckles whitened. "It was a long time ago."

Olivia swallowed hard. She didn't expect that, but prison changed people "Did you love him?"

He jerked around to face her. "What?"

She took a deep breath. Like her father said, in for a penny, in for a pound. "This Lenny. Did you love him?"

Hank's mouth opened, but nothing came out. He abruptly closed it and raked his hand through his hair. "God, no, it wasn't like that."

Although Olivia considered herself an open-minded person, relief swamped her. "So who was Lenny?"

Hank sagged against the corral. "My first cell mate. He was a kid, just turned eighteen. By then I knew enough to realize what would happen to him in the exercise yard." He toed the ground. "So I put the word out that he was mine."

Olivia glanced away. She'd put more than one boy like Lenny behind bars. "What did Lenny do?"

Hank grunted. "When he found out, he was pissed. Said he could take care of himself. He made it clear that he wasn't anyone's bitch. A week later he was found in the shower. Before he was stabbed in the gut, he'd been gang raped."

Bile rose in Olivia's throat, and she put a hand to her mouth. After a few moments of breathing deeply, she said, "I'm sorry."

Hank shrugged, affecting nonchalance. "Save your sympathies. I hardly knew him."

"But you tried to help him."

"Hell of a lot of good it did."

She rested a hand on his forearm. "But you tried," she repeated. "That's more than most people would've done."

Hank's gaze followed the stallion in the next corral. "I never tried again."

"You didn't have any friends in prison?"

"There were a couple of guys I got along with when I was working with the mustangs, but it didn't pay to get close."

Moisture blurred Olivia's vision, and she cleared her throat. "So why did Mantle say what he did?"

"Because I think he was one of the men who raped Lenny." Rage radiated from Hank's taut body.

Olivia's stomach curled with revulsion. "How did someone like him get chosen for the work release program?"

"Because he knows how to play the game." He didn't bother to mask his disgust.

"I'll talk to Dad in the morning and get him to send Mantle back to prison."

"On what grounds? He hasn't done anything, and I can't prove he had anything to do with Lenny's death."

Olivia's stubbornness and innate sense of justice wouldn't let it go. "His behavior has been inappropriate, and he's threatened you on more than one occasion. The early release work program wasn't created for men like him."

The firm set of Hank's lips told her he didn't approve of her meddling, but it wasn't just for him she was doing this. Because of her father's support of the program, any trouble within it would reflect badly on him. Olivia wouldn't let Mantle destroy what her father had created with the best of intentions.

The silence stretched out, and Olivia sighed. "I should get back to the house."

Hank nodded and escorted her across the yard to the porch.

"Will you be all right?" she asked.

He appeared startled by her question. "I'll be fine. How about you?"

She smiled with a trace of embarrassment. "I have a feeling I'll sleep like a baby."

The sound of Hank's light laughter lifted her spirits.

"Me, too," he said.

They stood motionless, and she swayed toward him, expecting him to kiss her good night. Instead, he pivoted on his heel and strode to the prisoners' barracks.

Olivia remained standing on the porch, uncertain if she was disappointed or relieved that he hadn't kissed her. Growing cold, she went into the house.

Despite what she'd told Hank, she doubted sleep would come easily.

CHAPTER EIGHTEEN

OLIVIA awakened with a start and blinked in the darkness. It took her a few moments to figure out she was in her bedroom. However, instead of the nightmare that usually woke her, this dream was far from nightmarish.

She squeezed her thighs together and tried to ignore the erotic brush of her nightshirt across her sensitive breasts. The remembered feel of Hank's gentle touches merged with the kisses of dream-Hank as he made love to her with infinite tenderness.

As she lay there, the vestiges of her dream wisped away, leaving her wide awake and restless. Turning her head, she read the clock's lighted numbers: 2:04. Great.

Mom's hot chocolate isn't going to help me this time.

What—or, more accurately, who—could help her was sleeping in another building.

Tossing back her covers, Olivia rose. She slipped on her robe and slid her feet into a soft pair of moccasins. Her stiff knee made her move slowly, but she refused to dig her cane out of her closet.

As she limped down the dark hallway, the phantoms from her assault hovered around her. She reassured herself with the knowledge that her father's revolver wasn't far away, but the obsessive need to review in painstaking detail how long it would take to retrieve was waning. She smiled to herself as she crossed the living room to the large windows covered by drapes. The curtains hadn't been opened since she returned home.

Taking a deep breath to alleviate her trembling, she pulled the drapery cord, and the long curtains separated. A three-quarter moon lit the yard, and she forced herself to confront the darkness. As her eyes adjusted to the dim light, she picked out familiar shapes. Nothing moved save the occasional horse in a corral.

She leaned her forehead against the cool glass, and relief filtered through her. Although she knew a killer was out there somewhere, right now there was nothing lurking in the shadows. Not even the phantasms that had stalked her day and night since her attack.

A shuffling sound caught her attention, and she turned to see her father enter the living room. She was pleased to note that her heart hadn't tried to leap out of her chest. "What're you doing up, Dad?"

He joined her at the window. "I was just going to ask you the same question."

She shrugged, but elation bubbled up within her. "I was challenging my demons."

He tilted his head. "And who won?"

She smiled. "I finally took a round."

He gazed down at her. "I'm glad, Liv."

"Me, too." She blinked aside her tears and noticed how her father held his bent left arm close to his torso. "Are you all right?"

He smiled wryly. "Just some heartburn. I popped some Tums, so I should be as good as new in a few minutes."

Faint unease rippled through Olivia, but she returned his smile. "As long as you're sure it's just—"

"It is." He patted her shoulder. "You came in late last night."

Heat bloomed in Olivia's cheeks. "Cleanup took longer than usual."

"Right. Cleanup." The corners of his lips twitched.

She never could get anything past him and sighed in surrender. "I was with Hank."

He held up a hand. "No details, please."

She chuckled, but her humor faded as she recalled how the evening had ended. "Why did you choose Mantle to be part of the program?"

He seemed startled by the question. Then he shrugged. "His record was good, and Bob Vincent, the warden, recommended him. When I spoke with Mantle, he seemed sincere in trying to turn his life around. Why?"

Olivia crossed her arms. "He was waiting outside the barn when Hank and I, uh, came out. He was rude and tried to goad Hank into a fight."

Concern etched her father's brow. "Hank didn't take the bait, did he?"

"No, but if Mantle keeps pushing . . ." She worried her lower lip between her teeth. "Mantle's acted inappropriately around me at other times, too."

Her father stiffened. "How inappropriate?"

"Crude remarks and gestures. He hasn't tried to touch me. Yet."

"Why didn't you tell me?"

"I thought you might think I was overreacting." Olivia lifted her chin. "I also didn't want you to think I was just coming up with another argument against the program. I'm starting to understand why you support it so fervently."

He stared at her a moment, then pulled her into a hug. Contentment surged through her, and for a moment she felt her old self click into place. But then an echo of fear washed through her, shattering the illusion of normalcy.

"I'll talk to Mantle in the morning, then decide what to do. If he's not working out, I'll call Bob Vincent to have him send someone up here to take Mantle back," her father said.

Olivia drew back and looked up at him. "And if Mantle lies through his teeth?"

"Have some faith in your old man," he said with a twinkle in his eyes. "I sat on the bench long enough to recognize a load of manure when it's shoveled my way. And this time I've been forewarned."

She leaned into him and tightened her arms around his waist. "Thanks, Dad," she whispered.

He patted her back, then loosened his hold and stepped away. When she met his somber expression, anxiety made her heart skip a beat.

"When I talk to the warden I'll have to tell him about the murders and Hank's possible involvement," he said regretfully.

Her apprehension graduated to full-blown alarm. "Why? Nothing's been proven."

"And I'm going to stress that when I speak to Bob. I'm going to recommend Hank stay here until the evidence is sorted out."

"Do you think he'll take your recommendation?"

"He has in the past."

Olivia hoped her father's persuasive skills hadn't dulled since he stopped practicing law. She mentally crossed her fingers and couldn't help but ask, "You believe he's innocent, don't you?"

"I wouldn't lay my reputation on the line if I didn't." He eyed her closely. "Do you believe he's innocent?"

She glanced down, remembering the glide of Hank's hand over her skin and the warmth of his body over hers. But mostly she remembered the tenderness in his eyes when he'd asked her if she was certain. She met her dad's questioning gaze. "He's not a killer."

"No, he's not." His smile was interrupted by a yawn. "This old man is going back to bed."

Olivia kissed his cheek. "Good night, Dad."

She watched him leave, then turned back to the window. A movement near the barn caught her attention, and a large shadow glided away from the building. A cloud passed over the moon, darkening the yard, and when it cleared, the shadow was gone. She stared at the barn, trying to make sense of what she'd seen. A breeze stirred against the window, making branches move and shadows shift. She smiled in relief. It was merely a branch swaying in the wind.

Sleep lured her and, after taking one last look outside, she went back to bed.

OLIVIA yawned as she placed the last of the bowls filled with scrambled eggs on the tables. As she headed back toward the kitchen, the men trudged in for breakfast. She remained in the dining hall, proving to herself that she could. Smiling to herself, she couldn't stop her gaze from latching onto the main reason of her reemerging confidence. However, Hank looked as if he'd slept as well—or unwell—as she had.

Reminded of last night's incident, she searched for Mantle. Her gaze swept across the other convicts—Lopez, Johnny Barton, and Reger—over Buck, Rollie, and the other men, but she didn't spot Mantle. *Maybe he overslept, which will be another mark against him,* she thought with more than a hint of wicked satisfaction.

"Olivia, could you make some more toast?" Dawn asked as she sailed out of the kitchen bearing a plate piled high with buttered toast.

Putting Mantle out of her mind, Olivia entered the kitchen to man the toasters.

Later, as the hired men left the dining hall, Olivia caught Hank's attention. He stepped over to join her by the kitchen. "Good morning," he said in a low, husky voice, evocative of the night before.

Quivering inside, Olivia was envious of his cool calmness. "Morning. Sleep well?"

He smiled, and his gaze slid down to her breasts, then back to her face. "I could've slept better."

Olivia had no trouble translating, and her nerve endings sizzled with awareness. "Me, too." She licked her lips and was disconcerted when Hank followed the movement with heavy-lidded eyes. "I-I talked to Dad about Mantle."

Hank straightened, and wariness displaced his languid sensuousness. "And?"

"He's going to talk to Mantle this morning."

Hank scowled. "So Mantle will do his lap dog act, and the judge will decide it was all your imagination."

Olivia's temper climbed. "Dad didn't get to be a judge by being a pushover."

"Whatever," he said, clenching his jaw.

Olivia didn't both arguing with him. She had faith in her father. "Have you seen Mantle this morning?"

"His bunk was empty when I got up."

A commotion outside caught their attention, and Olivia and Hank hurried to the open door.

"Somebody get the judge!" Buck hollered.

Olivia and Hank exchanged apprehensive looks and joined the milling men.

"What's going on?" Hank asked Lopez.

"Mantle's dead," the swarthy Hispanic replied.

Olivia gasped. Although she despised Mantle, she hadn't wished his death. "What happened?"

Lopez shrugged. "Don't know, ma'am. Somebody found him in the barn."

"Shit," Hank swore under his breath.

Olivia's mouth lost all moisture, and dizziness made her weave momentarily. Had Mantle pushed Hank too far? No, she refused to believe it.

Barton joined them. "No loss, if you ask me."

Startled by his unexpected fierce expression and voice, Olivia wondered what Mantle had done to him. Then she recalled Hank's belief that Mantle had been involved in raping Lenny, another young man. She swallowed hard, hoping Barton had been spared that violation.

But if he was raped by Mantle, wouldn't that give Barton a hell of a motive for killing him? It would take the pressure off Hank, but she found that scenario did nothing to ease her mind.

Her father's arrival scattered the disturbing thoughts. His face was pale, but his eyes blazed with intensity.

"Olivia, go into the house and call the sheriff," he ordered her.

She swallowed hard and nodded. She glanced at Hank. Unable to articulate her jumbled feelings, she squeezed his hand in reassurance, then hurried across the yard to the house.

Since Sheriff Jordan had been on his way to the ranch already, he arrived within minutes after she made the call.

Olivia rejoined Hank, who had distanced himself from the throng. Dawn, her face strained, was standing beside Barton. By Hank's rigid stance, it was obvious his sister's presence at Barton's side hadn't escaped his attention. At least he was sensible enough not to make a scene.

"I'm going to the barn to see if I can find out what happened," Olivia said close to Hank's ear.

"No," he said, his eyes flashing.

Shocked by his sharp response, she glared at him. "Why not?"

His eyes widened with angry disbelief. "You think I killed him?"

Olivia jerked as if struck by a physical blow. "I didn't say that."

"You didn't have to."

He pivoted on his heel, and she grabbed his arm. The stark betrayal in his face swept away whatever she was about to say. For long moments, they simply stared at one another.

Hank glanced away first. "You've already seen one dead body. You don't need to see two."

"You're worried that I'll freak out?"

He scowled. "No. But you might have nightmares."

Was he truly only worried about her? Or did he have something to hide? As much as she wanted to believe he had nothing to do with Mantle's murder, a pesky inner voice reminded her that anyone was capable of committing a crime of passion. But if she followed that line of reasoning, Hank might be guilty of murdering the two women, too.

She shoved aside her doubts and managed a smile. "They couldn't be any worse than the ones I've had the last few months."

His glower deepened, telling her he didn't appreciate her attempt at levity. But he didn't argue.

Olivia wanted to reassure him that she believed him, but her voice wouldn't cooperate. Squaring her shoulders, she circled the men and headed for the barn.

The red-haired deputy, Kyle, guarded the door.

"Is my father in there?" she asked him.

Kyle nodded and said apologetically, "Yes, but I was told to keep everyone out to preserve the crime scene."

"I've been at crime scenes before." Usually it was long after the body was taken away and forensics had completed gathering evidence, but Kyle didn't have to know that. She took a step closer to the young lawman. "Ask Sheriff Jordan."

Indecision played across his freckled face until he turned his head and called out, "Can I let Ms. Kincaid in?"

Olivia noticed that he avoided looking inside the barn. He obviously didn't want a repeat of his reaction to Melinda's body.

She wasn't able to understand the muffled conversation in the barn until Jordan said, "Let her in."

The deputy stepped aside, his face paling. "It's not a pretty sight."

Feeling far older than her years, Olivia said, "It never is."

Although the lights were on, it took a moment for her eyes to adjust after the bright morning sunshine. She spotted her father, Buck, and Jordan standing by the body, partially blocking it from her view. Preparing herself with a mental shake, she joined them.

The smell struck her first. Mantle's bladder and bowels had voided when he died. She resisted the urge to cover her nose with her hand and settled on breathing through her mouth.

She forced herself to look at Mantle's corpse, the bluish tinge around his lips and the marblelike cast of his narrow face. Then she spotted the leather strap wrapped around his neck . . . just like Melinda's body. And the one found with Sandra Hubbard's remains.

Everything she knew of serial murderers told her they rarely broke their pattern, and usually they were gender-specific with their victims. But she also knew that serial murderers followed their own twisted logic.

"Same MO," Sheriff Jordan said quietly.

"Except for one detail," Olivia said, equally soft. "The previous victims were women."

"Maybe it was one of them copycat killings," Buck said.

Suddenly she remembered the shadow she'd seen last night. What if it had been the killer?

Her palms dampened with sweat. "I might have seen the murderer."

Jordan's hawklike gaze speared her. "When?"

Olivia cleared her dry throat. "Last night. I woke up about two and couldn't get back to sleep, so I went into the living room. I was looking out the window when I saw a shadow moving away from the barn. I thought it was just a tree branch."

Her father's eyes narrowed. "You didn't mention this last night."

"I saw it after you went back to bed."

"How certain are you it was a person?" Jordan asked.

She pictured the fleeting shadow. "It was too dark to make out much more than a shape. But now that I think about it, it was larger than a branch."

"Was it the size of man?"

"Yes." Her fingernails dug into her palms as she wondered if she'd seen the murderer.

"Can you remember anything more, Ms. Kincaid?" Jordan asked.

"If it was a man, he was big, bigger than you." Her breath caught. "Maybe the size of Rollie."

Joredan eyed her suspiciously. "Your father told me that Elliott argued with Mantle last night in your presence. Is that true?"

"What does that have to do with what I saw?" she demanded.

The lawman shifted his weight from one booted foot to the other. "It's no secret that you don't believe Elliott had anything to do with murdering the two female victims. It's also clear that you've taken a personal interest in him."

Righteous anger flooded her veins. "You think that I made up the shadow to take suspicion away from Hank," she stated rather than asked.

The sheriff shrugged. "It wouldn't be the first time a person lied to protect someone he or she cared about."

"My daughter doesn't lie, Caleb," her father said with an edge of steel.

The State Crime Scene Unit arrived, interrupting their heated conversation.

Olivia, her father, and Buck shifted out of the way while Sheriff Jordan conferred with the three techs.

"I didn't lie, Dad," Olivia said in a low voice.

He wrapped his arm around her shoulders. "I know that, Liv."

"But why would Rollie kill him?" Buck asked, scratching his jaw. "From what I seen, Rollie and Mantle got along fine." He grimaced. "Birds of a feather."

"Maybe they had a falling out," Olivia suggested.

"Over what?" her father asked, puzzled.

"Maybe they were both involved in Melinda's death."

"Then how do you explain Sandra Hubbard?" Sheriff Jordan asked as he rejoined them.

"Was Mantle really working in Omaha when she was killed?" Olivia asked.

Jordan nodded. "He was employed there for nearly a year before he was fired."

"Why was he fired?"

"The man I spoke to said he was suspected of embezzlement, but it couldn't be proven."

Olivia didn't doubt Mantle had been guilty of the crime.

"I'm going to start questioning your hired men," Jordan said to her father.

"Of course. Would you like to use the dining hall again?" her father asked.

"That'll be fine. Don't send any of the men out to work until I've talked to them. And I want to speak with every single person who was on the ranch last night." He clenched his jaw. "I'll start with Rollie."

Yes. Olivia resisted the urge to pump her arm.

Before following the men out of the barn, she took one last critical look at Mantle.

Who killed you?

Outside, Olivia searched for Hank but didn't see him. It was probably best that she didn't talk to him now anyhow. Sheriff Jordan was already suspicious of her relationship with Hank. She didn't want him to think they were collaborating on an alibi.

She followed her father and the sheriff to the dining hall while Buck rounded up Rollie. Anticipation quickened her pulse. If Rollie had killed Mantle, it would take the investigation in another direction, away from Hank.

Jordan claimed the same table he'd used yesterday.

"You're welcome to stay," the lawman said to her father.

"I'm afraid I have to make a phone call," he replied with a weary shake of his head.

"The warden?"

Her father nodded. "He's not going to be happy he was kept out of the loop."

Olivia jumped to his defense. "It's not like any of what's happened is your fault, Dad."

"I know that, Liv, but Bob's going to want to know why I didn't contact him right after Ms. Holcomb's body was found." He smiled crookedly and patted her shoulder. "I've known Bob a lot of years. After he gets the mad out of his system, he'll listen to reason. Don't worry."

Her gaze followed him as he shuffled out of the dining hall.

"Has he been feeling all right?" Jordan asked.

Startled by his concern, Olivia shrugged. "Other than being a little tired and having some heartburn, he said he's fine."

Jordan rubbed his brow. "These murders have been hard on everybody, but especially your father."

She didn't bother to agree, since it was obvious. "Do you mind if I sit in on the questioning?"

"That might not be a good—"

"I didn't lie about what I saw last night, Sheriff." She took a deep breath and admitted, "But I can't honestly say it was Rollie either." Something clicked in her memory. "Did you ever verify Rollie's alibi for yesterday morning when those bales came down on Hank?"

Jordan shook his head. "I haven't had time. I can ask Slim when I question him about his whereabouts last night."

She tipped her head to the side as something tickled her memory. "Slim?"

The sheriff tugged the notebook from his pocket and flipped through it until he found what he was looking for. "Roland Pepper said he was cleaning the barn with Slim at the time of the incident."

Olivia's tickle graduated to realization. "Who were you questioning when Hank came in here to report the murder attempt?"

Jordan scowled, probably not liking her assumption it *was* a murder attempt. He glanced at his notebook again and his eyes widened perceptibly. "Son of a bitch. It was Slim."

Adrenaline pumped through Olivia, giving her a heady feeling she hadn't experienced in a long time. "Which means Rollie doesn't have an alibi when those bales were pushed down on Hank."

The sheriff's features hardened as he nodded. "You can sit in on the questioning, Ms. Kincaid, but you let me do the asking."

"Fair enough," she said, her euphoria making her agreeable to most anything.

Five minutes later, Rollie swaggered into the dining room. When he spotted Olivia sitting beside the sheriff, he frowned. "What's she doing here?"

"I'm taking advantage of her experience in interrogating witnesses," Jordan replied with a cool smile. "Does her presence bother you?"

Rollie glanced at her, then shrugged. "Nah." He dropped into the chair across the table from Olivia and Jordan. "I didn't kill Mantle."

"Where were you at approximately two a.m., Mr. Pepper?" Jordan asked.

Rollie crossed his arms and leaned back in the chair. "Sleeping in my bunk."

"Are you certain of that?"

Rollie scowled. "Unless I was sleepwalking."

"You were seen by the barn at that time," Jordan bluffed.

"What?" The big man's shock seemed genuine.

"You heard me. Someone saw you last night by the barn where Mantle was found. Do you want to change your story?"

Rollie leaned forward and planted his fisted hands on the table. "I wasn't anywhere near the barn last night."

Jordan mirrored the hired man's aggressive lean so he was only inches from Rollie's face. "Just like you weren't anywhere near the shed when those bales came down on Hank Elliott?"

Something flickered in the hired man's eyes. "I told you I was cleaning the barn with Slim."

The sheriff stared at him a long moment, and a cold smile spread across his face. "Slim was here with me when you were supposedly working with him."

Olivia held her breath as her heart hammered against her breast. Rollie had pushed those bales down on Hank. It was possible he'd killed Mantle. But what about the two women?

Rollie's heavy breathing was the only sound in the expectant hush. Suddenly Rollie struck the table with his fists, and Olivia jerked back in shocked fear.

Rollie exploded. "You're damned right I tried to get Elliott. He killed Melinda."

Olivia's head swam. "Did you see him do it?"

Rollie swung his wild-eyed gaze to her, and she shrank away from him before she could stop herself. "No, but everyone's saying he killed both Melinda and that other woman."

"That hasn't been proven," Jordan said firmly.

"I couldn't let him get away with it," the hired man muttered. He shrank into his chair, and his face crumpled. "I loved her."

Olivia shot Sheriff Jordan a puzzled look, but he seemed as bewildered as her.

"You loved Melinda Holcomb?" Jordan asked Rollie.

The big man's eyes glimmered with moisture, and his earnest expression reminded Olivia of a puppy. "It was only a matter of time before she noticed me."

"So you tried to kill Elliott?"

"The bastard wasn't even hurt."

"What about Mantle? Did you kill him?"

A tear rolled down Rollie's cheek, and he appeared genuinely confused. "Why would I want to kill him? He didn't hurt Melinda."

Olivia slumped in her chair. She believed Rollie. His grief and anger seemed too real. He hadn't murdered anyone, and his assault on Hank was caused by the oldest motive in history: love.

Which meant the murderer was still at large.

CHAPTER NINETEEN

HANK watched Olivia enter the dining hall with the judge and Sheriff Jordan. Had she discovered any evidence in the barn? As much as he would have liked to permanently wipe the smirk from Mantle's face, he hadn't killed him. If Olivia told the sheriff what happened between him and Mantle last night, Hank had no illusions that he'd be the prime suspect. Again.

Dammit. He couldn't buy a break.

A horse whinnied, and he noticed Ted having some trouble with a mare. Hank slipped between two corral poles and approached the farrier.

"Need some help?" Hank asked.

Ted glanced up, and his broad, gleaming face split with a smile. "Sure could."

Hank spoke softly to the mare while Ted ran his ham-sized but gentle hands over the horse's flanks and belly.

"Something wrong with her?" Hank asked, keeping his voice low so he didn't startle the mare.

"Whoever used her yesterday didn't loosen the cinch all day. She's got some sores from the strap."

"Who'd be stupid enough to do that?"

"Got me. But if I find out, I'm going to give him a piece of my mind." The farrier's mouth twisted into an angry scowl.

"Get in line," Hank muttered.

While Ted rubbed ointment on the raw spots, Hank scratched the mare's forehead and kept her calm. He glanced up to see Rollie go into the dining hall.

"I heard someone was killed in the barn," Ted commented. "Who was it?"

Hank brought his attention back to the farrier. "Mantle. He was one of the prisoners."

"The one that looks like a big rat?"

Hank couldn't help but grin crookedly. "Yep, that's him."

Ted grunted. "If I was Sheriff Jordan, I wouldn't put in much effort finding his killer."

"Yeah, well, Jordan takes his job seriously."

"I guess someone has to do the dirty work." Ted straightened and capped the ointment tube. "That should take care of her, but I'll tell Buck to let her have a few days off." He patted the mare's neck. "You been thinking about what I said about me taking you on as an apprentice?"

A bitter taste filled Hank's mouth, and he turned his gaze to the mountain peaks. "I've thought about it, but things aren't looking too good right now."

"How's that?"

"You heard about the murdered woman?"

Ted grimaced. "Kind of hard not to."

Hank stroked the soft hair under the mare's jaw. "The sheriff thinks I killed her and another woman eight years ago. Now Mantle's dead, and it's no secret he and I weren't buddies."

Ted laid a meaty hand on Hank's shoulder. "I think I'm a pretty good judge of people, and I can't see you killing anyone."

Although he was grateful for the farrier's faith in him, it didn't ease the coil of desperation in Hank's gut. "Thanks, Ted. I appreciate that."

Ted squeezed his shoulder and nodded.

Hank glanced up to see Sheriff Jordan escorting Rollie onto the porch, and the hired man's hands were handcuffed behind his back. Olivia stood framed in the doorway watching them.

Had Rollie killed Mantle? And the women?

"Looks like you might be off the hook," Ted commented.

Hank didn't reply but ducked out of the corral and strode across the yard. The sheriff led Rollie to the county patrol car and settled him in the backseat.

"What's going on?" Hank asked Jordan.

The lawman cast him an annoyed look. "Mr. Pepper is being charged with assault."

Hank tipped his head to the side, trying to figure out who Rollie had attacked.

"He pushed the bales down on you," Olivia said as she approached.

Startled, Hank's gaze flew to the hired man, who stared out the side window. He could see damp streaks down Rollie's cheeks. "Why?"

"Revenge for killing Ms. Holcomb," Jordan replied stiffly.

"But I didn't—"

"He thought you did," Olivia said. Her expression turned pitying. "He loved Melinda."

Hank's mind raced, trying to assimilate the startling information. "So he didn't kill anyone?"

"We don't believe so," Jordan answered. "Which means the murderer is still around here." His hooded gaze leveled on Hank, his meaning clear.

So Hank wasn't off the hook; in fact, that hook just dug in a little deeper.

Sheriff Jordan called one of his three deputies over and spoke in low tones to him.

"So he just confessed?" Hank asked Olivia, unable to curb his skepticism.

"After some incentive from Sheriff Jordan." A small smile tugged at her lips.

Although taken aback by the lawman's effort to find his assailant, Hank was more concerned about the recent murder. "How do you know he didn't kill Mantle?"

She darted a glance at Jordan, then moved closer to Hank. "Let's just say that Mantle's murderer is probably the same person who killed the two women. Rollie has an airtight alibi for the first victim, plus there's no motive for him to have killed any of them."

She'd obviously seen something that made her link the killings . . . like maybe *how* Mantle was murdered. "He was strangled, too, wasn't he?"

After a moment of surprised hesitation, she nodded.

Dark foreboding pressed down on him. "Did you tell Jordan that we ran into Mantle last night?"

"I told Dad, and *he* told the sheriff," she admitted. "But that's hardly enough to charge you. How did Mantle get along with the other prisoners?"

Frustration clawed at him. "How do you think?"

Her lips thinned in irritation. "Could one of them have killed him?"

"Maybe. But then he'd have to have murdered the women, too."

Olivia shook her head. "Not if he copied the killer's method to throw suspicion off himself."

He knew she was trying to help, but her theory only further muddied the waters. The urge to escape the whole mess nearly overwhelmed him. But he couldn't do that. Besides making him look guilty, running went against the principles he stubbornly clung to. And Judge Kincaid trusted him. Hank didn't want to disappoint him or Olivia. It'd been a long time since he cared what other people thought of him. Since others believed in him.

Sheriff Jordan rejoined them as the patrol car with Rollie in custody pulled out of the yard. "Your father should be told about Pepper," he said to Olivia. "Do you want me to tell him, or would you prefer to do it?"

Olivia sighed. "I'll do it."

Jordan gave a short nod, then turned to Hank, and his

expression lost its hint of compassion. "Since you're here . . ." He motioned toward the dining hall door.

Sooner or later, Hank knew he'd be in the hot seat. Better to get it over and done with than prolong the agony of waiting.

"Hank."

Olivia's voice stilled him, and he glanced at her, his pulse leaping at the concern in her eyes.

"Remember, you don't have to say anything," she said quietly.

Sheriff Jordan's tight-lipped mouth told Hank he didn't appreciate Olivia's advice. *Tough.*

Hank garnered a reassuring smile. "It'll be okay," he said to Olivia.

She didn't seem all that reassured but gamely nodded and headed to the house. Pride washed through Hank as she walked with her shoulders erect and her head high despite her limp. She was no longer the frightened woman he'd met when he'd arrived at the ranch. Somehow, even amid the murders, she'd regained a strength of purpose.

"Come on, Elliott," Jordan said, and Hank almost believed the lawman's voice held a note of understanding.

A movement inside the dining hall caught Hank's attention, and he spotted Dawn ducking into the kitchen. She obviously didn't want anything to do with him. Clamping down on his disappointment, Hank dropped into the chair Jordan indicated.

The lawman took a seat across the table from him.

"What's going to happen to Rollie?" Hank asked, stalling the inevitable questions.

"He'll be charged with assault. Again."

"Again?"

Jordan nodded. "Eight years ago he was in a Montana prison for beating up someone in a bar."

That Rollie had a prison record didn't surprise Hank. "So he'll get hard time?"

"Probably. Pepper thinks you killed Ms. Holcomb, the

woman he loved but who didn't give him the time of day."
Jordan rolled his eyes heavenward. "His lawyer could try
for diminished capacity."

It might have been funny, except Hank could almost
sympathize with Rollie.

Jordan picked up his pen and leaned forward. "I heard
Ms. Kincaid tell you that I know about the . . ." He paused
and deliberately eyed Hank. ". . . argument between you
and Mantle last night."

Hank held the sheriff's gaze, allowing the silence to
lengthen. "Is there a question in there?" he finally asked in
annoyance.

Matching irritation flashed in Jordan's face. "What time
was this argument?"

"Around nine thirty, maybe ten o'clock."

"What was the argument about?"

Although Hank knew this question was bound to be
asked, he still didn't know how to reply without hurting
Olivia's reputation. What would happen if it became common knowledge that she had slept with a con?

"I'm waiting," Jordan said, drumming his fingertips on
the table.

"Mantle made some crude remarks," Hank finally
answered.

"Surely someone who's spent six years in prison is used
to hearing them."

Hank tensed. "This isn't prison."

Jordan narrowed his eyes. "Did what he say have anything to do with Ms. Kincaid?"

Damn. He was more perceptive than Hank gave him
credit for.

"Yes."

Jordan glanced down, and a red flush touched his
cheeks. He'd obviously figured out some things on his
own and was reluctant to hear the details, which made
Hank's attitude toward him thaw a bit.

"Mantle had a dirty mouth," Hank said in a low voice.
"He said some things to Oli—Ms. Kincaid that weren't ap-

propriate." He shrugged. "She stopped me from giving him a lesson in manners."

"So maybe you decided to teach him that lesson when Ms. Kincaid wasn't there to stop you."

Jordan just lost the points he'd gained, and Hank growled, "I didn't kill him."

"All I have is your word on that."

Anger surged through Hank. "What evidence do you have that says I killed him?"

Jordan held his gaze for a few moments longer, then glanced away. "Nothing yet."

Because the crime scene investigators are still in the barn, Hank thought. He stood. "I choose not to answer any more questions."

Jordan came to his feet. "If you're innocent, you have nothing to hide."

Familiar bitterness surged through Hank. "That's what they said six years ago, and look where talking got me then." He shook his head. "I didn't kill anyone, Sheriff." He spun on his heel and strode outside.

Trembling, Hank stood on the porch and sucked in a deep breath. He gazed out at the high plains that stretched to the mountains, enticing him to disappear into the wild land where he'd be free. It took every ounce of his self-control not to start running and never stop.

OLIVIA'S father was on the phone when she came into the house to tell him about Rollie. She paced outside his study, listening to the low timbre of his voice. As soon as she was certain the conversation was over, she knocked on his door, which was slightly ajar.

"Come in, Liv," he said.

Uncertain how her father would take the news of Rollie's crime, she entered hesitantly.

Her father smiled, but the gesture didn't touch his eyes, which were troubled. His complexion was pale, almost gray. "Don't worry. I won't shoot the messenger."

Olivia's throat tightened. As worried as her father was, he still tried to ease her tension. "Sheriff Jordan arrested Rollie Pepper for pushing the bales down on Hank."

He blinked in surprise. "Why did he do it?"

She explained his motive and ended with, "He says he didn't kill Mantle."

"That doesn't mean he didn't murder Melinda Holcomb."

"True." Olivia clasped her sweat-dampened hands. "But I don't think he killed anyone."

Her father leaned back in his high-backed chair, and the springs creaked softly. "So we have a killer who strangles his victims with a leather strap, and we don't know who's next because no motive has been determined."

Olivia inhaled and let it out slowly. "That about covers it."

"What did Mantle, Melinda, and the first victim all have in common?"

She huffed out a humorless laugh. "If Sandra Hubbard was Mandy Hubbard, I'd say it was people with an M in their name."

Her sarcastic comment brought a small smile to her father's wan face. "It won't be long before the FBI will be involved in this case. In fact, when I spoke to Warden Vincent, he was surprised they weren't already conducting the investigation."

Olivia frowned. Three murders by presumably the same person in two states would make it a federal case. And the last two bodies were found on the ranch, which meant the murderer was close. Far too close for comfort.

"Bob will be here first thing in the morning," her father announced.

It took a moment for Olivia to connect the dots. "How did he take the news about Mantle?"

Her father grimaced. "About as well as a man whose job might now be in jeopardy. I talked him out of immediately taking the remaining four prisoners back to the facility. He's coming here because he wants to check out the situation himself."

"But he could still decide to send them back to prison?"

"I'm afraid so, Liv. I'll do what I can to make sure that doesn't happen, but it might be out of my hands at this point."

Despair dulled Olivia's thoughts. "What if he does send them back, and someone else is murdered? That would mean none of them was the killer. Would they be able to resume their positions here?"

Her father shook his head. "I don't know." He rubbed his chest and coughed. "There's nothing we can do now. Why don't you go fix lunch for the men?"

Although restless, Olivia knew mundane tasks would help keep her occupied. She studied her father a moment, not liking the creases in his brow or the way he kept his hand pressed to his chest. "What about you?"

He managed a smile, but Olivia saw through it. "My accountant has been after me to get last month's expenditures to him, so I'll work on that. It'll be all right, Liv."

She didn't know if he was trying to convince her or himself.

He gasped suddenly and squeezed his eyes shut.

Olivia's heart skipped a beat. "Dad?"

"It's n-nothing," he stammered, but the lie was evident in his pain-etched brow and the sweat that suddenly beaded his forehead.

Olivia hurried around his desk and squatted down beside him. "Is your chest hurting?"

"Just some heartburn."

This was more than heartburn. A hell of a lot more.

"Is the pain in your left arm, too?" Olivia asked through the dryness of her mouth.

"Tingles." He closed his eyes and gritted his teeth as pain crested through him again.

Hysteria threatened to steal Olivia's composure. She pushed herself to her feet and hurried outside. Her knees nearly buckled in relief when she spotted Buck and Hank.

She called out to them and the two men turned as one toward her.

"Come here. Hurry!" she shouted.

Hank didn't hesitate, and Buck followed after a scant second or two. Hank jumped the stairs to the porch and grabbed Olivia's arms. "What's wrong?"

"Dad. I-I think it's his heart," she said, her voice shaking as much as her hands.

"I'll call nine-eleven," Buck said.

"Where is he?" Hank asked Olivia.

She didn't answer but led him to the study in the house. Her father's pallid face gleamed with moisture, and his eyes were closed.

Olivia's vision blurred. "Oh, God," she whispered.

Hank immediately went to her father's side, and the judge's eyes fluttered open. "Is it your heart?" Hank asked.

"I think s-so." Her father's mouth twisted into a grimace of agony.

Hank speared Olivia with a sharp look. "Do you have any aspirin?"

She nodded, her gaze locked on her father.

"Get it," Hank ordered, snapping her out of her stupor.

Moving on jellylike legs, she stumbled down the hall and into the bathroom. She carried the aspirin and a glass of water back to the study, past Buck who stood nervously in the doorway. "Here," she said to Hank.

"Good," he said, giving her a quick smile.

Olivia watched him place an aspirin in her father's mouth then hold the paper cup to his lips. He swallowed convulsively.

"Just relax, sir. Take nice, easy breaths," Hank said in a soothing tone.

Hank had unbuttoned the top buttons of her father's shirt to make him more comfortable, but the older man's gray complexion frightened her. She couldn't lose him . . .

"It's okay, L-Liv." Her father's muffled voice brought her out of her misery. Her gaze met his. He was still trying to be strong for her.

Dammit! It was her turn to be strong.

"Is there anything I can do?" she asked.

"Pray the ambulance gets here soon," Hank whispered.

"Olivia," Jordan called.

"Over here," Buck said.

The sheriff skidded into the room, and his gaze landed on her father. "How is he?"

Olivia glanced at Hank, who replied, "Hanging in there. When will the ambulance be here?"

"Twenty minutes," Buck replied.

"Can we take Dad in your car and meet them halfway?" Olivia asked Sheriff Jordan.

"That would cut the time in half," Hank added.

Suddenly her father groaned and arched upward in the chair. His face grayed even more, and tears rolled from tightly closed eyes.

"We need to get him on the floor. I think he's having a heart attack," Hank barked.

Firmly but gently he moved Olivia out of the way, then he and the sheriff lowered the judge to the floor on his back. Olivia pressed herself against the wall and stared down at the unfolding nightmare.

Hank laid two fingers against her father's neck. "I can't feel a pulse." A faint blue appeared around the older man's mouth.

"Stay back," Hank said to the sheriff, then brought his clenched hands down on her father's chest.

Olivia flinched at the dull thump. She knew Hank and the lawman were talking, but she tuned out their words. Her entire concentration centered on her father. Her fingernails dug into her palms, but the pain was negligible compared to the piercing anguish of watching her father die.

But, no, he wasn't dead. Hank and Jordan didn't stop. First compressions, then mouth-to-mouth. One set right after another. She could tell the two men were growing tired, but their fierce absorption didn't waver.

More noise came from the front of the house, and Olivia realized the ambulance and EMTs were finally here.

"In here," she shouted.

A gurney loaded with equipment was wheeled into the

study. The man and woman replaced Hank and the sheriff at her father's side.

Olivia was dimly aware of Hank coming to stand beside her, but she couldn't draw her gaze from her father. As long as she didn't look away, he wouldn't die. She wouldn't let him.

"Got a pulse," the female EMT suddenly said.

The other EMT nodded. "Okay. Let's get him hooked up."

In a matter of minutes, Olivia saw her father's heartbeat on the EKG monitor. Her knees buckled, and only Hank's strong hold kept her upright.

"Is he on any medication?" the woman asked.

Olivia tried to swallow, but her mouth was parched. She nodded. "I'll get his bottles."

"I'll get them," Sheriff Jordan said. "Where are they?"

She told him, and he went to retrieve them. The female EMT asked more questions, and Olivia answered them mechanically. After the woman had written down the medications, they loaded her father on the gurney.

"You can ride with him in the ambulance, if you'd like," the male EMT offered Olivia.

She nodded. "Thanks."

As she, Hank, and the sheriff followed the gurney out of the house, Olivia became aware of the silent group standing outside the porch. At the front of the crowd was Buck, Dawn, and Ted, their expressions somber. She felt like she should say something but wasn't certain what.

"The judge is stable right now," Sheriff Jordan announced. "He may have had a heart attack, but they'll know more after he gets to the hospital."

The sheriff's voice broke her mute despair and fired her determination. Her father needed her to ensure the ranch and men were taken care of. She hurried over to Buck and Dawn. "Do you think you can handle getting dinner ready, Dawn?"

Biting her lower lip, Dawn nodded.

"Good. Connie is supposed to be back sometime this afternoon. She's the regular cook I told you about."

"Okay," the girl said.

Olivia turned to Buck. "Warden Vincent is coming here tomorrow morning, so make sure we don't lose any more of the prisoners before then. When the sheriff is done questioning the men, get them back to work."

"Yes, ma'am."

She nodded, then ran back to the ambulance and climbed into the back. Her gaze caught Hank's, and she realized she didn't want to wait alone . . . she wanted Hank's quiet strength. "Can you come to the hospital?"

"I don't—" Hank began.

"I'll bring him," Jordan volunteered, then glanced at the EMTs. "Yampa Valley?"

The woman nodded. "Closest one."

"We'll follow you."

"Is there anything you need from the house?" Hank asked.

"My purse. It's in my bedroom," Olivia replied.

"We'll bring it."

The ambulance doors were slammed shut, leaving Olivia with the female EMT and her unconscious father.

Only one other time had she felt this alone and helpless—when she was eight years old and watched her mother's blood seep across the dirty floor of a convenience store.

CHAPTER TWENTY

It felt odd for Hank to be sitting uncuffed in the front seat of a police vehicle. Déjà vu washed through him as he remembered the night he'd been taken from his family's ranch. He'd thought it was a practical joke until they arrived at the jail and no one was laughing.

He shook himself free of the uncomfortable memories and glanced at the sheriff, who followed the ambulance with the same dogged determination he'd used when interrogating him. "How much farther?"

"Another ten or fifteen minutes," the sheriff replied. He shot Hank a sideways glance. "Where'd you learn CPR?"

"They offered a course in prison."

"And you took it?"

Hank bristled at his skepticism. "Why not? It wasn't like I had anything else to do."

Sheriff Jordan grunted.

Hank dismissed the lawman and locked his gaze on the ambulance ahead, envisioning Olivia sitting close to her father. Just remembering the anguish he'd seen in her face made his gut twist into knots. When had her pain become his?

"She trusts you," Jordan suddenly said.

Hank didn't know if it was a question or a statement. Either way, it ticked him off. But then, when *didn't* Jordan tick him off? "What's your point, Sheriff?"

Jordan clenched his teeth. "The point is, if you killed those people, she'll be devastated."

"Since I didn't murder anyone, that's not going to happen." Hank turned slightly to eye the sheriff. "Besides, why are you so worried about Olivia?"

He shrugged one shoulder, but his fingers tightened on the steering wheel, belying his nonchalance. "She reminds me of my kid sister."

Hank thought of his own sister and the protective instincts she evoked. He felt much the same way about Olivia, yet there was one big difference; nothing about Olivia conjured brotherly feelings.

"When she was in college, she was raped," Sheriff Jordan said, his gaze focused straight ahead.

For a moment, Hank thought he meant Olivia, but then realized it had been Jordan's sister who'd been raped. He was surprised the sheriff would reveal something so personal, but it explained Jordan's solicitude for Olivia. "I'm sorry."

"Yeah, me, too. It happened seven years ago. She's never gotten over it."

"It's not something a person gets over quickly." Hank stared at Jordan's profile. "For what it's worth, although Olivia was assaulted, I don't think she was raped."

Sheriff Jordan shot him a sharp look, but his expression eased into relief, and he nodded his gratitude.

They entered the edge of Steamboat Springs, and minutes later they were parked by the Yampa Valley Medical Center Emergency Department entrance. Hank grabbed Olivia's purse and jumped out of the sheriff's vehicle. With her arms wrapped around her waist, Olivia stood off to the side of the ambulance as her father was lifted out and rolled into the ED.

"How's he doing?" Hank asked her.

She blinked, and it took a moment for her to focus on him. "He's stable. They gave him some nitro, and the pain eased."

Relief washed through him. "That's good news, Olivia." He held out her purse. "Here."

She accepted it with a weak but sincere smile. "Thanks."

The gurney disappeared through the double doors and Olivia, Hank, and Sheriff Jordan followed.

Olivia was given a clipboard piled with forms, and she completed them while Hank and Jordan alternately paced. Over the next two hours, they all took turns pacing, sitting on the floral tapestry furniture and watching the headline news on the TV. And drinking coffee—lots of coffee.

Finally, a lumpy man with graying hair, a bulbous nose, and a compassionate expression entered the waiting area. "Olivia?"

She stood, and Hank and the sheriff flanked her. She eyed the doctor closely. "Dr. Norby?"

He smiled. "That's right. It's been a few years."

Olivia managed a shaky smile. "It has. How's Dad?"

Dr. Norby sobered. "Lucky to be alive. Blood tests indicate that he did indeed have a heart attack."

She closed her eyes and swayed. Hank placed his arm around her waist to steady her. After a moment, she pulled away from him as if afraid of leaning on someone and focused on the doctor.

"I'm going to admit him to the cardiac care unit and run some more tests," Dr. Norby said. "We're fortunate to have Dr. Cotton, a cardiologist, in the hospital today—he comes up from Denver twice a week. He'll make the final assessment, but I believe Andrew has some major blockage in a coronary artery. If that's the case, Dr. Cotton will probably want to do a balloon angioplasty and place some stents in the artery to keep the clogging from recurring."

"Is it dangerous?"

Dr. Norby smiled gently. "It's the least invasive procedure. Dr. Cotton has performed hundreds of them."

"How is Dad?"

"He's conscious and complaining about all his attach-ments," Dr. Norby said with a tiny chuckle. "Would you like to see him?"

"Yes, please." Olivia surged away from Hank.

"Follow me."

She paused long enough to say, "Thank you" to Hank and Sheriff Jordan.

Once Olivia was gone, Hank sank into one of the re-cliners. "That was close."

Jordan nodded but remained standing. "I have to make some phone calls."

"I'll wait here for Olivia."

Jordan stared at him a moment. "I'm trusting you, El-liott."

Hank locked his gaze on the sheriff's and nodded. "I won't run." He paused. "There's no reason to. I'm innocent."

Jordan's lips quirked upward. "You're starting to con-vince me."

Hank gaped after the sheriff's retreating form.

OLIVIA entered the emergency room cubicle and spotted her father, his eyes closed, lying on a wheeled bed. She recognized much of the medical equipment from her own hospital stay. A blood pressure cuff was wound around his upper right arm and connected to a machine mounted from the ceiling at eye level. His heart and breathing rate were being monitored from wires attached to his chest. An oxy-gen level indicator was clipped to his left forefinger, and an IV needle, connected to a blinking pump, was taped to the back of his left hand. A clear plastic tube fed him oxy-gen. His face was pale but not nearly as washed out as it had been earlier.

With silent footsteps, she neared the bed, and her father's eyelids fluttered open.

"Liv," he said with a raspy voice. "What're you doing here?"

Olivia barely restrained herself from rolling her eyes. Instead she laid her hand on his right one. "When a woman's father almost dies, it's logical that she'd be with him."

"Guess it wasn't heartburn, huh?"

Olivia swallowed her receding fear and managed a smile. "Afraid not. Dr. Norby said you probably need an angioplasty."

Her father made a face. "Doctors."

Unaccountably angry, she said, "You almost died, Dad. If not for Hank and Sheriff Jordan, you wouldn't have survived until the EMTs got to the ranch."

"That bad, huh?"

Olivia nodded and forced her irritation aside. She glanced around and spotted a rolling stool. Hooking it with her foot, she pulled it closer and sat down. "How are you feeling?"

"Better." He absently touched his chest. "Earlier it felt like someone was sitting on my chest."

Surprisingly, the hum of equipment soothed Olivia's frazzled nerves. "Did Dr. Norby tell you he's admitting you?"

"Yes, which means I won't be getting any sleep tonight. Nurses will be waking me up every hour to torture me," he grumbled.

This time Olivia did roll her eyes heavenward. "Be glad you can still wake up," she said more sharply than she'd intended.

Her father's expression turned to chagrin. "I'm sorry, honey. I guess I should've been more suspicious of the chest pains. After all, my father died of a heart attack when he was sixty-two."

"I didn't know that."

"You were only a baby then." Her father sighed and glanced up at the quietly beeping monitor. "The nurse gave me a shot of anticoagulant in my belly. Hurt like a son of a—a lot. And she put a nitro patch on me."

Olivia glanced down at the round patch that wasn't attached to a wire. "It must be helping. You're sounding like your old cantankerous self."

A twinkle touched his tired eyes. "Who says I'm old?"

She laughed, but her own chest felt tight. They'd been lucky this time. But what about next time? Her dad was going to have to make some major life changes after this close call. And he was going to have to find a way to lessen his stress.

Like terminate his involvement in the work release program.

She'd been against the program from day one, and now she had the chance she'd been looking for. Yet she could no longer deny that if even one prisoner—like Hank Elliott—received a deserved break, the program was worth it. But if the choice was between her father's life and helping an unknown prisoner, it was an easy decision to make.

"How're things at the ranch?" her father asked, drawing her out of her dismal thoughts.

She grimaced. "Chaotic. Buck said he'd get the men back to work as soon as possible."

He nodded. "You're going to have to talk with Warden Vincent tomorrow morning when he arrives at the ranch."

"Can't I just cancel the meeting?"

"If you do that, he's going to send a van for the prisoners right away." He clasped her hand, and his fingers were cold and dry. "Convince him that nothing should be done unless hard evidence is found against one of the prisoners."

She stared down at their hands, remembering how she used to walk beside him, her small hand in his, and how big and powerful her father had seemed then. In fact, it had only been a few weeks ago when she'd felt the same as that little girl. But now he looked like a worn-out man past his prime, and she hated that he'd grown old without her realizing it.

She thought about his words. "I'm not sure that's the right thing to do. What if the murderer is one of them? We're only giving him another chance to kill again."

His eyes narrowed, and although they were dimmed

slightly by the medications, they were still piercing. "Innocent until proven guilty, Liv."

She glanced away, knowing that legally, her father was right. But she also couldn't help but wonder if the prisoners had added to her father's stress after the murders. Had they indirectly brought on the heart attack?

A smiling nurse arrived and announced it was time to move him to the cardiac care unit. After kissing her father's brow and promising to be up to see him after he was settled, she went to find the sheriff and Hank. But she found only Hank sprawled in a waiting room chair.

"Where's Sheriff Jordan?" she asked.

Startled, Hank scrambled to his feet. "He had to make some phone calls."

"Uh, well, they're moving Dad to the CCU. Did you want to see him?" Olivia asked, unaccountably ill at ease.

"If you don't mind," Hank replied, obviously picking up on her nervousness.

"No, not at all." She forced a laugh. "Dad would appreciate the company. He knows better than to look for sympathy from me."

Hank shrugged and followed her to the unit. They remained in the background until the nurse was done asking her father a multitude of questions. Since Hank wasn't a family member, the nurse gave him only ten minutes to visit, then left them alone.

"I'm glad you're here, Hank," her father said. "You can keep an eye on Liv."

"As if," Olivia said with a sniff.

"You should go back to the ranch. There's nothing you can do here except watch an old man drool while he sleeps."

"Sorry, but you're stuck with us until Sheriff Jordan comes back," Olivia said, not the least bit contrite.

Her father harrumphed, then turned to Hank. "Olivia said thanks to you, I'm still alive and kicking."

"Sheriff Jordan helped," Hank said. "I learned CPR in prison. Used it once there."

"Maybe you should think about going to med school instead of vet school."

Hank chuckled. "No, sir. Animals don't complain as much as people."

"Are you trying to tell me something, son?" her father asked with a feigned scowl.

Hank made some reply, but Olivia's thoughts were caught up with what her father had called him. *Son.* She'd known he liked Hank, but she hadn't realized the extent of his fondness.

Silence brought her out of her musings. Her father's eyes were closed, and his face relaxed in sleep. She caught Hank's attention and motioned toward the door. He walked out, and she joined him in the hallway. His hazel eyes were warm and sympathetic as he gazed at her.

"As soon as Sheriff Jordan is ready, I'd like to go back to the ranch and get some things for Dad," Olivia said.

Hank glanced over her shoulder. "Here he is now."

She turned around and spotted the sheriff striding toward them down the corridor.

"How is he?" Jordan asked.

Olivia gave him a rundown of what the doctor had said, then asked, "When are you going back to the ranch?"

"That's what I came to tell you. I need to get back now. If you're not ready, I'll send Buck or one of the other men to pick you up."

"No, that's all right. I'd like to go now," Olivia said. "Just let me check on Dad."

She returned a few minutes later to find the sheriff and Hank leaning against opposite walls. For once they didn't look like two dogs defending their territory.

The drive back didn't seem to take nearly as long as the ambulance ride to the hospital. Arriving in the ranch yard, she was surprised to see a dark sedan parked by the barn alongside a county patrol car.

Olivia and the two men got out of the sheriff's SUV.

"That black car wasn't here earlier," Olivia commented.

"It's probably the FBI," Jordan admitted. "They finally

sent someone from the Denver office. They'll be taking over the investigation."

Olivia gritted her teeth. Her father had warned her, and she'd known, too, but she hadn't been prepared for the reality of the suited FBI agents on the ranch. Or the caged look in Hank's expression.

"Will they be doing all the questioning, too?" Olivia asked.

The sheriff nodded wearily. "They'll probably want to talk to everyone themselves, even if I've already questioned them."

Olivia rubbed her throbbing brow where a headache had taken residence. "All right." She eyed Jordan. "With my father in the hospital, I want to be kept in the loop, Sheriff."

Jordan smiled dryly. "Depends on if they keep *me* in the loop." He turned to Hank. "I'll make sure they only get the facts."

Hank's eyes widened slightly, then he nodded. Ever since her father's collapse, a truce seemed to have formed between Hank and the sheriff.

"I'd best get this over with." The sheriff squared his broad shoulders and strode toward the scene of the latest crime.

"Do you need any help with your father's things?" Hank asked Olivia.

She shook her head. "I can handle it. But I would appreciate it if you'd help me find Buck."

Hank nodded. They found the foreman five minutes later in his room in the bunkhouse, working on his computer.

"How's the judge?" Buck immediately asked.

Olivia gave him the short version and ended with, "I'm going to drive back to the hospital as soon as I get some of his things in an overnight bag. Did you see the FBI come in?"

"Yeah. They wanted to talk to your dad but ended up with me. They said they're taking over the case."

Olivia nodded. "They'll probably want to question all

the men again. Cooperate with them. If anything comes up, let me know."

Buck stared at her a moment, then shook his head as if he was dazed. "Uh, yes, ma'am. So you'll be filling in for your dad?"

Olivia ignored the thumping of her headache and the sliver of hysteria that lodged itself in her chest. "That's the plan. Anything else?"

Buck shuffled his big, booted feet. "I assigned someone to each of the prisoners, to work with them and keep an eye on 'em. Do you want me to do the same to Elliott?"

Hank's jaw clenched, and his lips flattened with anger. Although Olivia hated to do it, she couldn't afford to show favoritism. "That's a good idea."

Hank remained silent, but his taut body language spoke eloquently. He believed she didn't trust him, but she didn't dare reassure him. Not in front of Buck. Besides, was she one hundred percent certain he was innocent of all three murders? When she heard Mantle was dead, Hank had been the first person to come to mind. Yet hadn't Hank been the one she wanted at the hospital with her, too?

She didn't have time to sort out her emotions now. Her father was in the hospital, and she needed to get back to him. "What about tonight?" she asked Buck. "Will they be guarded then?"

"I'll make sure they are," Buck replied.

"Thank you. Go round up the men and let them know what's going on," Olivia said. She glanced at Hank. "Mr. Elliott will join you shortly."

Buck's gaze darted between her and Hank, then he nodded. "Yes, ma'am."

They followed Buck into the main part of the bunkhouse but remained there while the foreman went out to gather the hired men. Olivia turned to Hank, who stood stiffly, his arms crossed and his jaw tight.

"It's for your protection, too," Olivia said without preamble.

"Right." Hank's tone implied the opposite.

She tried to swallow, but her mouth was too dry. "What if another body is found? You'll have a built-in alibi."

"You don't trust me."

Olivia blinked at his bluntness. She met his eyes but couldn't hold his gaze. "I trust you."

"Bullshit. You think I killed Mantle."

As much as she didn't want to believe he did, an insistent little voice of doubt nagged at her. "Did you?"

Fury darkened Hank's expression, and Olivia instinctively took a step backward, away from his wrath. His anger evaporated, replaced by disappointment.

"You've never been scared of me before, Olivia. Why now? Do you really believe I could kill someone?"

She studied the almost desperate look in his eyes, wishing she could give him the unconditional trust he wanted. But her background as an ADA and the attack that had stolen a vital part of her wouldn't let her believe him without reservation. "I believe people can get carried away and do something they regret seconds after they did it. It doesn't make him or her a cold-blooded killer, but it does make that person a murderer."

Frustration and helplessness sharpened Hank's features, and he took a step toward her. Although Olivia's heart threatened to escape her chest, she held her ground and tipped her head back to hold his fierce gaze.

He raised his widespread hands and placed them on either side of her throat. Here, alone in the bunkhouse, she knew how easy it would be for him to snap her neck, but just like her nightmare, she was frozen in place.

His eyes held her captive as his fingers caressed the exposed skin above her collar. He leaned impossibly closer until they shared the same air. "How does it feel to place your life in someone's hands, Olivia?"

His fingers tightened perceptibly around her neck, and she gasped. Then, just as quickly, he released her until only his fingertips brushed her neck. "What about your heart—has anyone ever held your heart in his hands?" He bent down and kissed her throat with light, butterfly touches.

Olivia shivered, but this time it wasn't fear. Dear God, it was arousal ... swamping her senses and bringing tingling awareness to her most private places. Without thought, she wrapped her arms around Hank's neck and pressed herself against his rock-hard body. She moaned as he continued to kiss an imaginary line up her throat, beneath her jaw, over to her chin, and finally ...

She opened her mouth to his without hesitation, and their tongues mated in a frenetic dance of desire. Olivia's thoughts lost coherency, and all she could feel was want ... need.

Hank suddenly drew back, and Olivia tried to follow, to continue the soul-searing kisses.

"No," he said hoarsely.

Thwarted, she stared at him until rational thought replaced the erotic images that he'd fanned to life. "Why?" she asked, unable to articulate any further.

"Because I wanted you to know how *I* feel." Then he spun on his heel and strode out of the bunkhouse.

Olivia stared after him as her hand went to her throat. He'd held both her life and her heart in his hands. Then he'd given them back to her.

Could she promise to do the same?

CHAPTER TWENTY-ONE

RIGHT after Buck's meeting with the men, Hank watched Olivia place an overnight bag in her father's vehicle. She'd changed into black jeans and a green blouse, which would've looked plain on another woman, but not Olivia. Even with her limp, her steps were firm and her face resolute. He could almost see the crystalline blue of her eyes.

She looked around the sunlit yard, and their gazes met momentarily. Hell, what'd he expect? His fool stunt could've set back her recovery by weeks. Or she could've had him arrested for assault. Or both. So why did he do it?

Because he wanted her to know how helpless he felt. Because he wanted her to know that trust went both ways.

Because he wanted her.

Christ, he was pathetic—a convicted felon who'd fallen for the judge's daughter who just happened to be a big-city assistant district attorney. It sounded like a fucking fairy tale. Only fairy tales were for children, not for a man who'd spent six years in the pen. And who'd probably end up back there for the rest of his sorry life.

The stallion neighed from the corral, and Hank watched it trot around inside the pen. The horse stopped and stared toward the mountains. Then he tossed his mane and continued to follow the same route around and around.

If Hank was convicted of murder, he'd become like the stallion—caught in a cage with no prospect of ever leaving it, with freedom just beyond his bars. Fear squeezed Hank's heart, and he fought the pressure growing in his chest.

Olivia drove away, giving him something else to focus on. He watched until even the plumes of dust disappeared.

"Did you see the judge at the hospital?"

Hank turned to see Barton standing beside him, and he answered irritably, "Yeah, I saw him."

"How was he?"

"Alive."

Barton frowned. "Think he'll be all right?"

Hank shrugged, hiding his concern behind a bland mask. "You heard what Buck said."

Barton kicked a corral post. "I hear that the Feds are taking over Mantle's case."

"You worried?"

Barton glanced up sharply. "Should I be?"

"Depends. Did you have anything to do with his murder?"

"Hell no. Not that I didn't wish him dead more than once, but I didn't kill him." His face reddened. "Besides, if I need an alibi, I have one."

Surprised, Hank studied the younger man, and comprehension flooded through him. "You son of a—" He grabbed Barton's shirtfront and shoved his face close. "You were with my sister."

Barton's cheeks turned bright red. "We didn't do anything."

Fury surged through Hank's blood, and the urge to throttle Barton with his fists nearly overcame his self-preservation.

"Something going on here I should know about?" Buck asked in an overly casual voice.

Hank stared at Barton for a moment longer, then released him, shoving him back. "Nope. Nothing."

Buck narrowed his eyes and turned his attention to Barton. "You got anything to say?"

The youngest convict shook his head as he smoothed his shirt. "Like he said, it was nothing."

Buck gave them each a critical once-over and stopped on Hank. "You'd best watch yourself, Elliott. If Barton turns up dead next, there isn't going to be any doubt who's been doing the killing."

Hank's gut twisted painfully, but he kept his expression blank. However, he couldn't prevent his sarcasm. "So you actually have some doubts?"

Buck narrowed his eyes. "Don't push it, Elliott, or I'll have you cooling your heels in the old root cellar."

Hank lifted his head and held Buck's stare. Finally the foreman grunted and strode away, allowing Hank to gulp in air. He became aware of Barton still standing nearby.

"Dawn says you didn't do it," Barton said.

Shock rippled through Hank, and he met Barton's eyes. "She said that?"

"Yeah." He smiled slightly. "More than once."

"Do you have any idea who killed him?" Hank asked to cover the emotion threatening to clog his throat.

"No. Me and Dawn were in the hay shed and didn't see or hear anything."

Hank's temper rose again as he pictured his baby sister alone with the felon in the middle of the night. "She's my sister, Barton." Resentment made it come out in a growl.

"I know, and that's why I'm telling you. I swear, we were only talking."

Although he still didn't appreciate Barton hanging around his sister, the kid had been honest about it. At least, Hank hoped he was. He curbed his animosity and nodded reluctantly. "If you really care for her, you'll stop seeing her. She deserves better than an ex-con."

"Don't you think that's up to her?"

Knowing Barton was right but not liking it, Hank didn't reply. He and the younger prisoner remained on the fringes of the milling men, but Hank noticed two of the hired hands standing nearby. They tried to act nonchalant, but Hank recognized them for what they were: his and Barton's guards. He wondered if Barton, Reger, or Lopez noticed their babysitters.

Olivia was right. If there was another murder, he and the other three convicts would have alibis. He looked around, studying each man and trying to determine who might have done the killings. He didn't trust Reger or Lopez enough to rule them out, although his gut told him neither committed the crimes. It had to be someone who'd lived in the area for at least the last eight years.

His gaze found Buck amid a small group of hired men. The foreman had worked for the judge for years. He was in a position where he could come and go as he pleased. Some of the hired men were long-timers, too—he'd heard them talk. Determining which ones had worked here the longest was something he could do. From there, he might be able to narrow the list of suspects.

He spotted Ted measuring a mare for shoes. Since the farrier had worked around the area for quite a while, he might have some information Hank could use. It was a good place to start.

LEANING against the kitchen counter, Olivia smothered a yawn as she poured herself a second cup of coffee. She was glad Connie was back, otherwise Olivia would be in the dining hall. Of course, that would give her something to do instead of thinking about Warden Vincent's impending visit or her father, who was having more tests run this morning.

Or Hank's brief display of power yesterday. He'd said he wanted her to experience the helplessness he felt. For a split second with his fingers wrapped around her throat she had, and it wasn't a pleasant feeling. However, his kiss had shown her a different form of vulnerability, one that was infinitely more dangerous to her heart.

She couldn't afford to think about him and her reeling emotions. Her father was her paramount concern now.

After she'd left him in the hospital last night, she'd driven home in the absolute darkness. The drive, as well as the day's events, had left her jittery and unable to relax when she'd arrived home after ten. Thinking about Mantle's murder and the fact that the killer was out there hadn't done anything to calm her, either. She'd parked as close to the house as she could and dashed inside. Immediately locking the door behind her, Olivia had retrieved her father's revolver, then went to check on Dawn. The girl had been asleep in her bed, bringing Olivia a wash of relief. She'd kept the gun on her nightstand while sleeping and had placed it back in its case this morning.

A knock on the door startled her, and she shot a glance at the clock—only seven thirty. Warden Vincent wasn't supposed to arrive for two more hours.

Taking a deep breath, she limped to the door and peeked past the curtained window. Two men dressed in suits stood on the porch. She recognized the ill fit of their coats due to the slight bulge beneath each one's arm. It appeared the FBI was getting an early start today.

She opened the door. "Yes?"

The two men flipped open their badges in unison, as if they'd choreographed for hours. The tall, thin man spoke. "I'm Special Agent Thornton, and this is Special Agent Bush. We're with the FBI."

Olivia studied their badges, then looked back at them, comparing their pictures with their faces. Satisfied, she asked, "What can I do for you gentleman?"

"We'd like to ask you some questions, Ms. Kincaid," Special Agent Bush, the short, stocky one said, his manner polite but brusque.

"Ask away."

Laurel and Hardy—minus the slapstick—exchanged surprised looks.

"It might be better if we do this in a private place," Thornton said.

Olivia wanted to refuse them entry, but she had no legitimate reason. She stepped back reluctantly and motioned them inside. Leading them into the kitchen, she asked, "Would you like some coffee?"

Both agents said yes, and Olivia carried steaming cups to the breakfast nook where they sat. Each man laid out an open notebook and poised with identical pens in hand. She had, on more than one occasion, worked with the FBI in Chicago. She used to think the DA's office was the epitome of bureaucratic idiocy, but the FBI's tangled red tape made theirs look like child's play.

As she waited for them to begin the inquisition, her palms dampened with sweat. She resisted the urge to wipe them across her jeans and sat down. She'd done nothing even remotely criminal.

Half an hour later, after repeating the same answers she'd given Sheriff Jordan three times, Olivia sighed in exasperation. "I'm not going to change my answers, so you can stop any time."

Laurel glanced at Hardy, and the two agents capped their pens and placed them in their breast pockets. Simultaneously.

"If there's anything else you remember, please call us at this number." Thornton handed her a business card with his name and cell phone number.

She accepted the card and laid it on the table.

"We understand that your father had a heart attack yesterday," Thornton said.

Olivia nodded, disinclined to offer any more information.

"Is he well enough to have visitors?"

She shook her head. "He nearly died. I won't have you upsetting him."

"We're investigating three murders, Ms. Kincaid. Two of the bodies were found on your father's ranch. Being a prosecutor, I'm sure you understand why we have to speak with him," Bush said.

"My father is a highly respected retired judge who has never had a single black mark against him. If you insist on questioning him, I'll be forced to call some of his old friends." Olivia had no idea if any of them could help, but she didn't want the two agents anywhere near her father until he was out of danger.

Thornton held up his long, skinny hands. "There's no need for that, Ms. Kincaid. We have enough to do for the next day or two that we can hold off on speaking with him."

Olivia relaxed marginally. "So I assume you'll be questioning everyone who works here."

"That's correct," Bush said.

Thornton's cell phone buzzed. "Excuse me." He pulled his phone out of his pocket as he moved away.

Olivia tried to listen in on the conversation, but Bush interrupted her eavesdropping. "Is there anyone you feel might have murdered Ms. Holcomb or the prisoner Mantle?" he asked.

"No," she replied. "I hardly knew them."

Special Agent Thornton rejoined them. "I think we should begin speaking with your workers. I'd like to start with one of the convicts on the work release program. Hank Elliott."

Olivia's heart missed a beat then raced to catch up. "Why him?"

Thornton's smile was plastic. "Where is he, Ms. Kincaid?"

Olivia didn't like the predatory look in the agent's eyes. He knew something about Hank. Had the phone call revealed something?

"I'll go with you to find him." She leveled a gaze at him. "I'm also going to sit in on your interrogation."

"I'm sorry, Ms. Kincaid, but that's not allowed," Bush said.

"It is if I'm his lawyer."

She headed to the front door, not caring if Laurel and Hardy were behind her or not. She wasn't going to throw Hank to the wolves. This wouldn't become a repeat of what happened to him six years ago.

Walking as quickly as her bad leg allowed, she spotted Buck and asked him where to find Hank.

"In the barn. We were told the authorities were done in there," Buck replied.

Olivia wasn't surprised to see the two federal agents flanking her as they made their way to the barn. Pausing just inside the door, she glanced at the place Mantle's body had lain, and her memory supplied the details. She shivered and forced herself to look away. She immediately spied Hank among the four men cleaning the stalls.

"Hank," she called.

Setting aside his pitchfork, he joined her. His wary gaze moved across the agents.

"Special Agents Thornton and Bush with the FBI. They'd like to speak with you," Olivia said without preamble.

Hank merely sent them a curt nod.

"We can go into the tack room to talk," Olivia suggested.

She pressed against Hank's side as they followed the two agents. "Give me a dollar," she whispered to him.

Although puzzled, Hank stuck his hand in his jeans pocket and produced a crumpled dollar bill.

"You've just put me on retainer as your lawyer," Olivia said as she slipped the money into her own pocket.

Hank's eyes widened, but a moment later she could see that he understood.

Once in the room loaded with halters, bridles, and saddles, the agents didn't waste any time.

"Mr. Elliott, I understand you're a prisoner at the state

correctional facility and are currently working here under the work release program. Is that correct?" Thornton asked, his notebook and pen in hand.

Hank glanced at Olivia, who gave him an encouraging nod. "That's correct."

"Where were you the night of October twenty-sixth, eight years ago?"

Hank sighed, and over the next forty-five minutes answered the same questions again and again. Olivia read frustration in Hank's curt tone and brittle expression, but there was nothing she could do.

"So you say despite the argument with Mr. Mantle two nights ago, you didn't kill him," Agent Bush said.

Hank nodded and raked a hand through his dark hair, which was growing out in thick waves. "I never saw him again after our disagreement."

"Then why were your fingerprints found on the leather strap that was wrapped around his neck?" Thornton asked, lifting an eyebrow.

Olivia gasped, and the room wavered in and out of focus. Hank's fingerprints were found on the murder weapon? There had to be an explanation. Surely she hadn't been that terribly wrong about him.

"I don't know." Hank's face flushed with anger or fear, or both. "I didn't kill him."

"Then how do you explain your fingerprints?" the agent pressed, taking a step closer to Hank.

Olivia's mind snapped back into lawyer mode. "Have you ever worked in the tack room?" she asked Hank.

"Yes. Last week I spent a day cleaning and repairing the equipment." He glared at the agents. "Ask Buck."

"It's obvious how his prints got on the leather," Olivia said to Thornton and Bush, who didn't appear convinced.

"Or maybe you knew you could use that defense when your prints were found," Bush stated.

"If he thought of that, he would have wiped his prints off it," Olivia said in exasperation. "We all know you don't have enough to arrest him."

"We have a motive, and we have his fingerprints on the murder weapon," Thornton said with the first sign of impatience.

"You don't have any witnesses who can place him at the murder scene," she argued.

"Ms. Kincaid, you know as well as I do that this is strong circumstantial evidence," Bush said. "And along with his admitted relationship to Sandra Hubbard, the proximity of her remains to his location at the time, and the fact that he'd seen and knew of Ms. Holcomb, we have enough to arrest him."

"Where's your arrest warrant?"

The agents glared at her, but Olivia didn't give an inch. "It seems to me that before you make such a hasty decision, you ought to interview all the suspects," she said. "I should think you'd know better than to conduct a sloppy investigation, especially with such a high-profile case."

She scored a direct hit on their professional pride.

"Ms. Kincaid, can you assure us that your client won't run?" Thornton asked stiffly.

"Yes," she replied without hesitation.

Knowing she'd won this round, Special Agent Bush glowered. "We'll talk with you both at a later time."

Olivia watched them leave with a sense of satisfaction. But when she turned to Hank, apprehension fluttered through her.

"Thanks," Hank said, his voice rough.

She forced a nonchalant shrug. "You're welcome. When they said they wanted to talk to you first, I thought it would be a good idea for you to have counsel."

Hank scrubbed his face with his hands. "Either somebody's setting me up, or I'm the unluckiest bastard in the country."

Despite the kernel of doubt, she couldn't ignore her need to hold him. She hugged him, and his arms came around her securely. "Maybe it's a little of both."

She stepped back and was glad to see she'd coaxed a slight smile out of him.

"It's only a matter of time." His expression turned grave. "A day, maybe two, but they're going to arrest me."

"You don't know that."

He smiled without pleasure. "Yes, I do. And so do you."

"It's all circumstantial, except for the fingerprints, and those can be explained."

"Right." Hank wasn't buying it. "I talked to Ted Shandler. He told me a few things about Buck and some of the others who've worked here for awhile."

Intrigued, Olivia asked, "Like what?"

Slim stuck his head in the tack room's doorway. "Ms. Kincaid, there's someone out here who wants to talk to you."

Warden Vincent had arrived.

"I'll be right out," she said to the hired man, who nodded and disappeared. She turned back to Hank. "I want to hear what Ted had to say. Maybe we can meet later."

Hank's hazel eyes darkened with desire as he nodded. "All right."

Olivia rested a shaky hand on his arm. "Don't panic yet. We still have time."

Raising his hand, Hank brushed her cheek with the backs of his fingers. "You'd better go."

Olivia fought the heat of his touch and forced herself to step away. Before she lost her resolve, she walked out through the barn and blinked in the bright morning sunshine. A maroon sedan with state government license plates was parked by the house. A tall, distinguished-looking man wearing a suit stood on the porch. She took a deep, steadying breath before walking across the yard.

"Ms. Kincaid?" he asked, his voice a resonating bass.

"That's correct. You must be Warden Vincent," she said, accepting his firm handshake.

"That's right. Where's your father?"

Oops. She hadn't even thought to notify him yesterday. "He's in the hospital."

Vincent's eyes widened. "What happened?"

"He had a heart attack. If not for Sheriff Jordan and

Hank Elliott, I would've lost him," Olivia said, hoping to sway him in Hank's favor. "Why don't we go into the house and talk?"

Five minutes later, Olivia felt a sense of déjà vu as she poured them each a cup of freshly brewed coffee and joined him at the table.

"I'm sorry about Andrew, but this is a sticky mess, Ms. Kincaid," the warden began, plucking at the sharp crease in his trousers. "One of our inmates dead, murdered while out on the work release program. It doesn't look good, especially if one of the other prisoners killed him."

Olivia clenched her coffee cup between her hands, trying to keep her temper reined in. "It doesn't look good for whom, Warden?"

He had too much politician in him to blush. "Your father and everyone else involved in the program, including myself. Something like this can ruin it, take away the opportunity it affords deserving convicts."

Three months ago, she would've agreed with him, would even have added her own arguments to end the program. But it was different now. She finally understood why her father poured his heart and soul into it. "But what if the killer isn't one of them?"

"At this point, it doesn't matter. Leo Mantle died while involved in the program." He said it like it explained everything.

"So we should pull the rug out from under other prisoners just because something like this might possibly happen again?"

"Do you accept the responsibility of someone else being killed?"

Olivia knew what her father would say. "Yes."

Vincent took a sip of his coffee. "Mantle's isn't the only death I'm concerned about. What about the young woman?"

She glanced away. "There's been no evidence to link Melinda Holcomb's murder to any of the prisoners."

"True," the warden admitted. "But then there's been no

evidence linking *anyone* to her murder. Do I leave the remaining four prisoners here and take the chance none of them were involved? Or take the chance that one of them might show up dead tomorrow morning? Or do I remove all risk and take them back to the facility?"

Olivia didn't like his suave politician speech, but she couldn't dismiss his questions outright either. It was time she pulled out some of her own political tricks. "If you have them returned to prison, you're admitting that you don't have any faith in them or your program. Wouldn't it be wiser to leave them here, since no one's been accused of any crime?"

Warden Vincent studied her. "You have your father's persuasive skills, but do you have his commitment to the program? With him in the hospital, the responsibility falls on your shoulders."

Olivia had known that would happen, but hearing it spelled out by the warden made it real. She either backed her father or she didn't. Although her mouth was dry, she said firmly, "I accept the responsibility."

Warden Vincent scrutinized her, probably trying to decide if she could handle it. "You'll have to be approved by the trustees to assume your father's position in providing work and security for the prisoners. I'll call you after they come to a decision."

"When will that be?"

"Sometime tomorrow." Suddenly he stood and rebuttoned his suit coat. "I'd like to speak to the prisoners before I leave. I want to make sure they each want to stay here."

Olivia rose. "Fine."

"One other thing, Olivia," Vincent said. "If one of them is accused of murder, I will have them all returned to the facility immediately." He paused. "And I will shut down the program indefinitely. Is that understood?"

Olivia met his hard look, determined not to show her misgivings. "Yes, sir."

Warden Vincent smiled. "Good. I'm glad we're on the same page. Now tell me about your job in Chicago."

Trying to ignore the rising dread in her belly, she pasted on a smile and told him what he wanted to hear as they strolled outside.

CHAPTER TWENTY-TWO

RETURNING from the hospital that evening, Olivia stepped out of her father's SUV and leaned against the vehicle to gather her strength. Fortunately she didn't have to track down Buck and give him an update, since she'd called him from the hospital.

From the FBI agents to the prison warden to the cardiologist, Olivia had endured more than her share of taxing meetings throughout the day. Right now, all she wanted to do was crawl into bed and forget about the murders, Warden Vincent's ultimatum, and her father's heart attack. But there were decisions to make and a ranch to oversee. And she'd promised Hank that she'd try to find the murderer.

She straightened and look around, hoping to catch a glimpse of Hank. For a moment, she ached to be with him, his arms around her and his body providing a comforting sanctuary. She didn't see him, and disappointment erased the expectancy, leaving her drained.

Olivia retrieved her cane from the vehicle. Although she could've done without it, she was tired enough that she didn't want to take the chance of stumbling.

As she plodded across the yard, she noticed the farrier in the corral. Fascinated by the contrast between Ted's brawniness and his gentle touch with the horses, she paused to simply observe him working. Her father had remarked one time that Ted cared more for horses than people. Olivia figured that was merely the nature of his job.

She wondered what Hank had learned from him. For a moment she considered wandering over to the farrier and talking to him herself. But then she wouldn't have the excuse to see Hank later . . . alone.

Expectancy buoyed her as she limped to the dining hall. As she approached the building, she took an appreciative sniff. Smiling to herself, she figured the men were glad to have Connie back. Olivia, herself, planned on eating dinner here rather than in the house. The lonely silence would only remind her of her father's absence.

The sound of Connie and Dawn's voices, along with the rattling of pans, brought a twinge of regret. She'd come to enjoy the cooking and the camaraderie she shared with Hank's sister. The job had been her stepping-stone out of the whirlpool of depression she'd been caught in. It was here her self-confidence had been given a chance to regroup and gain momentum as she'd experienced a renewed sense of accomplishment. However, after everything that had happened lately, she was grateful for Connie's return. And thankful Connie's mother was recovering from her stroke.

Connie caught sight of Olivia and hastily wiped her damp hands on the towel around her waist. "Sit down," she ordered, motioning to one of the chairs by the small kitchen table.

Olivia sank into it gratefully.

"How's your dad?" Dawn asked, her usually smooth brow creased in worry.

Olivia smiled. "He's doing fine. In fact, he wanted to come home today, but Dr. Norby vetoed it."

"What have they found?" Connie asked.

"The tests showed a nearly eighty percent blockage of

a coronary artery. They're going to do an angioplasty tomorrow."

"So he's going to be all right?"

"Almost as good as new. Of course, he's going to have to change his eating habits. The dietician has already talked to him." Olivia rolled her eyes heavenward, remembering her father's opinion of the new diet. "He's also been warned to take it easy for a month or two. Dr. Norby doesn't want any undue stress placed on him until things have stabilized."

"I hope there aren't any more killings," Connie said, visibly shuddering. "That's hard enough on people with healthy hearts."

"When did the FBI agents leave?"

"Around three," Dawn replied.

Olivia nodded. She knew what would happen next. The agents would pull together their interview notes and the forensics evidence retrieved from the three murders and start putting the puzzle together. They would take their reports to their supervisor, and the decision would be made whether to file an arrest warrant or not with the current evidence. As much as she wanted to deny it, she suspected it was only a matter of time until Hank's name showed up on a warrant.

"It's almost time for the men to eat," Connie said to Dawn.

Olivia considered offering to help, but she didn't have the energy to get to her feet again. So she remained in the corner, out of the way, as Connie and Dawn completed the final preparations for the meal. Moments after they were done, the men arrived for dinner.

Tucked away in the kitchen, Olivia could see into the dining room. She found Hank and drank in her fill of his denim-clad slim hips and lean legs, and his soft chambray-covered shoulders and chest. She recalled all too well what the well-worn jeans and shirt hid. But more importantly, she remembered the tenderness veiled behind his cool veneer. That was the man she was fast losing her heart to, despite her inability to set aside the pesky doubts.

A plate was placed in front of her, and she glanced up to see Connie's concerned face.

"Eat," Connie said, leaving no room for argument.

Olivia gave in gracefully, since she was hungry. After cleaning her plate and emptying her glass of milk, she glanced out into the dining room to see most of the men had finished their meal. A few sat around drinking coffee and talking, but the majority left, probably to either watch TV or use one of the two computers in the bunkhouse. Hank was one of those who stayed, although he sat back, not participating in the conversations, only listening with his head cocked to the side.

She had to set up a meeting time tonight so he could tell her what he learned from Ted. The anticipation of being close to him, if only just to talk, clashed with unwanted wariness. She didn't believe he killed the two women— *couldn't* believe it. However, Mantle was another matter. That Hank hated him was obvious, and his fingerprints on the leather strap were damning. But would he go so far as to murder him? Would he risk his chance of freedom?

"Do you need some help?" Olivia asked Connie and Dawn.

"No. Go to the house and rest," Connie replied with a shooing motion.

Olivia smiled and pushed to her feet. "Thanks. I'll see you tomorrow." She glanced at Dawn. "I'll see you later in the house."

There were only a handful of men remaining when Olivia ventured into the dining room area. Hank did a quick double take. Obviously, he hadn't realized she was in the kitchen. He stood as she approached the table.

"You're using your cane again." His eyes revealed the concern that was absent form his voice.

"Been a hell of a day," she said with a tiny shrug. "Walk me to the house?"

"Sure," he said offhandedly.

Olivia contemplated his coolness and wondered if it was because of their shadow, the man Buck had assigned to watch Hank. Or if it was caused by the lingering hurt she caused when she'd been unable to give him her total trust.

Unwilling to upset their precarious truce, she remained silent as they strolled to the house in the cooling evening air. He brushed her arm with his, and awareness shot through her. Hyperaware of his proximity, Olivia tried to distract her growing arousal. But flashes of their lovemaking made it impossible to ignore the liquid heat spreading through her veins.

He walked up the porch steps behind her as Olivia attempted to cool her stampeding desire. She glanced into the lengthening shadows and couldn't help but see Hank's "escort."

"We need to talk." Hank kept his voice low.

Olivia nodded. "How about tonight?"

Hank eyed her. "Are you suggesting I lose my guard and meet you?"

She didn't know if the shivers slaloming down her spine were caused by anticipation or fear. "That would be an accurate assessment."

His lips quirked upward in a crooked grin. "Spoken like a true lawyer." He glanced away. "The hay shed at midnight?"

Her heart warred with her mind. Was she naive enough to meet him alone in the middle of the night? Of course, she'd been alone with him before—numerous times—and he'd treated her with respect and gentleness. Besides, the temptation to be near him and free of prying gazes was too much to resist.

She nodded. "All right. I'll be there."

He gazed at her a long moment, as if he'd witnessed her internal debate. "Don't oversleep." Then he spun around and strode away without looking back.

Olivia sighed and entered the house. She might as well try to catch a nap before midnight.

The phone rang, and she hobbled over to answer it. "Hello."

"Ms. Kincaid, it's Sheriff Jordan."

Her stomach dropped. Had he learned something more about the murders? "Good evening, Sheriff."

"How's your father?"

"Fine. They've decided to do an angioplasty."

"When?"

"Tomorrow." Olivia suspected her father's health wasn't his chief reason for calling. "How is the investigation coming?"

A long pause increased Olivia's apprehension.

"The FBI hasn't made any decisions regarding the two women's deaths," he replied as if picking his words carefully.

"I thought all the victims were murdered by the same person."

"That might be so, but there isn't enough to arrest anyone for all three."

Olivia's hand tightened around the phone, and she closed her eyes. "They're going to arrest Hank for killing Mantle, aren't they?"

"Not exactly. *I'm* the one who has to serve the warrant."

Olivia stumbled back and dropped into a chair. She forced herself to think like a lawyer rather than a lover. "They're treating Mantle's death as a separate crime, which takes it out of federal jurisdiction."

"That's right." Jordan paused. "I'm sorry, Olivia."

She resisted the urge to lash out at the messenger. "I am, too. Will you be here tonight to pick him up?"

"Actually, since no one is around to sign the warrant, I'll have to wait until morning."

Olivia sat up straight. Sheriff Jordan could easily have gotten the needed signature that night, but he was giving Hank one more night of freedom. "Thank you," she said quietly.

"To be honest, I think he's innocent."

"What changed your mind?"

"I finally started listening to my gut." There was a reluctant smile in his voice. "I'm trusting you to make sure he's still there in the morning, Olivia."

"He will be," she promised. "And I want to warn you, he's already retained a lawyer."

There was a second of silence, then a rueful chuckle. "Switching teams?"

Olivia thought about that a moment, then shook her head. "No. I've always been on the side of justice."

"You have a lot of your father in you. I'll see you in the morning."

"Good night," Olivia said and punched the Off button.

She laid the phone on the counter and massaged her temples. Sheriff Jordan had put his job on the line to postpone Hank's return to jail, as well as warning her of the impending arrest. In fact, it seemed she and the sheriff had switched roles. He was now certain of Hank's innocence, and she was the one with doubts. But not enough to miss her midnight assignation with Hank.

After taking some aspirin, she went to lie down. Despite the mélange of thoughts racing through her mind, she drifted off to sleep.

HANK knew the door would be locked, just like last night. He suspected Olivia didn't realize Buck was locking the prisoners in their barracks overnight. That way the guards could get some rest, too.

He rose from his bed with a silent, fluid motion. Carrying his boots, he tiptoed to the door and tried the knob, although he'd heard Buck turn the key in it earlier. Definitely locked. Setting down his boots, he reached into his pocket and withdrew two pieces of wire. He squatted down and eased one wire into the keyhole, then the other one.

When one of his prison mates had offered to show him how to pick a lock, Hank had gone along with him just to kill some time. He never thought he'd be using the skill.

Five minutes later he heard the distinct click of the lock disengaging. He grasped the knob, and this time it turned easily in his hand. With muffled footsteps, he slipped out and closed the door behind him. He tugged on his boots and kept to the shadows as he made his way to the hay shed.

He entered it warily. Not that he expected Olivia to set a trap for him, but her inability to trust him made him cautious.

Empty silence greeted him, as well as the near blackness of the shed's interior. Moonlight shone in through two windows, and Hank's eyes adjusted enough that he could make out the hay tiers.

"Olivia," he called out softly.

There was no answer. Obviously, he'd arrived before her. Remembering what happened to Mantle two nights ago, Hank cursed himself for agreeing to meet Olivia here in the dead of the night. What if the killer was out there, waiting for another unsuspecting victim?

He slipped across the yard and found a dark corner by the barn, where he could see the front door of the house clearly. He'd ensure that no harm came to Olivia.

Leaning against the barn, he crossed his arms and ankles and breathed in a slow, deep rhythm to calm his racing nerves. The thought of being alone with Olivia sent an arrow of heat straight south of his belt buckle. He'd spent a lot of time thinking about their lovemaking. And every time he did, his body reacted. It was like some damned Pavlovian response. Hell, maybe all those years in the pen had made him more animal than human.

No. He didn't buy that. Being honest with himself, he admitted his lust for Olivia, but there was much more to it than animalistic urges. When he'd walked her to the house earlier that night, he'd wanted nothing more than to embrace her. Of course, if he could've gotten a kiss out of the deal, he wouldn't have refused. Instead, she'd kept her arms wrapped around herself like she'd done when he first met her. She was protecting herself . . . from him.

He had to find the real murderer if not for any other reason than to get Olivia to trust him again. Reviewing what he'd heard between the men and what Ted had told him, Hank waited for Olivia to come out of the house.

Some minutes later, the door opened. He straightened and watched Olivia step onto the porch. Her motions were tentative, and she lifted her head, looking around like a wary, wild creature. How much courage did it take for her to step into the darkness after her assault? Especially after the murders that had occurred here?

He tried to take a deep breath, but his chest felt tight. She was doing this for *him*—to help *him*. It was the strength of her convictions, of believing in right and wrong . . . and justice.

Not wanting to frighten her, he moved out of the shadows and called out softly, "Olivia."

Her head came up sharply. "Hank?"

"Yes. Come on."

She approached him without hesitation, and he took her hand in his. It was cool and dry. Without speaking, he led her to the hay shed, to where some bales were stacked at just the right level to sit comfortably. She lowered herself to one, and he sat down beside her, leaving about a foot between them.

"Did you have any trouble getting away?" Olivia asked.

"No," he replied, not elaborating.

Turning a bit to face him, she asked, "What did you learn?"

So she was going to play it that way. No time for casual chitchat. No comments about the last time they'd been alone at night. No touching allowed.

Stifling his disappointment, he replied, "I know of six men besides Buck who've worked for your father for over eight years. It puts them in proximity of all the murders."

"What about motives?"

"Buck's divorced. Twice. From what I heard, he can't seem to settle on one. Then there's Blanchard. He likes to shove women around. He's been arrested twice, but both times the charges were dropped."

He went on to repeat what he'd learned of the other men. Olivia listened but kept silent. Once he was done, he waited in the increasingly uncomfortable quiet.

"So what do you think?" Hank asked when he couldn't stand the suspense any longer.

Olivia shook her head. "That would explain the women's murders, but not Mantle's."

"Unless Mantle saw one of them murder Melinda," he said stubbornly.

"Then why did he wait so long to confront the murderer?" She rested her chin in her hand. "The murders smack of a serial killer—three victims that we know of killed in the same way. Melinda wasn't raped, but forensics couldn't determine if Sandra Hubbard had been, and Mantle didn't have any marks on him besides the ones on his neck."

Impatience flared in Hank. "So where does that leave us?"

"Searching for a motive. What did all three of the victims have in common?"

"Nothing."

"There has to be something."

Hank let out a frustrated sigh but tried to come up with an answer. "The women's bodies were buried, but Mantle's wasn't."

"Why?"

"Maybe he buries his female victims, but not the male ones," Hank threw out.

"Or maybe something interrupted him with Mantle."

Hank suddenly recalled what Barton had told him about having an alibi that night. "Dawn and Barton were in here the night Mantle was killed. What if they were walking past the barn when the killer was in there?"

Olivia's face lit up. "They might have scared him off before he could take the body away."

The air rushed from Hank's lungs. When he could get a breath, he said, "Dawn was that close to the murderer."

Olivia grasped his arm. "It's okay. Barton was with her. She was safe. She *is* safe."

"For now. But what about the next time?"

"We have to make sure there isn't a next time," she said, conviction ringing in her tone.

Unable to sit still, Hank jumped to his feet and paced. "And how do we do that? We're no closer to the killer than we were a week ago."

"That's not true. We know it's probably someone on the ranch, someone who's been here for at least eight years."

"So why did he kill them?" Hank shoved a hand through his hair in frustration.

"That's the big question. Once we answer it, we can stop him from killing again."

Hank abruptly sat down beside Olivia. "Do serial killers actually have a reason for what they do?"

Olivia nodded. "I've read some case files. They aren't all like Dahmer or Gacy. In fact, there are probably more out there than we realize. It's just that the crimes haven't been connected."

Hank plopped an elbow on his knee and rested his chin in his hand. "You really think we have a chance of figuring this out?"

"Yeah, I do," she said, with a trace of surprise. She turned toward him. "Sheriff Jordan called me this evening."

There was a warning note in her voice that made him tense. "Why?"

Olivia threaded her fingers together and stared down at her joined hands. "He's been directed to make an arrest for Mantle's murder."

It took Hank only a second to determine who would be arrested. He sprang to his feet, his hands fisted at his sides. "Goddammit." The curse came out as a bare whisper as anguish threatened to choke him.

Olivia stood and grabbed his arms to halt his frenzied motions. He hardly noticed her. His mind filled with the prospect of his remaining years spent in the hell he'd hoped to leave behind.

"Hank, listen to me. Please." She laid her warm palm against his cheek. "Look at me. Come on, Hank."

Slowly, his fury abated, leaving him trembling. He gazed down into her moisture-filled eyes, and her sorrow pierced him. "I'm sorry, Liv."

"You didn't do anything to be sorry for," she said, her eyes now glimmering with anger. "Damn it, Hank, we're going to fight this together."

He stared down at her, at her firm but soft lips, at the determination in her expression and the concern in her eyes. Framing her face between his palms, he lowered his mouth to hers and kissed her tenderly. He felt the brush of moisture on his nose and drew away to see a tear rolling down her cheek. Thumbing it away, he dropped a featherlight kiss on each eyelid. "Please don't cry, Liv. I'm not worth it."

Anger returned, bringing a dark flush to her cheeks and sparks to her silvery eyes. "Don't you dare say that, Hank. You *are* worth it. Just because the system screwed you once doesn't mean it's going to happen again. This time you've got Dad and me in your corner."

The last time he'd been accused of a crime, he'd had no one on his side but a thirteen-year-old sister. Even his court-appointed lawyer hadn't believed him. But the stakes were higher this time around. This time it wasn't accessory to a felony; this time it was murder. If he went down for this, there'd be no chance of reclaiming the life he'd been denied.

"Please, Hank. Don't do anything stupid. Sheriff Jordan told me he doesn't think you're guilty. But he's bound by the law to take you in. And if you run, it's going to make you look guilty," Olivia said, her face so close her breath warmed his jaw. Her expression intensified. "Trust me."

Trust. That was the bottom line. He'd given up on trust when he'd been thrown in prison six years ago. It had been waylaid by betrayal and bitterness. Studying her pale face, he realized Olivia had lost her trust the night she was assaulted. Yet here she was asking him to trust her. But there remained one question.

"Do you trust me?" he asked in a husky voice.

Her gaze never wavered. "Yes."

The simplicity of her answer convinced him, and the bands around his chest disappeared. He swooped her up in his arms and carried her to where some broken bales were thrown. Setting her gently on the loose hay, he knelt beside her and kissed her as he removed her jacket, then unbuttoned her blouse. He spread them on the hay behind Olivia, then took off his own shirt and added it to the pile. Easing her back to lie on the makeshift bed, Hank immediately found her mouth with his again and swept his tongue between her open lips.

Her breathing grew labored, and he forced himself to draw back so she could fill her lungs. But she grabbed his arms and pulled him back over her. "Love me," she whispered in a passion-laden voice.

And Hank did with long, wet kisses from her head to her toes until he entered her with a gentleness he didn't even realize he possessed. He rocked within her welcoming cradle, prolonging the sweet loving until neither he nor Olivia could deny the inevitable ascent. Her completion dragged him over the precipice.

After regaining his breath, Hank eased out of Olivia and disposed of the condom. He settled by her side and tried to memorize her passion-sated features.

Olivia lifted her hand and brushed his hair back from his face. "I won't let you go back there, Hank," she vowed.

He managed a shaky smile. "I know you'll do your best, Liv, but don't make promises you can't keep."

She closed her eyes to hide the truth from him. But he knew all too well that sometimes the good guys didn't win.

Reluctantly, he rose and offered her a hand. He pulled her to her feet, then into his arms. Skin against skin made his groin stir with renewed interest, but he stifled the temptation.

"You should get some sleep, Liv," he said tenderly. "You need to be with your father tomorrow."

Her face showed indecision. "And you need me when they come to arrest you."

"I'll just tell them I won't say anything without my lawyer present," he said, injecting lightness into his tone.

Although she wasn't completely reassured, Olivia nodded, turned away, and began to dress. Hank gathered his clothing and did the same, keeping his gaze averted from the smooth curves of her moonlit skin. When they were clothed again, they simply gazed at one another. Hank thought he should say something, but what was there to say?

He took her hand and led her out of the shed. The yard seemed almost bright after the shed's darkness. Hank was fairly certain no one else was awake, so he didn't bother to keep to the shadows as he walked Olivia to the house.

As he guided her up the porch steps, a frisson of unease slid down his spine. Surreptitiously, he looked around, expecting to find someone watching them. But there was no one to see. Unless the person was intentionally concealing himself.

Hank stifled a shiver. He was probably imagining things.

"What time will Sheriff Jordan be here?" he asked.

"He didn't say. I'd guess it'd be close to nine or ten, though."

I have less than ten hours of freedom.

Ice water slid through his veins, freezing his heart in a spasm of pain. But he couldn't let Olivia to see his desperate fear.

"Okay." Hank caressed Olivia's smooth face, then kissed her, barely brushing her lips. "I'll see you in the morning."

"You will," she promised, then turned to unlock the door.

Hank shouldn't have been surprised that she'd thought of Dawn alone in the house.

"Lock the door as soon as you're inside," Hank reminded.

"I will." She paused in the doorway. "Good night."

"Good night."

He stood on the porch long enough to hear the deadbolt click into place, then headed toward the prisoners' barracks. Halfway across the yard, he froze.

What if Olivia was wrong? What if justice kicked him

in the ass again? Terror iced his veins at the thought of returning to prison.

His mind filled with the image of the penned stallion. At this moment he was as free as he'd ever be. Mexico wasn't far away. He could make it down there in a day.

Hank ran.

CHAPTER TWENTY-THREE

OLIVIA tossed and turned in her bed. It was nearly six
a.m., but since her tryst with Hank, what little sleep she'd
managed left her restless and headachy. It might have been
better if she hadn't slept at all.

Giving up, she rose and tugged on her robe. She curled
her toes on the chilly floor and slid her feet into her fleece-
lined moccasins. Limping into the kitchen, she opted to
leave the lights off and leaned against the sink to stare outside. Despite the coral tint of dawn, she could see stars
flickering high in the heavens, creating a canopy where the
mountains met the sky.

It looked quiet and peaceful, in stark contrast to the bru-
tality evidenced in the barn two mornings ago. A tremble
skated along her nerves. In a short time Sheriff Jordan
would arrive and take Hank to jail in handcuffs. Her eyes
filled with tears, imagining Hank's stoic expression. But
she'd come to know him too well. She'd see the hurt in his
eyes and in the set of his shoulders.

Angry with herself for her pessimism, she grabbed a
pad of paper and pen out of the nearby junk drawer. There

was enough light to jot down some notes, things to ask Sheriff Jordan and the FBI agents.

Glancing up from the paper, she spotted Ted entering the barn. Although Hank had related to her what the farrier had told him, she had some questions she'd like to ask him herself.

She quickly changed into jeans and a sweatshirt, and pulled a comb through her bed-tousled hair. Squaring her shoulders, she walked to the barn.

Once by the door, she froze. This was where Mantle had been murdered. But big, gentle Ted was in there to protect her. Forcing herself to move, she pulled open the door and found the farrier in a stall with one of the mares.

He looked up and smiled. "Morning, Ms. Kincaid. You're up early."

She shrugged, feeling safe with the friendly man. "I had a hard time sleeping."

He shook his head sympathetically. "You're worried about your father."

"Yes. And other things." She approached the stall and noticed that Ted held a tube in his hand. "What're you doing?"

"Putting some medicine on the mare's sores."

"What happened?" Olivia asked, peering over the stall at the horse.

"Cinch burns. The idiot riding her a few days ago didn't loosen the cinch the whole time she was saddled." Anger vibrated in his bass voice.

Matching indignation spread through Olivia. "Everyone knows better than that. Or at least I thought they did. Who was it?"

Ted smoothed ointment over the horse's healing wounds with soothing motions. "Mantle."

Olivia frowned. "He must've done that the day before he was killed."

Ted nodded. "He deserved to die." He continued massaging in the ointment, speaking in low, comforting tones to the mare.

Olivia stared at him and dread curled in her belly as suspicion flared. She thought about Melinda and how she'd struck the stallion. "What about Melinda? Did she deserve it?"

"She hit the stallion."

Self-preservation instincts told her to run, but she wasn't certain. She had to learn the truth. Willing herself to remain calm, she said, "People who hurt horses should be punished."

Ted straightened and capped the ointment tube. "You understand."

"Understand what?"

The farrier moved closer, and only the wooden stall door stood between them. "That someone has to protect them."

"How do you protect them?" Olivia's heart pounded.

He shrugged. "By making sure those people won't hurt them again."

"People like Mantle, Melinda, and Sandra Hubbard?" She could barely speak past the lump in her throat.

Ted slipped the tube in the pocket of his leather apron. "Them and others."

Ted's the killer.

Terror iced her insides. She and Hank hadn't even considered the gentle giant, yet he'd had the opportunity and the means. It was only his motivation they'd lacked.

He opened the stall door, and Olivia scrambled backward, but her bad knee gave out, and she instinctively reached out for something to stop her fall. She latched onto Ted's arm.

He caught her around her waist with a thick arm. "Are you all right, Ms. Kincaid?"

He was a cold-blooded killer, yet his concern for her was genuine. Olivia's hands shook, and as soon as she regained her balance, she moved away from him. Fear rose in her throat like burning bile, and she choked it back.

"What's wrong?" The distress in his voice was real.

"Uh, nothing." She backed toward the door, or where she hoped the door was. "I haven't eaten breakfast yet."

Ted suddenly frowned. "No wonder you're looking a little pale. A small woman like you needs to eat."

His worry for her contrasted sharply with that of a cold-blooded killer. The situation was bizarre, and Olivia wondered if this wasn't another nightmare. But, no, this was real, too damned real.

She forced a laugh. "You're right. I am a little dizzy. I just need to go back to the house and have some food."

"I'll walk you over." Ted touched her shoulder, and she couldn't help but jerk away from him. He studied her, and his lips turned downward. "I thought you were like me. Like Hank."

Olivia stilled as her heart took another leap. "Hank?"

"He cares about the horses, too."

Her mouth was so dry she could barely speak. "Does he take care of the horses like you do?"

"Not yet, but he will," Ted said with absolute certainty. "He's going to be my apprentice, and I'm going to teach him."

Although shocked, Olivia shook her head slowly. "The sheriff is coming to arrest him this morning for Mantle's murder; then Hank is going back to prison for a very long time."

Ted appeared dazed. "No. He can't."

"He is," Olivia said firmly. "Hank is going to prison for something you did."

"It wasn't murder," Ted insisted. "I was taking care of the horses."

"But the law doesn't see it that way. You need to tell them, convince them that it wasn't wrong." Olivia was surprised she could speak so coherently. Her muscles threatened to turn to oatmeal, and her heart pummeled her chest.

Ted curled his hands into ham-sized fists. "No. They won't understand." He took a giant step toward her and caught her arm before she could escape. "I thought you'd understand."

"I do," Olivia lied.

"No. I won't let you stop me."

Even though she knew it was futile, she tried tugging out of his grasp, but it was no use. In fact, Ted didn't even seem to notice her struggles. He dragged her back toward the tack room . . . where the leather straps were kept.

She opened her mouth to scream, but only a stuttered cry escaped before Ted slapped his huge palm over the lower half of her face. Memories of that night in Chicago, of not being able to breathe, of being helpless, besieged her. She fought to escape, but as before, she failed. Only this time she'd most definitely die.

HANK lifted his head from his arms, which rested on the truck's steering wheel. It was still dark, but he knew the sun would be rising soon. So why was he still sitting here, less than ten miles from the ranch? When he'd found the keys in the pickup, he figured it was destined that he make his escape. But with each mile he drove, more and more doubts clamored at him, until all he could hear was his conscience.

Judge Kincaid trusted him. Olivia trusted him. Even Sheriff Jordan trusted him. And what did he do? Like an animal caught in a trap, he tried to escape at all costs, including chewing off his own leg. Except instead of a leg, it was his sense of honor that he'd left behind.

But what good did honor do him in prison? That was one of the first things that was lost when a man entered those four walls. Honor. Integrity. Self-respect. All became liabilities in prison.

What about out here? All he had was his honor, integrity, and self-respect. If he continued on to Mexico, who would arrive there? Only the empty husk of Hank Elliott. Is that how he wanted to live the rest of his life? As a man with no principles?

How would Dawn remember him? And Olivia and the judge? As a coward who turned tail before the fight even began?

His shoulders shook with bitter regrets—of the six

years he'd lost, the sister he'd deserted, and the woman he cared about. By running to Mexico, he might be escaping prison, but he was also losing everything. Was freedom worth it? Or was he only entering another kind of prison— a prison of his own design?

What about the murderer?

Hank clenched the wheel so tightly his fingers cramped. With the killer still free, Dawn and Olivia were at risk. What if one of them was murdered, found with a leather strap around her throat?

Hank blindly grabbed for the handle and shoved the door open. He stumbled out of the truck and fell to his knees as he retched. He vomited until there was nothing left but bile that burned his throat.

Falling back onto his butt, he sat there with his elbows on his knees and his head cradled within his hands. This wasn't who he was. Even though others may see him as a criminal, he *knew* he wasn't. The Hank Elliott he was— and who he wanted to be—possessed principles and integrity.

He dragged his sleeve across his mouth and struggled to his feet. After he got back in the truck, he turned the key in the ignition and started driving . . . back to the ranch.

Feeling a sense of urgency, he pressed harder on the accelerator, and the pickup kicked over the dirt road. The sun peeked over the eastern mountains, casting a coral-rose glow across the land.

The ranch came into view, and Hank knew he'd made the right decision. He parked the truck where he'd found it and was relieved to see it was early enough that he wouldn't have been missed yet.

Hurrying across the yard to his barracks, he heard a cry from the barn. He froze and listened, but no other call sounded. Had he imagined it? Or had the murderer chosen another victim?

He raced to the barn but paused before entering. Laying his ear against the wood, he listened and was rewarded with muffled movements. He opened the door slowly but didn't see anyone and slipped inside. Then he heard it again, a woman's cry from the tack room.

He dashed across the floor and through the doorway. Ted held Olivia with one arm around her waist. The other held the ends of a leather strap tight against Olivia's neck.

"Nooo," Hank shouted and charged.

Ted shoved Olivia aside and held up his hands as if surrendering, but Hank didn't try to stop his momentum. He plowed into the huge man, using his head as a battering ram. It was like running into a stone wall. He bounced off the farrier and fell backward, landing on the cold floor.

"What're are you doing?" Ted asked, his voice puzzled rather than angry.

Hank stared at him in disbelief. "You were going to kill Olivia."

He nodded, but it was with sad resignation. "She wants to stop us."

"Us?"

"You and me from taking care of the horses."

Hank shook his head, wondering if he'd sustained a concussion. He glanced at Olivia, and his bewilderment scattered at her lost look. She sat on the floor, her head drooping and her limp hands in her lap. She didn't seem to be aware of anything. Maybe he was too late—maybe the strap had cut off her oxygen for too long.

Hank scrambled to his feet. "What the hell are you talking about?" he demanded, knowing he had to take care of Ted before he could help Olivia.

"Why are you so angry? I thought you cared, too." Ted appeared confused.

"Of course I care for horses, but I don't kill people."

"But they deserved it."

Even though a part of Hank knew as soon as he'd seen Ted with Olivia, full comprehension shocked him, driving the blood from his face. "You killed them? Mantle, Sandra, and the other woman?"

"Others, too. I couldn't let them live, not after what they did."

Hank had admired Ted, had even saved his life his first day on the ranch. To learn he was the killer staggered him, but another look at Olivia brought rage surging in his blood. "You murdered them, Ted. And you almost murdered Olivia." He cleared his throat. "You have to pay for what you've done."

"I took care of them. Like I was going to teach you."

That Ted planned on showing him how to strangle people made Hank's stomach churn. "I'm not a killer, Ted. I could never do that, not even if they hurt a horse."

Ted stared at him as if trying to determine if Hank was speaking the truth. The change, when it came to Ted's face, was horrifying to behold. No sign of the farrier Hank knew remained in his features. His eyes were cold, almost dead. "You were the first person I thought I could trust. The first one I thought wanted to help the horses, too. But you're just like everyone else. You'd turn your back and let them escape their punishment."

Hank held out his hands to try to appeal to the man, even though he suspected Ted was too far gone to save.

"He won't listen to you," Olivia suddenly said with a raspy voice.

Hank risked a glance at her, and she seemed aware of what was going on. "Stay back, Liv. He's crazy."

"No," Ted roared then rushed toward Hank, his arms outstretched in front of him.

Hank sidestepped and tried to run past him, but Ted caught him by the arm and swung him around. Hank crashed against a wall lined with bridles and halters, sending some to the floor. His shoulder was numb, and his head felt like he'd been kicked by a mule. He slumped against the wall as he tried to get his body to answer his commands.

Ted reached for him again, but Hank eluded him, ducking beneath the big man's arms. He scuttled away, but kept far from Olivia's position. "Get out of here," he shouted to her. "Get help."

Her eyes impossibly wide, she climbed to her feet clumsily.

Ted grabbed Hank and wrapped his massive arms around his chest. The farrier squeezed, and Hank couldn't draw air into his lungs. Ted's hold tightened even more, threatening to crush Hank's ribs.

Abruptly Ted released him, and Hank dropped to the hard floor. The farrier's howl of pain made him look up to see a pitchfork stuck in the back of the man's thigh. Olivia stood behind him, weaving like a drunk on a three-day binge. Her face was chalk white, and the bruises on her neck were already standing out in harsh contrast.

Keeping one arm around his ribs, Hank labored to his feet. A pitchfork wasn't going to keep Ted out of action for long. He reached out to Olivia and snagged her wrist. "Come on."

She stumbled after him, her limp more pronounced. Hank regretted her pain, but if they didn't get out of the barn, away from Ted, they'd both end up dead. They were almost to the door when Olivia was snatched away from him. Ted shook her like a rag doll.

"You spoiled everything!" he said to her.

Hank spotted a piece of twine on the floor and grabbed it. He threw himself behind Ted and wrapped the twine around the man's thick neck. Using every ounce of strength that remained, Hank held the rope tight.

Ted shoved Olivia away and groped at the twine. His movements lessened until he slumped, and Hank released the rope, allowing the farrier to drop to the floor. The up and down motion of his chest assured Hank he wasn't dead.

Hank lurched to Olivia's side and wrapped an arm around her shoulders and the other around his ribs. "Let's get the hell out of here."

She gazed up at him and nodded.

Together, they wobbled out of the barn and into the amazingly bright morning sunshine.

STANDING in the dining hall, Sheriff Jordan said, "I think you both need to see a doctor."

Although he tried to mask his concern behind a gruff tone, Olivia recognized it for what it was. She laid her hand on his forearm and shook her head. "We're fine." She knew, however, that her scratchy voice didn't reassure him.

Jordan merely shook his head in exasperation and pointed at Hank. "You could have some broken ribs."

"Nah, just cracked," Hank replied with a loopy grin.

Olivia couldn't help but smile despite the sore twinges in her neck. She was simply grateful they were both alive.

Buck had seen them stumble out of the barn and had taken command, getting some of the men to guard Ted. Then he called Sheriff Jordan, who called the FBI. Olivia and Hank were taken to the dining hall, where Connie proved she was as good at first aid as at cooking.

Special Agents Thornton and Bush had come and gone, taking Ted, who'd regained consciousness, into custody. Their first stop would be the hospital to have the farrier's leg treated—the pitchfork had left three nasty puncture wounds. The agents had gotten initial statements from Olivia and Hank, but Ted incriminated himself immediately, going on about protecting the horses. He'd obviously gone over the edge. Like most serial murderers, Ted would receive a psych evaluation. Olivia suspected the eval would reveal things in Ted's past that had turned him into a killer.

Olivia glanced at Dawn, who stood by her brother instead of Barton. The girl gazed at Hank with something akin to hero worship, but it was the love and contentment in Hank's eyes when he looked at his sister that nearly made Olivia cry. It seemed the healing between brother and sister was well under way.

Sheriff Jordan's cell phone rang, and he moved off to the side to answer it.

"I knew you couldn't have done it," Dawn said to Hank.

He smiled. "Thanks, Dawn. That means a lot to me."

She shuffled her feet and gazed at the floor. "I knew you would be here."

Olivia shot a confused look at her and Hank.

"What do you mean?" Hank asked.

"Even though I didn't keep in contact with you this past year, I called the warden asking about you. When I heard you'd be working here, I came to the area to look for a job. It really was sheer luck that I ran into the judge in Walden." A shy smile graced Dawn's lips as she shrugged. "I might have been angry with you, but I've always loved you."

Olivia's eyes filled with tears as Hank hugged his sister. She could imagine how much Dawn's confession touched Hank.

Dawn drew away from her brother. "Well, um, I need to help Connie in the kitchen."

"We'll talk later," Hank said.

"A lot of laters," Dawn promised and kissed his cheek.

Warmth filled Olivia as she observed Hank following his sister with his gaze.

When Dawn disappeared into the kitchen, Hank turned to Olivia and grasped her hand. "Are you sure you're all right?"

"I'm fine." She grinned at the croaky sound of her voice. "Honest. In fact, I'd say that I've never been finer."

Hank tilted his head to the side in question.

"When Ted grabbed me, I flashed back to that night." She paused, glad for his quiet strength. "I kept mixing up Ted for the man who assaulted me. I couldn't seem to move, even though I knew I should fight."

"You did fight." He kissed the back of her hand. "If you hadn't used that pitchfork on him, I'd be dead."

Pain pierced her at his casual comment. "And if you hadn't shown up when you did, I'd be dead."

He glanced down at their clasped hands. "I thought I was too late."

"No." She raised his chin so he met her eyes. "Just like any good hero, you arrived in the nick of time."

Instead of smiling, Hank drew away from her, and his expression clouded. "I'm no hero, Liv. You know where I was while you were solving the murders? I was ten miles away in one of your dad's pickups, debating whether to continue to Mexico or not."

Surprised but not shocked, Olivia laid her hand on his shoulder. "But you came back."

"What if I hadn't?"

The anguish in his voice nearly undid Olivia. "It doesn't matter. You did, and that's what counts." She met his gaze squarely. "You're a good man, Hank Elliott."

Sheriff Jordan interrupted them with a quiet clearing of his throat. "Olivia, that was Warden Vincent. The Feds must've called him, because he knew all about Shandler. He said to tell you he's sending a van for the prisoners. It should be here in a couple of hours."

Her heart lurched. "But they weren't involved in the murders."

Jordan grinned. "He said you'd say that, and he told me to reassure you that the early release paperwork has been started for the prisoners. They'll only be in prison long enough for the paperwork to go through—three or four days."

Olivia clapped in delight and would've cheered, but her throat hurt too much. She looked over at Hank, expecting to see his face lit with joy. Instead, he appeared preoccupied. "Did you hear?" she asked him.

He nodded and smiled, but Olivia saw the effort behind it. "That's great news."

"So why are you acting like it's not?"

"I have to get back to the office," Sheriff Jordan said somewhat awkwardly. "Tell your dad I'll stop by to see him tomorrow."

Then he shook their hands and left, leaving Olivia and Hank alone in the dining area.

"He turned out to be a pretty decent guy, for a sheriff," Hank said.

"Yes, he is." She wasn't going to allow him to change the subject. "What's going on? I thought you'd be thrilled to get your walking papers."

"I am."

"But . . ."

Hank stood and went to one of the windows to look outside, giving Olivia his back. "There are a lot of decisions I have to make. What kind of job to look for, how Dawn and I are going to work things out." He turned to gaze at Olivia with a hint of a smile on his lips. "What about you? You're ready to go back to Chicago and tackle the bad guys."

"I'm not—"

"Yes, you are," he said firmly. "Trust me."

Tears stung Olivia's eyes. "Damn it, Hank. That's not fair."

He walked back to her and grasped her shoulders, holding her at arms' length. "We both have a lot of thinking to do. I care for you, but I'm a country boy at heart, Liv." He smiled to soften his words. "Let's just see what happens, okay?"

She closed her eyes and leaned forward, resting her forehead against Hank's chest. "I thought the hero rode off into the sunset with the girl at the end," she whispered, holding her tears back by sheer force of will.

"Only in fairy tales." He embraced her, laying his chin on her crown. "Follow your dream, Liv. Be the best damned district attorney in the history of Chicago."

She wrapped her arms around his waist and breathed in his familiar scent. Suddenly she wasn't certain of anything, not even the goal she'd strived toward ever since she was a child.

What if my dreams have changed?

CHAPTER TWENTY-FOUR

Six weeks later

HANK Elliott shifted the old Ford truck down to second gear as he turned onto the driveway leading to Judge Kincaid's ranch. His new blue jeans had already been washed a few times, but the pale blue shirt and tie were brand-new. Except for the one other time he'd worn them.

He smiled to himself even as his insides quaked with nervousness. Owing Judge Kincaid big time for his swift acceptance into the veterinary medicine school at Fort Collins, he wanted to thank him in person. The judge had been ecstatic to hear he was coming to visit and insisted that Hank stay for dinner and spend the night.

Judge Kincaid had sounded good—just like his old self. Hank had talked to him a week after the angioplasty, and the judge had sounded good, really good. When he'd hung up the phone, Hank had scrubbed at the damned irritating moisture in his eyes. Since then they'd talked every few days. If Hank didn't know better, he'd think Judge Kincaid had adopted him.

The only topic the judge and Hank didn't discuss anymore was Olivia. Judge Kincaid said she'd gone back to Chicago two weeks after he'd returned home from the hospital. Although Hank had told her to follow her dream, her departure without saying good-bye, even over the phone, had hurt.

There was no doubt he loved her, but he couldn't live in a place like Chicago. It would be too much like a prison for someone who'd grown up on a ranch, and Hank had had more than his share of prison. The one thing he did do, though, was follow his own advice. He'd be thirty-five by the time he got his veterinary license, but he wouldn't let bitter regrets cloud his future.

He'd considered blacksmithing, but Ted Shandler's specter would always be there. On last count, Ted had confessed to murdering six women and three men in an area encompassing Montana, Wyoming, Colorado, Nebraska, and Kansas. The bodies had been buried in remote areas, the locations of which Ted had given to the federal agents.

Judge Kincaid told Hank that Ted had been abused as a child, locked in the barn by his mother for days at a time. His only friends had been the horses locked in with him. Ted's first victim had been his mother, who'd ridden a horse lame, then had it put down. The horse had been one of young Ted's companions. Now Ted would spend the rest of his life in a mental institution.

Hank shoved the gloomy thoughts aside. There was too much to look forward to, including seeing Dawn again. She still worked at Judge Kincaid's ranch but would quit in two weeks to return to college in Fort Collins. He'd talked to her often on the phone. After he assured Dawn he wouldn't be an overbearing big brother, she agreed to rent an apartment with him while they attended school. It would be a good way for them to become reacquainted.

The only dark spot in Hank's future was Olivia's absence.

He made the final curve, and the ranch came into sight. A rental van was parked in the yard, and he wondered if the judge was getting rid of some things. He found a place to park out of the way and stepped out of his truck. Buck and Slim were each carrying a box from the van to the house.

"Look who finally made it," Buck greeted him. "Grab the last box and bring it on in."

With a chuckle, Hank loosened his tie and unbuttoned the top two buttons of his shirt. He picked up the deceptively heavy box and nearly groaned. It had to be books. He carried it to the porch and paused a moment. This was the first time he'd been back since the prison bus had taken him, Reger, Lopez, and Barton back to await their freedom.

"You going to stand around all day or come on in?"

Hank spotted Olivia, wearing jeans and a T-shirt, standing in the doorway. His heart leapt into his throat at the vibrancy in her eyes and face. Unable to speak, he followed her inside, noticing her limp was barely discernible.

"Just set it with the rest of them." Olivia motioned to a stack of three boxes by an empty bookshelf in the living room.

Moving like a robot, Hank piled it on the others. The stack shifted precariously, and he grabbed at the top box to steady it. Olivia's hands closed over his, also intent on keeping the boxes from toppling.

"Thanks," she said softly.

"I'll set it on the floor," Hank murmured.

She stepped back so he could do so.

Once the crisis was past, Hank couldn't help but study Olivia, remembering how soft her lips had been, the little cries of passion as they'd made love, her fierce need to help him. "What's going on, Olivia?" he asked, wishing his voice sounded steadier.

She shrugged and looked away, but not before he spotted the flush in her cheeks. "I've moved back."

Shock washed through him. "But your job . . ."

"I quit." She brought her gaze back to his. "I went back and realized it wasn't what I wanted anymore." She wrapped her arms around her trim waist and gave him a quirky grin. "In those immortal words of somebody, the thrill was gone."

Hank didn't know what to say.

"I'm going to help Dad administer the work release program, and I'll be working part-time in Fort Collins as an assistant district attorney," she confessed. She looked up at him. "I hear you've been accepted into the vet program at Fort Collins. Funny how that worked out."

Hank never thought of himself as slow, but he'd been about a mile behind Olivia. He finally caught up. His lips tugged upward. "Yeah, funny."

Olivia brushed her foot across the carpet and took a casual step toward him. "I think Dad's expecting you and Dawn to come home over the holidays and semester breaks. Weekends, too."

Hank stepped forward. "He is, is he?"

Olivia moved another foot closer. "Oh, yeah, definitely."

"What about his daughter? What does she expect?"

Her toes touched his. "I think she expects you to kiss her." She grasped his tie and tugged.

Grinning, Hank cupped her face in his palms and met her expectations, plus a little more.

"You know I love you," he whispered.

"I kind of figured that out." She traced his lower lip with her finger. "I figured something else out, too."

"What's that?"

"I love you, too."

"I kind of figured that," Hank said, brushing the tip of her nose with his.

"Did you figure out that Barton is working here?" she asked.

Hank rested his forehead against hers and groaned softly. "My sister and an ex-con."

"Ex-cons aren't bad. I happen to find a certain one pretty damned hot, myself."

Olivia kissed his neck, and Hank decided he'd postpone the big brother talk with Dawn. Indefinitely.

Turn the page for a special preview of
Maureen McKade's next novel

A REASON TO LIVE

Coming soon from Berkley Sensation!

LAUREL Covey's thin bonnet was little protection against the hot Tennessee sun, and she felt the tickling sensation of sweat rolling down her back. She ignored the irritation. It wasn't difficult. She'd had two years to learn how to overlook annoyances.

The memory of the hospital tent filled with wretched moans invaded her thoughts. Her nose wrinkled at the remembered odors of blood, sweat, urine, and rotting tissue. Laurel held her breath, and when she finally gulped in air, there was nothing but the scent of damp soil. With a shaking hand, she wiped the beaded perspiration from her brow. Funny how the stench hadn't bothered her during the war, but now her stomach roiled simply from the memory.

She shifted her backside on the buggy's unforgiving oak seat, glad for the discomfort to keep her thoughts from straying again. She glanced down at the cloth bag that held her precious journal. Soon, she'd be passing on his final words to his loved ones—to Jenny and his parents. Instead of merely names scrawled in her book, they would become real people. There would be tears and anger, just as there

had been at the last nine places she'd taken messages from
dead sons, husbands, or brothers.

For a moment, desolation swept through her, bringing
black emptiness. Despite the heat of the day, she shivered.
She reminded herself that the war was over and had been
for nearly three months. There would be no more soldiers
dying, and no more words to record and pass on to loved
ones. There were only those remaining messages in her
journal.

Promises to keep.

The pockmarked road ran through a thick copse of
trees, which opened as Laurel rounded a curve. A small
shack, made of warped wood, weathered gray by the sun
and rain, stood amidst three rooting pigs and a dozen
scrawny, scratching chickens. She halted the mule and remained seated in the wagon. Although there was an air of
poverty surrounding the home, it didn't look like it had
been touched by the ravages of war like so many others.

A lean, stooped man wearing faded overalls and carrying an ancient rifle came out of the house. A stained floppy
hat with more than one hole covered his head and shaded
his face. The way he held the gun told Laurel he was the
distrustful type. Not that she blamed him. It was difficult
to tell the difference between friend and foe nowadays.

"Whaddya want?" he called to her in a gruff voice,
keeping his weapon aimed in her direction.

"Is this the Hoskins home?"

He spat a stream of brown tobacco juice onto the bare
ground. "Who wants to know?"

"My name's Laurel Covey, and if you're Mr. Hoskins, I
have a message from your son Jeremiah."

His grip tightened on the rifle as pain flashed through
his gaunt face. "My son's dead. Got me a telegram that
said so."

Laurel glanced down at her gloved hands and blinked
away the moisture filming her eyes. Taking a deep breath,
she raised her head. "I know and I'm sorry for your loss. I

was with him when he died. He asked me to pass on a message."

Hoskins remained as still as a statue, and Laurel could
feel his measuring gaze. Despite the urge to look away, she
kept her own eyes steady. One of the pigs wandered closer
to the buggy, and his snuffling shorts distracted her and
gave her something on which to focus.

The rifle barrel wavered and finally lowered. "I'm Jeremiah's pa." His voice echoed with weariness. "C'mon in.
The missus just put on some coffee."

He turned back toward the house, leaving Laurel to
clamber down from the wagon alone. She set the brake and
tied the reins, grabbed her journal, and followed Hoskins'
hunched figure into the shack.

Laurel stepped across the door's threshold and blinked
in the abrupt darkness. Greasy smoke hazed the room,
blurring the corners and the simple, hand-hewn furniture
that occupied it. A movement caught her attention, and she
spotted a thin woman moving about the kitchen. Another
woman, younger and with a rounded belly, kneaded bread
dough.

"Says she got words from Jeremiah," Hoskins announced to the two women.

The younger one ceased punching the dough and stared
at Laurel. The older woman, probably Jeremiah's mother,
froze for only a moment, then said, "Sit. Would you like
some coffee?"

Laurel nodded. "Yes, please." Three small steps carried
her to the table, and she lowered herself to a rough chair
gingerly. She removed her gloves and laid them aside.

Mrs. Hoskins brought two cups of coffee and set one on
the table in front of Laurel. The other she gave to her husband, then she stepped back and eyed Laurel.

To allow herself a moment to gather her composure,
Laurel sipped the coffee that tasted like hot dishwater.
Keeping her expression blank, she laid her hand on the
journal that she'd set on the table. "I was a nurse during the
war," she began in the suffocating silence. "Jeremiah was

wounded during the battle at Hatcher's Run and brought to the tent hospital where I worked."

The young woman, obviously in a family way, wiped her hands on a threadbare towel and joined them. "So you seen him afore—" she glanced away. "Afore he passed?"

Seeing her close up, Laurel was shocked to find the young woman was actually a girl, maybe thirteen- or fourteen-years-old. She stifled her surprise and nodded. "Yes, I was. Are you Jenny?"

"Yes, ma'am." She lifted her dainty chin. "Jeremiah was my husband."

For a moment, Laurel felt much older than her twenty-seven years. She managed a smile. "I didn't know him well, but I could tell he was a good man." *Even if he was only a boy himself.*

Jenny's lower lip trembled, and her eyes glittered with tears before she blinked them back. "He died a hero."

Laurels' stomach churned. He'd died fighting a war the South was destined to lose. There was nothing heroic about that. But she forced herself to nod. "His last words were for you and his parents."

Mrs. Hoskins gasped and moved closer to her husband. "Wh-what did he say?"

Laurel opened the journal to where she'd left a small blue ribbon to mark Jeremiah Hoskins's entry. She licked her lips and read his words, "Tell my Jenny I love her, and tell Ma and Pa I made them proud."

Jenny covered her mouth with her hand as her expression paled and two tears trickled down her cheeks. Mrs. Hoskins tried to stifle a sob, but Laurel heard and felt it, like a knife twisting in her heart. Jeremiah's father looked away, his lips curling into a grimace of anguish.

Laurel stared down at the words in her journal, but all she could see was a vivid picture of Jeremiah's final moments. The futile desperation and horrible realization that death was close at hand had brought tears to the boy's eyes. He'd sobbed his last words to her and died with panic etched in his face.

Mr. Hoskins cleared his throat, bringing Laurel back to the present. She lifted her head and met his watery gaze.

"He was a good boy," the man said with an emotion-roughened voice.

Although Laurel hadn't known him, she nodded.

"He was so damned scared the war was gonna end afore he could sign up." Hoskins drew a gnarled hand across his eyes. "Didn't wanna be left outta the glory."

Glory. There was no glory in drowning in your own blood.

"Me and him married a week afore he left," Jenny said, a hand curved protectively over her round belly. "Said he'd come back a hero."

Bitterness rose in Laurel's throat, but she choked it back. "He died doing what he believed was right," she said, careful to keep her voice even.

Mrs. Hoskins threw her arms out and resentment spilled through in her voice. "He was a damned fool. I told him he ought to stay home with his wife and not go gallivantin' off to war."

Jenny clasped her mother-in-law's hand. "Don't, Mama Hoskins. He's gone. Ain't nothin' going to bring him back. And it don't do no good to be blamin' him."

The older woman snapped her mouth shut, and her fury fled, replaced with grief.

Laurel eyed the girl, taken aback by her mature words. She swallowed her own anger and tried to ease some of the sorrow that filled the tiny cabin. "Jenny's right. Jeremiah's last thoughts were of his family, so I know he loved you all very much."

"Did he suffer?" Hoskins suddenly asked, pinning her with a penetrating gaze.

Laurel glanced down and ran her hand over the smooth surface of her journal. "No," she lied.

Hoskins stared at her for a long moment then nodded. He straightened his spine. "Would you like to stay for dinner?"

Laurel's belly protested the thought of food, and she

shook her head. "No, thank you." She stood. "I should return to town." She faced Mrs. Hoskins, who was being
held by her petite daughter-in-law. "I'm very sorry for your
loss."

Jenny managed a slight smile. "Thank you, Miz Covey.
It comforts me to know my Jeremiah had someone by his
side when he died."

He shouldn't have died. The angry words leapt to Laurel's tongue, but she pressed her lips together to keep them
from springing forth. Instead, she merely nodded.

Hoskins walked her out, his damning silence preying on
Laurel's conscience. He awkwardly helped her climb up
into the buggy, then he shoved his hands into the sides of
his overalls. "I 'preciate you lyin' 'bout how my boy died.
His ma and wife don't need to know he suffered in the
end."

Laurel licked her dry lips, surprised by his astuteness.
She looked over his shoulder, to the peaceful setting of
green trees and the colorful flicker of flitting birds. It was
a scene she'd despaired of ever witnessing again. "If it's
any comfort, Jeremiah faced his death like a man."

Hoskins's chest puffed out. "I didn't raise no crybaby.
Taught him to be tough, like a man."

Afraid to say anything more, Laurel released the brake
and slapped the leather reins across the mule's rump. As
she drove away, she wondered if she'd done the right
thing. But then, what was another white lie or two if it gave
a grieving family some solace? Speaking the truth would
only bring more pain. No, she had no reason to taint their
memories with the harsh realities of war.

Her thoughts roamed as the mule plodded along the
road back to town. Ten families contacted with only eleven
more to go. Not that there were only twenty-one soldiers
she'd watched die, but those were the ones who had last
words to pass on to their families.

What else was left for Laurel besides delivering
deathbed messages? Her own parents had disowned her.
They'd made it perfectly clear that the Massachusetts

Monteilles were not traitors to their country, unlike Virginia-born Richard Covey who'd died at Gettysburg. Laurel had chosen her husband over her family and continued to pay the price for her loyalty.

The sudden cessation of bird trills brought Laurel out of her dark musings. The mule's ears pointed upward, and he kept swinging his knobby head to the right, toward the heavy woods that lined the road.

Icy tendrils of alarm spread down Laurel's spine, but it was still a shock when two men on horseback abruptly charged out into the middle of the road in front of the mule. She instinctively drew back on the reins, halting the skittery animal.

Stiff with tension, she gazed at the men dressed in familiar ragged gray pants and shirts. They'd obviously been soldiers in the Confederate army, but that observation brought no comfort. Desperate times bred desperate men.

"Afternoon, ma'am." The older of the two drawled a polite greeting.

Laurel nodded, her pounding heart lodged in her throat. "Good afternoon."

They continued to stare at her, their hungry gazes resting on her breasts. Dread slithered down her spine. With their horses blocking the road, she didn't have a chance of escape. "Can I help you?" she asked, keeping her voice even.

"Reckon you can," the younger ruffian said. "After you give us your money and fancy jewelry."

His meaning was obvious, and Laurel shuddered with revulsion and more than a trace of fear. "Please, don't do this." She hated the pleading in her voice.

As the men shifted to opposite sides and moved toward her, she struck the mule's rump with the reins. The animal jumped and brayed, then surged forward. The younger outlaw reached down to grab the mule's traces, halting the animal. Metal jangled and hooves hammered the ground, but there was no getting away from the brigands.

Laurel's heart plummeted.

The older one approached her and leered, revealing brown teeth. "Now that weren't very friendly of you. We ain't even got to know each other yet."

The stench of his unwashed body wafted across her as her breath quickened in terror. Had she survived the conditions of the hospital camps only to be robbed and assaulted by two men she might have nursed during the war? If the situation weren't so dire, she would've laughed at life's irony. Still, maybe it was a fitting recompense for someone who'd lived when so many others had died.